'This powerful, subtle novel is packed with explosions of violence . . . The novel's meaning, and what makes it as fresh now as it must have been 36 years ago, lies in the complex intransignance of its protagonist and his inability to settle in to any role. History itself provides a savagely unsettling and still unsettled ending.'

– *Sunday Times*

'It's a very powerful, enthralling and informative novel. But what is especially fascinating about it is that it offers, as it were, a missing piece of the jigsaw. It's an Indian-eye view of the Raj, of the struggle for independence, all the horrors of Partition – an Indian-eye view written in fiction that is very, very naturalistic, completely different from the post-colonial style, the magic realism that Salman Rushdie patented and very many Indian writers now imitate . . . In this novel you see things from the inside. For instance, right at the centre of of this book there is a scene at Armritsar in 1919 when General Dyer ordered his troops to open fire on a group of unarmed Indians. Now, Paul Scott charts the moral, emotional, social responses and repercussions of the Raj, the way it leads to disillusionment and disgust in some people and chauvinism in others. What Abdullah Hussein does is put you right at the centre of it, you are told what it was like to be there, so it's a very different experience from reading Paul Scott. And again it's different from the approach of Rushdie. In *Midnight's Children* there is a cameo set in Armritsar. It's very artificial, very distancing – lots of cinematic images, jokey stuff about a man being saved by sneezing at the right moment . . . Hussein's style is much more humane, much more direct . . .'

– Peter Kemp (*Sunday Times*), *Front Row*, BBC Radio 4

'Hussein is a wonderful storyteller . . . the narrative moves at an exciting pace, with its brief, unusual lives of the socially insignificant. These vignettes also evoke the volatility and violence of the last days of British India . . . the novel is a grim reminder that little has changed in the Indian sub-continent: tyranny continues to prevail and Naim's struggle is repeated, generation after generation, by the weary generations, by the inheritors of British India's troubled legacy.'

– *Literary Review*

'His decision to recast himself in English may be an attempt to create a new work, relevant to our times, which, universal in its particularity, forces us to look back and remember. The First World War, in which Naim loses an arm, is powerfully evoked . . . Hussein's strength lies in the rich, sombre depiction of war, nationalist upheaval and exodus. The author has the ability to remind us, by turning this century's raw and agonizing events into moments of collective epiphany, that history and story are in many languages the same thing.'

– *Times Literary Supplement*

'Well worth a read by anyone interested in what life under the Raj was like for the vast majority of Indians . . . The couple's marital quarrels symbolise the contradictions, disillusionment and cynicism underlying the Indian fight for freedom and, by inference, the future failure of Pakistan.'

– *The Times*

'A sort of *Doctor Zhivago* for Islamic India.'

– *Scotsman*

'Altogether a brilliant work: one of the great fictional portrayals of the Raj and a sobering, very moving human document.'

– *Kirkus Reviews*, USA

'Should be read by every Indian . . . It is a grave reflection on the coming of age of two nations, India and Pakistan, and the violent ripping apart of a syncretic culture. This is not the kind of novel to breeze through in a day or two: it needs to be savoured and thought about.'

– *Outlook*, New Delhi

'Retains its uniqueness . . . The pain, yearning and weariness of desperate generations of Indians who survived partition are brilliantly showcased in a novel that shimmers with life and hope in the face of utter anguish.'

– *Observer of Business and Politics*, New Delhi

'The religious frenzy post-Partition, not long after Cyril Radcliffe brandished his pencil to carve out two nations from the sub-continent, came like the flood waters, leaving over a million people dead in its wake – the scars of which we still carry 50 years hence. Abdullah Hussein found his muse in Partition and created an evocative first novel . . . It is not without reason that Hussein's novel . . . has never been out of print.'

– *The Indian Express*

'Dexterously translated by the author, bringing out the tapestry quality of the 1963 original . . . Very little seems to have changed since the time of Hussein's novel. There is a languid quality to the whole book which gives a tragic tone to the entire story. One must also give credit to the author's translation which readily brings the many emotions, narratives and historical landscapes to life.'

– *The Asian Age*

'A story of hope and utter anguish. It captures the pain and the yearning of a people.'

– *The Telegraph*, Calcutta

ABDULLAH HUSSEIN was born in 1931 in Rawalpindi, a city incorporated into newly created Pakistan after Indian independence in 1947. He published his first Urdu novel, *Udas Naslein (The Weary Generations)* in 1963, for which he won the prestigious Pakistani Adamji Prize.

His novels and short fiction have been translated into several Indian languages as well as into English and Chinese, and in 1996 the BBC based a feature film, *Brothers in Trouble*, on one of his novellas. Regarded as the leading novelist in the Urdu language, he lived in Britain from 1967 until his recent return to Pakistan.

The Weary Generations

By the same author

In English

émigré journeys – novel

In English translation from the Urdu

Stories of Exile and Alienation

Night and Other Stories

In Urdu

Udas Naslein (The Weary Generations) – novel

Ba'agh (The Tiger) – novel

Nasheb (The Fall) – novellas and stories

Qaid (Imprisonment) – novel

Nadaar Loge (The Dispossessed) – novel

Abdullah Hussein

The Weary Generations

Translated from the Urdu by the author

Peter Owen
London and Chester Springs

Peter Owen Publishers
73 Kenway Road, London SW5 0RE

Peter Owen books are distributed in the USA by
Dufour Editions, Inc., Chester Springs, PA 19425-0007

UNESCO Collection of Representative Works

Translated from the Urdu *Udas Naslein*

First published in Great Britain 1999
This paperback edition 2003

ISBN 0 7206 1187 3

Printed and bound in Great Britain by
Bookmarque Ltd, Croydon, Surrey

For my grandson

Ali Bahadur

Acknowledgements are due to
Dr Amer Sarfraz and Zahoor Ahmad Khan
who gave help with computer work in the
production of this book.

BRITISH INDIA

And [the people] shall look into the earth;
and behold trouble and darkness; dimness of
anguish; and they shall be driven to darkness.

– *Isaiah*

CHAPTER 1

A man on horseback, holding aloft a leaking jar of honey in his hand, had staked out a large tract of land and laid claim to it. In the middle of this expanse he, Roshan Ali Khan, had founded a village and called it Roshan Pur after himself. In all these years, the village had not grown beyond a hundred dwellings, the houses leaning, as if for mutual support, against each other, sharing walls and roofs of grey, uneven mud dug out of the earth. Narrow dirt paths led to the village from several directions, criss-crossing each other at unnatural angles, formed not by deliberate effort but as a result of the natural course of journeys undertaken by the villagers each day between the houses and the land they tilled. A stranger travelling on these paths would often get confused and, bypassing his destination altogether, end up in the wrong village. But the inhabitants of the 'wrong village', long used to errant travellers, would cheerfully offer him a pot of lassi and a cot to rest his weary back on before putting him back on the right track. Most of the time the paths lay quietly baking under the harsh sun, their belligerence showing only when an ikka or a bullock-cart passed over them, its wheels crushing the earth, which billowed upwards in the form of a dust cloud that hung forever in the still air, stinging the faces and eyes of men and women like hot needles.

Prior to the laying of the railway line that connected the town of Rani Pur to Delhi on one side and cities to the north on the other in the late sixties, years before even the 'Mutiny' that took place in 1857, it was already a crossroads for travellers in these parts thanks to the location it occupied right on the main road, the ancient, wide dirt track that ran for hundreds of miles from the south to the north of the country. Many paths, of different widths and angularity, proceeded from the town, leading to the two hundred outlying villages in the surrounding country. Taking one of these paths, you rode out, or walked, westwards to Roshan Pur. Outside each village that lay on the way, you met with dogs. Regarding every passer-by as an invader, the dogs, ill-fed and ill-tempered, stirred from their slumber and, keeping their distance, uttered barks of terrible ferocity. Some among the travellers would stop and bark back or throw stones at them, making the beasts all the more persistent in their vociferous attack, while others who knew the habits of these animals and wished not to be diverted into erring on the muddled paths ignored the dogs and passed by. Travelling thus for full fourteen miles, you reached Roshan Pur unharmed, although not uncovered by layers of thin dust from head to foot.The population of the village was divided into two communities of roughly equal size: the Muslims and the Sikhs. For purposes of land administration and taxes the village was part of UP, short for the United Provinces, although its actual location was a matter of dispute and folklore. Harnam Singh, head of the Sikhs, claimed that the village in fact lay within the bounds of the province of the Punjab, while Ahmed Din, the oldest resident and chief of the Muslims, maintained that it was indeed part of UP. It was a topic of ongoing argument, frequently contested by the two sides in the village chopal, more by way of passing time of an evening than as a point of principle. It may, however, be safely assumed that the settlement lay at some undefined spot on the very border of the two provinces.

No more than sixty years having passed since the settlement, and thirty from the time the canal was dug that now irrigated the lands, the old men who came to till the lands as young lads were still alive. Their sons and grandsons now working the land, as share-croppers or farm labourers just as their fathers had done, for Roshan Ali Khan, the owner, known simply as 'Roshan Agha', a title he had inherited from his late father, the original Roshan Ali Khan I. Roshan Agha lived in a large house in Delhi and seldom visited the village. The story of the beginnings of the village was thus young and still fresh in the memory of the first tillers of the wilderness. The account of it heard from the mouth of Ahmed Din was accepted by all as true. It went like this: at the time of the 'Mutiny', one Roshan Ali was a clerk in the District Collector's office in Rohtak. Being 'Middle Pass', he was considered an educated member of his small community. He lived in an inner mohalla of the old city with his mother, a wife and infant son. As the armed Indian troops rose up against their British officers, the population was seized by a sense of terror. People gathered in their mohallas, keeping their ears pricked all day for rumours coming from the direction of the cantonment. In the evening of that day, Roshan Ali was returning from the street next to his after a visit of condolence to the family of a friend who had been killed in an accident. As he emerged from the house of the deceased, Roshan Ali saw a dark figure running up the street. Suddenly, it stumbled and fell. Roshan Ali went up to look. Night had fallen and all that he could make out was that it was a man who had wrapped himself up in a blanket. Thinking that it was some poor creature come to the end of his tether, Roshan Ali, a strong man of thirty, gathered up the fellow in his arms, flung him on his shoulder and carried him home. As he lowered the man on to a bed, Roshan Ali saw that it was a fair-haired white man in a British officer's uniform, a revolver in its holster tied to his belt at the waist and his uniform soaked in blood. Roshan Ali's own clothes, he now saw, were spattered with spots of blood. His mother and wife started weeping. Roshan Ali bade them to be silent and give him help in tending to the wounded man. The women handed him towels and brought tubfulls of water and clean clothes, but beyond that they would do nothing for the 'farangi'. Indeed they would not show their bare faces near the man, covering themselves with thick cloth with only the eyes showing through slits, although the sick man was unconscious. Roshan Ali had to remove the man's uniform, clean the long breast wound inflicted with a sharp object, although luckily not too deep, and wrap a sheet of cotton tightly round his chest to stop the bleeding, all on his own. Then he dressed the man in his own suit of white cotton shalwar-kameez. After he was finished, Roshan Ali covered the log-like but still breathing body with a fresh blanket and slipped the revolver under the pillow. He had hardly had the time to change his own clothes and hide them, along with the uniform of the white man, who had not gained consciousness, in a large trunk under many old clothes before Roshan Ali heard a commotion out in the street, followed quickly by a fierce knocking at his door.

What he saw through a crack in a side window made Roshan Ali's blood run cold. There were a dozen Indian sipahis, armed with rifles and daggers. One of them, who was holding a hurricane lantern in his hand, was pointing to the trail of blood that led to the house. The soldiers were talking of breaking the door down. Roshan Ali could not find the energy even to go and put objects against the door to stop it opening. He stood transfixed, knowing the futility of such efforts in the face of twelve murderous soldiers. At that moment, five men, the oldest in the street – two Muslim, two Hindu and a Sikh – appeared out of their houses and cautiously, fearfully approached the mob, coming within talking distance just as rifle butts began to fall on Roshan Ali's door. The soldiers stopped. What they told the old men was this: a farangi officer had broken out of the mutineers' lines and, shooting down four Indian sipahis and suffering a sword wound in return, had managed to escape. He was pursued, and the trail of blood from his wound entered this house. If the farangi officer was not handed over to them, said the soldiers, they would break the door down and set fire to the house. The elders, fearing that the whole street would go up in flames, took their heavy turbans off their heads and, placing them at the angry soldiers' feet, begged them to stay their hands while they tried to get the culprit out of the house.

From this point on, the story line got snarled; rather, it grew into several different strands. One version was that Roshan Ali, brave man that he was, stood his ground and said he would rather lay down his life than betray a man who had taken refuge in his house; another that Roshan Ali had dug a hole in the ground of the small courtyard in the back of the house while the negotiations were going on outside and 'buried' the wounded man in it by covering him loosely with bricks from the courtyard, upon which the door of the house was opened and the soldiers failed to find their quarry. Yet a third version, perhaps the least credible, told how Roshan Ali flung the unconscious white officer on his shoulder once again, took the revolver in his hand and, shooting ahead of him, fought his way out to the safety of the cantonment with his charge. All versions sought, however, to reinforce Roshan Ali's virtue and provide anew a focus that would take the story forward.

For it so happened that the young British officer was a member of the English aristocracy with 'high connections'. His rescue thus earned the gratitude of the viceroy, who summoned Roshan Ali to present himself at the Delhi darbar and, in a befitting ceremony, bestowed upon him a khil'at that bore the title of 'Roshan Agha', in addition to granting him the right to go and round up as much uncultivated land as he could manage inside of seventy-two hours anywhere in the country. To the question of why and how Roshan Agha came to pick this particular spot for his land, miles away from anywhere and many more from his native town, the teller of the tale had no definite answer. So he hummed and hawed and quickly went over to the more intriguing episode of how Roshan Ali, single-handed and without any material resources, went about setting bounds to the territory he claimed. According to Ahmed Din, he gave his full attention to the problem for many hours before settling on a plan. All he needed was a horse, a large metal jar with a pinhole in its bottom and the purest honey he could find to fill the jar. The problem of money arose. What with his trip to the darbar in Delhi and fancy clothes to be bought for the occasion, Roshan Ali was left with little money for the purpose of putting his plan into action. He had to borrow the money from a colleague of his, a neighbour and good friend, for the horse, the utensil and the substance. Thus equipped, he started off. Holding the jar aloft, transferring it from hand to hand as the arms got tired, Roshan Ali rode for sixty hours, day and night, stopping off only three times during this period for a bite to eat from his bag and a few minutes' rest. That was all that the horse and the rider could do before the two of them got too exhausted to go on. But enough had been accomplished. The honey, leaking drop by drop through the tiny hole, had attracted ants and other insects of all kinds and sizes wherever it fell. Millions of these creatures not only outlined the surface of the earth, but most of them could not free themselves from the dense stickiness of honey and died there, forming fixed borders to Roshan Ali's land. Roshan Ali had become Nawab Roshan Agha not just in name but in substance as well.

Regardless of the implausibilities of the story, it was considered of no consequence to doubt the veracity of the story, for there was the solid evidence of a landmass of ten thousand acres, now irrigated by the cutting of a canal from the river and covered with living crops, sustaining some hundreds of human and animal lives for all to see. Roshan Agha built himself a brick house in the middle, leaving fifty yards of ground on each side where he planted a garden of mango and citrus trees and banks of scented flowers, in a perfect circle all the way round. It was to be called 'Gol Bagh' – the round garden. Beyond the tall garden hedges grew the village on all sides, except for a path on one side that cut through the mud houses to the brick house. Some years later, when the income from the produce of the vast landholding began to materialize, Roshan Agha also built, over many years and at much expense, a grand house in the best part of Delhi and named it 'Roshan Mahal', although he never lived there for any length of time, visiting it for increasingly brief periods before returning to his beloved garden.

Roshan Ali, being 'Middle Pass', was an educated man in his time and much valued the acquisition of education. He sent his only son, a bright boy, to good schools with private tutors, also briefly to England, although the boy was never to acquire any higher qualifications there except for a facility in spoken English and polite manners. Upon his return, however, the son committed an act of impropriety so serious, that is, he independently married a woman of unsuitable character and class, that the displeased father banished him from his ancestral home in Roshan Pur. Thenceforth the son, Nawab Ghulam Mohyyeddin Khan, made Roshan

Mahal his permanent home in Delhi. Roshan Agha did not see his son until the very last few weeks of his life when he was persuaded to forgive his son and accompany him to Delhi for medical treatment. His son's unsuitable wife had died a few years after the marriage but not before giving birth to a son and a daughter. The arrival of grandchildren greatly pleased Roshan Agha and was said to be the reason for his forgiving his son at the end of his life. The dead wife's widowed sister was invited to Roshan Mahal to look after the two small children. As Nawab Ghulam Mohyyeddin never remarried, his sister-in-law eventually took permanent residence at Roshan Mahal.

The only other brick house in Roshan Pur was located at one corner of the village and belonged to the family of the Mughals. The story of the Mughals, again from Ahmed Din's mouth, went thus: Mirza Mohammad Beg was the man from whom Roshan Ali borrowed money to buy the horse he took to round up the land. As Roshan Ali's transformation into Roshan Agha, with all the attendant riches, took place, he did not forget his old friend and benefactor. Roshan Agha transferred five hundred acres out of his ownership to Mirza Mohammad Beg by legal deed, invited him to come and live in Roshan Pur, built him a pukka house, although smaller than his own, at his own expense and told him to get on with cultivating the land. Mirza Mohammad Beg came from a long line of Mughals whose ancestors came to India with the first Mughal warriors from the north ten generations back, and he had the noble features of pure northern blood about him. Rumour had it that Roshan Agha was greatly enamoured of the unmatched beauty of his friend's wife and that it was this that had impelled him to show such largesse to Mohammad Beg; and even that Mohammad Beg's eldest son was the product of this attraction that had translated itself into a liaison in due course of time. But the very nature of rumour is wild, stretching itself to say even that Roshan Agha's only child, Ghulam Mohyyeddin Khan, who had pale grey eyes and a fair complexion, had come to be as a result of a tryst between Roshan Agha's beautiful wife and the very same Captain Johnson, later Colonel, whose life was saved by Roshan Agha and who became firm friends with his benefactor, coming to visit and stay, from as far as England, in Roshan Pur, the two going together to hunt wild boar and stag, the white man returning on occasion at odd hours, at times alone to the house, etc. etc. In the absence of solid evidence, however, what price mere rumour! No one, in the event, gave much thought to such gossip, except, in the dark and desolate corners of privacy, to lend some colour to dreary lives.

Mirza Mohammad Beg was a hard-working man and had an interest in metalwork. Besides agriculture, he also started a little workshop, where he was later to make all the tools used in working the land. He was not even forty years of age when bad luck befell him. After a brief illness, Mirza Mohammad Beg died, leaving behind wife and two sons. The eldest, Niaz Beg, grew to be a strong and handsome young man under the tutelage of Roshan Agha, living a comfortable life on the lands. He had inherited his father's love of working with metal objects and spent much time in the workshop Mohammad Beg had built. His mother married him off to a good-looking girl from a Mughal family she had known from her old town of Rohtak. There was no issue until, fifteen years after the marriage was consummated, a son was born. It was said that the old woman, Mohammad Beg's widow, was seized with such overwhelming joy at the birth of a grandson that she died on the spot. With the removal of his mother's iron hand, Niaz Beg felt free to take a second wife, a girl from a lower class and much younger than himself.

Mohammad Beg's second son, Ayaz Beg, had the love of books. He went to a madrissa in a neighbouring village for some time, but did not like it. He stopped going to the madrissa and began spending most of his days wandering around or helping his older brother make tools in the workshop. After a few years, Ayaz Beg got bored with village life and ran away from home. He joined up with a group of travelling people roaming the vast country and ended up way out in Calcutta. There he joined the East Bengal Railways as a labourer in the yards. After a time, a sudden change came over Ayaz Beg. He started reading pamphlets and magazines of a technical nature, chiefly to do with the railway systems. All the boredom of life went out of his bones and with years of hard work and application, teaching himself to read English, he rose to be a mechanic and kept rising through the ranks thereafter. He did not return home.

Then an incident occurred in the village which radically changed this family's fortunes. On the charge of having committed a grossly illegal act, Niaz Beg was arrested and sentenced to twelve years of rigorous imprisonment. The authorities did not stop at that; they also confiscated most of the lands belonging to the two brothers in their joint names, leaving only enough for the two wives of Niaz Beg to get by. Ayaz Beg then came to the village for the first time since he had left it and took his brother's young son with him to Calcutta, where he had by now risen, despite his lack of formal qualifications, to the very considerable position of engineer, educating himself besides in a wide range of general subjects, acquiring a rounded and sophisticated personality all the more remarkable for a man with his background. He never married. Now he had got something to do: to educate his nephew. He sent the boy to good English schools, giving him the best education available at his level.

Roshan Pur has a central position in this story; for the first few days, however, our narrative takes us to Delhi, the capital city of the Indian Empire, where, the old Roshan Agha having died recently in his eighty-sixth year, the title was going to be transferred to his son, Nawab Ghulam Mohyyeddin Roshan Ali Khan, in an elaborate ceremony held at Roshan Mahal. These were also the days when the struggle for the political independence of India had begun to take shape.

CHAPTER 2

The large house, set back from the road, stood in vast grounds at the corner of Queen's and Curzon roads. The two men, one elderly, the other young, got down from the behli a short distance from the main gate. Approaching the house, they could see the bunting strung overhead, the breeze ruffling it gently, and little multicoloured lanterns twinkling in trees and bushes. The light of the day was dying. The surface of the long drive leading from the gate was covered with freshly crushed, bright red gravel, marked on both sides by neat chalk lines defining the borders of the banks of summer flowers going right up to the wide patio. On the veranda were placed two tables, one bearing white napkin cloths, the other bare. Around the bare table were gathered several young people of both sexes, busily making up loose-knotted napkins but in a way that seemed not a job but an entertaining game to pass the time. Chairs and tables were being laid on the lawn by servants. A girl stepped aggressively from the lawn on to the patio. Going up to the veranda, she spotted the two guests and stopped, looking up as if startled.

'Hello, Uncle,' she said. 'Adaab. Papa is in the drawing room. Please go in. We are,' she laughed, 'making napkins.'

Taking a quick glance at her wrist watch, she went up the four steps and joined the others. The girl had hazel eyes.

'Look, Azra,' a girl in red silk dress said, holding out a jumbled-up white cloth. The first girl took the cloth and, exhibiting the same aggression that was in her step, held it up.

'Wrong. Absolutely wrong. Look, everybody. Pervez,' she cried, pointing to the tallest boy in the crowd, 'makes it like this,' and rolled up the cloth into a misshapen ball.

Everyone laughed.

'The maulana ties it like this round his head to lead the namaz,' a plump boy said from the other side of the table.

With her head thrown back, the girl was laughing, causing the back of her neck to roll up in a tight little rope of young, wheaten flesh, her face, flushed with the rush of blood, stretched in mad hilarity, making her finely ribbed throat tremble ever so slightly, her eyes beginning to water thinly, mockingly fixed on her brother, Pervez, the tall boy.

'I am not a girl,' the boy said, embarrassed. 'It's a girl's job. Or a bearer's.'

In this unfamiliar milieu, Naim's heart began to beat rapidly. He wanted to go and join this crowd, yet he couldn't. He followed his uncle, Ayaz Beg, into the house.

Nawab Ghulam Mohyyeddin was sitting on a tall delicate stool in front of a roll-top bureau, writing in a heavy notebook. He had a fair complexion, gold-tinged hair, a high, straight nose and pale-grey eyes. He extended his hand to Ayaz Beg.

'Come, come. When did you arrive?'

'Only an hour back,' replied Ayaz Beg and shook hands, bowing low. Naim had never seen his uncle greet anyone with such deference. 'I am sorry, couldn't attend Roshan Agha's funeral. Job held me down.'

'Of course, of course, for a conscientious officer like you.' The nawab turned to Naim. 'And the young man?'

'Nephew,' Ayaz Beg replied.

'Oh,' the nawab said. 'I see.' He kept his gaze upon the boy for a few seconds. Naim thought that the older man's powerful face had imperceptibly tensed. 'I see,' he repeated. 'Resembles his father. You know, we grew up together.' He paused. 'Is he back?'

'Yes.'

'How long was it?'

'Twelve years.'

'Oh!' The nawab got up from his seat and started pacing the room. Looking at Naim, he asked, 'Is he at school?'

'He has just done his senior Cambridge,' Ayaz Beg informed him.

'Have you seen your brother?'

'No.'

'Will you be seeing him?'

'No,' answered Ayaz Beg.

All three sat down on sofas. Ayaz Beg finally broke the brief silence that followed their last exchange. 'I hope everything is in place for Tajposhi.'

'Yes, yes. Insha'allah. Plenty of people. You will enjoy meeting them. Gokhle sahib is coming. So is Mrs Besant. I know you are a rank theosophist. Ha, ha!'

Ayaz Beg smiled.

'You know,' the nawab continued, 'I would have liked Niaz Beg to come for this . . .' his voice sloped off.

After a pause, Ayaz Beg said quietly, 'Yes, yes, of course.'

Naim was beginning to feel uncomfortable; never before had he heard of his father being talked about like this. When Ayaz Beg changed the subject and the two men began to talk about the political situation in the country, Naim felt relief. He started looking around. The nawab's glasses seemed embedded deep into the flesh of his nose. In contrast, his hands were delicate, with perfectly tapered fingers, which he moved prettily as he talked. He was a man of ordinary features, yet appeared imposingly attractive because of the manner in which he conducted himself. The room was opulently furnished. Directly behind Naim's chair stood a mounted tiger, looking alarmingly alive. The floors were covered with the deepest-pile Kashmiri rugs Naim had ever seen. Tall camel-skin floor lamps stood in four corners of the room. As the two older men conversed, a servant had silently entered to switch on the lamps, their soft light falling on the intricate wine-and-fawn patterns of the carpets. The nawab's eye-glasses glinted. After a little while, the nawab got up and went to the window that opened on to the veranda and the lawn beyond. After having had a look, he turned to tell his guests that the seating outside was nearly in place. Then he excused himself for having to go inside and change for dinner.

Out on the lawn, all the napkins, now properly done, were placed beside the crockery and cutlery, and bearers in starched white uniforms were moving among the tables making the last arrangements. There was no one else. Ayaz Beg sat down in a chair and started fiddling with his camera, which he had brought along especially to take pictures of the evening's ceremony. Naim was wandering along the edges of the lawn, looking at rows of flowers, when a group of girls and boys came out of the house and scattered over the lawn in twos and threes. The tall boy, after offering a respectful salaam to Ayaz Beg, approached Naim.

'My name is Pervez,' he said, extending his hand. 'You have come from Calcutta, right?'

'Yes,' Naim said in reply. He shook hands with the boy and stood quietly looking at him. During a lonely, unthreatened upbringing it had become his natural manner not to feel the compulsion to say something and yet appear anything but impolite.

'Let's go and meet others,' Pervez said.

As they approached the first two people, the rest of the youngsters started joining them. They had all changed into formal dress.

'This – this is Naim,' Pervez introduced him. 'He – he has come from Calcutta. This,' he pointed to the hazel-eyed girl, 'is my sister Azra,' then pointing to the rest, 'and they, I mean, are all members of family or friends.'

Naim kept silently touching the tassel of his red Turkish cap.

'Happy to meet you,' one of them said. 'Let's sit down.'

They sat down in chairs.

'Do you not speak at all?' asked Azra, her eyes dancing.

'No – no. I mean, yes,' Naim said.

'Nice name,' a thin boy spoke in English. 'I like it.'

Although their playfulness was gone, Naim discerned a vaguely mocking manner in them, which they used with each other as well. Only Azra kept talking in that frank and fearless way that could be taken as a shade too assertive. She was wearing a white silk sari.

'Do you know how to fold a napkin?' she asked.

'No,' Naim said.

'Actually,' she said, 'none of us does. We only discovered this today.'

'Aw, that isn't fair, Azra,' the thin boy said. 'You might as well say we don't know how to wrap a sari around us.'

Some of them laughed quietly. Naim felt that they weren't laughing at what was actually being said, just amusing themselves because they were in a certain mood, as if carrying on a private engagement. There was wilfulness in their exchange.

Ayaz Beg called out to Naim. He wanted help with fixing the camera, of which Naim perhaps knew more than his uncle did. It was a big box camera with a light-bulb flash, and Naim could take it apart and put it together again. It took them several minutes before it was loaded and the shutter working properly. Guests had started arriving. Nawab Ghulam Mohyyeddin stood at the entrance with a handsome middle-aged woman, receiving the guests. Azra stood alongside them. First came the foreigners, most of them British. Some of them wore top hats and long coats, under which they were sweating. They handed their hats and coats to the servants and were led to the best sofa chairs in the seating area, where they sat smoking cigars and talking in low voices, their women in high-neck dresses smoking long cigarettes stuck in equally long holders held aloft. The women laughed loudly, feeling free. The Indian guests arrived a little later. They were in various attires, marked by their area of origin, but chiefly by religion: Muslims in tasselled Turkish caps and long gowns, Hindus in hitched-in-the-middle loose dhotis and turbans, only a few of them in non-denominational sherwanis. They paid scant attention to the servants and went and sat silently on one side, bunched together, not caring to remove their large, loosely wound turbans and holding their canes straight up on the ground in front of them between their legs. They had all come in two- and four-horse behlis, only some foreigners and very few Indians arriving in automobiles. An Indian, in a shiny, gold-worked sherwani and tight turban, with a young man in Western dress trailing him, arrived in a car. The nawab met him, executing a deep bow. Someone said it was the Maharajkumar of Partap Nagar and the young man his secretary. He handed his gold-topped cane to the young man, who hung on to it. The Maharajkumar went and sat with the Britishers. An Englishwoman, sitting three seats away, leaned forward and waved to him. The man waved back.

As Mr Gokhle arrived, all the Indians and two British people stood up to greet him. Ayaz Beg mentioned his name. Naim went and stood close to him. He had heard the name before, but it was the first time he had set eyes on the man. He had on a sherwani-type half-coat, buttoned up to the neck, over pantaloons, both in black, and wore a cap, the kind Naim had seen on Tilak's head in photographs in Calcutta. A long narrow muffler was thrown freely round his neck. Wearing gold-rimmed glasses, the man might have been considered good-looking were he not so weak, thin and pale. Among the younger people, Naim was the only one who stepped forward and shook hands with him. Mrs Besant was the last to arrive. She wore a bright yellow sari and went and sat with the Indian guests. Upon her arrival, a hesitant conversation began in that group. Some British men stared at her. Servants were offering fruit juices to the guests. Naim stood under a young pomegranate tree, looking up in the subdued glow of a Japanese lantern hung among the branches to the shimmering red buds that had begun to appear. It's a winter fruit, Naim thought absentmindedly. What's it doing here in May?

'Hello,' Azra said, emerging from behind the tree. 'Have you had something to drink?'

'No,' Naim replied.

'Have this.' Azra proffered a tumbler full of fruit juice. Naim immediately lifted it to his lips.

'Do you never take off your hat?'

'No. Oh yes, I do,' blurted out Naim, taking a quick gulp of the drink.

Azra shone her eyes, which seemed in the half-darkness to have become almost black. 'Take it off then.'

Naim took his tarboosh off and began to stroke its tassel with his thumb.

'Here, you look much better without it, don't you think?'

For the first time, Naim had the presence of mind to answer, 'I don't know, I can't see myself.'

Azra smiled. 'Undo these,' she said, pointing to the top buttons of his sherwani.

'What?'

'Come on. Open up.'

As Naim undid the top three buttons, Azra suddenly blushed. 'Don't you feel hot bundled up like this?'

'No,' Naim said.

'Look, our sweet peas, they are already wilting. Well, I have to go in the house. Go and talk to some people, won't you? See you later.'

She was still red-faced as she walked away from him. Beautifully wrapped in the sari, she seemed an altogether grown-up, simple young woman after all, and for the first time since stepping into this house Naim felt comfortable. He reached out and plucked a flower that had dried up on its stem. He looked at it for a moment and let it drop to the ground.

The talk among the guests had now started in earnest. The Englishman with a huge head was talking animatedly, a finger raised above his head as if in admonition, to the man sitting next to him, while two others, leaning forward, listened intently. Next, in a four-seater, damask-covered couch, sat the Maharajkumar, flanked on one side by the Chief Commissioner, on the other by Nawab Ghulam Mohyyeddin and another British gentleman. In his hands the Maharajkumar had a deck of playing cards which he was trying to organize in a certain order.

'This is not the time or place for a game of cards,' he was saying, 'my apologies, nawab sahib. But I want to show you a fantastic trick I learned from a lady on my last trip to Paris.'

The Maharajkumar couldn't set up the cards as he wished and handed the deck to his secretary, who had stood behind him all along, to do the job.

'It is not strictly a trick,' he said to the Chief Commissioner, 'not a one-off, but a "game" of tricks. I'll tell you the basic rules . . .' An Englishman, sitting on the other side of the Chief Commissioner, was showing great interest in the intricacies of what the Maharajkumar was explaining, while his secretary shuffled and rearranged the cards like a professional. Waiting for the cards, the Maharajkumar began nervously to reminisce. 'You know, in the hotel in Paris where I was staying, I saw a strange sight. As I came out of my room one morning, a man, stark naked but for a towel thrown across his shoulders, passed me in the corridor. I said, "I am sorry." The man paid no attention to me. He went down the passage and into his room. Next morning, as I stepped out at the same hour, I was confronted by the very same man, once again in the altogether, coming down the veranda from

God knows where. Loud enough for him to hear, I said, "I am sorry," and withdrew from his path. He appeared not to have seen me at all, much less respond to my apology.'

The Englishwoman blushed. 'Few of them understand English,' she said apologetically.

'Surprising,' the Maharajkumar said, 'considering that the French coast is only a few miles from England.'

'Correct,' replied the woman. 'Isn't it amazing?'

'But that is not all,' the Maharajkumar continued. 'As the man passed me the second day, I turned back to look. And what do I see but a lady coming up from the opposite direction. This lady, would you believe, appeared to notice neither the naked man nor me, and passed us both as if nothing existed in front of her but the ground beneath her feet. Well, after that,' he paused, 'I got used to Paris.'

The Chief Commissioner smiled. The Englishman sitting next to the nawab, leaning forward, spoke in a tone of exaggerated importance. 'Frenchwomen are not like Indian ladies, after all.'

'No, no,' the Maharajkumar said, appearing thoughtful. 'They are hard-working women.'

This induced laughter all round. The secretary handed over the deck of cards, properly arranged. The Maharajkumar started showing the trick to his audience.

Naim moved on. The huge-headed Englishman, now on his feet, paced up and down in front of his listeners, and, most unlike his race of people, still talked on with much animation. On the first of the Indians' seats, two men in very large and loose turbans and dhotis, who looked like a higher class of trader, sat discussing the prices of commodities and other matters of the market. Outside the main gate the waiting motor cars and polished behlis with their colourfully decorated horses, just visible from the lawn, had attracted the street people and children, who stood around to view them in fascination. The police that had accompanied the British officers, and the Chief Commissioner's own guards, were busy shooing them away with threatening curses and lathis raised overhead. But the viewers of this finery, with their customary stubbornness, would shift from one spot to another, refusing to go away. The sky was now completely dark, with only the glimmer of stars scattered far into the warm cloudless night. On a sofa, in the Indians' area, Ayaz Beg was deep in conversation with Annie Besant, as was a man with very pale skin and dark hair.

'But, Mr Beg, at this point I disagree with Madame Blavatsky,' Mrs Besant was saying. 'She contends that beings in the stars are not material but only spirits, and wants to prove their existence by invoking supernaturalism. But the point is that they are indeed material bodies, and can be proved by physical phenomena. The introduction of physical sciences does no harm to theosophy.'

'I did answer this point in my letter to you last January,' Ayaz Beg said to her. 'The time has not yet come that physical sciences may be imposed upon . . .'

'There is no question of "imposing", Mr Beg. The point is . . .'

Naim stopped listening. He had heard all this from his uncle often enough and had long ago lost interest in it. He kept looking at Annie Besant, though, whose white hair made a kind of close-knit hat on her head and who had one of the most alluring voices Naim had ever heard. The girl who had left him standing under the tree a short while back wasn't to be seen anywhere. Suddenly, a sense of melancholy, to which he was given on occasion, seized Naim. He wandered on.

Nawab Ghulam Mohyyeddin had shifted to another sofa where he was now sitting beside the handsome woman who had earlier been acting as the hostess at the reception point. There were two Englishmen and an Indian by their side; the five of them formed a group of sorts and were listening to the Indian gentleman who had just been handed, by one of the nawab's servants, a long-barrelled heavy pistol with a wooden handle. The Indian, a man with a nice, intelligent face who was the last one to arrive by motor car and had entered the house leaning heavily on a walking stick, dragging an obviously gammy leg behind him, had been received warmly by several people, including the Chief Commissioner, and was now sitting with his leg, presumably wooden, straight out in front of him, admiring the handgun, handling it in a way that showed his familiarity with guns. Naim overheard Annie Besant behind him saying to her companion, 'I would like to speak to Mr Gokhle. He looks so weak . . .' Shortly afterwards she got up and walked across, Ayaz Beg and another man following her, to where Gokhle was sitting. People sitting over there made room for the three to sit beside Gokhle. Naim followed them at a short distance. As he passed the lame Indian he heard him say, 'The Germans, they make such wonderful machines. There isn't a single screw or even a rivet in the whole piece. A work of art. When I went for the tiger-hunt last year . . .'

Moving on, Naim came to where Gokhle was sitting and was surprised to see how quickly they had got into the thick of the conversation.

'This is exactly what I was saying,' Mrs Besant was telling Ayaz Beg, 'that my quarrel with Mr Gokhle's Servants of India Society is only to the extent of its title. But then names and titles matter so much. Why not, for instance, Servants of Humanity Society?'

'Or Servants of Theosophy Society,' a man said with an impish smile.

Annie Besant, ignoring the interjection, continued. 'You will agree that the word India does somewhat limit the movement.'

Gokhle rolled his cane round and round in his fingers. He took off his spectacles, cleaned the glasses and put them on again, fixing them firmly on the bridge of his nose.

'Theosophy, Mrs Besant,' he said in a sedate voice, 'is neither science nor politics. You could possibly call it, if you stretch it, a minor branch of philosophy, although I am not sure that serious philosophers will not challenge the notion. However, politics is the name for winning a few material benefits, such as better food, better clothing and better forms of abode, and the way to go about acquiring them for the populace. Material things have a certain mass and occupy a certain space. They are, by their very nature, finite. We cannot make politics infinite. The principles of Servants of India may not be purely materialistic, in the sense that those who serve them shall have to be prepared to give up many worldly comforts and conveniences. But they serve for the betterment of others, and these others are the people of India. That is how the word India gives a material form to the politics of the Servants.'

Annie Besant paused for a moment, then said, 'Why are you so fearful of greater targets?'

'Because your greater targets, by which I dare say you mean higher ideals, are appreciated only by people of your standard of education and sense – say, nawab sahib or Colonel Walcott – but not by the great multitude of common people in my country. They are not cultivated enough to come running for the betterment of the world; they will continue to work their little patches. But they will come for the sake of their brothers, wives and children. They may not understand high principles, but they are far from stupid. That is India.'

At that moment, the nawab, who was passing, stopped to listen. 'Ah, talk of politics going on all round. Splendid. You are looking a little pale, Gokhle sahib. I hope your diabetes is under control.'

'I am not bothered about my health, nawab sahib, nor even about dying, but only about love.'

'Love?' the nawab asked.

'The day I was born,' Gokhle replied, 'I fell in love with sweet things. Now it has been years since I have tasted any . . .'

'Ha, ha! Well said. In love with sweet things! Aren't we all? But you looked very well at the Congress affair in Bankipur last Christmas.'

'Did you go to Bankipur?' asked Annie Besant.

'Yes, yes. Gokhle sahib was there, and Maharajkumar, and Mr Sinha,' the nawab replied, indicating with his head the man with a wooden leg.

'Oh, I wasn't in India at the time. How did it go?'

'Very well, very well. Big conference.'

'Was there a resolution about the partition of Bengal?'

'Er . . .' The nawab halted. Trying to think, he looked up straight at Naim standing behind the sofas.

Gokhle laughed. 'Fear not, nawab sahib, Bengal united or divided, your tiger-hunts shall go on for ever.' There was only the slightest hint of irony in his voice.

'My memory is beginning to falter now,' the nawab said apologetically and excused himself to go towards the house.

'What did you think of Bankipur, Gokhle sahib?' Annie Besant asked.

'What do I think!' answered Gokhle sarcastically. 'It was a party, just like this one. Great people, beautiful, up-to-date people. Gossips all round.'

'Ah, Mr Gokhle, aren't you being a bit negative?'

'It wasn't that bad,' the man with pale skin and dark hair said. 'I was there, reporting for my paper.'

Gokhle turned to him. 'Was there anyone from your newspaper in South Africa?'

'Indeed there was. But seriously, you can't compare South Africa with here.'

'What do you mean?'

'In India politics is in the hands of people with a knowledge of history, etc.'

'And of English? Whole proceedings conducted in a language only a handful of people understand in this country?'

'Come, come,' the newspaperman said, 'does you no harm to do that. After all it's the leadership that has to lead and . . .'

Naim, who had been standing at the back crushing his red velvet cap in his hands, could contain himself no longer. He leaned forward and spoke calmly. 'Is that why less educated people are put in gaols? What about Tilak? He is in confinement.'

Everyone turned to look. The newspaperman's face became flushed with anger, causing pink stripes to appear on his cheeks. He made an effort to control himself. 'You call him a politician, young man? Well, about his politics the Chief Commissioner can tell you more. But as a reporter on such matters I can tell you that he is not even a good newspaperman.'

Ayaz Beg had turned pale. Both his legs shook with nerves. A gust of warm wind passed through a lit-up tree and the shadow of leaves, magnified many times, moved across Ayaz Beg's quivering feet. Almost immediately everyone started getting up for dinner. They had to cross over to another part of the sprawling lawn. Gokhle was still talking to Annie Besant. As they passed, Naim overheard him saying, '. . . although I was impressed by some young men. Motilal's son was there. Just back from England . . .'

The newspaperman stood in his place for some time, as if trying to calm himself. The man with the wooden leg passed, talking and laughing, balancing himself expertly on his sturdy walking stick. Naim got his handkerchief out of his pocket, wiped the sweat off his brow and joined the crowd.

There were two very long tables laden with fine china crockery, and enough leather-bound dining chairs were lined up on both sides to accommodate all the guests. Roasted young chicken and partridge, mounted on long thin wooden legs, stood all along the tables. In between them, twelve kinds of cooked food were placed in correct order in covered pots of sterling silver. The last item that was to be brought out later was pulao, although its saliva-inducing smell had already permeated the air, announcing the unlidding of its huge cast-iron degs in yet another part of the lawn concealed from view, the spaces for it being left vacant on the tables. In these spaces also stood little candles in small china saucers. These candles, not the regular smooth wax sticks nor the fat miniature columns of the same shiny stuff, but finger-thick knobbly little bars of an opaque, dark brown lardy substance that looked to have been hastily rolled and squeezed in the fingers of a hand when still warm, stood upright on flattened bottoms, unlit and mute, rather like the cut-off trunks of dwarf trees, as if put there to ward off the effects of the evil eye with their ugliness in the midst of such extravagance of sight and smell. At the top of the table was seated Nawab Ghulam Mohyyeddin. He seemed to have availed of the briefest of intervals to change into a red silk attire comprising a long, tight gown-like coat buttoned up to the neck over a billowy shalwar of many folds made of the same material, a gold satin cummerbund from which hung a long curved sword in a gold scabbard, and gold-wire-spun soft Indian shoes. He sat in a high-backed chair upholstered in red velvet alongside an old man in ordinary sherwani and white cotton shalwar and flanked by Pervez and Azra on either side of the top two chairs. Immediately in front of the nawab was placed a saucer which held the biggest knobbly brown candle, also unlit. A servant had brought and carefully laid down on one side of the candle a tray of black wood holding a tall, soft hat of blue velvet with an intricate design of narrow gold leaf worked in the cloth. Further down the table, on one side, sat the handsome woman, the Chief Commissioner, then other foreign guests, and on the other the Maharajkumar, the lame gentleman and the rest of the British men and women. Around the other table were seated all the Indian guests, including Mr Gokhle, the only foreign face among them being that of Annie Besant. Everyone properly seated, the old man at the top chair stood up. There was silence. The old man started to speak.

'Today, the thirteenth day of the month of May in the year of 1913, is the last day of the three months that have passed since the passing away of Roshan Agha. The words of the deceased, setting down the tradition, call upon me, as the closest friend and ally of the late lamented, to fulfil my duty and announce the passing of the name bestowed upon him by the grace of God and the British sarkar to Nawab Ghulam Mohyyeddin of Roshan Pur, the rightful heir and henceforth to be the holder in trust for the coming generations of the exalted title "Roshan Agha". Amen.'

Having come to the end of the speech, he picked up the blue velvet hat and placed it on the nawab's head. Two or three foreign guests began tentatively to clap but were cut short by the old man raising his hands in a brief prayer, in which all the Indians, Muslim as well as Hindu, and one or two of the foreigners, joined, raising their hands in the air in front of them in a gesture of supplication to their God. At the end of the prayer, they wiped their hands across their faces, signifying successful completion of the ritual. A part of the ceremony still remained to be performed; it was to do with the brown candles. The old man struck a match and handed it to the nawab, who lit the big candle with its help. As the flame rose from the wick and the nawab threw down the burnt-out match, Pervez and Azra cried 'Roshan Agha' and hugged and kissed him. Then they took up the brown candles in front of them and lit them from the flame of the big candle, placing them carefully back in their saucers. The handsome woman and the Maharajkumar followed, lighting their candles from the same source and bringing them to their saucers. Then all the foreign men and women, who under the pretence of congratulatory gestures were in fact laughing heartily at the unusual garb of the nawab, took up their candles too and lit them, each one of them in turn, from the big candle in an orderly fashion. Some of them, after lighting their candles, stood there carrying them aloft in their hands, chatting to others, only coming back to their seats when they noticed the Indians from the second table holding back in respect. Once the first table was done, the Indian guests crowded round the top, lighting up and laughing, nodding their heads. An aged Englishman with a booming voice still stood to one side, candle in hand, talking to the journalist.

'It would have been much more convenient, don't you think, had the whole rigmarole been written down and copies of it distributed in advance.'

'No, no,' whispered the newspaperman, 'it's not as if it was an ancient tradition. They are putting down the roots of it now for the first time, strictly according to the instructions.'

'What, by the dead chap?' asked the Englishman.

'Exactly. You see, in order to ensure its status it has to be presented as sacred and confidential. Can't be printed.'

The Englishman nodded doubtfully, staring sadly into the flame of his candle. All the candles having been lit and put back in place, the dinner began in earnest. Great oval dishes of steaming rice were brought out from the degs. There were four different kinds of cooked rice: three brown pulao, with chicken, partridge and quail, and the fourth a multicoloured biryani of young lamb. The eating was done in silence. The sky of mid-May was half-lit by a misshapen late moon. The wind had stopped in the trees and half the population of the great city had taken to their beds. Tall eucalyptus trees stood like stilled ghosts. A fountain at the other end of the lawn was noiselessly pumping up thin streams of drops, joined together and yet separated along lines curving down with the force of gravity in the regular shape of a fan. Naim looked up from his plate and was struck by the fragrant, dimly lit atmosphere that seemed as if suspended in a magic spell, its silence punctuated only by the sound of masticating jaws, or, at intervals, by the quiet, sated voice of the man with a wooden leg.

'Hunger,' he was saying, 'being the wildest passion of man, makes the act of eating the noblest human activity.'

The man sitting on the left of Naim leaned over. 'I heard what you said about Tilak,' he said. It was the same Englishman Naim had seen earlier pacing the ground before his friends. 'Are you aware of Tilak's activities against the Muslims? The Society to Ban Cow Slaughter? Permission to play music in front of a mosque and all that?'

Receiving no reply from Naim, the man changed tack. 'You see these candles? They say this particular wax has been in the family's possession for a hundred years. I wonder what they will burn when it is finished.'

Naim stopped eating. Putting his spoon down, he asked, 'How did you know I was a Muslim?'

'Oh, easy,' the man said, moving his head, 'you wore a tarboosh earlier in the evening. Right?'

Naim gave no response to this. It discouraged the Englishman from continuing his conversation. Instead, he was spoken to by another foreign guest sitting on the other side of him.

'I say, did you say something about this wax? Damn unusual stuff, wonder where it comes from, what?'

'Came from the beehive from which the honey came,' answered the Englishman.

'What honey?'

'No idea. Apparently there is talk of some honey along the line.'

'Damn unusual stuff.'

The feast was nearing its end. People were getting up and crossing over to the seating area, to sit in sofas and easy chairs, smoke and sip cardamom-flavoured kahwa brought to them by servants. Nawab Ghulam Mohyyeddin, now 'become' Roshan Agha, was finally left alone in his chair at the dining table. He got up. Staring in a grave mood for a long minute at the candle in front of him, he looked, in those clothes, at once graceful and ridiculous. Then he bent low and blew out the flame. Immediately his special servant appeared and began blowing out all the other candles one after the other and collecting them in the black wooden tray. Carrying a cup of kahwa in his hand, Naim wandered into the shade of a low, fat-trunked tree the thick branches of which spread out horizontally into the air without bending downwards. He balanced his cup of kahwa carefully on a branch and looked around. Just then, once again, Azra appeared unseen by his side.

'Why are you loitering all by yourself?' she asked, a mischievous glint in her eyes.

Startled, Naim didn't know what to say. Instead he picked up his cup and drank a mouthful of scalding kahwa.

'This is my favourite tree,' said Azra, stroking a branch. 'I spend whole days in it during our summer holidays. Before we go to Simla.'

In the weak, flickering light from up in the tree, her eyes were dark grey, hair brownish and her skin the colour of wheat. Her arm, resting on the branch, was healthy and round, its flesh seemingly trying to wriggle out of the tight half-sleeve of her blouse, making a round, ridged fold. Naim felt like reaching out to touch it there.

'Your kahwa must have gone cold. Do you want another one?'

'Oh, no,' replied Naim, 'it's hot. Too hot, actually.'

She laughed. 'Did it burn your mouth?'

'It did,' he said, making a painful face.

'Good!' she said.

As she laughed with her head thrown back, her neck flattened out and her throat quivered, causing Naim to imagine a small animal shivering in the cold. Placing her own kahwa cup upon the branch beside Naim's, she put both her hands on the branch and swung on it, then immediately checked herself. 'I mustn't do this. Papa wouldn't like it. Not tonight, what with all the guests and me in a sari. You didn't mind my little joke, did you?'

'No. But you are drinking my kahwa.'

'Oops, am I? I am sorry. Let me get you another cup.'

'No, no.'

'You don't want any more kahwa?'

'I'll drink from my cup.'

'From this?' she asked, opening her eyes wide.

'Yes.'

She paused, looking up at him, and suddenly the look of aggressive playfulness had gone from her face. 'The cups,' she said, embarrassed, her voice almost vulnerable for a fleeting moment, 'are so much alike.'

They stood sipping kahwa in silence. The uncertain May wind had begun to rise once again, gently playing with a tuft of hair on Azra's forehead.

'Very interesting – er –' Naim said.

'What?'

'The ceremony.'

'Yes. From today Papa is Roshan Agha. As Abba was.'

'Who was the old man?'

'The one who placed the hat on Papa's head? He is – was Abba's very old friend. From childhood, I think.'

Naim thought that the old man probably knew his grandfather as well; he had seen that Ayaz Beg was one of the very few who had been greeted warmly by the man.

'And the lady?' he asked.

'She is my aunt.'

'I didn't see your mother.'

'She passed away.'

'I am sorry.'

'It was a long time ago. Listen, do you have Western clothes?'

Feeling bold, Naim jested. 'I can have them made.'

It took Azra a second to catch on. 'No, don't. Look, we are having a party on Sunday to celebrate Pervez's passing his BA. Will you come?'

'I'll try,' Naim said.

'Oh, do come. Five o'clock. Don't forget. You will come, won't you?'

'Yes.'

'Good night,' she said, and walked away, crossing over to where her father was sitting with the guests wearing the conical blue velvet hat, the top of which moved floppily as he talked. After a while Naim went and sat beside Ayaz Beg, who was talking about the architectural flaws in a well-known building in Calcutta, to the man with a wooden leg who, in turn, was more concerned with the aesthetic faults in the enormous pile.

It was near midnight when the guests began to depart. Saying good night to the nawab and Azra's aunt, they went, yawning and some of them burping loudly, each to his manner of mount. A few of the street people, who lived in huts not far away, were still up, watching the motor cars start up and leave in billows of smoke. Following Ayaz Beg, Naim approached their behli. Before stepping into it he couldn't resist a last look at Roshan Mahal. A dozen servants were busy among the sofas and chairs quietly picking up the crockery from low coffee tables. There was no one on the veranda. The lights swayed in the wind that moved through the trees, making a desolate sound. Naim put a foot on the pedal and heaved himself on to the seat.

'Azra has invited me to a party on Sunday,' he said after a while.

A huge mosquito struck his cheek. He looked at his uncle. Ayaz Beg's was an open face on which every flicker of emotion could be clearly read. Naim saw unhappiness.

'You weren't taken there to deliver a speech,' Ayaz Beg said. 'You well know that even a mention of Tilak is tantamount to terrorism. Had we not been in Roshan Mahal the matter wouldn't end there. You could possibly be arrested.'

'I am sorry, Uncle,' Naim said. 'He is such a hero to us all.'

For a while, the two were silent. Then Ayaz Beg spoke, not in anger, but slowly, haltingly, in remorse. 'Our family has been destroyed just because of such things. I took you away – educated you – put my life's ambition in you –'

They swayed and swung in their seat, holding on to its sides, as the behli left the area and travelled along pitted roads.

CHAPTER 3

It was an unusually warm day. On the lawn of the big house the party had already begun. At the main gate stood a high-roofed black car. Pervez was standing there chatting to the car's owner as Naim arrived. Pervez introduced him to the young man. His name was Sahibzada Waheeduddin. He had been a year senior to Pervez at college, had recently passed the Civil Service competitive examination and had been posted to the Department of Education. The three of them were walking along the driveway when an English girl crossed over from the left wing of the house. Pervez introduced her to Naim.

'Sorry; my hands,' she said, rubbing the soot off her hands with a duster. 'Glad to meet you.' She stepped on to the lawn.

There was a loosely dispersed crowd under a century-old bargad tree. No chairs or tables were to be seen on the lawn, just a couple of low stools on which sat talking two boys and a girl. Next to them, two slightly younger people lay on their stomachs on the grass leafing through picture magazines. A few paces away Azra was trying to light a large oil stove. She was surrounded by four or five boys and girls, dispensing instructions. Two girls were coming up from the left wing, one of them carrying a cane basket, the other holding a large iron kettle by the handle. The English girl kneeled down on the grass beside Azra and whispered to her.

'Look, your handsome friend!'

Azra looked up. Her eyes lingered on Naim for a few seconds.

'But today,' continued the other girl, 'he is looking a proper person without his red cap.'

'Shush, Lydia,' Azra said to the girl. 'Salam alaikam,' she said to Naim and immediately took his hand, unconsciously transferring some of the soot from her hands to his.

'It was Lydia's proposal to make tea out here on this silly old stove. That will make it a "real" picnic party, she said. And look what happened.' She spread her hands.

She had come away, leaving a bunch of them to struggle with the stove. Her face was red from working. Her mouth stretched a bit too wide as she smiled, thought Naim; but the full lips made his heart fly.

'Waheed,' a girl in a straight-cut pyjama trousers and kameez said, 'you haven't thrown us a party to celebrate your appointment.'

'Yes, yes,' enjoined Lydia, 'now you are in employment, you owe us a party. Come on, pay up, Miser Tom.'

'You've had so many from me and you call me a miser?'

'But not one for crawling out of a state of unemployment.'

'What is it about Mrs MacMillan, Waheed?' asked Pervez. 'You go to the Civil Club.'

'What about her?'

'Rumours that she forced her husband to resign?'

'Rumours, yes. I don't know the whole story.'

Bored with the boys' conversation, the girls walked away. Finding himself with just Pervez and Naim, Sahibzada Waheed lowered his voice. 'It's true.'

'Is it?'

'Got too big for her boots, started behaving as if she was the Governor's lady and not the Deputy Commissioner's. Those Patel boys made it worse for her, going round every day for salaam and sitting at her feet as she played bridge and what not. She couldn't get me or Nawabzada Aftab or magistrate Kalloo to do it. Eventually, in utter frustration she made her husband resign. Was from the wrong class.'

Pervez nodded in agreement. A group of five had climbed up the bargad and were sitting there comfortably. The boy on the stool was reading the palms of two girls. Another girl was getting cups and saucers out of the basket and placing them on a durree spread on the ground. Lydia was carefully picking out little cakes from another container and arranging them on plates, licking the crumbs off her fingers.

'Come, children,' Azra shouted. 'Tea's ready.'

Pervez, Waheed and Naim came and stood by the kettle.

'Send up our tea over here,' shouted a boy from up the tree.

'Oh, no,' Azra replied. 'No pigeons here to take your food to you. Come and get it.'

'We're not coming down,' several voices shouted back. 'It's nice up here.'

'Ignore them,' the girl in straight-cut trousers said sharply. 'Let's start our programme.'

Azra fixed her straying hair with hairpins, covered her head with a dopatta and got up. 'Ladies and gentlemen.' Her voice was drowned by the noise others were making. 'Waheed, tell everyone to be quiet, please.'

Waheed, who was still talking to Pervez, heard the order and cried in an authoritative tone, 'Silence! Azra Begum wants to say something.'

Azra began by reciting an old Persian verse, misreading it. Naim couldn't suppress his smile.

'Speech shall not be in Persian,' someone interrupted.

'It'll be in English,' Lydia said.

'Yes, yes.'

'All right,' said Waheed. 'In English then, stop interrupting.'

'Today,' Azra began again, 'today –'

'Is Sunday,' said someone from up the tree.

'Hear, hear!'

Several people, concealed in the branches of the tree, started whistling the tune of 'Happy Birthday'.

'Shut up,' Azra said angrily.

'Silence! Silence!'

'Today, on the occasion of Nawabzada Pervez Mohyyeddin's success in his graduation exam, I herewith announce the opening of the tea party in his honour.'

Azra then handed a half-full cup of tea to Pervez and added a spoonful of sugar to it. Everyone, including the tree people, who had reluctantly climbed down, followed a prescribed procedure. They came one by one and added their spoonfuls of sugar to the cup, until the tea spilled over into the saucer and the cup filled up with sugar to the brim. Pervez had to take a nibble at the wet sugar.

'Clap,' ordered Waheed.

Solemnly the girls clapped while the boys slapped their thighs lazily. After that, proper tea was served.

'Right. Listen, everybody,' announced Waheed. 'Whoever climbs the tree with a cup full of tea in hand without spilling it shall get a prize.'

'What's the prize?' they asked.

'That will be announced later.'

'No, now.'

'Oh all right. He or she will be taken on a ride in my car to the river.'

'Fine.' A girl called Ghazala, a gymnast and also captain of the college basketball team, came forward.

Balancing herself and the cup in hand, she started, slowly, expertly to climb, amid a clamour of discouragements from the ground. Diverted by the noise, she slipped just as she had reached the first branch. She let go of her cup of tea and sat, legs dangling in defeat, on the branch, glaring at the crowd hounding her from below. A boy and a girl continued the contest by starting to climb from opposite sides of the tree. One of them didn't even make the first branch, while the other did but gave up the effort. 'Chicken!' arose the jeers from below. Some others began half-hearted attempts at accomplishing the feat. Soon a scattering of upended cups and broken china covered the grass under the tree. Bored with the game, Pervez wandered off towards the right wing of the house, where his aunt was talking to the head gardener. Naim and Azra and a few others sat by the kettle drinking tea. Lydia was talking to the girl sitting next to her on the grass.

'These Indian nawabs, it will do them a world of good if they are sent to my country for a short while. Listen, Jamila, my family too has an estate in Scotland, and the price of a tea-set is the same to us as to these people here. But the value of it is different. If we break it intentionally, we are punished.'

The sky had been threatening since the morning. The clouds were getting lower, turning blacker, causing a close, sweaty, windless day. It began to drizzle. Leaping off the tree and jumping up from the lawn, everyone ran to the shelter of the veranda. Naim looked towards the dwarfish tree on his left.

'You said it was your favourite place,' he remarked.

'It is,' Azra said.

'Why did you not take up the challenge then?'

'Because the bet was for the bargad, sleepy brain.'

'Why didn't you go for the bargad?'

'Because I wasn't sure I could do it,' she laughed. 'I hate losing.'

'Let us go to your tree,' Naim suggested.

Azra thought for a moment. 'Yeah,' she said. 'Let's.'

Teacups in hand, they ran to the tree and stood the cups on a low branch.

'They're again exactly the same,' Azra said.

'What?'

'The cups.'

'So they are.'

'They weren't. I had one from a different set at first.'

'Where did that go?'

'I changed it with Jamila's.'

'Why?'

'Just so they get exchanged again,' she said, laughing.

'I don't believe it.'

'Yes, yes,' she said emphatically.

'Let's exchange them.'

'No,' she said. 'They have to be exchanged accidentally.'

'Well, let's exchange them accidentally.'

Without warning, Azra began to climb up the tree. Naim followed her. Azra's round pink heels were close to his eyes, her foot almost touching his face. The wind, full of tiny drops of rain, swept across her, losing raindrops in the tree. Her mauve silk dress of shalwar-kameez fluttered, defining her calves, thighs and hips, their firm flesh straining against the heave. Reaching the middle of the tree, she sat herself snugly in a nook formed where two thick branches joined, her feet wedged against a third. Naim sat beside her, dangling his legs.

'You asked me whether I had – er – what was it, Western clothes?'

Her face, already red from the climb, became flushed.

'Well,' said Naim, 'how do I look in jacket and trousers?'

'You still look funny.'

'Why?'

'You are the only one with a jacket on. It's hot, you know, or haven't you noticed?'

For the first time the old mocking tone had crept into Azra's voice. Naim blushed.

'Well, did I not have to show you my proper Angrezi libas?'

Azra looked at him intently for a moment in the semi-darkness of the tree. 'You really looked funny with that tassel bobbing about on your head.' A moment later she laughed.

It was the same brief laugh with a hint of hoarseness, rather like a gust of wind through thorny shrubs, that seemed forever to be enclosed by her lips, ready to emerge even when there was little cause for it. Looking back at her through the wet, dark leaves, he suddenly saw the resemblance between her and her father. Both had a certain something – a wildness that imparted a shade of brutality to their eyes and the corners of their lips.

'What about your father's hat the other night?'

'That was only ceremonial,' she said, laughing again. 'I must say he looked funny as well.'

There was a commotion in his heart. He tore off a sprig and waved it in the air. It bounced the drops of rain resting precariously on the leaves of the tree. He laughed.

'Why are you laughing?' asked Azra.

'I never ask you why every time you laugh.'

'Two errors,' she said. 'First, I never ask you each time you laugh. Second, why does it make the question unnecessary?'

'I remembered monkeys up a tree in Calcutta Zoo.'

Slowly, a smile spread on her face. The rain became heavier. The others had all gathered on the veranda, looking at the rain and singing.

'Why do you throw your head back when you laugh?' he asked.

'Do I? I don't know. Why?'

'I like it.' He kept looking at her quietly. 'Your mouth opens when you laugh.'

'Doesn't yours?' she asked.

'Not as much. It's your lips. They make me want to touch them.'

'You come from Roshan Pur,' she said suddenly.

'My family live there. I live in Calcutta.'

'Will you go there?'

'Perhaps.'

'When?'

'I don't know.'

He reached out to touch her lips, running his fingers on them, then on her nose, eyes. Next he pressed the base of his hand on her cheeks, feeling the bones underneath, the jaw and the chin, as if trying to capture the memory of her looks in his fingertips, while the peculiar smell of the wet tree entered his nose, warm and humid.

From the veranda came the sharp sound of her aunt's voice, calling out to her. After a moment's pause, staring at him with unblinking eyes, Azra said, 'Let's go,' without moving.

'Stay here,' Naim said thickly.

'No,' she said, and jumped down from a great height. 'Uff,' she cried as she landed, looking up at him fixedly again for a moment, as if in terror. Then she got up. Naim climbed down and followed her, running, to the house.

Looking at Naim, a shadow passed over the aunt's brow, although she only said to Azra gently, 'You've been out in the rain, bibi.' They had all gone into Pervez's room, except for Waheed. He stood talking, in his usual conquering-hero style, to Lydia, the Bishop's daughter, who sat in an arm-chair below him, gathering up her feet, against the rain coming in with the wind.

CHAPTER 4

It was a small house that Naim's grandfather had built long ago, and it was inhabited permanently by a distant relative, an old man who had stayed single all his life, a grace-and-favour resident doubling as caretaker and general servant in the house now used by Ayaz Beg on his very occasional visits to the city. Naim lifted the side of the mosquito-net to look. His uncle still lay half-hidden behind his own net, partly covered by a thin cotton sheet, but was already stirring and coughing, a sign that any moment now he would slip his hand under the pillow and take out a packet of his small cigars and light one. He would cough some more, inhaling deeply, and before you knew he would step down from the cot and into the lavatory. In there he would make much noise. Emerging, he would go into the bathroom to make more noise, to cough out the phlegm from his throat and to fiercely blow his nose many times until he was breathing clear, while the half-smoked cigar was left behind on a ledge in the lavatory, slowly turning to ash and spreading all around its acrid smell, which Naim would find both familiarly satisfying and unpleasant as he took his turn in that small space. Ayaz Beg had ordered his life according to regular habits that had hardened into rituals, ceasing to exist as functions of the day in that Naim never noticed them; he simply waited for the day to begin.

He went and stood at the edge of the roof where they had slept through a warm night. Looking emptily down into the street, he saw the milk shops opening to cook a breakfast of halva-poori for their regular customers and street vendors returning from the main market with their pushcarts loaded with green vegetables and fruits of the season. A young lad ran up the street, carrying a jug to collect the day's milk from the shop with a popular street song loud on his lips, the tune rising along the wall to greet Naim, blinking away the sleep amid bits of early morning dreams and memories still fresh in his mind . . .

Lighting another cigar after his first cup of tea, Ayaz Beg surprised his nephew with a sudden remark. 'You have been going to Roshan Mahal every day.'

Naim looked at his uncle's open face, trying to fathom the meaning of what he had said.

'I have not visited the place since the evening of the ceremony,' Ayaz Beg continued. 'You know why?'

'No,' replied Naim.

'Because our family has been disgraced in Roshan Pur.'

Naim searched for something to say. 'I didn't go to see the nawab.'

Ayaz Beg ignored his reply. 'His children,' he went on, 'are the issue of a woman of the street. Ghulam Mohyyeddin married her. Then her sister came to stay. The nawab got interested in her and rivalry began between the sisters. After some time the wife killed herself. Her sister now takes her place – without marriage. But who bothers about that? The masters of land can get away with anything. Ghulam Mohyyeddin, although a man of cultivation, nevertheless listened to his heart instead of his head and introduced rotten blood into his family. It was different for us. Our family was respectable but did not have enough property to cancel the wrongdoing. Your father –' Ayaz Beg got up in agitation and went to the window that looked out on the street. When he returned to his chair, his voice had calmed down.

'Your father also followed his heart, bringing ruination upon us.' He lit another cigar, pulling deeply at it before he spoke again. 'You are old enough, it is about time you knew what happened. Ours was the only family in Roshan Pur that wasn't servants of Roshan Agha. Our father, when he went to the big house, sat in a chair and not on the floor. He was a brave and hard-working man. But Niaz Beg, my brother,' Ayaz Beg stood his cigar on the edge of the ashtray and spread his hands, as in a gesture of remorse, on the table, thick fingers stained with tobacco, 'oh, he too was a brave and hard-working man. But he had madness in the brain. Along with the workshop that our father had built, my brother also acquired a passion for making things. It wasn't ordinary fondness for using tools with his hands, he was completely taken with it, absolutely and entirely at one with the job. He started making guns. This is the truth, that the way he made a twelve-bore barrel and fitted the works to it and polished it, even the English guns couldn't match it. Oh, he was an artist. He made them and kept them with the care and attention that other people reserved for children. I remember the day the police came. They searched our house and found several guns without licence. Niaz Beg was trying to explain, begging them to let go.

They grabbed him by his beard and slapped him on the face. They dragged him away with them.'

Ayaz Beg's hands now rested on the table like two wounded birds, quivering at the tips. 'A few days later, he returned. The skin on his cheeks was black from blows, and half his beard had been pulled out. Any other man would have stopped. But not my brother, no, sir, not him. As I said, there was madness in his heart. I only want to tell you the truth of how it was, so that you know the real nature of your father and not end up hating him. When he moulded those objects from cold iron, they turned into living things in his hands. It was like love; if he stopped making them, his life would ebb away. How could they take that from him? Soon he was at it again. Roshan Agha the elder said to him, "Niaz Beg, you will bring destruction upon the whole village." Your father took the tools from the workshop into a room in the house where wheat chaff was stored, shut himself in there and carried on. He made ten-chamber revolvers that nobody had ever seen. Well, this time a whole police guard came with a white officer at the head. It was as if the villagers knew that they were coming. People had disappeared into their houses, shutting the doors behind them, and cattle wandered in the streets unattended. They took all his firearms, got every single thing in the house, including cots and clothes, made a heap outside the house and put a torch to them. My brother spread his hands before them, saying that these were his "toys", that he only played with them. "No bullets. I make no bullets," he said, weeping, "I don't know how to. Not a single bullet has been fired from them. These are toys. My ornaments." The British officer took his revolver out and fired into the burning heap. "I will burn the whole village down," he shouted, so that those inside the houses could hear. Then they took him away. In the end he was sentenced to twelve years of rigorous imprisonment, on a charge of mutinous treason, plus confiscation of all our lands, save a few acres.'

Ayaz Beg covered his face and wept silently for several minutes. His voice had been pressing on Naim's heart as if a massive stone were being lowered slowly on it. He felt relief when that voice broke down. Before he got up to go out of the room, Ayaz Beg spoke his last words. 'Your parents want to see you. You can go. But you must come back soon. I can't go. Even today, if the government comes to know that I see him, I will lose any position that I have earned.'

Naim climbed up the stairs to the roof and lay down on his cot. After a while he went to sleep. He woke up only when the sun crept up and started to burn his skin. He dragged his cot to the shade of the parapet.

Tossing and turning, he went back to sleep. He was drenched in sweat when he awoke. The sun was setting on a hot day. He took off his shirt, made a ball of it and pressed it on his face and chest to dry himself. Ayaz Beg had come up several times to look while Naim slept. Hearing the noise of his waking, Ayaz Beg climbed up to the roof once again to ask whether Naim would like to accompany him on a stroll. 'I don't feel like it,' was Naim's answer. He sat on the cot where he had slept for a long time, his limbs feeling leaden, until the sun went down and stars began to appear one by one in the clear sky. Ayaz Beg was long gone on his evening walk. Naim got up, put on a clean shirt and walked straight out of the house.

Azra was sitting by the fountain out on the lawn reading a book in the light of a table lamp brought out on a long flexible wire.

'What have you been doing today?' she asked.

'Sleeping,' Naim answered.

'Sleeeeping!'

'Yes.'

'Why?'

'It was hot.'

'You should have taken a bath,' she said, laughing. 'We all waited for you.'

'Who?'

'Who what?'

'Who waited?'

'Pervez. Jamila.'

'Not you?'

Azra silently extended her hand to catch the cool drops of the fountain on her fingers.

'Why not you?' asked Naim.

'Why, why!'

They laughed quietly. For the first time in all these days, Naim felt that through the jokey exchange and the low self-conscious laughter they had suddenly become aware of one another as never before.

'You haven't even washed your face today,' Azra said to him.

'How do you know?'

'I have good eyesight. Wash it in the fountain. It's clean water.'

Naim put his hand under the fine drizzle of the arcs the fountain made and wiped it across his face. He went and lay down on the grass beside Azra's chair and realized that he had walked out of the house wearing only slippers on his feet. Surprisingly, it didn't bother him. He closed his eyes and felt the cool of the grass through the thin muslin shirt on his back. Behind the dark eyelids he saw, unaccountably, the image of a mountain lake he had never seen.

'Come here,' he said.

Azra kept looking at him intently without moving. Resting her elbows on her knees and her chin on the heel of her hand, she sat leaning in her chair in such a position that the wind blew needle-tip drops from the fountain on her face, where they flickered like tiny stars. Naim put his hands on the grass and sat up.

'Have you ever seen a harbour?' he asked.

'No,' she said.

'It's wonderful. Thousands of lights swimming in water.'

'I wish I could go and see them.'

'I want to go and live on a ship,' Naim said.

'How can you live on a ship?'

'I can join a merchant ship. What I really want to do is join up with the Navy.'

'Oh, but –' Azra checked herself.

'Will you come with me?'

'Where?'

'When I join the Navy?'

'Women can't go and live on a ship,' Azra said. She took out a pen and began to draw lines with its tip on her fingernails.

Roshan Agha appeared in the veranda from the left wing, glanced at the two of them and passed through another door a few paces down.

'Roshan Agha is unhappy today,' Azra said.

'What about?'

'Pervez's marriage. Everybody wants him to marry Jamila. He says no.'

'Why?'

'He doesn't say. Except that he has known Jamila from childhood as a relative and not as a wife.' She uttered her short laugh and went back to the pen on her fingernails.

With the nightfall the delicate, slim-fingered leaves of the shreen tree had closed up around each other and hung limply like an empty glove, the heavy, damp fragrance of its flowers spreading the feel of summer in the dark. Out on the road, behind the tall hedge of the lawn, a bullock-cart was passing on its slow journey, the lazy-toned peasant voices of its passengers rising above the creaking of the cart's wheels. The wind passing gently over the wet grass was pleasantly warm. 'Will you?' Naim asked.

'Will I what?'

'Come with me to the sea?'

Without looking up from her nails, Azra paused before speaking. 'Will you go to Roshan Pur?'

'Perhaps,' Naim replied.

'You'll go to see your parents.'

'Maybe. Why do you ask?'

'I just ask. What's the harm in that?'

'The harm is that you haven't answered my question.'

'I can't.'

'Why not?'

Azra looked up, her eyes widening blankly. 'Auntie told me you cannot join any government service.'

The fingers of Naim's hands, white and fragile, paled suddenly and spread out on the grass as if pulled apart by strings. A servant appeared by Azra's side, bearing a message from Roshan Agha that she was to come inside the house.

'I'll be a minute,' she told the servant.

Naim lifted himself off the ground and started walking away.

'Will you come tomorrow?' Azra called after him.

He didn't answer. Azra kept looking at his receding back until Naim walked out of the house. At the gate the chowkidar said something to him. A heavy, foul-smelling object had settled in his stomach like a clenched fist. Once on the road, a sudden anger rose up to his brain like a curled column of smoke. He leaped over the narrow moat that ran along the boundary wall of the house and thrust his face through the hedge.

'Your aunt is a bad woman,' he shouted.

There was no one to be seen on the great lawn. As he jumped back, the chowkidar came towards him.

'Go,' he roared at him.

Then he turned and started running down the road.

CHAPTER 5

Naim's train journey was marked by an incident which, although it did not directly concern him, occurred right before his eyes between the station of Ali Kot and the next train stop of Rani Pur, Naim's destination. As the train started to leave Ali Kot, Naim, who had earlier left his seat to go and stand in the doorway to escape the stuffiness inside the compartment, saw an old peasant running along the platform in an attempt to board the train. His entire baggage, a small loosely tied-up bundle, was hooked to one end of a wooden staff that he carried on his shoulder, holding the other end tightly in his hand. It did not look like he was going to reach the third-class compartment he was chasing as it raced further and further away from him. In desperation, he clutched at a handle nearest to him and with a last, awkward leap climbed on to the footboard of a first-class compartment, still hanging precariously as the train gathered speed. He began to knock repeatedly at the closed door of the compartment with his staff. Eventually, the door was unlocked from inside and a bare-bodied white man appeared from behind it. The room was cool and dark inside. The white passenger, who appeared to have been woken from sleep, had a vile expression on his face. Seeing the sunburnt, withered face of the old peasant at his feet, he shouted in his mixed Hindustani-English, 'Nikal jao. Get out. This dabba fust class, reserve for sahib loge, naeen for you, naeen hai. Go . . .'

'Saab ji,' the peasant begged, 'my wife is on the train. In the name of God, pity me. I will go when the train stops.'

The peasant heaved himself on to the lip of the compartment. The first-class passenger, whom the old man's action had caused to draw back a step, became furious. At first he tried pushing the intruder out by closing the door on him. But the peasant had gained a hold on a space as narrow as a two-inch ledge and clung to it for dear life. The earth a few feet beneath him was flying away backwards. On his creased-up face, terror began to appear.

'I will not come inside, saab ji. Let me sit here on the floor . . .'

The white man, getting angrier, withdrew into the compartment for a minute. When he returned, he had heavy boots on his feet. He started kicking the old man in the back with all his force. 'Soo'er, pig, smelly pig, nikal jao, jao, go, go . . .'

The peasant's staff flew out of his hand, taking with it the bundle of dirty thick cloth tied to its end as the man held on to the two side handles of the carriage with both hands. The round bundle struck the earth and rolled along the sloping ground, the impact undoing its loose knot and revealing a small quantity of gur and a few raw cobs of corn, before it was left behind by the train and disappeared from view. The old man saw his meagre stuff scattering away and a terrible moan emerged from his throat, 'Haaa – my daughter – it was for my daughter . . .'

The first-class passenger kept kicking him, shouting, 'Take a soo'er for your daughter, a pig, take a pig . . .'

Under the blows, some of them falling on his head, the peasant yielded his place on the edge of the carriage but kept a hold on the outside handles by passing his arms through them and knotting them together while balancing himself on the narrow footboard in the face of the rushing wind, which pressed him back. Gradually, the effort of clinging to the speeding train drew the life out of his spent body, although he still managed to tighten the vice-like knot of his arms around the handles. He hung on like a limp rag flapping in the wind, his eyes slowly shutting on him and blood, mixed with tears, trickling down his face, curling through the creases of his ancient skin to his chin, the drops flying in the wind, spattering the side of the carriage. There he stayed until the train arrived at Rani Pur. Two Anglo-Indian sergeants of the railway police came to force the peasant's arms from the carriage handle and put him down on the station platform, where he lay in a lifeless heap, looking quite naked without his staff and his bundle of possessions. Within fifteen minutes Naim had seen a man deprived of his whole world. An old woman with an equally beaten-in face came and bent over the body, looking at it in disbelief. She poked at it a couple of times, saying, 'Get up!' quietly, then kneeled beside it as if in prayer and, gathering it in her arms, began to utter low, animal-like moans.

One of the two sergeants knocked at the door of the carriage. The white passenger lifted the two wood and glass panes of the window. The sergeants talked to the man. Naim, disembarking, went and stood by the policemen. Half a dozen other people gathered round the body. The man in the carriage looked at them angrily. The last words that Naim heard the sergeant say were, 'You will have to answer some questions at the end of your journey, sir.' The passenger dismissively waved him away and dropped the window.

'He is going to be charged,' Naim said to the man standing next to him.

With great sarcasm, the man nodded his head repeatedly and said, 'Yes, oh yes, yes indeed. Who will be the judge and who the jury? Not your uncle, young man, not your uncle.' The man hastened away.

Naim was met by a kammi of his father's who had brought a severely ill-nourished mare for Naim to ride. Naim rode the wretched animal for fourteen miles to the village while the kammi walked alongside, talking without pause.

'. . . Chaudri Niaz Beg raised his wheat by his own hands this year. It was a heavy crop, everybody says there is God's will in his hands. Gave me three maunds, just to me, you see, full three maunds only to me. And he bought this fine animal.' He struck the horse with the flat of his hand, but it paid not the slightest attention. 'She comes from a fine line, believe me, but she was with the weavers of Jat Nagar, and they brought her to this condition. The weavers, may God take them from this earth, keep ever a tight fist with their animals. To be cruel to a tongueless creature is a crime against man and God. In his absence, Niaz Beg's lands had gone to the devil. It is good now. Oi, you low-caste dogs, we are not going to stop in your godless village, go away. There were not enough rains and not enough water in the canal this year so the rice crop was light. But not to worry . . .'

Dusk was falling as the trees of Roshan Pur came into view. 'Do not worry,' the talkative kammi went on, 'these are our dogs. They bark from habit, but once they recognize us as one of their own they will stop. Ah, here comes Chaudri Niaz Beg . . .'

The dogs of Roshan Pur never recognized Naim and kept yapping at his heels. But Niaz Beg did. He jumped up from under a kikar tree, threw away a thin stick that he was carrying and, despite the dimness of light in his sight, had no difficulty in running straight to Naim, putting his arms round his son's body and kissing him, first on the chest, then on his face several times, mumbling unintelligibly as he did so. Naim felt his rough whiskers and the smell of sweat and fresh grass from his father's body. Above a hard, gaunt body the old man had a ruined face.

Niaz Beg immediately started admonishing the servant. 'What kept you so long? I know, you jumped on the mare and made my son walk, didn't you? Don't I know the nature of you kammis?' He got hold of the horse's reins and started walking ahead as the servant, spreading his hands before him, tried to explain that the railway train was late by many hours, which Naim knew wasn't true and that there had been no delay in their coming.

'Lies, lies,' cried Niaz Beg. 'Don't I know you, don't I? People like you have a dark heart and a lit-up tongue. Just you come begging for a share of wheat next time and I will give you the dung of an ant, just you wait and see . . .'

Outside the house, two women, one old and the other much younger, stood weeping loudly. Niaz Beg addressed them angrily. 'Did I not say we should not send this talkative merasi for this important job? Now look, he has spent all day talking to himself. Did I not say I will go myself and get my son back before sundown?'

'Not on the weavers' mare, chaudri . . .' the servant said.

With his wiry, light body, Niaz Beg executed an astonishing leap, landing clean on top of the horse. Digging his heels in the animal's flanks, he rode it round the two weeping women in a tight circle and jumped back down. He picked up a light little stick from the ground and started beating the horse with it. 'Miserly weavers, gave you nothing to eat, took my money and sold me a dead donkey . . .'

The older of the two women threw her arms around Naim and held him tight for a long time. Then she began passing her hands all along his body, feeling his features with the tips of her fingers like a blind person trying to figure out through touch the appearance of her son. Two dogs started fighting near them. Niaz Beg ran after them with a raised stick in his hand, uttering terrible oaths. After driving the mongrels 'to the ends of the earth' as he had promised, he returned on the trot. People were coming out of their houses with lanterns in their hands to look. Taking his hand, Niaz Beg pulled Naim towards the house.

'Pay no attention,' he said, pointing to the two women with his stick, 'they are silly, they know nothing.'

A young Sikh lad called out. 'Chacha, has your son arrived?'

'Yes, yes,' answered Niaz Beg shortly, then said to Naim, 'Pay no attention. These are people with no education.'

In the courtyard of the house, two buffaloes sat chewing cud and two bullocks stood eating from fluffy heaps of cut grass with their mouths in the trough. 'This one,' Niaz Beg said, patting one with his dry, calloused hand, 'I bought for the price of four maunds of wheat two months back. It got a paper from the gora saab at the last cattle fair. Finest blood. Well, Dittay, true or not?'

Ditta merasi agreed. 'Sixteen annas true, chaudri. No answer to it within twenty miles. Famous bull of Jat Nagar's chaudris cannot finish an acre before it starts crying for its mother. This one tills an acre and a half again by the time the sun even begins to go down.'

'True, true,' said Niaz Beg proudly. He turned to the two weeping women. 'Stop doing hoo hoo hoo, you silly women. Have you laid out the rice? Come,

Dittay,' he addressed the kammi, now patting him warmly on the back, 'eat rice with us.'

A large rough cloth with printed flowers on it had already been spread out on the ground of the inner courtyard. The women brought out a round tray of fired clay heaped with white boiled rice which they set in the centre of the cloth. The women, a twelve-year-old boy and Ditta merasi sat down around the tray. Before Naim could sit with them, Niaz Beg ran inside and brought out a low wooden stool for his son.

'Sit on it,' he said. 'I have made it with my own hands. Go on, sit, sit.'

Naim sat on the stool, above the others on the ground. The younger woman sprinkled raw brown sugar on the steaming rice and then poured on melted butter which quickly got absorbed by the fluffed rice. The four men, including the young boy, started eating around the large tray, gathering up rice in their fingers. After a couple of mouthfuls, Naim got tired of having to bend down each time he wanted to scoop up the rice. He knocked away the stool and joined the others on the ground. Hungry after a full day's journey, he ate heartily the delicious sweet rice fragrant with flavours of white buffalo butter and reddish-yellow shakkar. He hadn't eaten these things for years, and before he knew it the top of the arch he made in front of him in the heap of rice was approaching the centre of the tray. Naim pulled himself up. His mother took his hand and carefully cleaned the grease off his fingers with the hem of her muslin kurta. Then she poked the young boy in the ribs with the wooden handle of her fan.

'Stop eating,' she admonished him. 'Your bottom will start running again.'

'Who is he?' asked Naim.

'The old woman's nephew,' Niaz Beg answered.

'He is your uncle's son,' the woman gently told Naim. 'The low woman my brother married put a spell on him.'

'Don't tell lies,' Niaz Beg said to his wife. He turned to Naim. 'Pay no attention. She was the best-looking woman for ten villages around. Why would she let herself die if she had magic in her hand? Lies. They both died in the cholera epidemic.'

The old woman quietly gathered up part of the rice left in the tray in a little heap in front of her husband, upended the melted butter cup and, wiping the bottom of the vessel with her fingers, let the last drops of liquid fall over the rice. Niaz Beg began picking up great big dollops of rice to his mouth. Smoke from the slow-burning dung cakes was spreading in the still air, obscuring the little light that came from the single lantern. The dark circles around Niaz Beg's eyes touched his cheekbones, and below them the flesh on his jaws had dried up like parched earth. He ate with concentration, the bones of his face, from temple to neck, rising and falling prominently like a starving bullock's. It vaguely disturbed Naim to notice how much his own features resembled his father's. A baby began to cry next door. The younger woman stood up to go inside the other room.

'She was weeping just for show,' the older woman said to her husband, 'only to appear as if she was happy at my son's coming home.'

'Hunh?' Niaz Beg grunted.

'She will put a spell on us during the night.'

'What spell, hunh? Hunh? You are taking out of the heels of your feet where your sense is.'

'Who is she?' Naim asked diffidently.

'The other woman,' answered his mother. 'No need for you to have anything to do with her. She is a proper witch.'

'Stop barking like a mad bitch,' Niaz Beg said, bent over the rice, as if admonishing not his wife but the food in front of him.

By the time Niaz Beg was finished not a lot was left in the tray. He pushed it towards the two women, who began to pick at it. Niaz Beg wiped his greasy fingers on his beard and the few hairs that were still left on his head, burping loudly.

'When did you come back?' Naim asked him.

'In the sixth month of the last year,' Niaz Beg replied in a matter-of-fact way.

Although it was a hot night and the air was teeming with mosquitoes grown fat on the waste matter and dung of cattle tethered in the same courtyard where they all slept, Naim slept as soundly as he had ever done. He was surprised at how quickly the night had gone when he was woken by a shrill noise close to where he slept. The two women were fighting. The sudden shock of the clamour made Naim leap out of bed, putting his foot straight into a small pat of warm dung freshly deposited by an untethered buffalo wandering about his cot. Pulling back his foot, he jumped to clear the greenish mass and landed in a puddle of cattle urine, which splashed all around his ankles. Swearing under his breath and blinking in the early morning sun, he went to the water pump and washed himself. The women were shouting at each other.

'You lured him off to bed when it was I who cooked and fed him the day before yesterday, you dirty little bitch.'

'And who cooked and fed him last week when I had to go and see my sick mother, leaving him for you? Did you not lie down with him after I had slaved over my hearth to fill his belly?'

'So where would he go with all that food inside him? To lie with your mother? And hah, sick mother! Don't I know that you went to see your paramour who was dying for you back in your village, and you for him?'

'Hold your vile tongue, you shameless witch. Only yesterday your six-foot son came home and you warmed your bed with the man the very same night. God forgive me, have you no shame?'

'Hah, a fine one to talk of shame. He,' pointing to Niaz Beg, 'had not even been home for full nine months before you dropped a kitten.'

'I am not scared of your son. I only think of your white hair and stay my hand,' the younger woman said, shaking her head of black hair vigorously in the direction of Niaz Beg, who had come out of the older woman's room moments before and stood between the two women, looking nonplussed. Then he saw Naim across the courtyard and suddenly came to life.

'Shut up, shut up, you silly women,' he shouted. 'I will kick both of you out, I will beat you to the next world, bitches, barking like bitches, I will buy you two dogs to satisfy you. Will you be satisfied then?' His head trembled, his beard shook, and his arms were waving in the air like a vision of some wild village dance. His shouted threats had no effect on the women. Advancing on one another, they exchanged a series of fierce blows, pulling each other's hair, screaming obscenities. Giving up the struggle, Niaz Beg withdrew. He went up to Naim and, gently pushing him towards the door of the courtyard, said to him, 'Pay no attention, these are women with no sense, only full of urine and jealousy. Turn yourself away from them. Go, while I kill them and bury them in the devil's ground.'

Outside, two pups wrestled, a fat buffalo wandered aimlessly, two sparrows jumped up and down on the buffalo's wide back, picking fleas from the black skin. A suckling bitch sat sleepily watchful on top of a heap of manure, feeding her young. The Sikh youth Naim had seen the previous night stood yawning as if he were just out of bed.

'You are chaudri Niaz Beg's son?' he asked roughly.

'Yes,' Naim replied.

The Sikh youth picked up one of the pups by the ear and flung it into the pond. The pup, yapping loudly, climbed on top of one of the buffaloes that were bathing themselves in the dirty water. Some small boys, staying afloat by holding on to the buffaloes' tails, started crying in imitation of the pup and splashing water over it.

'Old women are fighting again,' Sikh youth said, laughing. 'They do it every other day.'

Controlling his anger, Naim asked, 'Why?'

'Chaudri often eats from one and sleeps with the other. Every time they fight, chaudri says he will kill them dead, but he has never raised his hand to them.'

Naim smiled wanly.

'Mind you,' the youth continued with simple cheerfulness, 'it only started after chaudri came back from gaol. All the time that he was away, the women lived in peace, like sisters, and never looked at another man's thigh.'

The Sikh boy started walking along the edge of the pond.

'Where are you going?' Naim asked him.

'To lift our wheat.'

Naim followed him. They turned left at the end of the pond and there at some distance before them were a couple of fields of ripe wheat, partly harvested. Most of the neighbouring fields had been cleared. The sun had crept up and covered the shorn fields with its hot white blanket. Wheat stalks were scattered in the harvested fields, and feathered creatures of every kind, from tiny sparrows to fat doves, pigeons and sleek crows, sat among them, picking out stray seeds of wheat along with insects that had lost their cover. Trees were only grown near and around the village, mostly sheesham and mango that provided dense shade, and under them the peasants tethered their cattle away from the heat of the sun while they rested on cots or sat and talked to while away the hours.

'Why is your crop still standing?' Naim asked.

'We sowed late.'

'What's your name?'

'Thakur Mahinder Singh.'

They walked on towards the standing crop.

'Have you come from the city?' Mahinder Singh asked.

'Yes.'

'Which city?'

'Delhi.'

'Is that where you live?'

'No. I live in Calcutta.'

'Kalkuttaah,' the Sikh repeated slowly. 'I know. My uncle went there.'

'What did he do there?' asked Naim.

'What business is it of yours?' Mahinder Singh said with no hint of malice in his voice.

Ruffians, thought Naim. Probably thieved in Calcutta, his uncle.

They were crossing the dry bed of a nullah whose sand had already become hot under the rising sun.

'Don't you want to know my name?' Naim asked.

'I know,' replied Mahinder Singh confidently. 'You are chaudri Niaz Beg's son.'

Following him across the nullah, Naim laughed quietly. They were now approaching the wheat field. The wind was gusting through the crop, moving it in waves that shone gold-like in the bright sun. Naim idly broke off an ear of wheat, rubbed it between his fingers to separate the grains, put one in his mouth and threw away the rest.

'You are a city boy,' said Mahinder Singh, who had been watching him. 'You don't know the value of anaj.'

'I do,' Naim said. 'The other grains are for the birds.'

Mahinder Singh smiled good-naturedly. A girl was coming up from the side, a tall, slim girl carrying a cane tray on her head and an earthenware, narrow-necked pot in her hand. Mahinder Singh blocked her way. She tried to squeeze past. The boy wouldn't give way. A frown and a smile appeared together on her face.

'Where have you been?' Mahinder Singh asked her.

'Took food for my bhapa.'

'I am hungry too,' Mahinder Singh said.

'Is your mother dead?' the girl taunted.

'Are you your bhapay's mother then?'

'Don't show your shameless teeth. Let me go.'

Mahinder Singh plucked the pot from her hand. It was empty. He returned it by pushing it into the girl's hard, flat belly. She bent over under the blow and grabbed the pot. Mahinder Singh didn't let go of her. The girl pushed back and with all the force of her chest and one arm she moved the young man several steps back. Mahinder Singh bit his lip and shoved her further back than she had done him. Drops of sweat had appeared on their faces and their breath came hard and fast through their heaving chests. One side of the sheet loosely tied around the girl's waist was swept up by a combination of the struggle and the wind, revealing a brown-skinned thigh of rounded, healthy flesh, young sinews straining against the weight of the young man.

'Come,' Mahinder Singh said to her, pointing with his head to the shoulder-high wheat crop.

'No,' the girl sank her fingernails into the boy's neck, 'swine, let me go.'

Mahinder Singh, now the stronger of the two, push-dragged her into the standing crop, saying shamelessly, 'Come lie with me, come . . .'

'Your bhapa is sitting over there,' the girl threatened. 'I am going to call out to him.'

'What can he do?' Mahinder Singh said fearlessly.

'He can break your bones.'

'He has to find us first.'

'You pig,' the girl cried. 'You smell.'

Mahinder Singh forced the girl down to the ground and for a moment they both disappeared from view. Suddenly, a heavy, rough voice came up from the other side of the field, calling Mahinder's name. Mahinder Singh's head appeared above the crop, then the girl's. Mahinder Singh swore and came out of the field. The girl followed, adjusting the sheet around her waist. She picked up her roti tray and fixed the lassi pot in the crook of her arm.

'I will see you here tomorrow,' Mahinder Singh said menacingly.

'I am going to Jat Nagar tomorrow with my bhabi and not coming back until sowing starts,' the girl said, arching her brow and smiling challengingly, before she went down the nullah's slope on her way back to the village.

Mahinder Singh swore some more after her. The girl turned once she was on the other side of the nullah and lifted the flat of her hand towards the boy in a gesture of taunting victory. Mahinder Singh stood looking at her as she went, swinging her arms, her back, hips and legs making a single movement of boneless elasticity like a long thin eucalyptus twig swishing through the air. Mahinder Singh's long hair had come loose from underneath his turban; thick tufts of it hung around his eyes, curved and stiff, framing his brow which was aflame with naked desire.

'Who was she?' Naim asked him.

'A slut.'

'Didn't look like one to me.'

'So did she look like your mother?'

'Shut up.'

'What else did she look like?' the Sikh laughed.

'Your mother, you swine.'

Mahinder Singh confronted him. 'Don't you try to talk back to me.' He pulled out a thick wooden flute from the fold of the sheet tied around his hips and started twirling it slowly in his hand. 'Don't you know me?'

'No,' Naim said bravely. 'I only see a stupid Sikh with a flute in his hand.'

Mahinder Singh extended his flute hand to Naim. 'Here, you take it. I'll still break your head.'

Naim stood his ground. 'Show me how you will do it.'

After a few moments of squaring up to one another, eyes screwed up and menace in their bodies, Mahinder Singh laughed.

'You only came yesterday. Drink your old lady's milk for a few days before you come and fight me.'

'Coward,' Naim said.

'I will fight you yet, but not today. We allow twenty-four hours to guests.' Mahinder Singh put the flute to his lips and started to blow, producing, to Naim's surprise, a nice sound.

Without taking the flute from his lips, Mahinder Singh started walking ahead. Following him still, Naim saw that the Sikh's arms and shoulders were scorched black by the sun while the skin under his dirty printed vest was of a lighter shade.

'Don't you ever wear a shirt?' asked Naim after a while.

Mahinder Singh turned to look at him without stopping and continued to blow on the flute. They turned to their right along the field and saw several men separating the wheat from the chaff with the help of huge wooden forks. Their black bodies shone with sweat in the glare of the sun. Mahinder Singh's father told him roughly to stop playing the flute and get down to work with the fork. Hesitantly, Mahinder Singh joined them.

Months passed. Despite several messages from Ayaz Beg, Naim did not return to him. He had started helping his father with work. The rest of the time he slept. His brain had become scrambled and a hazy, unaccountable anger hovered about it. He was gaining weight, and it bothered him. Niaz Beg encouraged him lovingly in his own way. Sleep was good for a young man in hot weather, he said to his son.

At times Naim talked to his father. Why didn't he start up his shop where he could make all the implements anyone wanted to work in the fields, like ploughs, forks, scythes. It was easier than working on the land, said Naim. The only emotion that showed on Niaz Beg's face in response was one of black-eyed fear, quickly replaced by the regular blank look that permeated his features.

'Yes, yes,' the old man would say, 'one day I will open the door of the workshop, but for now the land is good to us, gives us food to fill our belly.'

At times, too, Naim sought to advise his father. It was no good fighting with the women or letting them fight among themselves. They should all live in peace. And he shouldn't swear so much all the time, Naim said to him. This angered Niaz Beg.

'Have you come to read me a lesson? Keep your head to yourself. My head is heavy enough for me to carry around.'

For three days of the week they ate well. That was when Niaz Beg stayed with Naim's mother. The rest of the week they had indifferent food. Regularly on the seventh day of the week Niaz Beg would take his cot and some simple food from home and go out to sleep in the fields.

One evening as Naim was returning from racing his mare against Mahinder Singh's horse he found Ayaz Beg's servant waiting by the side of the path leading to the village. He had come all the way from Calcutta to see Naim.

'I went to your house, bhayya,' he said. 'Your father chaudri Beg saab swore at me and also threatened to kill me. I escaped with difficulty. Your uncle wants you to come back. He is much worried, has been to Dilli many times.'

Naim kept patting the mare's neck. 'How is his health?' he asked finally.

'He is all right, bhayya, but sick for you.'

'Is everything else all right?'

'Everything is well, bhayya. Thakur Darshan Singh has passed away. Roshan Mahal's Pervez mian is going to become big officer in –'

All at once, a great anger swelled inside Naim. 'I am not going back,' he said to the servant and dug his heels in the mare's ribs. Riding away, he heard behind him his father's voice shouting at Ayaz Beg's man.

'You servant, you slave, your master is a mason, a weaver. Tell him my son is not coming back, he is staying here. You mason's labourer, you bastard, you are not son of your father, go and ask your mother, the bitch . . .'

The man could no more bear the humiliation and lost his temper. He turned. 'And you, do you not eat from your brother's land? Come, give me an account of that.'

Naim rode his mount into the man, making him stagger and fall. 'Go,' he roared, turning again and riding away.

Niaz Beg was still screaming at the servant. 'Go tell your master the mason, the weaver, that he is no brother of mine, he is a disgrace to my father. Be off, off.'

Behind him the village was shrouded in the blue haze of dung-cake smoke, which was giving off its peculiar, acrid smell of a country dusk.

CHAPTER 6

Niaz Beg slept only half the night. Once the sowing was over, he would often go after midnight to his fields and sit watching the crop grow. Now, however, the sowing season was on. Niaz Beg and Naim had worked hard the past few days to prepare the soil. They only had one pair of bullocks. Mahinder Singh had offered to get them another pair, but suspecting that it would be stolen property they had declined. Father and son had tilled four acres with their one pair, leaving two acres for the second sowing of the rainy season later in the year. That was their total ownership: six acres.

It was more than three hours before sunrise when Niaz Beg left his bed. He changed the water in his hukka, pulled out a still-smouldering dung cake that he had buried in the hot ash of the hearth at night before going to bed and placed it firmly on a tobacco leaf in the hukka's headpiece. Within minutes he got it going by pulling deep into his lungs from the pipe. As the fire touched the raw-rubbed tobacco and its smoke hit his windpipe, Niaz Beg coughed. He sat there savouring the delicious sting of it for a few minutes and thought pleasantly of the coming night when he would sleep with his younger wife in the next room. From habit, he passed his hand over the loose flesh and dry bones of his elder wife who lay sleeping beside him. The old woman squirmed in her sleep at his touch. Although that body no longer lit a fire in the old man's loins, he felt a sense of security from its touch, as though it were a wallet that contained no cash but concealed important papers within its folds. The peculiar smell of sleeping bodies and stale breath hung in the room. In a corner of the room slept Naim, snoring lightly. Out in the courtyard, moonlight fell silently on the walls, creating shadows on their uneven surface. Niaz Beg went to sit on Naim's cot. The hukka's sharp gurgle near his ear caused Naim to wake with a start.

'I am taking the plough,' Niaz Beg said to his son. 'Get up and bring the seed out. Up, up! Farmers' sons don't sleep like women. Up you get.'

A katik moon threw a crisp, cotton-white light over all the earth. A dog by the pond barked lazily at Niaz Beg. A peasant lying on a cot nearby raised his head and asked sleepily, 'What are you about this early, chaudri?'

'To sowing, to sowing,' Niaz Beg replied.

'God be with you,' the peasant said and fell back.

'Yes, yes, with you too,' he answered shortly.

Everyone knew that Niaz Beg was impatient with God. He put his faith in a few of God's things, like his labour on the land and the food he grew, as well as his cattle and his two wives; but not much else. With the plough on his back and the bullocks' nose-lead in his hand, Niaz Beg still had the skill to carry his hukka in the other hand and to constantly pull at it through his lips to stop it going out, the inhaling of breath through the pipe and the rise and fall of his chest somehow keeping time with the pace of his steps, so that he was at one with the earth and the sound of bells around bullocks' necks tinkling delicately in the silent moonlit night. In the hour of his labour, the man was of the elements, and that was what made him impatient with men who uttered God's name and slept on, and with their God too. Under the kikar tree by the field, Niaz Beg unloaded his stuff, freeing his hands, and quickly hitched the plough between the two bullocks. Then he went into the field. He buried his hand in the soft earth that had already been ploughed and levelled. Bringing up the soil in his hand, he examined it: it bore within it just so much moisture that it broke up between his fingers in small round pieces and yet left traces of damp on them. 'Right, right,' he said happily, 'it's ready.' A shadow approached him in the night as he stood, feeling the wetness of earth beneath his feet, waiting for his son to arrive with the seed. It was a tall Sikh man. He spoke to Niaz Beg.

'Who are you talking to?'

'The soil,' replied Niaz Beg. 'It is ready. Look.'

The Sikh felt the earth in Niaz Beg's palm, rubbed it between his fingers and dropped it to the ground. 'Yes,' he said, nodding approvingly, 'it's ready.'

'Where to, Harnam Singh?'

'To water my field.'

'What, now?'

'My turn on the canal has only come now.'

'When will you sow, then?'

'Late. What else can I do?'

'Yes, yes, very late. Last year too you did not cut your crop until the sixth month. I remember, for it was the month I came back.'

'Still, it's a matter of my turn on the canal, Niaz Beg. Do you think I keep lying down with my woman? I only have one.' The Sikh laughed. 'Our guru did not allow us more than one, not like your guru did.'

'Damn the guru,' Niaz Beg muttered after the Sikh had left. 'Only excuses for lazy limbs.'

After waiting a few more minutes, he ran back to the house. Naim was spread-eagled on his cot, sound asleep. Niaz Beg poked him in the belly. 'When we were young, our father stopped our lassi as soon as the hot months were over, lest we should become addicts to sleep.'

'What are you shouting for?' Naim said to him. 'Half the night is still to come.'

Heavy with sleep, Naim pulled up his trousers, which ripped on one side with the force he used on them.

The two of them loaded the seed bag on to the mare and came out of the house. Niaz Beg had relaxed by now. Following in the footsteps of his son, who was walking alongside the mare holding up the seed bag from one side, Niaz Beg started singing an old village song.

'Nobody sings it nowadays,' Naim said.

'I sang it when it was new. Everybody sang it then,' answered Niaz Beg. 'What is wrong with old songs?'

'They are dead and gone.'

'Maybe,' Niaz Beg said. 'But not forgotten.'

Near the kikar tree a jackal stood motionless, watching the bullocks. Spotting it at a distance, Niaz Beg put a hand on Naim's shoulder and made signs to him to stop the mare and be absolutely still. Then he fell on his knees and leaned forward until he was lying on his stomach. Noiseless as a mouse, he started to crawl, concealing his movement behind stray wild bushes. He approached the jackal from behind and got quite near it before the animal became aware of his presence and ran away. Niaz Beg got up, swearing, and came back to where Naim stood with the mare like a statue in the night.

'Laloo's horse is stiff in the joints. He needs it.'

'What, a jackal?'

'Yes, its flesh has hot properties. Cooked and fed to the horse, cures paralysis.'

'What about people?' Naim asked with a smile.

Niaz Beg did not answer. He was already unloading the two-maund-heavy bag of seed. After standing it against the tree-trunk, he unfolded a cotton sheet he had brought with him and knotted its four corners, making a pouch of it. Into the pouch he poured several handfuls of wheat seed. Slinging it across his shoulders, he entered the field, driving the bullocks before him.

'Come on,' he said to Naim. 'This is your first sowing. Watch.' From one end of the field, he started sowing. 'Look,' he said, 'it's different from tilling the earth. The soil is already soft now, you don't put your weight on the handle and dig in, only just so the end of the pipe stays dipped in. Only just. Watch. Watch and learn.'

After a couple of runs up and down, he handed the plough, the sowing pipe and the seed pouch to his son and came to stand at the edge of the field.

'Hunh! Hoonh!! Keep the line straight, keep it straight, straight, straiiight . . .'

Swearing under his breath, Naim got on as best as he could, pursued by his father's relentless voice.

'. . . seed, look at the seed, it's dropping on the side, going astray, waste, pay attention, look, look . . .'

'Aren't your eyes sharp!' Naim shouted back. 'Seeing little grains in the night.'

Ignoring Naim's remark, Niaz Beg kept his sights fixed on his son's work. 'Twist the Blue's tail,' he instructed; 'drags his feet, the shirker, but when it comes to eating an acre's fodder don't fill his belly. Twist his tail hard, hard . . .'

Irritated to the limit after a time, Naim pulled up and walked out of the field. 'Go and do it yourself,' he said, dropping the half-empty pouch at his father's feet.

'The first day in my life that I did my sowing I got a kikar twig on my back one hundred and forty times from my father.'

'So now it's your turn to take your revenge? One hundred and forty times indeed! You can't even count beyond twelve.'

'Work, work, don't cry, sun is coming up any minute now, then you will say it is too hot, another excuse.'

'What, any minute? It will still be dark in two hours. You have no idea of the time, you never sleep.'

'Hah! It's those who don't wake that don't know the length of the night. Time doesn't live in the face of that dead watch on your arm.'

'Where does it live, then?'

'In day and night,' Niaz Beg replied. 'Or a season. Or life. Do you think I learned to sow between my mother's legs? No, sir, I worked days and nights, and season after season, and on my first day my father beat me more than he beat the bullocks.'

'You are lying. You were very small when my grandfather died. I know.'

'Don't argue. Night is going to end soon.'

Niaz Beg had refilled the seed pouch. He flung it on Naim's shoulder and pushed him back into the field. Naim resisted, made threatening gestures, but couldn't stop his father shoving him towards the plough. The first light of day was breaking in the eastern sky and the stars were fading, the fainter the quicker, when Naim, drenched in sweat, finished the third pouchful of seed. He was tired to the bone but had at last acquired the skill of sowing. Not a single seed from his last pouch fell outside the feed pipe and not a plough-line up or down went anywhere but straight ahead. It was Niaz Beg's younger wife's turn that day to get the food out to the fields. Naim picked up the pot of lassi and drank straight from it till he had his fill. There were two thick millet-flour rotis in the cane tray. The one with a greasy sheen to it had been buttered when hot. Niaz Beg claimed it and started eating hungrily. Naim got the other, dry roti. Both men ate their bread with cooked mustard greens. The baby started crying. The woman produced a fat milk-filled breast from underneath her kurta and thrust it in the baby's mouth. After sucking for a few minutes, the baby fell asleep. Naim finished eating, drank a couple of mouthfuls of lassi and lay down on his back under the tree.

'Here,' Niaz Beg pushed the hukka toward him, 'take a pull, helps with work.'

'I don't want it,' Naim said. 'And I am not going to work any more now.'

'Why not? Only two-thirds of the sowing is done.'

'We can do the rest tomorrow.'

'Hah, tomorrow! If you say tomorrow, tomorrow never comes. We finish it today. The quicker we sow, the quicker we cut. My mouth is bruised with eating this cursed millet flour. I am hungry for a soft wheat roti. Come on.'

'My limbs are aching, I am not working any more today, I have told you.'

Niaz Beg took one look at his son's face and got up. He filled the seed pouch and went into the field. To release his anger, he began to swear loudly at the birds that had alighted in the freshly sown field to pick at the seed, waving his arms wildly to drive them away.

The baby slept soundly in his mother's lap, the skin on one side of his face touched by the golden rays of the new sun. Naim reached out to lay his hand on the baby's slumbering face. It was as if the mother had been waiting for this gesture.

'Your mother thinks I am your enemy. Am I to blame now that Ali has come into the world? She says I am a witch.'

The baby's face was hardly a foot away and Naim could smell mother's milk on its mouth. It was the first time Naim had lovingly patted this baby, and the first time he had spoken to this woman who was a stranger and enemy to him in the same house.

'You shouldn't fight among yourselves,' he said to his stepmother. 'I have said this to my mother too. Feed all your milk to Ali, make him big and strong. Then we will compete in tilling the earth and father shall sit to the side and swear at us.'

He leaned over and, taking the baby's pink toe between his teeth, bit it gently. The woman, who too was looking at this strange young man this closely for the first time, suddenly started crying. 'For twelve years,' she said, 'we lived in peace. After my first husband died, my father gave me over in marriage to your father. I was his bride for twenty days before he was taken away by farangi soldiers. Your mother and I lived under the same roof and did not set eyes on another man's thigh. Now she is my enemy.'

Tired senseless, Naim dozed off listening to the weeping woman. The sun overhead had begun to slip away to the west by the time Niaz Beg came out of the field holding an empty pouch.

'Still nearly an acre left,' he said to Naim. 'We shall have to borrow seed. Tomorrow, you said. It has come true. You have a black tongue. Take the bullocks home.'

Roshan Agha's munshi was a fat, red-faced man who wore spectacles – a distinction, unique in the village, that lent him an added air of authority. He lived in two rooms which formed part of the outhouse of the haveli owned by the landlord.

'Come, chaudri, come,' he greeted the father and son as they went to call on him in the evening. 'How are you faring?'

'Not well, not well without a loan of seed from you,' Niaz Beg replied.

'Ask for my life, chaudri, I will lay it at your feet,' the munshi said, 'but do not ask for seed. May God burn me in hell if I have a grain of it left in my store.'

'Do not utter an oath too soon, you sinful man. It will be me who lays down my life for a finger-width of unsown land.'

A devious smile appeared on the munshi's face. He delivered a forceful slap to Niaz Beg's back. 'Same old satan, you are.'

'I want a half bag,' Niaz Beg said. The two men started talking in whispers as if hatching a conspiracy. Then Niaz Beg suddenly cried, 'One to ten, that's it, settled. Do not say another word.'

'One twelve, chaudri, one twelve.'

'I will not leave a single hair on your already bald head, you devil. Remember that I am not one of your field muzaras. I am Mohammad Beg's son, standing on my own two feet. One to ten, that's all.'

'One twelve.'

'One ten.'

'One twelve.'

They kept repeating their lines as if this were only a joke. Before they left, Niaz Beg and Naim loaded the half-full bag of wheat grain on to the mare, Niaz Beg swearing menacingly at the munshi.

'Shall we have to pay back twelve times this quantity?' Naim asked on their way back.

'Who says twelve? Only ten. Five full bags and no more. If he demands more I will show him that I am a full owner of land in this village.'

'What will you do?'

'First of all, I will break those things he wears on his nose.'

'You mean his glasses?'

'Yes, yes. That will make him blind.'

'We don't need as much as this for the field that is left.'

'I will keep some back for bread. I am starving for a wheat roti.'

'Why don't you keep back more from the crop?' asked Naim.

'We always have enough. But now there is one more mouth to feed.'

'Who?' Naim asked. Then, realizing that his father was talking about none other than himself, he said angrily, 'If you think of me as a burden, I will go.'

Niaz Beg was quiet for a moment. When he spoke, his rough voice was tinged with the quiver of a simple man's emotion. 'Since you are my flesh and blood, you can stay. But you will have to work.'

One cold winter evening a crowd of men gathered at Mahinder Singh's house. They were all friends and relatives of the Sikh family. They sat in three separate groups in the large room, each group being looked after by one of the Sikh brothers who offered the men unboiled milk in wide-mouthed earthen cups. They had all come bathed and washed, dressed in their best clothes and shod in heavy, uncured leather footwear, their hair rubbed with linseed oil and nicely gathered under fresh turbans. The Sikhs' house was by the side of the pond. It was a single-room house, and the room was used for all the functions of living – cooking, eating and sleeping – by the whole family. There was a small side room which served as a store for grain, straw, chaff and other things that needed to be put aside. The cooking things on this occasion had been shifted out to a corner of the courtyard that had the shelter of a simple tin roof standing on wooden legs and no walls, leaving the room free for the night's gathering. In the room, everyone sat on the floor, the only light provided by a lantern hanging from the wall. Mahinder Singh's elder brother was the groom of the party. Anxious to exhibit their clothes of raw cotton and homespun silk, the men had taken off the light blankets in which they had come wrapped from the cold outside and were sitting against the walls with their limbs spread out to show off their finery to good effect.

'My wheat crop is already high above the knees, Mahindroo,' Fakir Din, a favourite of the munshi's, boasted.

'And why not, Fakiroo. Hasn't the munshi's wife personally urinated on the root of each plant in your field! Soon even your fat bum will not be visible in the crop.'

Juginder Singh, busy with his duties as the main host, was running in and out of the room in shirtsleeves, feeling not a bit of the cold for the hard kikar liquor he had drunk. In the little storeroom a space had been cleared for a large earthen vat full of the stuff, and around it sat a few serious drinkers, dipping their cups in the vat and sipping from them.

'My Blue can keep going with the plough for six hours at a stretch even when he is not in full health,' announced Karam Singh, the middle brother.

'And easily tills the ground about two hands wide,' quipped an old fellow reclining against a heap of wheat straw stored for animal feed.

'Oh, hunchback, I will push you back up your mother's legs if you don't shut up,' said Karam Singh, emptying his cup of liquor on the old man's head.

Three other men sitting around started laughing, tilting their faces to the ceiling and clapping merrily with their hard, yellow-palmed, callused hands, drops of liquor and saliva trembling on their beards. Juginder Singh ducked into the room. 'This,' he pointed to the vat, 'I buried in the ground all of six months ago and got it out only tonight. It's older than your grandfathers, you old fools, drink it with care, a little is enough to make you crazy.'

The three men began to drink and laugh hysterically. Kuldip Kaur, a hefty young girl who was Juginder Singh's wife, passed by the door and screamed. Lal Din had earlier been blowing on the dying embers of his hukka to keep it going and a spark had fallen on the straw. The dry stalks had caught fire and were smouldering, producing smoke which the intoxicated men in the room had hardly noticed. Mahinder Singh and another man doused the fire by throwing a bucket of water over it.

'Who brought this enemy of guru into the house?' asked Mahinder Singh. 'Get it out of here.'

'Oi, Mahindroo,' Juginder Singh said to his younger brother, 'enemy of guru or not, Lal Din is my friend. Hukka stays where it is.'

Mahinder Singh looked at his brother's drunken face and turned away. Kuldip Kaur, who had the body of a workhorse and the face of a child, was intoxicated merely by being the centre of so many men's greedy eyes. She was rushing, hips swaying and breasts thrust out, in and out of the room at the slightest excuse.

'Feed the wet straw to the animals first,' she said to her husband, 'or all of it will rot.'

'Son of a bitch,' muttered Mahinder Singh, 'spoiled the whole mood.' He went out of the house.

Mahinder Singh was a loner, the only one he could call his friend being Naim. He met Naim out by the edge of the pond.

'What's happening?' Naim asked him.

'Juginder's getting his turban tonight. I told you three days ago, remember, I asked you to come?'

'Oh, yes,' Naim said. 'I forgot.'

The two of them entered the big room. Everyone in there was the landlord's servant, while Naim was the son of a landowner in his own right. The men in the room greeted him warmly.

'The way you beat Mahindroo in the horse race yesterday showed the quality of your blood,' a middle-aged man sitting next to Naim said to him appreciatively.

'His father was a brave man too, but the son, if you ask me, is one notch up,' another said.

'Who did you cross your mare with, chaudri Neem?'

'With the munshi's horse,' Fakir Din offered before Naim could reply, pushing his hukka at Naim. 'Have a pull.'

Naim declined the offer, saying he did not smoke.

'That is a useless animal,' said a weak-voiced peasant sitting in the back. 'He's dopey.'

'Who, the mushki?' Fakir Din asked loudly, aggravated.

'Oh, the mushki, no, no.' The peasant drew back. 'I was talking of the one he had before.'

In the glow of victory, Fakir Din began pulling furiously on the hukka pipe.

'Want a drink?' Mahinder asked.

'No,' Naim said.

'It's number one stuff.'

'No. Thank you.'

The heavy drinkers all had by now moved to the big room. A couple of them stood in the middle with their arms up in the air attempting a travesty of a dance. Seeing them make ungainly movements, some young boys among the guests who could dance got up. Fakir Din put his hand to his ear and began to sing a long-drawn-out village song out of time and step with the wild, limb-stretching, powerful dance of the boys.

'What's getting a turban mean?' Naim asked.

'Bhaya broke into a cattle yard.'

'What?'

'You wouldn't understand,' Mahinder Singh said proudly. 'This is the world of tigers.'

'You are drunk.'

'I am not drunk, chaudri saab. Until one of us lifts another man's property and brings it home he cannot wear a turban.'

'Don't you all wear turbans anyway?'

'These are guru's turbans. I am talking of a man's turban.'

The ceremony of succession that Naim had seen at Roshan Mahal in Delhi passed before his eyes. 'What did Juginder do?' he asked.

'Went to Ali Pur last night. The bastards woke up, though.'

'What happened then?'

'Juginder cut two of them with his kirpan and lifted a buffalo.'

'He is getting his turban as a reward for theft?'

'Cowards give their own names to things,' Mahinder Singh said, laughing. Then suddenly he became serious. 'Remember, one word out of you about this and you are finished.'

The dance and Fakir Din's interminable song came to a halt as the food was brought in. It was wheat-flour halwa, hot from the pan, cooked with raw sugar and fried in cardamom-seared ghee. All the men ate, balancing dollops of halwa dripping with ghee on their fingers before putting them in their mouths, where the soft and slippery substance slid down their throats with the greatest of ease, filling the room with hushed sounds of the gentle working of jawbones and the faint gurgle of swallowing interrupted only by Kuldip Kaur's footsteps as she came and went, fetching yet more cups of lukewarm milk straight from the udders of the Sikhs' buffaloes. A momentary thought passed through Naim's mind that mixed in these cups might also be milk from the buffalo that Juginder had thieved from the next village the night before. He saw a drop of sweat on Kuldip Kaur's cheek and he felt warm in the cold night. After the meal was over, an elderly Sikh wound a large turban of blood-red silk around Juginder Singh's head and each of the guests got up to shake hands with him and utter the words 'Greetings, Sardar Juginder Singh Ji'. The ceremony over and the meagre stock of simple farmers' chat and gossip quickly exhausted, they began to leave one by one, to go home and sleep.

The next day the police came to the village. They called up the team of elders, led by the munshi. They arrested Juginder Singh, Karam Singh and Arjun Singh, laid them down on their stomachs and beat them blue with a foot-wide leather strap on their bare backs. But nobody said a word, and no witnesses came forward to tell of the crime.

In Niaz Beg's house the two women were working in the courtyard, the elder spinning cotton on the wheel and the younger sewing a quilt spread in front of her on the ground. The young boy was giving the buffalo a bath by throwing water at it from a bucket. As he completed his chore and came back to sit by his aunt, shivering with cold, the elder woman said to him, 'Give the small buffalo a bath as well. It is your aunt's too.' The boy went off to fill the bucket from the water pump. The second buffalo was bigger but was called 'small' because it belonged to the younger woman. As the boy started doing his job, the younger woman threw an oddly loving glance at her rival for this act of kindness. It was the coldest season of the year and all of them, men, women, children and birds, had come out to sit in the late morning sun. The atmosphere was chirpy, light and cheerful. At that moment Niaz Beg entered the house in a state of agitation. His cheeks had turned blue and there was terror in his eyes. He made straight for the storeroom at the far end of the yard.

'Don't tell anyone, don't say a word,' he said, and locked himself in.

The two women got up in panic, stood a cot in front of the storeroom door and spread a quilt over it, concealing the entrance to the room. Then they sat in the yard, waiting. The boy ran out of the house, returning a few minutes later.

'The police have come,' he announced. The women made a sign to him to be quiet. The three of them sat there, looking out the door of the house. Chickens picked at the grain on the ground and at the insects in the air, making small contented noises.

Out in a field, Naim spotted Mahinder Singh engaged in what looked like a wrestling match with a buffalo. He went and stood looking at them. Mahinder Singh had a large black piece of clinker in his hand that he must have picked up from the brick kiln. He was making repeated attempts to get a hold on the buffalo's head. Each time, the huge animal jerked him away with such force that he fell back on his haunches on the ground. From there, Mahinder Singh jumped right back up to continue the fight. 'Have you not found a woman today?' Naim said, laughing.

Mahinder Singh gave no answer.

'You won't kill it with a brick,' Naim said to him.

'Shut up,' Mahinder said between gritted teeth, rejoining his battle with the buffalo.

Both creatures, man and beast, had the same animal wildness on their faces, the same desperation in their respective struggles. The buffalo, which at first had been trying to run away, now stood her ground, determined to fight as Mahinder Singh became more reckless with the passing of each second. Naim stood transfixed by the two warring beasts. Eventually, as the voices of some men, coming from the other side of the field, seemed to be approaching them, fear appeared in Mahinder Singh's eyes. With an enormous heave and a hoick that seemed to come from the very depths of his being, Mahinder Singh lifted the buffalo's head, parted its lips and with a savage blow of the iron-hard clinker, broke one of the buffalo's upper teeth clean in half. He threw the rock away in the standing crop and fell on his back, exhausted.

A constable and a villager appeared around the corner of the field. The constable untethered the buffalo and took the two boys with him back to the village, delivering a blow of his lathi to each of them as they went.

All the Sikhs' cattle had been herded outside their house and the three brothers were lying face down, bare to the hips, being beaten with a leather strap by two constables. Long, raw marks of the lash had come up on the skin of their backs and buttocks from which blood seemed about to ooze. As the small group of four men and a buffalo appeared from the fields, a farmer sitting near the police party jumped up and ran to them.

'Here it is,' he cried, 'my buffalo, this is it, they stole it, wounded my servants, murderers, thieves, dirty Sikhs.'

Mahinder Singh put his hand on the animal. 'Shut your filthy mouth, you liar, I will pull your tongue out. Look,' he said, lifting the buffalo's upper lip, 'I bought this mother of yours with a broken tooth from the market three months ago. Did your buffalo have a broken tooth?'

'Thieves, robbers,' the man wailed, spreading his hands before the head constable, 'let it loose and it will go straight to my home, its own home, it was born there, I swear, it is mine.'

Ignoring the man, Mahinder Singh was running around, identifying each of the cattle. 'This is my half-tail bull, tail cut off when it was a baby, and this – this my one-eyed cow, eye lost in fight with another cow, and this my horse with a cracked hoof . . .'

As he passed the head constable, the policeman felled him with a blow of his lathi. The constables forced him face down to the ground and started giving him the lash. Unlike his brothers who had borne the pain in silence, Mahinder Singh began to make a racket. Every few minutes the head constable would give a sign to the beaters to stop and ask the boy to tell the truth. Each time he would be answered with oaths of the most foul kind from the mouth of Mahinder Singh.

'Give him the smoke,' the head constable ordered finally.

They tied up Mahinder Singh's feet with a rope and strung him upside down by a thick branch of the shisham tree under which they were sitting. Then they burned red chillies under his nose. The evil smoke getting up his nostrils, Mahinder Singh cried out, 'All right, I will tell, in guru's name stop.'

The burning chillies were removed. Mahinder Singh sneezed non-stop for several minutes, at the end of which he let out a string of even viler curses at the police. The operation was repeated over and over, Mahinder Singh saying, between tears and sneezes, 'I don't know who lifted your fucking mother,' until he passed out. He was then let down and kicked ferociously while he lay unconscious. Not a word that would incriminate them could be got out of any of the brothers. The police, however, returned the buffalo to the rightful owner and went away without charging anyone for lack of witnesses.

The buffalo was of no value to the Sikh family; the point had been made and Juginder Singh had won his coming-of-age 'pug'. In the evening, relatives and friends came to congratulate the brothers, bearing gifts of home-made sweetmeats as gestures of support and jubilation for the victorious events of the day and night.

A friend was tending to Karam Singh's wounds. The medication consisted of a folded muslin rag, dipped in hot linseed oil mixed with powdered cloves, which was put on his sore back and buttocks. He was crying with pain.

Juginder Singh, sitting by his wife's side, mocked his younger brother. 'What a woman! Did we not get the same lash? Hunh, crying like a woman dropping a baby!'

Karam Singh's friend placed another piece of cloth dripping with boiling oil on his back. Uttering a cry of pain from the oil's sting, Karam Singh reached behind him and flung the dressing away. 'Stuff it up your mother's arse,' he said to his friend.

'Hunh! A woman,' Juginder Singh said contemptuously.

'Pig,' Karam Singh snarled at him. All the men laughed.

A short while later a stranger entered the house. He was a tall, black-bodied peasant, barefoot and dressed only in underpants. His legs were covered in mud, and he appeared to have travelled over rough ground.

'Victory to wahguru,' Juginder Singh said. 'What brings you here this time of night, Ram Singh?'

The stranger, who had been leaning against the wall, slid down it to sit without answering the greetings. Juginder Singh got up, frowning, and went to sit by the man. They talked in whispers. A sudden change came over Juginder Singh. He clenched his fists.

'When?' he asked.

'Last night,' said Ram Singh.

Karam Singh and Mahinder Singh stood up. They went to join the two men. All four started talking in low, agitated tones. Their faces had turned pale and their eyes red. Juginder Singh got up.

'All right, tonight,' he said to the others, 'this very night.' Fixing his turban with lightly trembling fingers, he went out.

The visitors, sensing a crisis, got up and left. Sitting where he was, Naim asked Mahinder Singh, 'What happened?'

'Our cousin got murdered.'

'What for?'

'Over water turn.' Mahinder Singh walked up to Naim. 'We are going to finish them tonight. Are you coming? Our friends come with us for revenge.'

For a moment Naim didn't know how to answer. Mahinder Singh was looming over him, swaying slightly. 'Unless they are cowards,' he said.

Naim looked at him angrily. 'I will come,' he said, and left their house.

Naim and Niaz Beg took turns sleeping out in the fields during this season to guard their young crop against marauding wild boar, foxes and suchlike. Naim had made himself a kind of machan up a shisham tree where he spent the night wrapped in quilt against the cold. Some time after midnight he dozed off for a few minutes. He was woken by the sharp point of a spear in his ribs.

'Who is it?' he asked.

'We are off,' Mahinder Singh answered from below. 'Come.'

Their black bodies rubbed with oil from head to the bare feet and dressed only in brief underpants, all four brothers carried full-length spears in their hands, sharp dagger-like weapons tied firmly to their ends, and a bellyful of kikar liquor inside them, its strong smell floating on their breath, protecting them from the cold. They were accompanied by their mother and Kuldip Kaur, the women carrying large cane baskets on their heads.

'Why are the women coming along to fight?' Naim asked Mahinder Singh in a whisper.

Nobody answered. They moved, shadow-like, quick and silent, through fields green with crops, several of them being irrigated through outlets from the canal. The still, cold air of the night, rich with the mixed aroma of linseed, alcohol and wet earth, seemed to be travelling with them. The soft ears of the wheat were just growing heavy with the milk-filled seed that would harden within weeks and turn to edible golden grain. The men and women were approaching their dead cousin's village along the canal bank in the pitch black night under an overcast sky. Mahinder Singh stopped at a certain spot.

'Here,' he said, pointing with his lance to the edge of a field that had been broken up; water from the canal had collected outside in a large puddle and had then been stopped at its source. 'Was feeding his crop right here. The pig – died with just one blow of a spade.'

'Shut your mouth,' hissed Juginder Singh.

'Pig.' Mahinder Singh spat on the ground where their cousin had fallen.

Further down, they spotted three people sleeping under heavy quilts in a clearing between a field and the canal bank. Approaching on tiptoe, the four men approached them while the women hung back, crouching behind a tree. It was quick, the whole thing over within a few minutes. They flung the quilts off the sleeping men with their lances and sank the blades into their chests. Juginder Singh grabbed a sword and cut off their heads with a single lightning blow to each of them. They died without a sound. The women came up. Juginder Singh took an axe from a basket, chopped the bodies into small pieces and threw them in the canal. The women scraped off the bloodied earth, filling the baskets with it and emptying them in the canal. The men levelled the ground with a spade and spread the dead men's quilts over it. Naim had gone off in the middle of all this to stand by the bank of the canal. A cold shiver had spread over his body.

'Come on,' Mahinder Singh said to him.

Naim followed them on unsteady legs. There was a taste of blood in his mouth. He felt as though he had swallowed a handful of pebbles, making his stomach heave. A few stars peeped through a break in the clouds, throwing the faintest of light upon dark earth. The seven shadowy figures sped through silky-green wheat crops standing in field after field. In a field of low green millet grown for fodder, Mahinder Singh stopped.

'I am going to cut some for my one-eyed,' he announced.

'Have you no sense?' Juginder Singh said to him. 'You want to be seen and caught, fool?'

'Go,' Mahinder Singh said in a loud, threatening voice. 'Go.' Juginder Singh and the others, if only to keep him quiet, hastened away. Mahinder Singh put out the long shaft of his spear across Kuldip Kaur's stomach as she passed him.

'Stay,' he ordered.

'What for?'

'Help me cut it,' he said, looking fixedly and pushing her with the weapon's handle towards the middle of the field. Juginder Singh stopped just for a moment to look at the two of them, then turned away, swearing as he went, the rest of the party following him. Pulling out a sickle tied up in his turban, Mahinder Singh started cutting the soft green plants, rapidly clearing an area. Kuldip Kaur followed him, bundling and tying up the crop with 'ropes' she made by twist-winding the stalks. The sound of the water in the canal reached them from afar. They heard someone approaching.

'Lie down,' Mahinder Singh whispered, 'down.'

Kuldip Kaur lay down flat on the ground. The man was a farmer tending to the watering of his field. Carrying a spade in hand, he passed by.

'I could see your chest above the crop,' Mahinder Singh said. 'What if that fucker saw it?'

'So? There just would have to be another one,' the woman said. 'Your dagger's still sharp, isn't it?'

'Don't shoot off your mouth. Come here.'

She sat up. 'Let's go. It will be daylight soon.'

Mahinder Singh grabbed her breasts.

'Animal,' she hissed in the dark.

'I am tired,' he said. Spreading his arms, he rolled over, landing with his head in her lap.

'I am cold,' Kuldip Kaur said.

'Come here.'

She lay down beside him. He put his arms around her. 'Are you still cold?'

'Your hair smells.'

'Bitch,' he said.

'Don't squeeze. I can't breathe.'

He laughed. 'I can squeeze the life out of you.'

'Pig. You are not stronger than me.'

'I am the strongest of all.' He wrapped his legs around hers and did several rolls on the ground, taking her with him in his arms. 'Son of a bloody cow,' she cried. 'Let go of me.'

'I am the strongest,' he said.

'Juginder is stronger than you. He cut them all tonight.'

'Bastard bitch.'

'Did he not?' she mocked.

He swore at her. 'Were they your fuckers, that you mourn them?'

He released her. Picking himself and his spear off the ground, Mahinder Singh stabbed at the roll of green millet leaves that Kuldip Kaur had made. The blade of the lance went right through the bundle.

Kuldip Kaur got up, pulled down her shirt, pulled up the lance and handed it to Mahinder Singh. Then she carefully placed the bundle of fodder in the basket and lifted it on to her head. They started off. After a short while Mahinder Singh started singing.

'Shut up,' Kuldip Kaur said, 'someone will hear us.'

He kept on singing. The morning star was shining brightly as they got home. Mahinder's mother was on her way to milk the cow with the milk pail in her hand.

'What kept you?' she asked her daughter-in-law.

'Why don't you give your sons a little less to eat so they stop bothering me like dogs all the time,' she said and went straight to her cot.

CHAPTER 7

Harvesting had begun. Every man, woman and animal in Roshan Pur was busy. Even the birds, seeing an abundance of grain on the ground, hovered in swarms, uttering shrill cries of hungry delight. Under the May sun, the bare bodies of men had been burnt black. In the women's jars at home, ghee was being finished fast as each cutter consumed a quarter seer of the stuff a day. The storerooms were emptying of straw and chaff, and the cattle were showing their ribs like curved swords under the loose, dull skin on their flanks. Dry white spots had appeared on the faces of the women, who gave everything they had – food, the warmth of their bodies at night – to the aching limbs of the labouring men in the hope of a year's subsistence. Yet the villagers, working in a hundred and twenty degrees of shadeless heat, with their deep-creased faces, sunken eyes and cheeks, were happy, for before them was the heavy, ripened wheat ready to be cut down, the fruit of their long, hard labour. Swinging their sickles in short fierce strokes against dry stalks, talking and laughing, mocking and swearing, they were leaving heap after heap of the felled crop behind them as they moved, squatting like two-legged tortoises, along the ground, clearing swathes of field in their wake.

By the end of the week most of the fields had been cleared. They lay flat, looking naked and white in the sun, lifeless without the standing crop that had swayed in the wind for months and was now gone, marked only by great mounds of cut crop scattered all over them. The women of the village, anticipating for the first time in a long while the end of their toil, had come out in a blaze of colour, the red and orange, yellow and green of cotton and cheap silk kurtas and shalwars or simple sheets wound round the hips and air-light dopattas of dyed muslin covering their jet black, oiled hair. Even the cattle, eating armfuls of straw given them as starters until the wheat grain was beaten out of the ears and the proper chaff and stalk tied up and hauled away to the storerooms, raised their heads and mooed, brayed and roared, the females among them getting restless and hot of blood and juices, ready to mate even before their ribs disappeared under layers of winter fat. It was a celebration.

Niaz Beg pulled up in his bullock cart by the Sikhs' field. Mahinder Singh came out to greet him.

'Your eye is red,' Niaz Beg said to him.

'Motherfucking sweat got in,' Mahinder Singh replied. 'Flows like lassi these days, you know.'

'True. Very true.'

Mahinder Singh glanced up. A grey haze hung in the still atmosphere, threatening a storm. Wide-winged kites wheeled high and low, crying with their tongues out as if warning of the coming wind through the lull. 'Signs are bad,' he said.

'They are,' Niaz Beg said. 'I came with a purpose.'

'Is your cutting done?'

'Done. We cut a good crop.'

'And you are complaining?' laughed Mahinder Singh.

'Not complaining. But our store is full and still a little bit is left out. You have a big store, will you take my surplus?'

'With the grace of guru, we have a heavy crop this year as well, chaudri.'

'My boy is a friend of yours, that is why I came to ask.'

'He is my friend all right. Yes, yes, I will talk to Juginder.'

'We will eat from it first, finish it in a month.'

'All right.'

'When I was taken away, you know, I gave a bullock to your father for safekeeping. Don't know what happened to it, I was away a long time. Maybe it died, like your father. There is no accounting for such things. But he was my friend, your father was.'

'Right, right. Don't worry, chaudri.'

Niaz Beg gave rope to the bullock, then flipped it hard on its back. The bullock didn't budge.

'It won't go, chaudri,' Mahinder Singh laughed. 'Feed it a cup of my daroo, then see how it goes.'

Niaz Beg began to beat the animal furiously. In the fields that were still being cut, they were beating the drums, the cutters swinging their sickles in time with the beat – dhum dhum dhum – dhumadhum dhumadhum – dhum dhum dhum – kept up by two professional drummers, their eyes closed and sweat pouring from every limb, completely lost in the rhythm of their hands and the sound they created. Equally lost in the drumbeat were the peasants, the farmers, the cutters, holding bunches of stalks in one hand and running the cutting edge of the sickle over them with the other, doing it for an hour or so without stopping, dropping their sweat on earth that had been wet and black, firmly holding the green shoots only six months before and was now grey and dry and weak, giving up its fruit to men as they desired. 'Halalala – dopey swine, come on – lazy-hand pig, faster, faster, halala . . .' Mock-swearing, they cheered and challenged each other to keep up the dance of the sickles on the roots of their food. As the sun reached its zenith, trying to break through the haze of dust, the women arrived. In their colourful dresses they poured out of their homes, balancing cane trays of thick butter-drenched millet-flour rotis and large round earthen pots of lassi which they held in the crook of the arm against the arc of their waist, eyes greedy and voluptuous for the almost bare fields and for their men. Once they were near the harvest they scattered in the fields, putting down food beside their men, and started gathering up little bundles of the cut crop that had been left behind by the cutters, laying one on top of the other to form high mounds from field to field. The drums stopped. The harvesters got up on tired knees and sunken bellies and leaped, hungry-jawed, upon the food.

The sun was setting when the wind rose, bucking the great grey sheet that had floated around all day, rumpling it up into huge balls of dust and flinging them to the earth. The dust-storm had arrived. The harvesters ran to their houses to fetch sewn-up gunny bags and whatever tarpaulin covers they could lay their hand on, even old quilts and heavy blankets, to cover up the little hills of crop and place stones on them all round to prevent them from flying away in the gusty wind. Those who couldn't find enough material for covers hauled the remaining crops on to their bullock carts and took off for home.

Fakir Din was trying to get his bullocks going.

'They are for the butcher, Fakiroo,' Mahinder Singh called out to him. 'They have had their day.'

Gravely offended, Fakir Din pulled at the rope-reins with such force that the bullocks' eyes bulged out. He eased a little, then pulled at them once again. The bullocks' nostrils flared, ears fluttered, muscles strained, and they started running.

'Butcher, eh?' Fakir Din shouted. 'Come on, let's see who's for the butcher. Here is the mile and there is the field. Halala . . .' and off he went, with Mahinder Singh coming up fast in answer to the challenge. The race was on, the two carts flying side by side, their wheels running astride the narrow path and into the fields on either side, as the bullocks were viciously beaten by their masters with rope-reins and lashes of long thin twigs cut from shisham trees, accompanied and followed by the cheering, challenging cries of supporters who had cleared the path and taken sides without malice, athletic youngsters running alongside the carts and some of them leaping on to them and throwing their arms up in the air, shouting 'Halalalala . . .' By the time they reached the edge of the pond, Mahinder Singh's cart was yards ahead. He pulled up. Jumping down from the cart, he slid out of the dhoti that covered his lower half. Standing naked, he started thrusting and gyrating his hips, making his genitals flip and flop in front of the oncoming Fakir Din, who, red-faced with anger and shame, swore loudly and turned his cart to head for home, while all around them swirled a fierce storm, blasting particles of hot dust into their bodies and faces, blinding and choking them.

They wrapped up their faces in sheets of cloth, leaving only slits for the eyes, and returned to the serious business of hovering in the fields around their heaped and covered crops, guarding them for half the night as they had done all their lives against the cruelties of the elements. When half the night had passed, the storm abruptly stopped. The men then returned to their homes, grateful that the storm did not bring in its wake the rain which could rob them of all they had toiled for.

By morning the dust had settled, the air was clear as glass and the sun, once again out of the shadow of dust, entered the streets of the village, quietly lighting up the chimneys and the edges of roofs. The men emerged, laughing and talking, driving their cattle ahead of them, the animals' neck-bells sedately tinkling as if both animal and man had found new energy and peace at the beginning of this day, ready for the threshing of the crop to separate the grain from the chaff. Little did they know at the time that another, deadlier storm awaited them that same morning. They had hardly been in the fields for an hour before everything came to a stop.

Niaz Beg ran out of his field and entered the house. He went straight to his storeroom. 'Shut the doors,' he shouted to his wives. 'Lock it. The lock's on the ledge up there. Don't tell anyone, you hear? Don't say a word –' Naim saw his father hiding in the storeroom and left the house. He saw a dozen policemen, rifles in hand, rounding up the peasants from all the fields. There were several horses and a military vehicle lined up along the widest path leading into the village. An Anglo-Indian sergeant and a thin-faced British officer, both in military uniform, stood by the vehicle. When all the men had been gathered in a cleared field where their cattle were tethered, the sergeant began, in a loud, harsh voice and broken vernacular, to address them.

'War is threatening to devastate our country. It is the duty of each one of us to protect the country and the government.'

There was complete silence among the villagers, broken only by the tinkling of a bullock's neck-bell as it shook its head to drive off the flies.

'We can only protect ourselves if we win the war. We have lakhs of men in our country,' the sergeant swept his arm across the breadth of the crowd. 'We can win with the help of fighting men. Now, everyone who joins up will be given Royal silver coins in wages and free food and clothing on top. When the war ends, men will come home and get a pension for life.'

'Have they stopped killing them in the wars now?' old Rehmat said with a little sarcastic laugh.

The sergeant's lips twitched. 'We don't want old men,' he said. 'Only young men may give their names.'

A buzz rose from the crowd. Two young boys started talking.

'Where is the war going on?'

'Don't know.'

'Yes, where is it happening?' Mahinder Singh asked the sergeant.

'Silence,' the sergeant ordered. 'War is threatening England and the British government, *your* government. We need you to fight for your King and country. Come on, come forward and give your names.'

'We are harvesting,' a man said. 'Our cut crop is still out.'

'We have no time,' the sergeant said severely. 'We have to cover the whole district. Step forward.'

The crowd stirred. Men's voices arose here and there. 'Who will thresh our wheat? The jackals?' 'What will we eat?' 'Have we laboured for a whole year for the pigs to eat our grain?'

'Look at my hands.' An old peasant extended his arms in front of him. Everyone standing beside him looked intently at his callused, dry-skinned hands as if they were seeing them for the first time. The sergeant was looking back at the thin-faced officer.

The officer quickly turned and went to his vehicle. He put his hand into the cab and brought out a sheaf of papers loosely held in a file-cover. After leafing through them for a minute, he handed them to one of the only three men who were in civilian clothes. They turned out to be a doctor and his two assistants. The officer then unfixed a bayonet from the rifle carried by a policeman standing next to him. He held up the weapon in front of the men. The sun caught the steel and exploded in the eyes of the bullocks, who jerked their heads in sudden fright. The officer paused for a moment, then spoke in perfect vernacular.

'You will now cut your crops with this,' he waved the bayonet, 'and do it on the field of battle.' With that he expertly flung the bayonet down so that it stood on end with its point sunk into the earth. 'Tell the soldiers to present the men,' he ordered the sergeant.

The constables, poking them with their rifle butts, began to separate the younger men and drive them to the front at bayonet-point. The men resisted, clinging to their animals. The bullocks rubbed back, mooing softly, not with hunger or lust but with the warmth of intimacy as if they understood the danger ahead for their masters. Naim calmly walked up to the sergeant.

'Put my name down,' he said in English.

The sergeant looked up, surprised. 'Are you educated?'

'I have passed senior Cambridge from Calcutta,' Naim replied.

'We want fighting men, farmers and peasants, not educated people.' The sergeant paused, then added, 'Er – not yet.'

The officer walked over and addressed Naim. 'Why don't you join the Education Department? It is equally useful, all round.'

'I am a farmer. I can ride, shoot and fight,' Naim answered.

The officer looked at him with interest from head to foot. 'Wait,' he said.

Naim stood there looking at the uncut wheat crop whose grain-heavy ears swayed drunkenly in the light wind. In the cleared fields, heaps of gathered crop lay motionless like huge tortoises sunning themselves. Wide-winged kites wheeled overhead, crying thirstily, as the hot wind of a summer noon swirled around the pushing, shoving, swearing and sweating men of the village. After two hours of effort, coaxing and bullying, the sergeant and his soldiers had only managed to extract names and particulars from two young men. The officer was in an obvious temper. He turned to Naim.

'So you want to enlist?'

'Yes,' answered Naim.

The officer nodded to the sergeant, who proceeded to take down the necessary details: name, domicile, father's name, occupation. Naim's tongue quivered as the name of his father was called for. But there was no reaction from either the sergeant or the officer. After he had been put through a cursory medical examination and enlisted, Naim felt as if he had already won his first battle.

The recruiting party did not leave; they set up camp in a field and demanded food for the night. Only the officer got into his vehicle and left, the wheels raising clouds of hot dust from the baking path in their wake. He returned the next morning, accompanied by Roshan Agha. All the men of the village – and some women, mostly old, who kept their distance – came out to greet him. They were joyous to see their supreme master, since he came to their humble abode so rarely that some young lads had never set eyes on him. They jostled to get near him, grateful as supplicants who wanted nothing more than to be in the presence of this near-deity they called 'mai-baap' – 'mother-father'. Without wasting any time, Roshan Agha got up on a chair and addressed the peasants while the officer and his men stood to the side, arms folded, as though they had nothing directly to do with all this.

'The English sarkar is fighting a war with our enemy. I want all young men to come forward and fight to save our country. As the gora sahib has already told you, coins of Royal silver shall be given to you every month, plus as much as you can eat of food, and uniforms with strong boots, guns in your hands for tha tha tha, free tickets for the railway trains for you to go where you want, and much more. But that is not all. On top of it, here is my word to you: everyone who goes to fight, his family will get double share of the crop they grow.'

Roshan Agha's word was law. Inside of two hours, sixteen young men were enlisted. The visitors, including Roshan Agha, left the village with eighteen fresh soldiers. Women wept, old men's chests fell in several layers, young girls lost all sense of tomorrow.

Niaz Beg kept himself locked in the storeroom for a day and a night. When he emerged the next afternoon, the terror of the previous day had given way to a vacancy in his eyes that had spread out to cover his whole face, like the vista of an empty, barren field.

'Naim gone?' he asked.

The old woman, sitting by the hearth, looked back at him with vast, desert-like eyes without answering. Niaz Beg cautiously approached the wall of the adjoining house and called out, 'Hussain gone?'

'Gone,' his neighbour replied from the other side of the wall.

'Who else?'

No reply came from across the wall.

Niaz Beg waited for a moment, then asked, 'Are you going out to the fields?'

Still no answer. Giving up, Niaz Beg picked up his hukka from the courtyard and went to the hearth. It was cold.

'No fire?' he asked.

His wife, silently waiting for his anger to rise, shook her head. Niaz Beg put the hukka down. He went off to a corner of the courtyard to pick up the sickle and a length of rope that lay on the ground. He stood there trying to fix the hand-scythe inside the folds of his turban. Looking at him working blindly on his turban with trembling fingers and failing, the woman's eyes filled with grief and pity, although they were still dry as parched earth. Eventually Niaz Beg picked up an identical implement lying near by that had belonged to his absent son. He threw it to the young boy.

'Let's go get some millet for the animals,' he said to his wife's nephew.

The twelve-year-old caught the scythe in the air and chirped, 'Yes, baba, I can cut. Yesterday I cleared half marla of greens with Neem before he left . . .'

On his way out, Niaz Beg was brought to a halt by the sight of the buffalo's teats swollen like inflated rubber tubes.

'Nobody milked the buffalo today?' he asked, addressing his wives although not looking back at them. He spread a hand under the distended udder. A few drops of milk fell on his palm.

This was a crime in his house. In the past, he would have jumped up and down with rage and shouted, 'You do this to a tongueless animal? Your own milk will dry in your breasts and your children will perish, bitches . . .' But on this day he dried his palm by wiping it on his beard and said weakly, 'The buffalo is throwing milk,' and went out.

The older woman made as if to get up to go to the buffalo, then fell back where she had been sitting on the ground. Covering her eyes with a hand, she began to weep.

Outside, all was calm. Some old men wandered about in the fields among heaps of the cut crop without touching any of it. The sun shone cruelly on a patient earth; the storm had passed through and taken away the heart of the village.

CHAPTER 8

129th Baloch, Duke of Connaught's Own, Ferozpur Brigade, Lahore Division

For two months the regiment stayed at headquarters, during which time they were given training – brief and brutal – in how to do battle, consisting chiefly in the use of .303 rifles, fixed bayonets for hand-to-hand fighting and grenade attacks. Apart from that, there were parades, never-ending parades; marches, quick marches and 'double-ups' carrying twenty seers of kit, left-turn here and right-turn there, stop here and about-turn. The peasants, village dwellers who could stop and start and execute a turn at will like birds upon the wind, took the discipline heavily to heart and broke under the shouted orders and having to learn how to walk in long trousers and strange boots.

It was the beginning of August and black monsoon clouds thundered overhead, making it the darkest of nights. Ali Pur's Abdullah, Naim's only friend in the platoon, was trying to mend a tear in his uniform. Four West Punjabi soldiers, carefully turned away from each other, were busy changing into their night shirts.

'Where did you disappear from the firing range?' Naim asked.

'I don't loiter,' Abdullah replied. 'I come straight home.'

'Home?' asked Naim with an ironic smile. He pushed his bedding roll against the wall with his boot and sat down on it. 'You were firing like a madman today. I was afraid you'd kill someone.'

Abdullah stayed silently bent over his needle and thread.

'If you do it again, you'll be shot,' Naim said.

Feeling tired after the day's training and weary of Abdullah's silence, Naim rested his head against the wall and shut his eyes. Outside it had started raining. A man sitting on the far side of the barracks began singing a song of barsaat that spoke of the onset of rains cooling the sunburnt earth and of women in pale dresses rising and falling on swings tied to ancient trees.

'Exactly a year ago,' Abdullah said suddenly, 'I caught a lovely fish.'

Naim opened his eyes. 'Did you eat it?'

'No.'

'What happened to it?'

'It was the most beautiful little fish I ever caught. How could I eat it? On its body, only as big as my hand, were thousands of spots of all colours, red and orange and blue. I can never forget it. Today I saw a stone in front of me as we were crawling on the range. This stone also had many, many coloured spots on it and was of the same size and shape as the fish. Suddenly, I felt like running off to catch a fish. This is the season for it. When the rains came, we went fishing in the ponds. That is why I fired on the stone.'

Wide-eyed, Naim looked at him. 'You wanted to kill the stone?'

'No.' Abdullah paused. 'You are a book-reader. You will not understand.'

'I will tell the sergeant,' said Naim, laughing.

'I will break the motherfucker's head.'

'You have a bullock's brain inside your head.'

'I don't know,' Abdullah said thoughtfully. 'But I have a bullock's heart.'

'Bullocks don't have a heart, they are rough and insensitive. Now horses, I know about horses, they have a heart.'

'Bullocks too. You know, when my brother died our Blue didn't eat for two days. My brother had brought him up from when he was little. I went out and he followed me. I took him to the millet field and he didn't once put mouth to it. I sat down under a tree. I bit into a mango and gave half of it to the bullock. That was the only thing he ate in two days. Afterwards he put his head on my shoulder and cried.'

'Cried!'

'He had tears in his eyes.'

'Good bullock,' Naim laughed. 'What happened to the fish?'

'Huh? Oh, the fish. Don't know, I brought it home and put it in a dish full of water. From there it disappeared.'

'Disappeared where?'

'Don't know. We all think the buffalo ate it.'

'You definitely have a buffalo's brain, if not a bullock's.'

The West Punjabis had taken off their night shirts and were bathing in the rain outside and laughing. Half of the recruits from across the barracks were out in the rain. Others stood on the veranda smoking and watching the bathers lit by flashes of lightning. Naim started humming a tune he had once heard in Roshan Mahal coming from what seemed a long time ago.

'Neem,' Abdullah raised his head again from his needle, 'when will the war start?'

'It has started.'

'When?'

'A few days back.'

'Have you read it in a book?'

'They are called newspapers. Why, are you in a hurry to die?'

'To fight. Even to die will be better than this. We have sisterfucking rifles and bullets but no one to kill. As soon as I hold a rifle I want to kill. You think a stone has blood under its skin? I shot it because I am fed up with the parade. Nothing but parade and more motherfucking parade.'

'Don't worry, you will soon get a chance,' Naim said.

Five days later the order came for the Brigade to move. There was commotion in all the barracks. They polished their boots to a high shine, oiled their rifles until even the shoulder-pieces sparkled, rubbed soda on their uniform buttons and finally massaged mustard oil into their washed hair and combed it. As a last touch they passed eye-pencils of kohl across their eyelashes to darken them further as if they were getting ready for a wedding. There were sounds of the opening and shutting of trunks, yet in the very centre of this noise there was silence among the men which seemed as though it would be broken with a bang at any moment: each of them felt as if the others would suddenly burst out laughing or else assault the men nearest to them for no reason at all. The order to move had triggered a force that rippled out through every muscle in their body; it was the expect-ation of freedom that they would have in the field of battle. After a while, the letter-writing began. The educated ones among them wrote their letters first and then wrote for the others. Naim had to write the most.

'Aren't you going to send a letter home?' he asked Abdullah.

'What is the point? If I am killed my wife will be looking for another husband even if she has three hundred of my letters.'

'If a woman does that in Punjab,' one of the Punjabis said, 'she is killed.'

'Punjab is full of junglees,' Abdullah said as he slid the bolt of his rifle in and out of its empty casing, making a sharp metallic sound familiar to them all. 'What were you saying?'

'Letters,' said Naim.

'Yes. Letters.'

'That is a silly thing to say.'

'What is?'

'That letters don't mean anything.'

'It's true. Once read, they are like dead people. Reading old letters and weeping over the dead is no use. It is like seeing yourself dying beforehand. Anyway, nobody in our whole family can read. They will have to go to other people to have it read to them. That is no use too.'

'Why not?'

'Don't want to tell the whole world what I am doing.'

'They already know you have been recruited into the army.'

'That is enough for them.'

There was a peculiarly secretive side to Abdullah that interested Naim. Naim was, however, the only one among them whose life had changed for the better. His time in the village had devastated not just his mind but also his body. The discipline of the past two months, which had given the peasants for the first time in their lives the feeling of boredom and listlessness, instead offered Naim a system of routines with which he had been familiar for most of his early life: he was again living as a regular, cheerful man.

Some time before midnight they embarked on a goods train. A layer of wheat straw mixed with leaves of corn and millet was laid on the floor of carriages for the soldiers to sit and lie upon. They put down their rolls of string-tied bedding along the corrugated iron walls of the carriages and sat on them. Sleep had vanished from their heads; their eyes glittered in the semi-darkness along with their cigarette ends, the only light in the carriage being provided by a low-flamed hurricane lantern hung high up in a corner. One soldier in Naim's carriage had a stomach-ache and was the only one lying down, uttering occasional cries with his head tossing on a thin bed of corn leaves. The train carried no goods other than the conscripts and didn't stop at normal stations, running at its regular half-speed pace for long periods of time. When it stopped it was only to let another train pass or to get water from a station pump. When the train stopped the carriages became stuffy and humid and the men gathered round the open door to breathe, attracting the attention of the people down at the station.

'What station is it?' a soldier would ask.

'Dharam Pasa. Where are you going?'

'To the front.'

'What front?'

'War.'

'Where?'

'Where your mother lives. Want to send a message?'

The soldiers would laugh.

'Will we get horses?' Abdullah asked.
'Don't think so,' Naim replied.
'I saw horses in a carriage up the train.'
'Probably for officers.'
'If they told me to bring my horse, I would.'
'Ask your wife to bring it,' someone in the carriage said. 'You will have two bodies to ride then.'
Abdullah ignored the taunt. He pulled a wheat ear from underneath him. 'Look,' he cried,' look what I found. The bastards took away somebody's ripe crop and threw it in here.'
Naim quietly took it from Abdullah's hand and rubbed it between his palms. The grains separated, and he blew away the chaff from his hand. 'The odd grain goes with the straw, doesn't it?'
'The odd grain? What about your whole crop, and mine? Who knows where it is? Thrown into trains like this or eaten by the pigs – who knows?'
'Maybe we too will be eaten by pigs soon,' a morose-faced soldier said.
'Stop talking like that. Here,' Naim offered the grains from his palm to Abdullah, 'eat them.'
Abdullah reluctantly took a few, leaving the rest for Naim. The wheat kernels were tasteless although slightly bitter, but crushed between strong teeth and mixed with saliva their flesh turned into sweetish milk. The two men's jaws were working in unison like the limbs of soldiers on parade.
'This turns into pure blood,' Abdullah said after a while.
Naim nodded in agreement.
Swallowing the thick liquid of raw wheat, Abdullah uttered an anonymous oath to the air. Four men playing cards laughed loudly at the very moment that the sick man emitted an agonizing cry, punching himself in the belly. He turned over and began to grind his teeth on strands of dry grass.
'Be patient,' the huge peasant, who had been telling a 'true story' to his companions, said to him. 'The train is going to stop soon.'
'How do you know?'
'I know. I have a feeling for these things.'
'So you can tell whether you are going to be killed or come back alive?'
'Stop this idle talk,' another said. 'Give the man some water.'
A soldier put his water-filled canteen to the sick man's mouth, but he pulled his face away, letting out a scream of pain.
'Hey, don't stand there looking at him like donkeys. Stop the train.'
'Why stop the train? You want to throw him out?'
'Yes, yes,' others agreed with the first man. 'Pull the chain.'

'The chain?'

'Yes, the chain. I have heard there is a chain and if you pull it the train stops.'

The story-teller took the lantern off its hook and went around the carriage looking up and down the walls. Many others followed him. Completing the round, he returned to announce: 'There is no chain.'

'This is a goods train,' a quiet-looking young boy said. ' Not for people. Goods have no use for chains, don't you see?'

The sick man had turned over on his back and lay straight, partially calmed, his groans now reduced to soft moans. After about a half-hour the train stopped. The soldiers congregated round the open door.

'What station is it?' They asked the usual question.

'Why do you ask which station it is? What does it matter?' the sad-faced men said.

'I would like to know,' the questioner said.

'You are not leaving the train here or anywhere. You're staying on it.'

'So?'

'So when your station comes you'll be taken off. That's it.'

'Oi, why are you blocking the door?' the sick man's attendant said. 'Clear a way, let the air come in.'

No one moved from the door. Abdullah got up and poked his elbow in the ribs of a man standing in the door. 'Get away. Let me out.' He jumped down. Several others followed him.

It was a small rural station. A dim lantern hung by the single door of the station building. Soldiers were jumping out of all the carriages on to soft, slightly damp earth that smelled freshly of rain. The steam engine, after emitting a couple of sharp hissing puffs, had fallen silent. They knew there was to be a 'cross' there, and they were sauntering up and down the station. A sudden noise arose from a carriage: 'Kill it. Kill it.' Shortly afterwards a soldier emerged with a small snake hanging by his bayonet. Everyone examined it and expressed his opinion: 'Very poisonous. Full of venom.' The man walked down the station and stopped in front of a carriage.

'Here, Bhopalis,' he said, offering them the snake at the point of the bayonet. 'A gift for you from Balochis.'

Someone from that carriage fetched the lantern to the door. After a moment's silence, there was laughter from the men. The man in the carriage knocked the dead snake off the bayonet with a kick of his boot and went back in.

'What regiment is this?' asked Abdullah.

'Ninth Bhopalis,' Naim said.

They walked on. Machine-gun barrels poked out of the MG Detachment carriages in their cloth covers. Soldiers, their legs sprawled across the barrels, slept. Next came the stretcher-bearers' carriage, where they sat talking against the stacked-up stretchers. The last ones were horse carriages. The passenger train coming from the opposite direction thundered down and passed without stopping, whistling furiously. Only a few of its carriages were lit, their ceiling fans whirring. In them the passengers were sitting up, reading newspapers or just looking out. A woman in a first-class compartment stood, bent over in the window with her head and naked shoulders out, looking at nothing. Only one fat man, who seemed to be sucking something, looked vaguely astonished to see a goods train full of soldiers in uniforms.

'Did you see her?' Abdullah asked afterwards.

'Who?'

'The woman.'

Naim quietly smiled.

'There was a woman in the train, I swear.'

'Yes,' Naim said.

They were unrolling their beds. The story-teller, his hand cupping his ear in the usual village-singer fashion, was singing the legend of Heer. As the train started to roll once again, the men began gradually, in the small hours, to fall asleep.

At Karachi harbour they boarded HMS *Weighmouth*. Naim's company was on the upper deck while the machine-gun detachment and half of the Bhopali Brigade were accommodated lower down. Most of the peasant soldiers quickly fell victim to seasickness and spent their days sucking on lemons and throwing up. Their first stop came at Aden. They stopped for twenty-four hours while shiploads of soldiers kept arriving from other Indian ports. Out of Aden, they became part of an armada of thirty-five ships. In the Red Sea they were joined by three battleships. Once they got over the sickness the peasants, coming from the water-starved plains, were wonderstruck at the sight of the sea. The limitless expanse of water that altered its colour with changes in the sky overhead, the seagulls that dived into it, the fishes of all colours that broke the surface and sparkled in the sun, the movement of water that went on and on until it met the horizon, and floating on this the dozens of ships, with their muffled hooters, each ship fifty times bigger than the village they had come from, ships like cities – all this excited and enthralled them and drove thoughts of war from their minds. But soon the voyage ended. At Port Said they disembarked and boarded railway trains that took them to Cairo. They encamped at Heliopolis Race Course outside the city. On one side were low yellow and grey stone hills on which goats roamed delicately under a naked sun, on the other was spread out the city, its roads traversed by bedouin driving their donkey- and camel-carts, some selling vegetables, fruit and milk. On another side could be seen a desert landscape. On the tinder-dry boulders of the hills and the shimmering cityscape, and upon the tired and tense faces of the soldiers too, a fierce sun rose each morning in full blaze, reminding the plains Indians of home. Once again, there were parades and more parades.

The company, having fallen in a half hour before, stood at ease awaiting further orders. Eventually, Captain Maclean appeared in the middle distance on a horse. The havaldar shouted 'Attention!' The soldiers shouldered their rifles and put out their chests to stand erect. The captain took two rounds of the company on his splendid Arab horse.

'I once had a horse like that one,' Abdullah whispered. 'It swelled up with bad wind and died.'

'Keep quiet,' Naim whispered back.

The captain had some difficulty controlling his mount. Finally able to calm it down, he addressed the company.

'Men, because of certain circumstances we have to stay here a few more days. I trust that we shall soon be on the battlefront. Keep yourselves fit and fresh. And you need not worry about your folk back home, they are being well looked after by the government.'

Through bared teeth, an angry sound came from the horse as it reared up on its hind legs. The captain, trying at the same time to control the horse and slip his hand back into the white glove that he had earlier taken off, dropped the glove to the ground. The havaldar ran to pick it up and hand it to the captain.

'Company, route-march,' came the shout from the havaldar's red face.

'I would fix that animal in a day if it was under me,' the soldier standing next to Abdullah said while Abdullah was saying to Naim, 'It is sister-fucking hotter here than at home.'

Route-marching, they crossed a stretch of sand and came to an oasis. A farmer, tilling a tiny area of land, stopped to look at them.

'Does it ever rain here, or is its piss quite enough for the crop?' a soldier asked, pointing to the plough-camel that cast a crooked silhouette against a blinding background.

Seeing the soldiers laugh, the Egyptian farmer smiled broadly, showing a gap where his front teeth once were.

'No talking,' shouted the havaldar.

'Swine,' a soldier said under his breath.

They returned from the route-march at noon. Abdullah took off his sweat-soaked shirt and flung it to the ground.

'It's four days since I last had a bath.'

A Punjabi soldier laughed bitterly. 'My nose is full of sand.'

'How do you breathe?' Abdullah asked him.

'Through my arse,' the soldier replied.

A Pathan soldier, spreading his shirt out to dry in the sun, said to him, 'Come and lie down here, you fill the tent with foul smell.'

'The officers get water to bathe every day,' someone said.

'They have to, because they only wipe their arses with newspaper,' said the Pathan.

They removed their clothes down to their underwear and lay down to smoke cigarettes.

Next morning, Naim was called up before the Brigade Major. He entered the major's office, a green canvas tent that housed the tables and other paraphernalia of the major and his havaldar clerk.

'I see that you are educated,' the major said to Naim.

'I have passed senior Cambridge, sir.'

'From where?

'St Xavier, Calcutta.'

'Had any machine-gun training?'

'No, sir.'

'Well, you will. I am promoting you to the rank of lance naik. Report to the section commander, MG Detachment.'

From Cairo, after six days, they were moved by train to Alexandria, where they did little else but route-march for a further few days before once again embarking on HMS *Weighmouth*. Finally they all had a bath aboard the ship, which was now part of a reduced armada of twenty vessels. The Bhopalis were left behind. An English battalion was travelling with them on the ship. One sunny day, amid much hooting and whistling, their ship dropped anchor at Marseille. Cigarette-smoking men and women in bright dresses welcomed the English officers by kissing them on the cheeks, the officers in turn asking them amid loud cheers, 'We are not too late, are we?' They were followed from the ship by the officers commanding the Indian troops: Captain Maclean, Captain Asher, Lieutenant Browning. The sun's pale rays out of the French sky slithered down the high brows and gold hair of the white officers whose nervous chins and blue-grey eyes shone with youthful life and health. These were the young men, some of them mere boys, for whom love burned eternally in many bosoms and whose rings gleamed many a year on young women's fingers. Within a few months they would all be dead, killed or reported missing in action.

'Les Indiens,' said the French to each other, pointing to the dark soldiers.

The 3rd machine-gun section was made up of two guns, ammunition, twelve mules, sixteen soldiers, Lance Naik Naim, Havaldar Thakur Das and Section Commander McGregor.

'The water here,' said Thakur Das, head thrown back and mouth pressed to the small round canteen, 'is sweet. And the food,' offering the canteen to Naim, 'is powerful.'

'Powerful?' Naim asked with a smile.

'Yes,' said Thakur Das. 'Makes blood in the veins. And the women.'

'They make blood in the veins too?'

'Ha ha ha!'

After weeks of travelling in ships and trains and living in grey, sun-baked lands, the dark, fertile earth and green vistas of France, its brightly dressed women and men who raised their hats in greeting to the troops, had brightened up the soldiers' mood, despite the tiredness in their limbs.

'We are going to get new ammunition tomorrow,' Thakur Das remarked.

'What kind of new?' Naim asked.

'Number seven bullet.'

'What happens to number six?'

'Rejected. Condum. Look,' he took a bullet from his belt, 'you see, this is pointed. Number seven will be flat in the front.'

'What difference will it make?'

Thakur Das paused for thought for a long moment, revealing his ignorance, before answering, 'Listen, this one goes like this,' he made an arc in the air with the bullet in his hand. 'The new one goes straight as an arrow.'

'What's the advantage?'

Thakur Das was beginning to show signs of irritation at Naim's questioning. He paused again. 'The one that makes an arc hits nearer than that which goes straight.'

Naim wasn't convinced by the argument but kept his counsel.

'We are also getting new bayonets,' Thakur Das informed him.

'What kind?'

'Same kind, only longer.'

'I see the advantage,' Naim said, smiling. 'The longer it is, the further it hits.'

'Exactly.' Thakur Das suddenly became serious. 'Are you making fun of me?'

'No, no,' Naim said.

Thakur Das lay down, facing the wall. 'Section commander showed me all this,' he said authoritatively.

They route-marched for miles the next day in a light rain. Then the rain stopped, the clouds lifted and by the time they returned to camp the sun had broken through. In his tent, Naim was trying repeatedly to strike a damp match. He was annoyed with himself. For the first time he felt bored.

'Put it out in the sun,' Thakur Das said, offering a dry box of matches.

'When are we going to the front?' Naim asked.

'Soon.'

'Soon, soon! Have you ever heard of anyone winning a war by route-marching?'

'Be patient,' Thakur Das said.

Imitating the havaldar, Naim repeated, 'Soon!'

Thakur Das turned round with a quick movement. 'Lance Naik Naim Ahmad,' he shouted.

'Yes.'

'Stand to attention.'

Reluctantly, Naim complied.

'How many rounds in a Maxim gun's belt?'

'Two hundred and fifty,' Naim answered.

'Weight?'

'About – er –'

'Weight of the gun?' Havaldar asked sharply.

'Sixty pounds.'

'At ease.'

Thakur Das went and stood at the tent-opening, his back to Naim. The light of the day faded suddenly. Clouds, thought Naim, absent-mindedly looking at the broad back of the havaldar that framed the opening.

Thakur Das came back. 'Don't ask too many questions. When war comes, it always comes too soon. Much too soon. When, where, how, all these questions, they make a coward of you. Sit.'

The two men sat side by side and lit cigarettes. Clouds chased each other across the sky, making the watery sun appear and disappear on the tent floor.

'Don't you ever ask questions?' Naim asked after a while.

'No.'

'You are not afraid of dying?'

After a moment, Thakur Das replied, 'I don't think about it.'

'What,' Naim said, trying to appear solemn, 'if I kill you now?'

Thakur Das made a tiny start. He began pulling at his cigarette. 'You will not do that,' he said in a slightly nervous voice.

'I am only joking,' Naim said.

Thakur Das finished his cigarette and leaned over to toss it out of the tent. 'You talk of going to the front,' he said. 'There everyone is the same, with guns and live ammunition, you can kill me as easily as I can kill you. But we don't, because it would be murder. Murder is different. You are going on your way and you kick over an anthill without giving it a thought. That is war. But if you see a single ant crawling up your arm, you don't kill it, it would be murder. You carefully blow it away to the ground.'

The sun was out and its rays were creeping up the tent once again. In the pale light, Thakur Das looked restless.

'You don't feel the pain of dying in battle?' Naim asked.

'I don't know. I have seen men dying like rats. You asked me whether I was afraid of dying. I don't know about that either. I have two children. I will have no control over my wife when I am dead. My wife has a boy from her previous husband. I don't, I have to tell you this, look at him as my own. When I die, my children will have no father. Or another father. I am afraid of that. A young boy like you cannot understand that. You only have fear of your own death.'

From Marseille they moved again. This time they were given the same kind of railway train that they got at the very beginning of their journey at Ferozpur: a goods train, the floor of the compartments covered with thick layers of hay. The train would stop at small stations for hours. They travelled for three days through beautiful country until they reached their camp in Orléans. They stayed there for sixteen days waiting for orders from headquarters, route-marching every day. The regiment consisted of nine British officers, eighteen Indian NCOs and seven hundred and ninety men. On the fifth day of their stay the Duke of Connaught's own son, Captain Prince Arthur, visited the regiment in person. Riding a white horse and dressed in an impressive uniform, this good-looking young man addressed the officers and men in the weak morning sun.

'I still remember the happiness I felt a few years ago when I visited the regiment in Hong Kong. To see Indian troops standing side by side with the British in Europe today makes me doubly happy. I will inform my father, the colonel commandant of the regiment, that you are in good form. I leave you now in the hope of seeing you again in a short while at the battlefront.'

Nobody saw or heard from him again until some time later when someone read in a newspaper that he had been killed in action.

On the seventeenth day they boarded another goods train and arrived at a place that abounded in paper-making factories. They found they were not alone there. Route-marching, they passed the camp site of 57 Frontier Force. Hawknosed and moustached Pathan soldiers, washing their utensils inside the barbed-wire perimeter, waved at the sight of passing countrymen and called out 'Hooa, hooa!' Next evening they saw a line of vehicles, crawling like ants, approaching from a distance. The 29th Connaughts, their excited hands on the wire fence, waited with a collective thumping heart. The lorries were not for them. Their hopes died when they saw the vehicles turning towards the Frontier Force camp site. They were to wait and continue route-marching for a few days yet.

'We shall be at the front tomorrow,' someone would say. 'Our lorries are coming.'

'I can hear the sound of cannon,' another would announce.

'Then you will die on the way,' a third would laugh, 'without ever seeing a bomb.'

'You never see a bomb anyway. Nor a bullet that hits you.'

'You may not see it but you will know it when it rips through your arse.'

The peasants, who had never seen a war, talked about it without terror or bravado, as though it were no more than a joke. One day the staff captain told them where the front was. 'It is two hundred miles away from here. In Belgium.'

'What, not in France?'

'No.'

Eventually they got their share of lorries. The vehicles travelled slowly, crossing the Belgian border and reaching their destination in twenty-four hours. They were lodged in the ghost town of Hollebeke. The battlefront was three miles away.

The town had been totally evacuated. All the best houses were commandeered by the white military – cavalry and artillery companies made up of three different nationalities: the Belgians, French and British. Two-storey houses were occupied by them, with their cooks, kitchens and boxes of dry rations. A few of the officers had their favourite horses in the ground-floor rooms as well. Headquarters staff were housed separately in a good large building. Then there were the shops, cleared of goods and their floors covered with corn stalks. Half the shops contained the horses and mules of cavalry and supply companies; the other half were reserved for the Indians.

The night sky hung low over the treetops, their leaves shivering in a light, cold wind. It was a narrow rectangle of a room, once a small shop, where the sixteen men of a machine-gun section, having eaten their dry meat and cheese rations, were lying down for the night. Some had promptly fallen asleep. A dim lantern hung in an alcove and two machine-guns stood by the wall; the ammunition was with the section commander.

'Are the mules safe?' Havaldar Thakur Das asked.

'They are,' Naim replied.

'Who is on the watch?'

'Spahi Ahmad.'

'Who will take over?'

'Riaz. At two o'clock.'

'Check it before you sleep.'

'I will.'

Naim had the familiar smell of dry corn stalks in his nostrils. The warm, humid breath of slumbering bodies was slowly spreading in the room. He undid his boots beneath his blanket and pushed them out with his half-warm feet. Thakur Das, who had made a small tent of his blanket by lifting his knees inside it and wrapping it all round him, including his face, and could even be heard snoring for a minute or two, suddenly poked his head out and asked, 'Have you a cigarette?'

Naim gave him a cigarette, requesting him to go and smoke by the door to avoid setting the dry corn alight.

'Let's go and sit there,' Thakur Das suggested.

'I am tired,' Naim said.

'Oh, come on, keep me company.'

The two of them, wrapped up in blankets, went to the door, half opening it, and sat there smoking.

'The floor is freezing,' Naim said.

'Will your complaints ever stop? Pull up some stalks. Let them catch fire. Who knows what will happen to the place when the attack comes.'

Naim slid some corn stalks underneath him and, feeling their comforting warmth, settled on them. 'I wonder why the front is so quiet. Only three miles away and jackals are barking.'

'The Germans haven't attacked yet,' Thakur Das informed him.

'Who is in our front lines now?'

'White troops. They are up against a whole enemy division.'

'How do you know?'

'Captain Maclean told me.'

Thakur Das threw his cigarette out of the door and wiped a huge hand over his two-day growth of beard. From the next shop came the sounds of mules' nervous hoofs on the floor, followed by one of the animals urinating noisily on the corn stalks. Naim stuck his head out of the door and called out in a controlled voice, 'Spahi Ahmad Khan!'

The soldier struck his rifle with the flat of his hand and answered back, 'Present.'

'Very good,' Naim said to the dark night.

A fine, silent rain was falling outside. 'This weather is bad for war,' Thakur Das said.

Naim quietly shut the door.

'In the rain that does not make a sound you don't know what is coming,' Thakur Das said again. 'The worst is snowfall.'

'Why?' asked Naim.

'First, it gets very cold. Then you slip on it.'

Naim laughed out loud.

'What is funny?' Thakur Das asked angrily.

'Nothing. Where did you see snow?'

'In the North West Frontier region. Action against the Afridis.'

They were diverted by a low roaring sound up above. Thakur Das opened the door and looked up. The noise got gradually nearer. A moving red light appeared in the sky, crossing from left to right. Following the point of light, the two of them, forgetting their blankets, got up and stepped out into the street, their mouths open and eyes fixed above them. The light and the roar disappeared quickly over and behind the rooftops. They stood there in the rain for a minute, looking at the featureless sky, then came back into the room.

'This was an aeroplane,' Thakur Das said confidently.

'Was it the Germans' aeroplane?' Naim asked.

'Don't know.'

'It had a red light.'

'They all have a red light,' said Thakur Das; then less certainly, 'sometimes a green light.'

'It makes more noise than cannons.'

'They do.'

'Have you seen it before?'

'No, they have only now started flying.'

'How do you know?'

'Why are you always questioning me? Do you doubt my word?'

'No, of course not,' Naim said.

Naim excitedly lit a cigarette.

'Finish your cigarettes here,' Thakur Das said to him. 'You can't smoke at the front.'

'Why not?'

'Why? Why? The bullet will come at the cigarette end and take your face away, don't you understand? Give me a cigarette.'

They sat smoking at their place just inside the closed door.

'Maybe we go up tomorrow,' Thakur Das said after a while. 'I am fed up with here.'

Naim looked at him with a smile.

'Don't try to be clever,' Thakur Das said. 'I feel worse than the mules in this place.'

'Yes,' Naim said, 'they only stand and urinate when they feel like it.'

'Listen, boy, I am really fed up. It's no joke. A man has got to be either facing the bullets or back home.'

'Do you miss home?' Naim asked him.

'I do. I miss my wife.'

'Do you love her?'

'I miss her, is that not enough? I know that she misses me as well. Missing someone is better than loving them. You know, we got together in a strange way. I used to be in the business of women.'

'Business of women?'

'Buying and selling them, that is what we used to do, Ram Singh and I. We lifted them from Ambala, Ludhiana, Rohtak and took them to Punjab. They fetched good money in Lyallpur, Sargodha, Multan, from bid landlords. We never had any use for them ourselves, we were well-known kabaddi players, only looked after our health and strength. But one day it happened.'

'What happened?'

'I heard that a kumhari had given out a call that should there exist a real man in the world, he may come and take her away. My moustache curled up at the sound of this. I found out that the kumhar, the woman's husband, was a champion wrestler in the area and his mother used to lock him and his wife in a room and didn't let them out till the morning. So going there at night was out of the question.' Thakur Das's voice was halted by phlegm in his throat. He cleared it and went on, 'So, going there at night was no use. I sent word through a go-between woman that I would be under a pipal tree a half-furlong from her village on a certain day at the time that the sun begins to slip from overhead, and if she is a woman of her word she may come out and meet me. That day I waited under the tree for an hour and she didn't come. I fell asleep from the heat of the sun. I was woken by the point of a stick being poked in my belly. I opened my eyes and saw a young man standing there. "What do you want?" I asked. "You send a message with pride and then you shut your eyes. Shame on you. It is not a man who sleeps as he awaits a woman," said the young man. Except that it was no young man, it was her in disguise. We started off together from there and spent the night at a friend's house in another village. In the morning she says, "Marry me." I promised to do so just to silence her and took her to Amritsar. There I sold her to a customer for one hundred silver rupees and escaped from there in the dark of the night. That was that, I thought. But no. I was sleeping in my own house a few days later when I was woken up again. Can you believe it, woken from deep sleep twice in a row by the same woman? This time she was sitting on my chest with a dagger in her hand.' Thakur Das stopped.

'What happened then?' Naim asked.

'What do you think? Could you say no with a knife at your throat?'

'You married her?'

'We have been married for fourteen years.'

Confused, Naim blurted out the question, 'But why?'

'Why what?'

'She had a husband, strong, a wrestler – I mean . . .' He ran out of words.

'Yes,' Thakur Das said, himself confused, as if he did not understand what the question was about.

In another shop a soldier began to sing, in a low, dry voice, a song of bereavement and departure. Naim threw the corn stalks from underneath him on to the nearest sleeping soldiers and went back to his bed. Thakur Das followed him.

'I know of women,' he said, 'who have six babies with one man and then run off with another. Surindri got me at the point of a knife, got the pandit at the point of a knife to marry us. You know, the two of us were on horseback and the pandit, trembling with fear, led the horse by the reins and took us through the rounds. Ha ha! But listen, since that day she has not raised her voice to me. She misses me. I know it here,' Thakur Das patted his chest, 'here. She speaks to me here.' He patted his chest again.

'I am going to sleep,' Naim said, covering his face with the blanket.

CHAPTER 9

The German attack came at Ypres. The battle continued until November. The Ferozpur Brigade marched to Belville where General French issued orders for the brigade to join the Second Cavalry Division. The 129th Duke of Connaught's Own was put under the command of Brigadier-General Vaughan who commanded the Third Cavalry Brigade. In the morning they reached the firing line and took over from the 5th and 6th Lancers. Naim's company was on the right flank by a vast wood whose dense trees, after running across the plain for a short distance, suddenly climbed a steep hill, looking like a herd of elephants going up to the top. Grass grew uncut everywhere, holding within it the fallen leaves of autumn.

Machine-guns were fixed in the trenches evacuated by the Lancers, who had left behind their empty ration tins, pieces of hard biscuit and cigarette ends. Eight men were deputed to each of the two machine-guns. Two more sections, with a gap of twenty yards between them, had taken up position, their four guns fixed in the already-dug foundations. The German attack had begun on the northern front, and sounds of artillery were reaching the southern positions. Ahead of the machine-gun pos-itions, at a slightly lower level, were the trenches of cavalry units. The Second Cavalry Division occupied a three-and-a-half-mile area between Hollebeke and the canal bridge. The trenches were a mile-and-a-half long. The left position was taken by the Third Brigade.

All day the sun shone on them and they sat there, waiting for orders. The trenches were cold and wet, and strange-looking insects crawled in them.

'Where is Havaldar Noor Mohammad?' Naim asked.

'At the outpost, top of the staff headquarters building,' Thakur Das answered, carefully picking up an insect and releasing it on the back of his hand.

'He was saying we will definitely attack this morning.'

'Yes, everyone thinks he is Brigadier-General Vaughan,' Thakur Das said. 'We will not attack, the enemy will. They did in the north too.'

In front of them the sun was going down on the broken landscape. The trenches camouflaged hundreds of soldiers' faces, red, brown and black, their ears cocked to the continuous low roar of artillery to the north, eyes glittering with the fever of a weary vigil.

'Motherfuckers,' Naim muttered, crushing a whole line of insects under his boot.

Thakur Das looked at him in mild alarm. Then he called out, 'Riaz, got the belts?'

'Got them,' the soldier answered.

'Gul Mohammad, you go now,' he ordered. 'Riaz and Ram Lal, you two take out the bullets and put them back in again. Practise, practise. Two hundred and fifty rounds go in three minutes, remember.'

Naim was killing the insects with the flat of his bayonet which he had unhinged from his rifle.

'Don't kill them, don't kill anything in your own trench,' Thakur Das said to him gently. 'There are rules in a field of battle.'

Naim gathered the dead creatures with his bayonet into a small heap on one side and raised himself on his knees. Gul Mohammad, crawling away behind the trench, passed the section commander and saluted him in a lying position. The section commander went on to speak briefly to a lean white officer and then came straight to the trenches. He stopped at each of the machine-gun positions and spoke to the men.

'Well done, men. We will attack tomorrow.' The officer tossed a packet of cigarettes to them before departing.

'Tomorrow, tomorrow,' Thakur Das said. 'This is the third time he has said it. The pig can't find some other place to go telling lies.' He took a cigarette out of the packet and gave one to Naim, throwing the rest to the others. The soldiers lunged at them. They lit their cigarettes. 'No head rises above the trench now, boys,' Thakur Das warned.

They smoked in silence. The clouds were hanging low and a biting wind blew over the earth, swirling in the trenches.

'You know,' Thakur Das said, digging the nail of his first finger into the mud wall of the trench in front of him, 'it was a cloudy day the time that Surindri and I were married. You should have seen the face of the pandit . . .' He laughed.

A sudden hard knot of resentment – of unknown origin, a throwback to what seemed many ages ago – gripped Naim's stomach. 'Fine place to talk of women,' he said, anger showing in his voice. 'What are you so happy about?'

Naim's reaction surprised Thakur Das. 'Any place is good enough to talk of women,' he said plainly. 'If you go looking for a place to be happy in, you will never find it.' Then with concern, 'Are you feeling all right?'

With an effort of will, Naim calmed himself. 'I am all right,' he said, pretending to cough. He spat. 'Perhaps this tobacco is bad.'

'English cigarettes, these are,' Thakur Das said.

About midnight it started to rain. It went on falling for four hours. There weren't enough tarpaulins to cover the trenches. Whatever they had – machine-gun covers, their coats – they tried holding up, wrinkling them to make channels for the rainwater to flow away. Nothing they did succeeded in keeping the water out. By the time the rain stopped they were standing in calf-deep water. They started to bail the water out with the help of empty ration tins. The section commander walked up and down the trenches, saying, 'Well done, men. Buck up. Good show.' In the midst of this they heard a drone overhead.

'Down,' Thakur Das shouted. 'On the ground.'

They dived face-down, their noses buried in runny mud, while the red light above quickly crossed the sky and faded away.

'Oh, get up, men, get up,' the section commander was saying. 'Those things are not going to attack you, they only come to look.'

Then they were standing up with their boots full of water, heavy coats dripping and bodies shivering.

'Come on, come on, buckets in and water out, buckets in and water out . . .'

The sounds of noses being blown and small tins being filled with water and emptied time after time arose all along the trenches that night until dawn came up, and the damp got into the soldiers' bones deeper than the Indians, reared in hot weather, had ever known before. A mile away they could see movement in the enemy lines.

The taste of the trenches had driven out the cheer that Naim had kept up for so long. He was in a nasty mood when Thakur Das told him to douse the small fire of damp twigs that he had managed to light in the trench.

'Leave me alone,' he said to the havaldar.

'We don't want to make too much smoke,' Thakur Das said as he went and crushed the half-lit twigs under his boots.

Naim tore off his helmet and flung it to the ground. Then he threw his rifle at the havaldar. The rifle brushed past Thakur Das and hit the mud, where it stood straight up against the trench wall. 'Here, take it away,' he shouted.

Thakur Das looked at him with a steady gaze for a minute, then he shrugged his shoulders and turned away. A soldier sitting by the second machine-gun, his face lined with dirt, said to his companion, 'The lance naik wants to be court-martialled.' The sun was up. The woods stood, peacefully green and still, above the sleepless, dirty, wet heads of the soldiers, and a thin steam was rising from the earth along the edges of the trenches. Some twigs were smouldering from an earlier fire where a soldier sat trying to dry his socks while Thakur Das chewed on a hard biscuit with mouthfuls of water from his canteen. When he had finished, Thakur Das picked up Naim's rifle.

'Do you think there are not enough enemies already in the field?' He tossed the rifle to Naim. 'Here, you will need this.'

Naim caught the rifle in the air and sat down in the trench to nibble on a biscuit.

The cavalry units were withdrawn that day, but no orders came for the machine-gunners. At night the sky became overcast, and soon afterwards it began to snow. It was the Indians' first sight of snow. Sticking their heads out of the trenches, they kept looking for half the night at the snow falling over the woods and settling there. They had covered the trenches with whatever pieces of cloth they could lay their hands on. When they tired of watching the snowfall in the still air, the soldiers sat and, in the slightly raised temperature, they felt encouraged to take off their shirts, vests and socks and hold them over the damp and dying fires, hoping to dry them. Thakur Das was trying repeatedly to scrape the mud off his boots with the help of his bayonet, unmindful of the fact that the mud had long been cleared and the bayonet point was beginning to score the leather. Naim stood, resting his weight on the bayonetless rifle stuck under his armpit, and looked out, remembering the time he first saw the snowfall in Simla when he was small. They were staying in the house of one of his uncle's friends during the long summer holidays. They had taken a trip one day up into the high mountains and he saw the snow falling there in the middle of August. Down in Simla, the house was built in the side of a hill and it has a wooden veranda overhanging a sheer drop of hundreds of feet. A cat had had kittens and lived on the veranda, and when it rained a kassi flowed right opposite the house with the water running from the top of the hill to the bottom and the water was so clear he could see the pebbles underneath from where he stood on the veranda. He had a friend his own age, the son of the house, what was his name? Yes, Deepak. As the rain stopped they would go down to the kassi to pick up coloured pebbles that had been swept down from the top while Deepak's sister Nirmal sat atop a boulder and played the harmonica. At that age they were Naim's only friends. Where were they now? What might have happened to them? Standing there, surrounded by a vast, hidden sea of men, he felt utterly alone. A slow, unaccountable anger that had been rising and falling inside him all day had settled in the pit of his stomach. His legs were trembling under him from standing too long, and he found that he was starving.

The attack began the next day. The plan was to go like this: No. 3 Double Company, which was in possession of the Hollebeke trenches under the command of Major Humphrey, would advance and encircle six hundred yards of the front; No. 1 Company under Captain Adair would take Rumbeke, and as soon as No. 2 Company came alongside they would commence the attack, the right flank heading towards the farm on contour 30; two platoons of No. 3 Company, along with the machine-gun section now led by Captain Dell, would support the fire coming from the trenches around the farm; No. 3 Company, minus the two platoons, and No. 4 Company would wait in reserve behind the farm. The firing started at three o'clock. They faced the enemy machine-gun and rifle fire. The artillery was still silent on either side.

Captain Dell, binoculars to his eyes, was walking along the machine-gun positions. The noise of firing was echoing from the western hills, and the air was weighted with the smell of gunpowder.

'Thirty-nine degrees south-east. Fire!' shouted Captain Dell.

Naim pressed the trigger. The bullets fell well short of the enemy trenches, throwing up small stones and larger pieces of earth.

'Blast,' said the commander and turned to look towards the OP's position. 'Idiot,' he said. 'Cease fire!' He fixed his binoculars once again at the enemy. 'Forty-two degrees south-east. Fire!'

This time their fire was right on target. The line of enemy heads disappeared below the trench line. A couple of arms were thrown in the air and a soldier leaped up as if he had been shoved powerfully from beneath. The second burst got him straight in the body. He rolled over for a yard and lay still and flat on level ground.

'Well done,' shouted Thakur Das. 'Fire!'

Naim felt the sensation of the blood circulating rapidly in his veins. He increased the pressure of his finger on the trigger. 'Load up the belt,' he said.

'Do not overheat the guns.' Captain Dell was speaking into his binoculars. 'They are your best friends, do not let them melt away, give them a break . . .'

Rifle and machine-gun shots were piercing the air, the atmosphere was hazy with dust and powder, and the sunlight reflected off the dead enemy soldier's helmet.

In late afternoon the artillery opened up from behind with rapid fire. The enemy fire stopped for a time. Adjusting and readjusting his binoculars, Captain Dell shouted the order, 'Company, advance.'

Two soldiers pulled up the machine-gun while Thakur Das handed its tripod to a third. Naim's soldiers picked up their machine-gun and ran forwards, crouched over. A burst of fire whistled over their heads. One of Thakur Das's soldiers threw up his arms, rose momentarily on his heels and fell to the ground. The entire detachment dropped to their bellies. A second burst of fire came inches above their backs. Gripped by terror, they tried at first to hide behind small stones, then dug their heads into the earth, but in the face of heavy and accurate enemy fire they eventually had to retreat. Half-wet earth and grit entering and blocking their nostrils, they were slithering backwards on their stomachs like wounded snakes. They were almost back at their trenches when a soldier, propelled upright by the impact of a burst of fire, spun round and fell back into the trench. A bullet hit the magazine of a machine-gun behind which Naim had been sheltering his face and smashed it.

They refixed their guns in the trenches and, following Captain Dell's sharp, angry orders, opened fire. The wounded soldier, holding his stomach with both hands, cried, 'Water.' Someone put their canteen to his mouth. He took a mouthful but the water flowed back out of the corners of his lips. He was looking with a fixed gaze at what seemed to be nothing at all. Casualties of the aborted attack: two men and a machine-gun.

A part of the company led by Captain Wilson lost its way and ended up to the right of 2 Company. At dusk the captain asked for assistance and was promised two platoons of 4 Company. But before they arrived he took a direct hit in the head and died instantly.

In view of more important events on the right flank, the break-up of the division became inevitable. The next morning the regiment was ordered to withdraw from their positions and go to the north of Hollebeke. In the evening two companies were called back to occupy trenches A and B again. For two days it went on like this. A third of the artillery, chiefly comprised of six-inch Howitzers, was knocked out. Then came the German attack.

The Second Bavarian Corps was massing its troops in the section where the Third Cavalry Brigade was dug in; 129's two companies were in the forward lines and were to be relieved at seven in the morning by the 5th and 6th Lancers, while No. 1 Company had just relieved No. 2, which was pulled back into reserve. The enemy attack added to the generally unsettled situation, and in the face of heavy artillery bombardment No. 2 Company had to retreat to take refuge behind the farm. Captain Dell's company was still in position. It had lost half its men, enemy batteries were pounding the position, and it was some time since the section commander's last round of the trenches, which were largely blasted and broken. In answer to the enemy's Big Berthas, the smaller six-inch guns were proving to be no match. The enemy front lines were fast advancing towards them. Five hundred yards away they could see soldiers in unfamiliar uniforms. The company had five machine-guns, all firing. One by one they soon fell silent. It was still a couple of hours before sundown, and the wind blowing over the previous night's snow carried a smell of blood and gunpowder along with the groans of the wounded and the dying. The noise of the artillery's continuous barrage bored holes into the men's brains, driving them to the verge of insanity.

'Put in a belt,' Thakur Das ordered.

Two soldiers quickly finished slipping in bullets and fitted the belt to the magazine.

'Is that all?' asked Thakur Das, looking at the heap of empty belts.

'Rahim has gone to fetch more.'

'How long ago was that?'

'About a half-hour.'

'Riaz, you go,' Thakur Das said.

The soldier hesitated for a moment, looking around, his eyes vacant with fear.

'Go on, only one gun's left. You want to die like a rat?'

Riaz heaved himself out and started crawling back to the ammunition hut. Thakur Das and Naim saw, along the barrel of their gun, the line of enemy soldiers showing signs of advancing towards them. Thakur Das hurriedly went over to the next machine-gun, where he found the bodies of four soldiers, their faces smeared with dirt and contorted in death. A half-spent belt hung by its magazine. Thakur Das tried its trigger. He swore and came back.

'Jammed,' he said.

'Can't we use that belt somehow?' Naim asked him.

'Have you not had MG training?'

'I have.'

'Why do you ask then?'

'Just asking,' Naim said, his silent gaze crowded with other questions.

A shell landed thirty yards behind the trench and Riaz flew up like a jumping fish and lay still. Thakur Das and Naim kept looking at him for a minute and saw no movement. A second shell came down three feet away from their faces and a wall of earth lifted Thakur Das into the air. He fell back, still inside the trench, his mouth and nose full of dirt. He lay there for a few seconds, too stunned to breathe. Then he started coughing and blowing his nose. Rubbing his eyes furiously to clear them, he sat up.

'Are you . . . ?' Naim inquired.

'Yes, yes, I am alive. I have tasted dirt in all my holes many times before.'

'The gully is demolished,' Naim said to him.

'I can see . . .'

A third shell dropped at a safe distance, but still buried them with clods of earth. The two of them dug the machine-gun out of the debris.

'No bullets,' Thakur Das said. 'Riaz is gone.'

Naim understood what he meant. Securing his rifle around his shoulder, he climbed out of the trench and started a slow crawl back to the ammunition dump. Rifle, machine-gun and artillery fire made a roof over his head. He passed the body of Riaz. Riaz's abdomen was open and part of his intestines was sticking out. Naim averted his face to avoid smelling the steam rising from the torn gut. Next he came across Rahim, who had been hit in the neck and blood had collected in a puddle, his sightless eyes staring from his head. Naim took a mouthful of snow from the ground and kept crawling. A few minutes later he approached the temporary hut erected with odd bits of wood and foliage from the forest hidden in a cluster of trees, where three soldiers were busy filling the bullet holes, taking the ammunition from wooden boxes and slipping them into the leather belts. Halting for a second outside the entrance, Naim heard them laughing. He made a noise that alerted the soldiers inside. They jumped up, rifles at the ready.

'Who goes there?'

'Friend,' Naim replied and stepped into the hut. He could see the laughter still hovering around their faces. 'Belts ready?'

'All ready, lance naik.'

'What is the joke?' he asked.

The men burst out laughing. 'Shams was telling us about this bull of his who used to kidnap cows and bring them home.'

'You talk about naughty bulls at a time like this?' Naim said solemnly.

The men went on laughing. 'Any time is a good time,' one of them said, 'and this is the best time, ha ha ha ha!'

Naim knew then that these men, hearing the earth blasted for days, had stopped caring. He was grateful that they hadn't stopped working. He slung four loaded belts on his back. 'Keep working,' he said to them as he went out. 'We shall need a lot more of these.'

The belts were one too many for him to carry. He gritted his teeth and kept crawling with them on his back up to the trenches. He passed an L-shaped trench where a machine-gun stood silent. 'Friends,' he called out, 'men, you want ammunition? You want bullets?'

He got no answer and carried on. Daylight was fading quickly. He was now in sight of his machine-gun, which was still firing. Thakur Das's head was bobbing up and down; he was using the last belt sparingly, firing short bursts at a time. Naim was exhausted but happy that he had enough ammunition on him to keep the gun firing for a good while. He knew that Thakur Das would be happy with his work.

He was a dozen feet away from his trench when he saw a whole line of soldiers from the opposite trenches spring up as if thrown out of the earth and come running towards him, their guns blazing. He dug his head into the ground and shouted, 'Havaldar, don't get up. They are coming –'

Thakur Das's head bobbed up for a second. Naim felt his left hand going numb. 'Don't get up,' he shouted, 'stay in the gully, run to the right –'

Thakur Das stood up. 'Naim, are you hurt?'

'No,' he said. At the same time he saw blood pouring out of his arm. 'I don't – know,' he stammered. 'Get down, Thakur, run to your right –'

Thakur Das climbed out of the trench and ran towards Naim.

'Ohh . . . go back,' Naim moaned.

At that moment Thakur Das was hit in the back by one bullet after another, his body jerking from head to foot three times in quick succession, until he opened his arms, as if to hug someone, and fell on top of Naim with all his weight. Naim remembered two things before he passed out: wishing Thakur Das would get off him, but Thakur Das, flat as a slab, wouldn't budge; and seeing, in the back of his mind, just as he heard a deafening explosion behind him in the cluster of trees, the laughing faces of three men talking of a kidnapping bull back in someone's village.

When he came to, he was still lying underneath Thakur Das and he realized that he had lost consciousness for only a few minutes. He also knew that their trenches were now occupied by the enemy. But no fire was coming from there. Behind him he could only hear the roar of his own artillery shelling the ground far beyond the trenches where he and Thakur Das had been. With a huge heave, he moved from beneath Thakur Das's body, threw off the ammunition belts and started a terrified crawl backwards, expecting the enemy fire to come at any moment. Night had fallen. In the dark, he reached a safe distance, stood up and started running until he reached the artillery batteries. He saw a horse bleeding from the chest and two men tending to it. He approached an officer.

'Friend,' he shouted. 'Lance Naik Naim Ahmad, 129 Baloch, machine-gun detachment, section number –'

'All right, lance naik,' the officer said, 'speak.'

'Our position has fallen to the enemy, sir. All the men are dead. The guns are in enemy hands.'

In the thin light of a sliver of moon, the officer wiped his brow with his white, faintly trembling fingers. 'Report to the adjutant,' he said.

Pressing his hand on his bleeding left forearm, Naim went towards where he thought the brigade headquarters might be.

CHAPTER 10

They fought on in Belgium and France for a year. In the month of July, the regiment was pulled out and ordered to go to East Africa. They spent a few days in Marseille where they were to board ship.

It had been a sunny, warm day and Naim had been out strolling along the city streets, which were crowded with men, women and children. A horse-cart, loaded with baskets of vegetables, passed. A few yards ahead, the horse's hooves slipped on the road surface and it fell awkwardly with its legs spread out in all four directions. People gathered on the roadside, women uttering small, brief cries of pity and horror. The farmer and his helper, putting the strength of their backs behind it, first helped up the horse and then started picking up spilled heads of cabbage, parsnips and other vegetables from the road. Some more people gathered on the other side. Suddenly Naim saw a figure in the crowd, walking away. He was a heavy-set man in a crumpled army uniform. There was something in the way he walked and the line of his shoulders that was recognizable. Naim caught up with him. The man turned round.

'Mahindroo!' Naim cried in surprise.

'Neem!' Mahinder Singh answered.

They grabbed one another's hands and kept pressing and shaking them for minutes on end without saying another word, their eyes twinkling with old warmth. Finally, Naim laughed and said to him, 'You are alive! And dirty. Great!'

Mahinder Singh laughed. 'I am going to have a bath today.'

'Good. Then you will be alive and clean.'

'What are you doing here?' Mahinder Singh asked.

'We are going to Africa. I am in the 129th Baloch. A machine-gunner. And you?'

'No. 9, Hudson Horse, Ambala Brigade.'

'Have you been fighting?'

'Yes.'

'Where?'

Mahinder Singh pointed in an indefinite direction with his hand. 'There.'

'Against whom?'

'Turks – Germans,' Mahinder Singh said vaguely, as if he was not sure who they were.

'Are you all right?' Naim asked.

'Yes. You?'

'I got a bullet. But only in the flesh. Healed quickly.'

They walked on in silence.

'You want to go and eat something somewhere?' Naim asked him.

'Er – no, I am going back to my unit. Come, there is a place where we can talk,' Mahinder Singh said.

Walking alongside one another, they left the neighbourhood. People, especially children, stopped to gape at this soldier with a beard and a turban wrapped round his head. The two of them entered a vast cemetery. Concrete-slab graves with headstones spread out from narrow red stone pathways on either side of which stood tended fruit trees. Looking at Mahinder Singh out of the corners of his eyes, Naim noticed that the young Sikh no longer had the agility in his limbs; he had grown fat and moved ponderously, like an old bull – something unlikely to happen to a soldier in the midst of war.

'Any news?' Naim asked.

'There were floods.'

'Somebody told you?'

'Ramzan.'

'The cobbler? He wasn't with us.'

'No, he was away when we were taken. He was caught six months later.'

'Where did you meet him?'

'He was sent to our regiment.'

'What else did he say?'

'It came for four days non-stop after we left. Crops washed away. Many houses collapsed under the rains, Ramzan's too. After the floods foot-and-mouth spread and killed many cattle. But our two best bulls were sold by Juginder in good time. Chaudri Niaz Beg also sold most of his animals before the disease came, so you'll be all right.' Bad though the news was, Mahinder Singh perked up as he spoke to Naim of their homes. 'After we came away many Roshan Pur girls ran off with boys from Jat Nagar who had hidden and escaped being taken. Ishtamal was done by the land department. Our barley field by the pond was exchanged with one of yours by the graveyard. Our field is good soil, you have nothing to worry about. Everyone's land is in one place now, what more do we want? Good for animals too, they don't have to go from one field to the other . . .'

In the growing dark of evening, they were the only two left in the sprawling cemetery. Much of their talk had been exhausted in the first half-hour. Still reluctant to part, walking up and down the paths in silence like ghosts from another time and another place, only occasionally breaking the quiet of the place with a word from Naim or a grunt from Mahinder Singh, they kept repeatedly looking at one another without words. As light of the day died, Naim stopped and put his hand on Mahinder Singh's shoulder.

'Mahindroo, are you well?'

After a pause, Mahinder Singh said softly, 'I am well. Only tired. Much tired.'

'Of the war?'

Mahinder Singh shrugged.

'I didn't think war would do you any harm,' Naim said, laughing. 'Remember back in the village? You could kill without blinking an eye.'

Mahinder Singh left the path and went to sit on the raised slab of a grave. 'That was different,' he said after a few long minutes. 'To avenge the blood of one of your own, even a rat can kill. Here we don't even know the people. It is like killing a pig, or a jackal in the jungle.'

'Well,' Naim said, 'that is what war is.'

Although supporting his weight on hands placed on either side of him on the stone, Mahinder Singh looked slumped, his back in the shape of a bow, his shoulders fallen, as if his body had taken on a different form.

'Tell me,' Mahinder Singh asked suddenly, 'why are we here?'

'Because of the war,' Naim said. 'The enemy has attacked.'

'What, attacked our village?'

'Attacked the British sarkar and their friends.'

'What is it to us?'

'They are our masters.'

'Our master is Roshan Agha,' Mahinder Singh said simply.

'Yes, and the English sarkar is Roshan Agha's masters.'

A brief hollow sound emerged from Mahinder Singh's mouth. 'How many masters do we have?'

Naim laughed. 'Well, it's just the way it is.'

Mahinder Singh got up ponderously, as if making an effort to carry the weight of his clothes. 'I like this place,' he said, gesturing towards the graves. 'Here good people are buried. With names.'

Naim didn't know what to say to awaken within Mahinder Singh the old friend he once had. Cheerily he pressed on. 'And dates.'

'Yes,' said Mahinder Singh. 'Some with the names of their fathers and mothers too.'

Naim laughed again. 'But, Mahindroo, you can't even read.'

'But I know. On the stones are names and dates.'

He thumped his sides, as if dusting his clothes, although there was no dust. Then he offered his hand to Naim. Naim grasped it in both hands and kept squeezing it as if to reach the inner places of the man.

'I will see you. Later,' Mahinder Singh said, freeing his hand.

'Yes, yes. When all this is over. Once we are back in the village we will snatch all the girls from Jat Nagar's scoundrels, won't we?'

After a long moment, during which Mahinder Singh looked around at the graves and their headstones, which had lost their contours in the dark, he said, 'Yes.' Without another word he walked away, quickly disappearing from view, leaving Naim standing there with visions of his village and the two of them as they had been, in past seasons so far back that it was hard even to recall them, although there was no more than a year and a half in between. In that time they had seen the face of a war they did not understand.

Africa

Making their way through six-foot-high grass with the help of bayoneted rifles, they emerged on the bank of a lake that divided the jungle into two halves. The sun was reflected like a conflagration on the waters of the lake.

'Bah oh!' exhaled Lance Naik Sajan, pressing a piece of cloth on to his face, which was covered with fine cuts that oozed tiny drops of blood. 'Sharp as swords it is, and they call it bloody grass.'

Naim, screwing up his eyes to scan the jungle on the opposite bank, suddenly felt his feet sinking into the earth. He looked down in horror.

'Retreat,' he shouted.

The soldiers jumped, fell, leaped in panic and pulled themselves out of the shifting earth, withdrawing quickly into the grass.

'Swamp,' Naim told Sajan.

Sajan swore. 'Strange country. My blood has turned black. Look.'

'Everything looks black in the shade.'

'No, no, I am telling you. It is the mosquitoes. You know, I have crushed a mosquito and its blood was black,' he said, uttering a forced, hollow laugh peculiar to men in battlefield.

They had been camping in this part of Africa, undergoing exercises to 'familiarize' themselves with the African war in grassland and small dense forests where the rule was 'fire first and apologize afterwards'. In this land of swamps, they lived among large mosquitoes that outnumbered them by a million to one. There were deaths from malaria. The condition of the white troops was worse, because they fell victim not just to malaria but to diarrhoea and skin diseases as well. Many died without firing a shot. The only 'healthy' troops on their side were the African battalions who, although reputed to be poor fighters, were not in the least affected by the elements. Across the lake, in the other part of the jungle, was the enemy. There had been no engagement so far. All night long the men stayed half-awake, fighting the bee-sized mosquitoes. One of their men died of snake-bite. When a death occurred among the ranks, the men of the platoon stayed up, remembering the dead and killing mosquitoes which they considered their first opponents in the war, more deadly than the enemy soldiers because they were always there and attacking.

'Such a useless death,' Lance Naik Sajan said to Naim as they sat around, tired but sleepless. 'I mean an insect that you can easily kill sneaks up on us and kills us.'

'No more useless than any other,' Naim said.

'Except those that come from God,' Sajan said with a certain satisfaction.

'So you think a death in war comes from God,' Naim asked after a while.

'No,' answered Sajan, 'I don't think so.'

'All right, why not?'

Sajan was quiet for a moment. 'You know, havaldar,' he said then, 'whenever I think I have killed someone, not hand to hand but even unseen, I feel the blood in my throat. Death that comes from God's will does not stick in anyone's throat.'

'I think we will have an engagement with the enemy tomorrow,' Naim said to change the subject, although he did not believe it. He had only had some doubtful information about their strength. 'They are massed over there on the western side of the trees. Intelligence says they have sixteen thousand troops. Two thousand white and fourteen thousand black.'

'Where do they get the blacks?'

'Don't know. Each company has two hundred men, sixty big guns and eighty machine-guns. We will have a job to do . . .'

'Motherfucking mosquitoes,' Sajan said. 'Oh yes, sir, big job to do. Havaldar, are there mosquitoes where the enemy is?'

'Of course, much more.'

'Good.'

Not long after, they had their first real engagement. There had been no word from Intelligence. They were on a routine exercise when it happened. Light-footed as forest foxes, they were advancing through thick grass when suddenly they came up against a company of white soldiers.

'Black Bird!' The company commander shouted the code word.

He was answered by rifle fire. The company hit the ground and returned the fire. Birds flew up from the grassland and small animals scurried away. After a few minutes' silence, a line of soldiers appeared virtually at arms' length from them and attacked. Hand to hand began. Naim, still on the ground, took aim at a soldier's chest and fired. The soldier, a husky, red-faced man, fell back and gathered up in the shape of a ball. He didn't get up. Finding attacking soldiers almost looming above him, Naim jumped up. A few feet away he saw a soldier running across, his bayonet pointing at the body of Naim's company commander. Without a moment's pause, Naim charged and sank his bayonet in the side of the soldier. The commander, alerted by the cry of the wounded man, turned and fired his revolver at him. The soldier slumped to the ground. The commander glanced round and fired again at a soldier attacking Naim. At the same moment Naim looked to his side and saw that his left arm was hanging by thin threads of flesh and veins just below the elbow. Before he lost consciousness he distinctly recalled thinking, why was it always his left arm that got hurt?

The hospital was in a building once used as a school. In a long narrow room, Naim lay among the other half-fallen, their heads touching others' feet, squeezed into spaces too small for them. Amid cries and moans from the wounded, the maimed and the near-dead, the old bandaged ones looked at the new arrivals as a buffalo would look, with uninvolved concern, at another in the agony of giving birth. A Pathan soldier lay beside Naim.

'How are you feeling, jawan?' a doctor on his round asked the Pathan.

'Son of a donkey,' the Pathan said to the doctor, glowering at him with red, swollen eyes. Then suddenly, he burst into tears. 'I have become lame – I will be a lame man, always –'

The doctor threw a tired glance at the soldier and moved on to Naim. 'Your last dressing will be on Friday,' he said, looking at the patient's papers, before moving on.

Following the doctor came Nurse Doris. 'Stop crying, you baby,' she said to the Pathan affectionately.

'He is not a baby, nurse,' Naim said, laughing.

'You are all babies here. When you arrived here last month you were crying too.'

'No I wasn't.'

'Yes you were. You have forgotten. You were very small then,' she said, sweetly mischievous, passing on to the next man.

Naim got off his bed and went to sit on the Pathan soldier's bed.

'What is your name?'

'Amir Khan,' the Pathan replied.

'Where do you come from?'

'Kaka Khel. Near Peshawar.'

'Where were you wounded?'

'Some place out there. Don't know the name.'

'Unit?'

'Frontier Force Rifles.'

During this exchange the soldier's gaze remained fixed upon Naim's arm. Naim smiled and showed him the bandaged stump. 'Yes. It had to be cut off.'

The Pathan soldier shook his head in aggrieved sympathy, looking from Naim's half arm to his own half leg for a few seconds, then smiled, as if taking strength from the other man who looked alive and well minus an arm.

After his discharge from the hospital, Naim reported to his unit, from where he was sent to brigade headquarters. He was sitting on a bench outside an office, waiting to be called, when he felt someone's hand on his shoulder. He looked up and saw it was Khalik from Jat Nagar. Naim stood up and they shook hands. Khalik kept looking at Naim's empty sleeve, knotted up below the elbow.

'Yes, this,' Naim said, moving his arm. 'I was wounded.'

'Bad,' Khalik said. 'Very bad. Do you remember the time we came to Roshan Pur for a kabaddi match and you broke my ear with a blow of this hand?'

'N-no,' Naim said, 'I don't remember. Where are you posted?'

'Here, in headquarters. I am with the supply corps.'

Khalik gave him a cigarette and helped him light it.

'What's the news?' Naim asked.

'My brother Tufail has made a havaldar. Darshan Singh became disabled and was sent home. Roshan Pur's Mahinder Singh died.'

The cigarette in Naim's fingers trembled. 'In action?'

'Yes. But not at the enemy's hand.'

'What happened?'

'His unit was ordered to advance, but he stayed put, wouldn't move. After many warnings, finally his company commander shot him.'

Naim inhaled deeply on the cigarette several times.

Khalik continued in a low, flat voice. 'He had, you know, grown a bit poor in the head. Oh, I don't know, don't want to talk bad about the dead. Anyway, there was something wrong with him.' He saw signs of distress on Naim's face and said, 'Mind you, he may have died in some other way. This is just the story that I heard.'

Naim's thoughts were still muddled as he was called in.

'You have been recommended for a medal for bravery, and we are all proud of you,' the adjutant told him. 'Final approval has to come from high up, takes time. Look, can you handle a rifle?'

'Yes, sir.'

'I mean, can you fire it?'

'I can,' Naim answered without thinking.

The officer looked at him as if he had doubts about the statement. 'Well, it doesn't matter. You will do guard duty on the enemy wounded.'

'Yes, sir.'

The wards of wounded prisoners of war were in a small church building. On the second day of his new assignment, Naim went down a corridor and stopped dead; it was as if the earth had gripped his feet. So far he hadn't looked at the wounded with any interest. To him they were like every other wounded man he had earlier seen in his own sick bed – except that these were the enemy. Bloodless and disfigured, they were mostly white and hence strangers to him. That day he first glanced at one who had a face swollen to the size of a large watermelon, his features lost in the distended, fluid-filled flesh. As he turned his face away, Naim caught sight of another, lying still, with his head propped up on a rolled-up piece of cloth that served as a pillow. Naim turned pale and quickly retraced his steps. It's him, he said to himself. I saw his face. He turned towards me for a second before he fell. His bayonet was inches away from the captain's ribs when I pushed mine into his side. He had on his face the grimace of pain as he looked at me. How can I forget his face, the imprint of his twisted face on my brain, the face of the first man I drew blood from under my eyes, near enough to touch him and smell his sour blood? Why the hell did he not die and disappear into the earth? He took a bullet from the captain too. Ya khudaya, how hard these bastards are!

Naim stayed away from that part of the ward for the rest of the day. The next day he tried to steady himself and passed by the sick man, who was looking straight ahead. Will he recognize me? he thought. Actually I have only exposed my profile to him, whereas he saw me from the front earlier in the grass. Is my face fixed in his eyes? I once heard a story that a police investigator looked into the open eyes of a dead man and saw the image of the man who had killed him. I don't really believe that story. Anyway, this man is not dead. But that is the whole problem. He is alive . . . On the third day, the foolishness of the situation dawned on him – that he, Naim, was now this man's master and had no need to fear him; that he held the weapon and the man was his prisoner and powerless. He looked the man straight in the face and passed on. The man, yellow-skinned, sunken-cheeked and heavily bandaged around the chest, looked back without a glimmer of recognition in his eyes. It's all right, thought Naim, we are completely different in appearance from these people and probably look all the same to them. He can never pick me out.

Satisfying himself thus, Naim went about his guard duties, gradually losing his self-consciousness until a couple of days later when he was brought to a halt again: he imagined that the man had smiled at him. Without stopping, he managed a wan smile back. On his next round the man spoke to him. In a heavy, thick voice, he said, 'Officer.' Naim stopped near him. The man knew few English words but made himself understood.

'Sun,' he said, pointing to the large window just behind him, 'all day. I burn.'

Naim nodded and hastily withdrew. Still, he couldn't keep himself from going to speak to the doctor in charge.

Doctor McDonald smiled sarcastically. 'Does he think he is in a hotel?'

'But, sir,' Naim said, 'he is badly wounded. At least we can stop the sun coming in. It is very hot in there and he is suffering.'

'Suffering, hah! Can you imagine how many people he may have made to suffer?'

'Very true, sir,' Naim said, but didn't go away.

The doctor looked at his amputated arm and relented. 'Don't look to me to do anything, I can only attend to his wounds. But you are free to do what you can.'

After a bit of looking around, Naim found a piece of tarpaulin that he hung up, with the help of another soldier on guard duty, a partly shell-shocked man who had the use of both arms, in front of the window. It stopped the sun coming in.

'Thank you,' said the prisoner several times, gratitude showing in his eyes.

From then on, Naim stopped by the man at least once in a day to ask him how he was, to which the man always replied, 'Thank you,' with a smile.

A few days later the man spoke to Naim once again. 'I Harold. Thank you for favour.'

'No favour,' Naim said to him, 'only my duty.'

'I return favour,' Harold said.

'Thank you. But there is no need.'

'I make hand.'

'Hand? What hand?'

'That.' The man pointed to Naim's empty sleeve.

'This?' Naim asked, raising his left upper arm. 'How?'

The man simply said, 'Yes, yes,' vigorously nodding his head.

Naim came away from there saying no more than 'thank you'. On the following days Naim did not stop by the man; and by generally ignoring him he tried to discourage the man from speak to him. Some days later, however, with the help of another wounded prisoner who spoke better English than Harold, Naim came to understand the prisoner's offer: Harold and his father, coming from a long line of cabinet makers, had worked all their lives in a factory that made artificial limbs before Harold was taken into the army. All he needed, the prisoner speaking on behalf of Harold said, was some tools and a piece of wood. Throughout this conversation, Harold, with a smile on his face, kept saying 'thank you' and pointing to the back of his shoulders and neck where the tiny boils that had come up on the skin from the heat of the African sun were already beginning to lose their angry red colour and were drying up. On top of his guilt, Naim felt embarrassed. Conspiring with another guard, he stopped going to Harold's ward altogether. Days passed without Naim setting eyes on Harold. The longer he stayed away, however, the stronger the image of the man with a pathetic smile on his lips impressed itself on Naim's mind. At the same time, as if by coincidence, the feeling of the loss of an arm became intensified inside him, obliging him in the end to give up his dignified resistance and go to the doctor once again.

'It is against the rules,' Doctor Major McDonald said. 'They cannot be given even the smallest sharp instrument. They can open up their wounds, or kill themselves right off. These people are fanatics.'

'I am sure he won't do any such thing. I trust him. Sir, it is a question of my arm.'

'We are setting up an artificial limb factory in India. You will get it properly done as soon as you are back there.'

Naim persisted. 'Sir, I think this prisoner can make a good one and quickly.'

It went like this, back and forth, between Naim and the doctor, for a few days. Eventually, perhaps again as compassionate gesture towards Naim, the doctor said, 'All right. I can use my discretion in this matter, but if anything untoward happens the responsibility will be entirely yours.'

The doctor decided that Harold should be shifted to a vestibule near the entrance so that he could not be seen by the other prisoners and that Naim should spend the whole time with him for the few hours a day that the man was using the tools he was given. Furthermore, he decreed that the tools should be taken from him at the end of each day's work and put away. After the job was finished, the prisoner would be shifted back to his previous place in the general ward.

This was done. Naim procured a few carpenters' tools and a piece of cured hardwood, of which there was plenty in those parts. He would take them all away from Harold in the afternoon and bring them back the next morning. Over the next two weeks, Naim saw that shapeless piece of wood take on the form, at Harold's meticulous hands, of a forearm almost exactly the size of the one Naim had lost, a wrist and a hand, complete with criss-crossing veins, bits of knobbly bone sticking out in the right places, the wrinkled skin on the wrist, finger joints and fingernails, all perfectly carved with nothing more than a penknife aside from a couple of bigger tools which he used initially to cut the wood to the proper size. Finally Harold asked to examine the stump-end of Naim's arm more closely for dents and depressions so he could work out where to cut into the joining end of the wooden limb. This took the longest time and required several fittings. The only thing Harold couldn't do was to fix the small metallic catches and hinges that would hold the attachment securely in place. For that Naim would have to go to a factory in India.

Naim took the wooden arm to the doctor. Although surprised to see the workmanship, the doctor said without a smile, 'Good. Move him back to the ward.'

Taking him from the vestibule, Harold's independent home for over three weeks, to the ward, Naim said to him, 'Sorry for this. And thank you.' He took the artificial arm and put it in his trunk, safely wrapped in woolly clothing.

Four weeks later Naim received his honourable discharge with a letter of commendation and a small pension. Before boarding ship for his voyage home, Naim paid a last call to the sick POWs. When he learned that Naim was going home, Harold produced the broadest smile that anyone had so far seen on his face. Naim lingered there. There could be no conversation other than broken phrases between them. But Naim had a question on his mind that he didn't want anyone else to interpret for him. Finally he asked it. 'Why did you do it for an enemy?'

Harold first answered with a pause and a shrug, as if he didn't understand the question. Then he said, 'I not know you enemy, only man.'

Twelve weeks after returning to Roshan Pur, Naim was called up to Delhi by the army authorities and decorated with Distinguished Conduct Medal. With it came an award of ten acres of land in his village, a promotion-on-retirement to subedar and an increase in his pension.

HINDUSTAN I

O Mir, Beyond bearing is the melancholy of a broken heart
Fan awhile with thy dress to rekindle its fire

– *Mir Taqi Mir*

CHAPTER 11

More than usual it had been a time of distress: a drought that burned the earth and whatever green it held to a dirty pale colour and then to ashen grey, followed by rains that fell without cease, causing floods as the rivers and canals broke their banks and destroyed whatever was left in the soil, demolishing the mud roofs of houses, bringing great hunger to the bellies and grief to the eyes of humans and beasts until they had the deranged look of great misfortune. Hindus and Sikhs sacrificed virgin goats to the hungry gods and goddesses while the Muslims kneeled down to pray to their one omnipotent God that water, the scourge, be transformed once again into the life-blood of the earth; they never let go of the hope, the last refuge of this patient breed, that this difficult time too, like so many that had come before, would pass, for such had been the fate of the Indian peasant from the beginning of time.

When Naim returned, the first and, as it turned out, the only one to come back alive from the war, he found the slow, sleepy rhythm of life beating steadily in the breast of the village as he had left it. The earth's topsoil, washed away by the rain, had been replaced by the floods that brought with them dark fertile earth from the banks of the waterways. Once the waterlogged fields dried out they exposed rich, glittering layers that cried out for seed. A few months later, the same peasants stood among knee-high crops and, reassured by the miracle of their hope, lifted their eyes to the sky in gratitude not for the accident of soil but to their gods who had made it shift. Naim had come through Bombay on the return voyage and got himself fixed up in a military-run factory with clips that securely attached his wooden arm to his stump. In the factory they marvelled at the artificial limb and asked questions about the factory where it was made and the kind of machinery they had. They shook their heads in wonderment when Naim told them the truth. As well as fitting the clips they treated the wood with chemicals and applied a special paint of a colour that almost exactly matched Naim's natural skin. Under a full shirt sleeve it would take a close look, or prior knowledge, to tell one hand from the other. Naim could not help his father with work on the land as much he used to do in the past, although he did whatever he could – he could work a plough, but only for so long, and he trained himself to ride as well as he ever did before. The only thing he was unable to do was cut green fodder with a scythe, which required the grip of both hands and, however natural-looking his left hand was, he could not make a fist of it. He did, however, begin to partake of all the normal events in the village – the prize-bullock races, the kabaddi matches and such. On biggish occasions of this kind, in his or a neighbouring village, he put on his army uniform and joined the festivities. Men bowed their heads in deference as they met him, women covered their heads with dupattas in the presence of this gallant man, although he was still only a boy, and young girls, who had heard his mother boasting that in countries across the 'seven seas' many women wanted him to marry them but that he had rejected them and come back to his village, surreptitiously uncovered their heads of thick black hair and did not move away from his path, looking unashamedly straight at his face. Upon his return, Naim was seen as a different man, as if a stranger had come to live in the village.

He was crossing the canal bridge when he saw three riders coming up from the other side. It was Juginder Singh and two youths from the village. They reined in their horses as they came alongside Naim.

'Where have you been?' Naim asked Juginder Singh.

'To see the pigs.'

'Did you find any?'

'Lots of them. We dug pits. Going on a hunt tomorrow. Want to come?'

'Yes.'

'Come to our dera when the sun is up to a spear's height. Have your lassi with us.'

'Right.'

Naim was awakened the next morning by a noise coming from outside the house. Slipping his feet into the old army boots that he found comfortable to wear, trying to yawn the remaining slumber out of his body, he walked over to the outer yard where animals were tethered beside their troughs. It was a bright morning, the sun had just come up and there was still time enough before he needed to start out for Juginder Singh's house. Approaching the mare from behind, he took hold of the thin, flat bones at the back of its knees and pressed them, one after the other, between his thumb and forefinger. The sudden, tiny kicks of the mare that ran through her body like a current told him that the animal was healthy and alert, ready to be mounted. He patted her on the neck, making her move her skin upon her flanks in a shiver as only animals could do. Ali had toddled over. Naim picked him up with one hand and sat him on the mare's back. The child clung to it, grasping the hair on the mare's neck and screaming with a mixture of fright and glee. The boy's mother ran over to grab her son down from his perch. Laughing, Naim examined the horse's reins and mouthpiece that were hanging from a nail on the wall.

'The reins are ripped a little on one side,' he said to his father.

The noise outside increased. Naim went out to look. He saw a handful of people gathered at Ahmad Din's door. Among them was the munshi, holding the reins of his horse, with two of his servants standing by him. Ahmad Din was shouting at him.

'I am not giving you a straw from my house. I have nothing for you. Go away and tell this to whoever you want. I don't care.'

The munshi spoke menacingly. 'We will search your store. I know you have grain.'

'You step into my house and I will pursue you till I am dead, you evil, heartless man. Be off!' One end of his turban trailing on the ground as if it had been torn from his head, his clothes dust-smudged and saliva running down his scraggy beard, he was speaking in a terrible, breaking voice. 'I will tell them that you and your servant dogs knocked me down and beat me. You beat an old man. I will go to court, I will beg mercy from the white man's law . . .'

Naim went over and stood beside the crowd. Ahmad Din spread his hands in front of him, as if begging for alms. The munshi took a look at Naim and checked himself.

'All right, no need to shout so much. We can talk about it another time.'

'What other time? I have no time for you. Not even the blink of an eye. Don't you dare come back again!'

The munshi was already walking away with his two men.

'What is the matter?' Naim asked Ahmad Din.

A man, another sharecropper, answered instead. 'They came for motorana.'

'What is that?'

'Motor tax.'

'I don't understand,' Naim said to the man.

'Roshan Agha has bought a motor car. We all have to pay our share.'

'Why? What share? It is not your motor car.'

The man simply said, 'We all have to pay.'

'How much?' Naim asked.

'It depends on how much land you till. I have twenty acres under me, so I have paid a half maund.'

'What? Twenty seers of wheat?' asked Naim, dumbfounded.

'We all have to pay,' the man repeated.

Ahmad Din pushed his crack-nailed, bent-fingered black hands under Naim's eyes. 'I will have nothing to eat if I give motorana. I will starve. I grew my wheat with these hands.' Tears began to flow from his eyes. 'All on my own, my son has not come back from the war, I am alone, I will not pay them even if they kill me . . .'

Naim put his hand on Ahmad Din's shoulder. 'Don't worry, chacha. I will talk to them.' He walked back to his house, leaving the old man whimpering, 'They beat me,' with his fists pressed to his chest.

In the house, Niaz Beg was mending the reins with the help of a leather-needle and strong cotton thread.

'Do you pay motorana too?' Naim asked him angrily.

'Hunh!' Niaz Beg made a sound of utter contempt in his throat. 'Motorana? We are the owners of our land and masters of our grain. I will put them to eternal sleep right outside my door if they come round here. We are not like other people. We,' he thumped his chest, looking at his son sideways, 'have won a medal for bravery. Who does he think he is?'

Reins mended, Naim saddled the mare.

Niaz Beg asked him, 'Don't you want your lassi?'

'I will have it at the Sikhs' dera,' he said. Mounting the mare and holding the reins and a spear in one hand, he dug his heels into his mount. The mare, taking to its heels, jumped over the high plinth of the open door and they were gone.

The hunting party, riding their best horses, approached the dense jungle, leading their mounts between the trees with great caution. This was a part of the forest where sunlight seldom touched the ground and the earth was covered with years of fallen leaves that made a damp carpet which killed all sound. Apart from the rotting foliage, this darkened world was permeated with the smell of layers of droppings from the crows, pigeons and parrots that came to rest among the thick branches of shisham, pipal and bargad at night, of generations of decomposing dead birds and the strong odour of large and small animals that lived on the ground – the mixed aroma of the jungle that excited a lust for blood in the hearts of the men. The previous day they had dug seven pits in which they could sit with only their heads showing above ground. The party consisted of fifteen men, seven for the kill and the rest to serve as 'beaters', all carrying spears forged with sharp arrow-heads at the killing end.

A horse neighed. The rider patted its neck to calm it down. 'The bugger will wake them up.' He began to tell Naim the rudiments of boar-hunting. 'After they have ruined our crops in the fields and had their fill in the night, they come back to sleep here at this time. When roused from sleep, a boar becomes blind. But if you give it time, only a few minutes, then it regains its sight and can see what is happening before it. You'd better join the beaters and stay with them. No, do not get me wrong, I only mean that a boar is a powerful animal, you need the strength of both hands to kill it. When a boar comes at you, do not run, stand still, and when it is almost upon you, jump aside. It's neck is stiff, it can't turn inside a circle of ten yards . . .'

Seven men sat in the pits with their spears laid along the ground at the ready. The party of beaters went around on tiptoe until they came upon two families of boar, some lying down, some sitting up playing with their young. At the sight of them, the beaters started making the loudest noise they could manage, shouting and beating spear upon spear. Taken by surprise, the boars sprang up and started running in all directions. Whichever way they turned, they were confronted by the semi-circle of men and their weapons and the terrible noise they were making. Eventually the boars were rounded up and driven towards the pits. In the first run, only one animal went straight into a spear carried by a youth, all the others missing them. In a state of excitement approaching panic, the beaters re-formed and were able after a time to encircle three adult boars, the rest having escaped into the jungle. Back at the pits, the one that was pinned down struggled a bit to get away but found that the spear head, which could only go forward into the pierced skin and through the layers of fat and flesh, wouldn't let it off the fatal hook. The boar stood there, looking at its captor through beady eyes, its snout exhaling great gusts of warm, desperate breath. The youth jumped out of the pit and pressed hard on the spear, pushing the boar backwards. The boar fell on its side, beating the air with its short, stumpy legs. A second man got out of his pit and started stabbing the boar in the stomach with a long, thick dagger. After a few minutes, amid the boar's last squeals, they cut its throat.

The three boars trapped by the beaters were heading blindly towards the pits. Two of them, perhaps remembering their first run, suddenly turned back and charged through the legs of the beaters, tusking one man in the leg. The third, a huge beast, ran on right down the line of Juginder Singh's pit. Fixing the grip of both his hands on the spear, Juginder Singh raised its front end, aiming at the boar's chest between its forelegs. A split-second before the impact, the boar turned ever so slightly to the side. The spear's point ploughed through the skin of the boar at full force from shoulder to hind leg and slipped out, exposing a thick layer of cotton-white fat along the boar's side. Juginder Singh had been unable to stop it. He swore. The beast fell headlong into the pit on top of a cowering Juginder Singh, ripping the skin on his back with an angry jerk of its tusk. The next moment it jumped out of the pit and disappeared, squealing wildly, into the trees. Both the hunter and the hunted had exposed one another's bodies and drawn blood. The beaters stopped and gathered round Juginder Singh's pit. As Naim, who had run off to the other side when the last two boars charged them, was coming back to the pits his eye caught two hind hooves sticking out from behind a tree. Quietly he went round and saw the wounded animal sitting there, his good side resting against the tree trunk, a wide sheet of skin hanging from the open side, dripping blood. With his spear raised to the level of the boar's chest, Naim approached the beast. The boar just looked dumbly at the man coming towards him. At the last moment Naim changed direction and, positioning himself on the side, quickly pushed the spear through the boar's open wound. The pig squealed. Those tending the two injured men around the pits came running. They saw shivers running through the boar's body and Naim pushing the weapon deeper and deeper into it.

'Push, push,' they shouted. 'Right on, keep pushing, hard, harder . . .'

With only one hand, an arm and a shoulder behind the long, heavy spear, Naim had to grit his teeth to dredge up the last of his strength to get the spearhead into the animal's vitals. The boar didn't struggle much. There was a moment when Naim, looking into the beast's glittering eyes, thought he heard the abrading sound, vibrating through the iron to his ear, of the steel point piercing far into the boar's trunk. He also wished at that instant that he had another hand to put behind it so that the business would end sooner. The last few seconds were the hardest for Naim, not for the strength that it required of him but because he couldn't take his eyes off the expressionless, slowly dying face of the boar, who finally let out a high, agonized cry and slumped to the ground, resting its snout lightly before it. A cheer went up from the men standing around.

'Gone through the heart,' one said. 'It puts its snout on the ground only when something breaks its heart in two.'

'How do you know about the snout?' another asked. 'They all die like that.'

'I know,' the first one said. 'My life is spent among pigs.'

'We know,' the second answered, 'you are almost one of them.'

Laughter arose from the assembly of men. Naim didn't bother to pull his spear out of the dead pig's body. He walked back to where Juginder Singh was lying in his pit. Two men were burning up a cotton cloth, mixing it with a man's urine and rubbing the stuff into his wound. Naim sat down at the edge of the pit and realized that he hadn't really wanted to kill the boar, only to test the strength of his arm, and that in the end, looking at the animal's helpless face, he had even wished that it would jump away from him and run.

'I have taken revenge for you,' he said to Juginder Singh.

'Good,' Juginder Singh said, smiling through a grimace of pain. 'If Mahindroo was here, he too would go after it and kill the bastard.'

Naim wanted to say, no, it was just luck. But he kept quiet. He felt the absence of Mahinder Singh deeply. The story he had told the village was that Mahinder Singh had died fighting bravely on the battlefield. 'Yes,' Naim said. 'He would.'

Dusk was falling as they returned to the village. Roshan Agha's new Ford car was parked near the haveli. Everybody in the hunting party saw it and quickly went off to their homes, except Naim, who turned his mare towards the haveli. On horseback Naim could see over the boundary wall. There were two chairs in the courtyard, one large, throne-like, on which Roshan Agha sat, and on the other sat the munshi. All the older share-croppers and field labourers from the village were sitting on the ground in front of the chairs. They had all put on their best clothes and starched turbans with high shamlas in honour of the Agha; the only one among the elders not present was Niaz Beg. Around the yard stood three tables, and on two of them, towards the sides, there were oil lamps with tall clear glass chimneys. The third table was set beside Roshan Agha's chair. There was a white china plate on this table filled with a small heap of dried fruit, although Roshan wasn't eating anything from it. There was a low hum of talk among the men. Suddenly a high-pitched voice from one side shouted, 'Ahmad Din.'

Ahmad Din got up from the middle and walked forward.

'Not like that,' the munshi said severely. 'On your knees.'

Ahmad Din hesitated a moment. The munshi gestured to his servants. Two young men came up and, grabbing Ahmad Din by the shoulders, forced him down to the ground, where he stood on all fours, looking up. Upon another silent gesture from the munshi, the men tore off Ahmad Din's splendidly wound red silk turban and knotted it loosely around his neck, holding on to the other end of it.

'Grass in his mouth.' ordered the munshi.

One of the men pulled up a handful of grass from the earth and pushed it in Ahmad Din's mouth. By now, all resistance had gone out of the old man.

'Now come,' the munshi said.

The servant with one end of the turban in his hand gave it a tug. Ahmad Din crawled for a yard, then fell flat on his stomach, shivering throughout the length of his dry old body.

'He got double his share, Agha Ji,' the munshi said to Roshan Agha, 'just as your janab gave your honourable word when his son went to war. Now, with one mouth less to feed, his store is full of wheat, and yet he refuses to pay motorana.'

Roshan Agha hadn't spoken a word the whole time. His face showed displeasure and he didn't look straight at what was going on. In the end he lifted his right hand and waved it as if fanning away the air from in front of his nose. The man holding Ahmad Din's turban dropped it instantly and withdrew. But Ahmad Din did not rise. He lay there, face down, as if trying to hide his head in a hole in the ground, shivering uncontrollably. Naim turned his eyes away. Riding home, he passed Roshan Agha's car. He had a thick twig in the hand that held the reins. With the full force of his arm, he threw the twig at the car. It skidded off the top of the car and fell on the other side. He was halfway to his house when he heard quick footsteps behind him. He pulled up and looked over his shoulder. In the growing dark of the evening he recognized the young schoolmaster Hari Chand. A primary school had been started in the village on Roshan Agha's orders in Naim's absence. Hari Chand was the only teacher, hired from outside, who taught some village children in a side room of the haveli.

'Naim sahib,' the teacher said to him, 'will you come with me for a few minutes?'

'Where?' Naim asked him.

'To my humble house. I would be grateful.'

Naim got down. After a brief pause, he started following in the footsteps of the schoolmaster. It was a single dark mud hut in which Hari Chand lived.

'Just a minute, sir,' he said, 'I will light the lantern.'

The glass casing of the hurricane lamp hanging from the wall was smudged with dirt. There was a misshapen hole in the ground that served as a hearth, and around it the walls had become blackened with wood smoke. A narrow cot, covered by a heavy, rough cotton durree, lay along one wall. Books, sheets of paper and pencils were scattered on the cot. More bound volumes and half-open copybooks lay irregularly on a bare table that wobbled on the uneven floor.

'Please sit down,' Hari Chand said, pointing vaguely to the cot. 'Do you like green tea?' Then without waiting for an answer he added, 'I will make a cup for you.'

Rearranging one or two books to make room, Naim sat down on a corner of the cot. The schoolmaster was breaking up some twigs. After placing them neatly in the hearth, he struggled for a minute with a damp matchbox, finally getting the twigs alight, and fanning the fire by furiously blowing in it. Smoke filled the room.

'Did you see that?' Hari Chand suddenly asked.

'What?'

'In the haveli.'

'Yes.'

'Were you upset?'

Naim took a minute to answer, then said quietly, 'Yes.'

'The Agha is not a bad man. I saw his face turn pale when the wretched old man was crawling like an animal on a leash. But what difference does it make? He won't do anything because his raj runs on such things. The whole thing is rotten.'

Naim sat without answering, watching the schoolmaster grind a cardamom pod on a hearth-stone to brew with the tea.

Hari Chand spoke again. 'Have you considered your father's position?'

A look of sorrow mixed with a kind of panic passed across Naim's eyes.

'He wasn't there tonight,' continued Hari Chand. 'He is a proud man and a brave one. But he is in a bad way. Who caused him to be like that? You tell me.'

The schoolmaster splashed boiling tea from one cracked earthen cup into the other to bring out the colour of the tea. He mixed raw sugar into the cups and, coming to sit beside Naim on the cot, handed one to him. They sipped the hot tea.

'What would you say if I told you that you can change all this?' Hari Chand said to Naim.

'Me?' asked Naim.

'You, me, all of us.'

'How?'

Hari Chand looked at him with a steady gaze. 'First you have to be ready to do it.'

'I can't be ready before I know how,' Naim said.

'I can't tell you. I have a particular job to do here. But you will meet our people.'

'Who. when, where?'

'One question at a time,' Hari Chand said with a smile. 'I will tell you in a few days. You will meet one man first in Rasool Nagar.'

'Who is this man? I mean, who are you working for? The Congress?'

'No. They don't approve of what we are doing, although our goals are the same.'

'It's a town,' Naim remarked idly after a while, enjoying the flavourful tea after a long day and wishing subconsciously to forget the whole evening and even Hari Chand.

'Only a small town,' said Hari Chand. 'Delhi is a big city. Even bigger is Calcutta, where you come from.'

'How do you know?'

'We know a lot about you. This man you will meet also knows you. We have talked about you.'

Naim was quiet for a few moments. Then he said slowly, almost absent-mindedly, 'I only come from Roshan Pur.'

'Are you ready for this?'

'Let me think about it.'

The schoolmaster had thick black hair on a pockmarked face with rough features. He had had the good fortune to go to school for a few years. But inside that simple peasant's body was a different heart. Shaking hands with him on his way out, Naim felt a deep sense of friendship with this man to whom he had spoken for the first time that night. He unwound the reins of his mare from the thick nail that served as the door-handle of the hut and said farewell. Before turning into his house he saw Roshan Agha's car starting off from the village and the munshi and a few others, unseen by their master, bowing at the tail lights as they disappeared into the dust thrown up by the wheels.

Following Hari Chand's directions a few days later, Naim knocked at the door of an old, narrow, two-storey house that seemed to have fallen into disrepair. It was situated in an equally narrow street which Naim, on horseback, could scarcely pass through. The door was opened by a white-haired man in old blue railway-type uniform.

'I have come from Roshan Pur,' Naim said to him. 'Hari Chand sent me. Master Hari Chand?'

'Yes, yes,' the man nodded. 'But nobody comes here on a horse. Look, tie it up by the wall. Here, there is a hook by the door, fortunately. And tell your horse to stand sideways so that it does not stop people getting past. Hee, hee. Can you control it? Come in when you have done it, the door is open.'

There was an inner door leading to a back room. By the time Naim had dealt with his mare, which he now regretted bringing with him, another man had emerged into the front room.

'My name is Balkamand,' he said, offering his hand to Naim.

'I am Naim Ahmad Khan.'

'I know, please come in, come with me.'

Balkamand led Naim into the back room. The room looked in bad shape. Most of the plaster had fallen off the walls, exposing small, thin bricks laid upon each other with mud instead of mortar in the old style. The dried mud had been pulverized over the years, causing the wall to crack and warp, bringing it to a state of near collapse. An old man sat on a stool, his elbows on a table before him, studying some papers. Balkamand introduced him to Naim. 'Kishan Das sahib, our Assistant District Secretary.'

The old man looked up.

'And this is Mr Naim Ahm–'

Before Balkamand could finish, old Kishan Das stood up to shake hands with Naim. 'I know. Naim from Roshan Pur. I got Hari Chand's message some days back. Sit down.' He offered Naim another stool. 'I saw you at Roshan Agha's party a few years ago,' he said.

Naim, halfway to sitting on the stool, stood straight up again in utter surprise. 'Were you there?' he asked.

'I only saw you from the other side of the lawn. But I heard what you said. I tried to contact you when we set up our branch here, but you had gone to the war by then. Please sit down.'

Kishan Das, completely bald except for a fringe of white hair around the base of his head, had an unusually young voice and a strong grip. The man who had opened the door brought two cups of tea which he set down on the table. Neither of the two men paid any attention to the tea. Kishan Das gazed at Naim quietly for a moment, then said, 'If you just consider your family's history – your father, grandfather – you will realize how treacherous these people are who represent this system, the system of poverty and slavery, these people who control all our lives. They will not bat an eyelid before betraying those who provide them with the means to lead their grand lives.' He paused. 'If you are prepared to work to change all this, you should know beforehand that it is risky and dangerous work.'

'I am not afraid of danger,' Naim said.

'I know. You fought bravely in the war.'

'Nobody sets out to be brave in war. It's just a –'

'I am talking of the risk involved. We are poor people and possess nothing.

But you have lands and awards from the sarkar. You have something to lose.'

'It doesn't matter to me,' Naim said to him.

'Mind you, it may not come to that. All you have to do is not get caught.' He laughed, and an expression as young as his voice spread across his face. 'Brave as you are, what we need most of all is educated people. We only have simple peasants and day labourers. We have very few people with any proper education to work in the field.'

Naim nodded in reply.

'Let me tell you how we can proceed,' Kishan Das said. 'You will spend two weeks here. Balkamand will tell you all about it. Then you will go out into the field. You need not see me until then, but do look me out when you are ready to go.'

They got up and shook hands. In the front room Balkamand pointed to a cot with a durree spread out on it, a cotton sheet jumbled up towards the foot and a thin, hard pillow with smudges of oil on it at the head of the bed. 'You can sleep here,' he said.

'Is it your bed?'

'Yes.'

'Where will you sleep?'

'Ooh – somewhere,' Balkamand said vaguely. 'Have some food, it's ready.'

'All right.'

Naim ate one roti with cauliflower cooked in mustard oil, thinking all the while that perhaps he was eating Balkamand's share of food. Balkamand was a tall man of middle years with a full head of salt-and-pepper hair. But his most distinguishing feature was his eyes, which had a shine in them that seemed to come not from the surface but from somewhere within.

When Naim had finished eating, he stood up. 'I will come back in a few days,' he said. 'I have to prepare my father. Also,' he laughed, 'I have to take my horse back to the village.'

'Of course,' Balkamand smiled, 'I had forgotten all about that.' He shook Naim's hand, his eyes shining more intensely. For a few seconds Naim couldn't take his eyes away from Balkamand's face.

'Do you want to ask me about anything else?' Balkamand asked.

'No,' Naim said, slightly embarrassed for appearing to stare at the other man's face.

'Look,' Balkamand put his hand on Naim's arm, 'if you have any questions, ask without hesitation.'

'No, no,' Naim said, 'it's just –'

'What?

'You have a remarkable shine in your eyes, that's all.'

Balkamand blushed like a young boy. They walked to the door. Naim untied the mare's reins from the door-hook. Some children had gathered in the street, looking at the horse.

'When you get to my age,' Balkamand said to Naim, 'the eyes change. They either make you blind or make you see further.'

'According to what they have seen?' Naim asked with a smile.

'No. Because of the kind of eyes you have.' There was a note of sadness in his voice.

After a few seconds, Naim said farewell.

Niaz Beg didn't prove as difficult as Naim had expected. 'You have been lonely since you came back,' he said. 'If you want to go and see your friends in the big cities, by all means go. It will make you happy. I am not yet too old to look after everything on my own in your absence.'

CHAPTER 12

Lying atop a thin cotton-wool quilt spread on the floor in a pitch dark room, Naim said to himself, 'It is the fortieth day.' He put his hand beyond the edge of the quilt and felt the cold of the stone floor. 'Forty days have passed and I have done nothing. I have merely become one of them. I haven't had the chance even to try to do what I came here to do. Who can get through to these illiterate idiots anyway? If only Kishan Das knew these people. "You are my son," he said to me before I left, "but first of all you are the son of Hindustan." Ho ho! If he knew what this son is doing for Hindustan!'

The wooden plank covering the hole in the wall that served as a passage between the two rooms of this mountain hut shifted to the side, casting a wide band of lantern light in the darkness of the room. Sheelah's round face appeared in the space.

'Ay, Wood-bound, how are you?' she asked.

Naim produced a grunt in reply.

'Why did you not go today?'

'I am not well.'

'Afraid of planting the powder?'

'Shut up.'

'Why, even I can fix the powder under anything.'

Naim didn't answer. A childlike smile appeared on Sheelah's face. 'Do you want a cup of tea, Wood-bound?'

'No.'

She stepped in and replaced the plank to cover the hole. Darkness returned to the room. Naim sat up, wrapping his arms round his raised knees. The girl came and sat down beside him. Naim peered into her face in the dark.

'What are you looking at?' she asked, fluttering her eyelashes near his face.

Naim stood up and went silently to the sole window in the room. This was a roughly cut small opening in the stone wall with a plank fixed in it, the holes around it filled with broken stone. He struggled with its rusted bolt for a minute.

'Don't open it,' Sheelah said, coming to stand by him.

'I need some air,' he said.

'Baba will be unhappy.'

'I can't figure out to this day whether Baba is on our side.'

'He is,' she said.

'Could be an informer.'

'No. Listen, Wood-bound –'

'Don't call me that. My name is Naim.'

'My brother told me that this,' she said, shyly touching his left hand, 'is made of wood.'

'So?'

'In our village there was a man with only one leg and another who was mad. We called the one who was lame Lame, and the mad one Mad.'

'Only idiots talk like that. We say Naim Ahmad Khan and Sheelah Rani. Say it.'

'Naim Ahmad Khan and Sheelah Rani.'

'Good.'

'Now am I good?'

'Yes.'

'Why don't you talk to me, Naim Ahmad Khan?'

'Just call me Naim.'

'All right. Why don't you talk to me?'

'I do.'

'In many months you have spoken to me only –' counting on her spread fingers, 'one, two, three, four, five, six times.'

'Only one month and ten days.'

'Do you count them?'

'I do. Every day.'

'Why did you come here?' she asked.

'I don't know.'

'You came here from many miles and you don't know?'

'Five hundred miles.'

'How could you count them, you didn't come on foot.'

'I read books. That is how I know. Look,' Naim touched her face with wooden fingers, 'this is your cheek, this your nose, these lips. I can feel them.' He kept passing his lifeless fingers over the girl's dark, spotless face and felt very clearly that he could in fact sense the touch of her skin, as though blood actually flowed through that piece of wood. Sheelah, stunned for a minute, looked up at him with wondering eyes. Then she laughed quietly with embarrassed pleasure and touched his left hand again, holding on to it for a second.

'It is warm,' she said. A bird of the night flew silently across the window. 'An angel passed,' she said, putting her hand breathlessly on Naim's arm.

'Only an owl. Or a bat.'

'Don't say that. It's a sin. I heard the sound of its wings. When it passes good things come to you.'

'Are you a good thing that has come to me?'

She was quiet for a moment. 'I don't know,' she said.

'So now it is you who don't know why you have come, see?'

'I know why you have come,' she said, laughing. 'You have come to do nothing but eat our food for free.'

'I have gone out with them and done my share,' Naim said.

'Only three times.'

'Were you counting?'

'Yes, yes.'

She had a strange face. On dark skin, her lips were naturally red. She was now looking out of the window at the distant hills where wooden houses, built one above the other like steps to an enormous palace, glimmered in the half-dark of a starry night.

'I had a village once,' she said.

'I know. Madan told me.'

'When?'

'When he and I went for the line the first time.'

'What else did he tell you?'

'Many secrets.'

'What, what?'

'That you used to run around.' Naim laughed.

'The cholera spread. First my father died, then my mother. Madan ran away. I was left alone with my aunt. Then Madan came back.'

'What happened then?'

'He had ideas in his head. He said, let's go. After two years we finished up here.'

'Did you have a boy as friend in your village?' Naim asked with a smile that she couldn't see.

'No.'

'Madan said that you did.'

'No, no,' she said fiercely.

They were quiet for a while, standing side by side, their bodies touching, looking out the window.

'Will you go with them tomorrow?' she asked.

'I don't know.'

I am not going again, Naim thought, enough blood on my hands, faces of the dead still fixed in my eyes.

'Will you go back then?' Sheelah asked.

'Maybe.'

'Don't go.'

Naim turned to look at her red lips glistening in the dark of the room.

'They will be coming back soon,' she said. 'I'll go now.'

But she made no move to go.

'Where do you sleep?' Naim asked her.

'By the door.'

'Behind the wood?'

'Yes, yes. It's months and months and you don't know?'

'It's not months and months, it's less, why don't you listen?'

'You snore. Sometimes I can't sleep for the noise you make. I feel like pushing the wood on top of you.'

Soon the three men returned to the hut. One of them started trying to light the already half-ashen twigs in the hearth. The others took off their damp clothes.

'How did you get wet?' Naim asked.

'We dived in the lake for fun,' Bannerji said.

'It's a clear sky,' Naim said.

'We weren't sitting at home like you. It's raining on the other side of the hill.'

'Is the powder wet?' asked Iqbal, spreading his shirt near the smoking twigs.

'It was under my vest on my belly,' Bannerji replied.

'Keep it away from the fire.'

Bannerji swore. 'How many times do you have to tell me?'

Iqbal took out the desi handgun from his waist and hung it by a nail on the wall. 'Got a cigarette on you?' he asked Madan.

'No.'

Iqbal shrugged and sat down, leaning his back against the wall. He closed his eyes. The lantern cast deep shadows on his skin-and-bone face, and he looked completely spent. Naim walked over and offered him a cigarette. Iqbal lit the cigarette and asked, 'How are you feeling now?'

'Better,' answered Naim.

'What did you do all day?'

'Nothing.'

'Nothing at all?'

'Just thinking.'

'Can you think?' Bannerji asked.

'Yes,' Naim said, looking at him menacingly.

'Better stop thinking. I have.'

'Just as well,' Madan said. 'Must have been a hard job for you.'

'Well, I am happy,' Bannerji said, dragging up his two blankets nearer to him.

'Can't stay away from his bed for a minute,' Iqbal said, screwing up his nose. 'Like a woman.'

'Can't even open the fucking window. What do you expect?'

Naim leaned towards him. 'Madhukar Bannerji, are you really happy?'

'Yes. Why are you looking so dreadful?' Bannerji said, tossing his half-alight cigarette into the fire. 'Bloody wet!'

'Should have saved your cigarettes instead of the powder,' Naim said.

'You are right, I should have.'

'Now smoke the powder.'

Sheelah came in carrying a pan of water. She put it down on top of the fire in the stone hearth.

'Is Baba giving us something to eat?' Madan asked her.

'Don't know,' she said.

'Sheelo,' Madan said to her mildly, 'I am starving.'

'I think he is cooking something.'

Sheelah stood there with hands on her hips. Naim thought that her mouth and nose had a close resemblance to her brother's. The old man entered from the outer room holding a stone cooking pot full of thick broth.

'Potatoes, boys, potatoes,' he announced and put the pot down on the ground.

The pot was black on the outside from wood smoke; inside it were potatoes broken and boiled in water, red with chillies, giving off an appetizing smell, a thin steam curling upwards from the surface.

'And bread?' two men asked at the same time.

'Oh, yes.' The old man produced from the pocket of his long, military-style old coat a packet of brittle maize rotis. After handing them the food the old man sat down to smoke his small, portable hukka, closing his eyes the better to enjoy the feeling as he pulled at it. Everyone ate hungrily and in silence, their jawbones working prominently in the lantern light, the only sounds in the room being those of their noisy chewing and the hissing of burning pinewood.

'Leave some for the girl,' the old man barked without opening his eyes.

The men frowned at him. But they stopped eating, leaving a little potato at the bottom of the pot and one roti on the cloth spread on the ground. They wiped their fingers with the cloth, drank cups of water and gathered round the fire.

'What happened today?' Naim asked Iqbal.

Iqbal turned away to put on his shirt.

'Done the forest office?' Naim asked again.

'Un-hunh,' grunted Iqbal.

'Can't you speak?'

'No,' answered Bannerji instead.

'Then what?'

'Just the chowkidar.'

'The chowkidar? You killed the chowkidar?'

'No. He will survive. We made a mistake.'

'Why the chowkidar?'

'I said a mistake was made, it all went wrong,' Bannerji said harshly.

Naim glowered at them, his hands trembling. He turned his face to the wall and tried to calm himself. Iqbal seemed to have gone to sleep in a sitting position by the fire, his head resting on the wall. Madan had unwrapped the strip of dirty cotton from around his old calf wound. Sheelah was washing it with warm water.

'I saw the chowkidar the other day,' Naim said in a quiet voice after a while. 'He was a poor old peasant. There was no need.'

Iqbal suddenly lifted his head off the wall and said angrily, 'A mistake is a mistake. They will be made until we get it right.' He put his head back on the wall and closed his eyes.

'He was innocent, only earning his bread for the day,' Naim said insistently. 'You may shut your eyes, but you will see his face behind them.'

'I am not seeing anybody's face, behind the eyes or in front of them,' Iqbal said without either opening his eyes or turning his head. 'Why did you not come with us if you are so clever?'

'I am not blaming you, only regretting injury to one who was just like us, poor and tyrannized. We are not achieving anything by attacking these people. We have to get them on our side. Numbers are important. What can we do by staying in small pockets of people, isolated and with no programme ahead of us, except to behave like beasts?'

'Look,' Madan said to Naim. He broke off, grimacing with pain from the hot brick that his sister put on the swelling on his leg.

'It's going down. Be still,' Sheelah said to him, 'it's gone down quite a bit.'

All of a sudden, Bannerji started laughing. 'Ho ho ho! Seeing behind the eyes. Why, Balay, are you seeing – ho ho – behind the eyes? Ha ha ha – are you –?'

Iqbal ignored him, staying still against the wall.

Madan spoke to Naim again. 'You say you learned things in the war. All right, did you go and talk to the enemy to get them on your side? Do you know what you are talking about? I have learned something in life as well. I will tell you what it is. I ran away from home and went to Nagpur. For six years I worked as a sweeper in a bookshop. You are not the only one who has read books, I read them too. From them I learned that in order to wake up those millions you have to knock them. Before you become a bullock to till the land and produce food, you have to become a beast. You know why? Because you are castrated.'

'That is where you are wrong. We cannot win by adopting the ways of the beast, because it is not just the landowners but those who own the landowners. And they have big guns. We have only one option and that is to get a million people together and show that we can defeat them by having the population on our side.'

'Listen, Naim Khan sahib, I am what you call an achhoot, given the respectable name of scheduled castes. In my village we ate with other people's dogs. That was the schedule of our caste. You have seen a year or two of war and boast about it. In my twenty-five years every single day was a war to stay alive with respect. I remember everything. If I join your millions and offer myself for prison, my sister will live on the street and go from hand to hand.' He poked a stiff finger in Naim's chest. 'You know what you should do now? You should finish your speeches and be off.'

Iqbal sat up from the wall. He pulled out a burning stick from the fire and struck it hard on the floor. It broke into small pieces of live charcoal that flew up and dropped on the ground around it. A spark fell on Bannerji's arm. He sprang up from the floor and started rubbing his singed flesh, hissing with pain, 'Sss – what the devil? Sss –'

'Shut up, all of you,' Iqbal shouted, 'I am trying to sleep.' He pushed the red hot end of the stick close to Naim's face. 'And you, shut your nonsense up. You are coming with us tomorrow, no more excuses, you hear?'

Naim got up and stepped across the gap to his room. Iqbal threw the stick into the fire, lifted up the glass of the lantern and blew it out. Naim covered the hole with the plank of wood. Darkness returned to the room. Lying on his blankets, he passed his hand over his thigh and felt the pistol in his trouser pocket. It gave him confidence.

He awoke at a slight noise in the room. The plank had been moved aside halfway and he could see the faint glow of the dying embers in the next room. The light was not sufficient to penetrate the pitch darkness of the rooms and he could see nothing else. He stayed under his blankets, listening to the rain falling on the window. After a while, he sat up and started crawling on all fours towards the gap, taking care not to make a sound with his wooden arm on the hard floor. He imagined himself walking like a four-legged creature, a calf, a bear or a wolf, and felt a sensation that, to his surprise, he did not find disagreeable. He poked his head through the space vacated by the plank and could just about make out the sleeping figures of the three men and hear their breathing in between the snoring of one of them. Someone tugged at his shirt, causing him to jump. Straining his eyes, sitting on his hind legs, he put out his hand to feel the face and hair of the figure sitting on his side of the plank and knew that it was Sheelah. He sat there, breathing hard. Then he took her by the arm and led her back to where he had made his bed.

Before she lay down beside him on the thin quilt, she went and soundlessly shifted the plank back to cover up the hole in the wall. They lay in the dark for many minutes as the sound of rain outside died slowly away.

'I am cold,' Sheelah whispered.

Naim pulled out his heavy army coat, which served as his pillow, from underneath his head and spread it over Sheelah. 'Pull your feet in,' he said.

Pulled up, Sheelah's knees dug into Naim's side. He felt her belly harden and shiver and knew that she was laughing silently.

'When did you wake up?' he asked in a low whisper close to her ear.

'I couldn't sleep.'

'How long was I asleep?'

'Some while.'

'It's way past midnight then.'

'Yes. Why were you arguing with them tonight?'

'Only saying some things.'

'Don't argue with them.'

'Why not?'

'They are dangerous.'

'I have to talk to them. That is why I came here.'

'They don't like talk. They killed a man for that.'

'Who? When?'

'Last year. He was sent to us, like you. From Bombay. We were in Bihar at the time. He talked to them all the while. Then Iqbal shot him.'

'Why?'

'He said he was fed up with the man making speeches.'

'Who was he?' Naim asked.

'Some man. I don't know.'

Naim felt her breath quickening. The sound of sobbing came from her.

'Quiet,' he said.

Gradually, she became very still. He kissed her.

'Your neck is very soft,' he said.

'In God's name,' she whispered, 'talk quietly.'

'Do you know how kisses taste?'

'How kisses taste? No.'

'Different, one from the other. Like water.'

'What do you mean?'

'If you are thirsty, they are sweet. If not, they have no taste.'

'You are strange,' she said, her hand passing over his flank. 'Why do you sleep with no shirt on?'

'Old habit.'

'You have no hair on your chest.'

'Nor have you.'

'Men who have no hair on their chest are faithless.'

'Is that true?'

'Naim,' she asked, 'you will not go away?'

'No.'

Suddenly she burst into tears. He wrapped his arms around her, trying to muffle the sound of her weeping.

'Don't. Please don't cry.'

She became very quiet.

'Why do you cry?' he asked after a while.

'I don't know.'

'You don't know?'

'I feel like it,' she said, 'sometimes.'

'Sheelah,' Naim said, pressing her to him, 'you are so young.'

'If you think I am young, then you are young. If you don't grow up with women, you never grow up.'

They lay naked under the blankets for a long while. In the dark, he saw the gleam of her eyes and lips.

'Your eyes have a light in them,' he said.

'What do you mean?'

'Nothing. I remember a man who had the same light in his eyes.'

'Who was this man?'

'A friend.'

'Was he as beautiful as you?'

Naim laughed quietly. 'I don't know.'

'I should go now,' she said.

He stayed silent. After a few minutes, she crept out of his bed and went into the other room, noiselessly replacing the plank that separated the two rooms.

CHAPTER 13

It had been three hours since Naim had come and settled under a huge mountain tree on a slope above the railway line. 'All you have to do is to note whether the goods train has passed and tell us when we come,' Iqbal had told him. 'Don't want to waste the powder on a bloody goods train.'

The train didn't come, nor did the boys. The time was long past and now Naim, having talked to himself, quietly at times and at times loudly, to keep away the boredom, was cold and hungry. Dark clouds had begun to gather overhead, making the night darker still. He was like a blind man who knew the location of things, the line, the tunnel, the path back to his hut. Just as he swore at them for the hundredth time, he heard the train's sharp whistle, warning of its entry into the tunnel. The train emerged from the tunnel and thundered away. It was a goods train. Drops of rain began to fall. Now, thought Naim, the passenger train would follow, and where are those idiots, what can I do, I've got nothing, they wouldn't trust me with the dynamite and I wouldn't do it anyway, I'd throw it away and tell them some story, definitely, I've had enough of it, oh my God, what do I do, shall I go back, I am already getting wet.

The wind had come up, driving the rain sideways so the shelter provided by the branches and leaves above him was gone. He heard a voice coming from the other side of the path and felt relief: they were coming, he had done his job and wasn't going to hang around, he'd go back as soon as they arrived. The voice came nearer. It was a peasant, driving his donkey carrying a load of forest wood ahead of him. In the heavily falling rain the peasant had his head covered with a conical hat he had made out of an empty gunny bag. He had in his hand the donkey's tail which he was twisting constantly, talking to the beast. 'Had you not spread your legs and refused to move halfway up, we would be home by now. Look what has happened, all the wood is soaked and what should we burn now, your mother's behind? You have bad blood in you. No surprise. I bought your mother from a cobbler and she immediately died, leaving you a baby. I have brought you up with these hands and you do this to me. No surprise. Cobbler's ass, bad blood.' Talking non-stop, the peasant went up the path, step by painful step in the driving rain. Naim just looked at them with eyes wide with fury until they disappeared. Futilely he cocked an ear to the other side of the path; there were no more voices. A few minutes later the passenger train passed, whistling in and out of the tunnel, raindrops dancing in its big forehead light. Naim got up and started back to the hut. Slipping and sliding over smooth stones in the black rain, balancing himself with the support of both hands and at the same time trying to stop his hand falling off his arm, he was wet through to the skin by the time he reached the hut, his boots full of rainwater, his body shivering with the cold. He found his two companions sitting calmly in the room. A stranger with a short hennaed beard sat with them on a pile of blankets, smoking a hukka.

'You never came,' Naim said to them.

'Rain,' answered Iqbal. 'Dry weather job, don't you know?'

'You could have sent someone to let me know.'

'Sent Bannerji,' Iqbal said nonchalantly and kept playing with his revolver, turning its magazine with flicks of his fingers time after time, as if enjoying the metallic clicks it produced.

'Nobody came,' Naim said. He took off his dripping coat and then his shirt, throwing them on the floor. He sat down on the floor to remove his boots and socks, upending the boots to empty them of rainwater.

'He'll have gone to the village to get drunk,' Madan said to Iqbal. 'Fine people you have collected. They'll be the end of us one day.'

'Anything to eat?' Naim asked Baba.

Everyone looked around blankly without answering.

'An extra guest today,' Baba said, pointing to the stranger with the beard, who sat pulling at the hukka as if he had nothing to do with all this.

Baba went out. Naim looked at everyone in turn and couldn't keep his temper. 'I was sitting there for over three hours and nobody bothered. All I saw was a donkey like me and a man who was worse than a donkey. I haven't eaten since this morning. What do you think I am?'

There was a pause for a minute. Then Iqbal said, 'Yes, tell us, who are you?'

'What do you mean?' asked Naim.

'You have been here for more than a month and we don't know anything about you. What made you come and join us? Who sent you?'

Naim's anger, as well as the hunger in his belly, evaporated. 'What are you talking about? I am one of you. All right, I was sent by someone. They are the right people.'

'Who?'

Naim felt that he had no option but to go where he was led. 'A man named Kishan Das.'

'Who is that?'

'He is the assistant secretary of my district.'

'The Congress?'

'Yes, and no.'

'What do you mean?'

'They have the same aims.'

'Do you agree with them?'

'I think they are the right people.'

'They have nothing to fight with,' Iqbal said, gathering up the fingers of one hand in the shape of a cone and repeatedly opening and closing them, 'except yap, yap, yap. They go to the parties given by white governors and eat their food. Yap yap yap.'

'They have no balls,' Madan said.

'They have brains,' Naim said. 'What you can't do with balls you do with brains.'

'And how do you do that?'

'By standing up and demanding your rights.'

'Hah!' Madan laughed sarcastically. 'I too read that in books once.'

'This is not written in books, Madan. It is carved in hands,' Naim raised his right hand, 'carved by the labour of hands.'

Iqbal had been quiet, looking at Naim through squinting eyes. 'That is not our fight,' he said. 'That fight is for cowards and cripples.'

'Shut up,' Naim shouted in a rage. 'I lost my hand in open battle, not by creeping up in the dark like you and slinking back to your caves.'

Iqbal did not answer. Fingering his gun, he suddenly raised it and fired. The bullet hit the clay base of the hukka, shattering it, the foul-smelling water splashing out and running all over the floor. Baba rushed in from outside, wild-eyed. 'What was that? Somebody killed?'

'Nobody,' the man with the hennaed beard said quietly, holding in his hand the crooked smoking pipe without its bottom.

Baba looked at the broken pieces of clay on the floor. 'This is no place for shooting,' he said angrily. 'Is this why I have provided you with shelter here?'

Keeping his hand in his trouser pocket, Naim went to his room. He lay down on his bed, removing, with effort, his finger from the trigger of the pistol. After a few minutes the bearded stranger cautiously entered the room through the gap.

'I have,' he said, extending his hand before him, 'some dates.'

Hesitating a moment, Naim took the bone-dry dates from the man's palm and started munching them. The stranger went back to the other room. After he had finished chewing up the dates, Naim went to the big room to wash them down with a glass of water. On the way back he slid the plank to cover the hole in the wall, isolating himself from the others.

Some time during the night Naim awoke and couldn't get back to sleep. He knew Sheelah slept directly on the other side of the plank, next to her brother. He listened for sounds; there was complete silence in the hut. He got up. Walking up to the plank in the dark, he took a whole minute sliding it to one side to uncover half the hole. Before he could reach out and touch her, Sheelah sat bolt upright, as if already waiting. She came into his room and the two of them put the plank back to cover the gap before pulling his blankets over them.

'Did you sleep?' Naim asked in a whisper.

'No.'

Curled up like a kitten against Naim, her warm, feverish breath seeped into his skin, making his bones ache. 'They might have killed you tonight,' she said.

'So what?'

She put her elbows on his chest and raised herself on them. 'I would have killed them,' she said.

'Would you? How?'

'I would put a burning coal on the bag of powder.'

'That would blow us all up.'

'The bag's under his head, he'd blow up more.'

Naim laughed silently. 'You are a foolish girl,' he said and kissed her on the shoulder, the neck, the lips.

'I would have, I'm telling the truth,' she said. 'Naim?'

'Yes?'

'You should go away now.'

'Where?'

'Back where you came from, your home.'

After a pause, Naim said, 'Yes, I think so too.'

'Where is your home?'

'In my village.'

'Will you take me with you?'

Naim did not answer.

'I will go with you,' she said again.

'All right.'

'What do you do there?'

'Work on the land.'

'We worked on the land too. Other people's land. But I can do everything, milk the cows and churn the milk to make butter, cut crops, make dung cakes to burn. I can also cook rice. Do you have a mother and father?'

'Yes.'

'I will do everyone's work for them. I will not just sit about. I will be useful.'

Naim was quiet. She shook him by the shoulder.

'All right?'

'Yes, yes,' he said impatiently. But in his heart he had a sense of grief, both immediate and distant. After a while, he said to her, 'Go back now.'

'Yes,' she said, kissing him on the chest, and silently went back to her room.

All during the next day, Naim roamed aimlessly over the hills. The clouds had cleared. He sat down under a tree for a brief period in the afternoon and slept in the warm sun. It helped to quieten his heart. He returned to the hut late at night. Baba was sleeping on his cot, wrapped up in his dirty quilt under the thatched awning of his hut. Naim sat down on a corner of the cot. Baba poked his head out of the quilt and asked him where he had been.

'Just walking.'

'Where?'

'On the hills.'

'Are you going away?'

'Why do you ask?'

'The girl told me. In secret. She said you were going away this night.'

After a while, Naim said, 'Yes.'

Sheelah came out of their hut. 'I heard you talking,' she whispered to Naim. 'They are still awake. Don't go in.'

'Why?'

'I heard them talking among themselves.'

'What about? I can deal with them.'

'No, please. Just do as I say.'

'My things are inside,' Naim said.

'I will bring them out. They are going to sleep soon. Don't worry. They don't know you are here. Stay out.' She went back. Baba whispered, 'Perhaps we should go inside. Come.' He picked up his quilt and led Naim into his one-room hut. He put some dry twigs on the still warm hearth and blew hard on them, bringing a cough to his throat. On the fire he placed a pan and warmed up some milk, which he gave in a clay cup to Naim with a rock-hard maize roti. Naim ate the roti by dunking it in the milk and drank the milk, emptying the cup. The two of them sat near the fire, talking occasionally in low tones.

Some time after midnight, Sheelah came into the hut carrying a bundle of Naim's blankets in which she had wrapped his bag and his second pair of boots, and she also had a small bundle of her own. 'Let's go,' she said to Naim.

Naim stared at her.

'I have two rotis for the journey,' she said, pointing to the bundle of her own blankets.

Naim got up. Gripping his rolled-up blankets under his left armpit, he put his right arm across her body and pushed her gently back. 'You stay,' he said thickly, and went out of the hut.

Sheelah ran after him. She put her hand on his arm and said, 'You said you'd take me with you.'

'I am not going back to my village,' he said.

'Where are you going?'

'Somewhere else.'

'I'll go anywhere,' she pleaded.

'No,' he barked back at her.

'But you said so . . .' She wept.

Naim left the path and went down a long, very steep slope, running and slipping at the same time over wet earth and small stones. Sheelah sat down at the top with her bundle beside her. She kept looking at him blankly for a minute. Then she put both her feet against a huge stone and pushed with all her might. The boulder rolled down the slope after Naim with dull thuds, narrowly missing him.

'Liar. Pig,' she shouted. 'Wood-bound. Cripple.'

At the bottom of the slope Naim saw a small pool of clear rainwater in a depression in the ground and felt a great thirst. He bent down on his hands and knees and put his lips to the still, cold water. He saw his dim reflection in the water against the sky and knew that he had several days' growth of beard on his face and wild, dirty hair on his head. He stood up and started walking. Up at the top of the slope, Sheelah lost sight of him in the dark night. She dried her eyes, picked up her bundle and turned away. After a few listless steps, the spring came back to her legs and she ran back to the hut.

CHAPTER 14

On Roshan Mahal's big lawn a dinner had been held the previous night, hosted by Roshan Agha, in honour of Pervez for having successfully completed various stages of the competitive examinations for the Indian Civil Service. It had been a long hard struggle for the young man. He wasn't particularly bright but had a talent for applying himself to the job. He had spent three years passing the examinations but not being selected in the competition for the available posts. Finally, on his last allowable chance, he had made it. All of Roshan Agha's friends, his usual contacts in politics and the high bureaucracy, had been invited. The next afternoon, as the house tradition went, the younger people, from the age of seven to twenty-one, were holding their own party – a very different affair from the grand khana the night before. They weren't allowed on to the manicured big lawn, which was still being cleared up and tended in the wake of the dinner, so they had all gathered on the smaller side lawn. Most of Pervez and Azra's relations and friends were there. The area was buzzing with the frantic cries of children and grown-up girls and the booming voices of young men, all of them busy at their games. Except for Azra. She had been among them, trying to organize the girls for the debating contest to be held shortly and at the same time overseeing the arrangements for the food which was being prepared for the guests in one of the kitchens, when Sahibzada Waheed, finding her on her own for a moment, bent over her ear and quietly recited a romantic Farsi couplet to her. It was as if the very state of her being suddenly altered. She smiled politely and moved away from the crowd. She walked around the tall sanatha hedge that ran between her partying friends and another strip of grass bordered by flower beds in that nook of the sprawling house. She picked up the hand-fountain bucket and looked in. There was a little water left at the bottom of it. Upending the bucket, she aimlessly watered a plant that had already been fed. She was hidden from view by the thick hedge. The others' voices, with which hers had been joined a few minutes back, now seemed to come to her from across a great distance.

Arshad was addressing his side. 'Gentlemen. Friends –'

'And countrymen,' someone interrupted.

'Be quiet. Friends –'

'Lend me your ears,' someone else said.

'Shut up. Gentlemen, this is not a game, it is a question of our nose.' Arshad put his index finger firmly on his nose.

'Rather a matter of –' a girl said.

'What?'

'A matter of nose.'

'Look,' Pervez said, 'don't poke your nose in our affairs, I mean matters. You attend to your own team . . . matters.'

The girl – Phoebe Gregson, Azra saw hazily through the fine mesh of the hedge – touched her nose lightly. All the girls laughed.

'It is a matter of shame for us,' Arshad began again, 'that today girls have had the nerve to throw a challenge to us.'

'Hear, hear,' the men clapped.

'I said it is not a matter for applause but a disgrace.'

'Hear, hear.' More clapping from the men.

The girls had begun to organize themselves.

'Four speeches each. Right?'

'No, five,' Pervez interjected.

'We agreed on four.'

'Nonsense. Five. We agreed on five.'

'One, two, three, four . . . Where is Azra?'

'She is probably in the kitchen.'

'I have just come from the kitchen. She isn't there.'

'Might have guessed, you glutton.'

'I only had a glass of water, I swear.'

'Liar. You smell of kebabs.'

'Let me be struck down if I lie. I didn't touch the food.'

'Oh God, where's Azra? Azraaa –'

Azra heard it as though it was someone else's name. She stood still, holding the empty bucket in her hand. Then she heard Sahibzada Waheed's short, light footsteps approaching from around the hedge and over to her side and she wanted to be somewhere else.

'Azra bibi, what are you doing here?'

For one moment she felt that her old friend was addressing not her but another person. She looked around, as if expecting to find a third standing there.

'Oh, look,' the sahibzada said, 'you've drowned the poor flower. Now it will die.'

Staring at a perfect jewel-like drop of water resting on a petal, she felt that the flower was looking back at her through that sparkling eye. 'No,' she said. 'It won't die.'

'Are you sure?'

'Yes. Look at that drop.'

'Oh, how wonderful!'

'How did you find me?' she asked.

'I have something of the bloodhound in me. I followed your smell.'

'Foul, was it?'

'No, no, the opposite. Most wonderful. You leave your perfume on the grass that you tread.'

She laughed. 'Fantastic exaggeration, as ever.'

'No, no, no.'

She wanted to run away.

'The speeches are on,' the sahibzada said.

'Yes, I can hear them. Let's go.'

'No. Let's stay.'

They walked up and down the narrow strip of grass. Azra didn't understand what had happened – she never did, although she was never surprised at it. It always happened, and at the most unexpected of times. At times like these, her heart filled up at once with the weight of a vague, unremembered sorrow and the lightness of joy: she became still and yet felt like crying out in an unfamiliar, two-tone voice.

'I don't understand you,' the sahibzada was saying. 'I never know what you are going to do from one moment to the next.'

'I know what I am going to do now,' she said, laughing, and tossing her head in a familiar gesture, sweeping back a strand of hair on her brow with the back of her hand. 'I'm going to join the speeches. I mean, we are, aren't we?'

She ran over to the other side. Shirin was standing on a chair, orating in her shrill voice, and the crowd were laughing their heads off. Several people turned to look at Azra. Shirin stopped for a moment, then resumed where she had left off.

'Well done,' Azra shouted.

'Where did you disappear to?' Arshad said to her. 'It's your turn next.'

'I am ready,' Azra replied.

This was the young generation of the Indian upper classes that, for a few years of their youth, mixed with each other, went to the same schools and colleges, spent long summer holidays at the same hill stations and had endless parties in vast houses full of light and air and servants. On this day, after the speeches, the applause, the hotly disputed judgement, the chaos, the boycotts, the food, the songs, the stories and the jokes, night fell and the party ended. In her bedroom, Azra changed into night clothes, threw a gown over her shoulders and switched off the light. Instead of going to bed, she went and stood at the open window, looking out into the garden where most of the lights had been turned off, save one or two at strategic points near the gate and the big lawn. The house had three floors, and Azra's rooms were at the top. Just outside her window was the top of the tallest eucalyptus tree in the garden. She could reach out and touch its leaves, as she had often done. But on this night she looked above the trees and the lights. The sky was becoming overcast with great puffy masses of cloud. She looked for the stars among the clouds and marked them – one, two, three . . . When all the stars disappeared one by one, she turned back into the room. A little diffused light from outside spread faintly through the room. She noticed that her collection of little bronze and china figurines on the mantelpiece was covered in a fine layer of dust. She calmly proceeded, without turning on the lamp, to clean each object in turn with her silk nightgown. After she had them clean and glistening dimly in the dark room, catching the light from the hidden source, she stood back and regarded them – those figures of metal and stone with which she had lived for years – as if they were living beings whose acquaintance she had made for the first time. The last thought she had before she went to bed was: Am I really strange? She did not need to ask herself. She knew that her strangeness had been part of her for as long as she could remember, and it was known and accepted by others. A hint of a troubled smile appeared on her lips, and she closed her eyes.

CHAPTER 15

It was a bitterly cold late January dawn when Naim reached the eastern edge of Roshan Pur's lands from where he could see the faint outlines of grey mud walls of the village in the distance through the fog that hung in the still air. Wheat and gram crops were already calf-high. There were patches of bare, tilled fields whose ruts were covered with hard frost. Naim had left the train and walked miles in the dark until daylight began to spread at his back and he had a view of the village for the first time in eighteen months. Wrapped up in his dirty long coat, woollen hat and heavy boots, all ex-army and long used, he stood under a shisham tree looking at his beloved home and felt the blood in his legs gradually run cold and the chill of the frozen earth rise through his feet, making him shiver. His tongue was dry from walking so far. He picked up a thin, sharp-edged piece of ice from the ground and put it in his mouth, letting it slowly dissolve into thick saliva. He pressed his tongue against the roof of his mouth to hold back the tiny particles of dirt while attempting to suck in the clear liquid. It proved an unsuccessful effort. He had to spit most of it out, but his throat was no longer dry. He came out from under the ancient tree that he had known all his life and started walking. The lands he was stepping on did not belong to him or his fathers, yet they were Roshan Pur's lands and they made him feel at home. He pulled his wool cap down on his brow and thrust his hands deep into the coat pockets, enjoying, as he stepped on it, the occasional crunch of frozen water that had begun to give off vapour with the gradual climbing of the sun, now just below the rim of the earth.

Men were already out, carrying ploughs on their shoulders and driving oxen ahead of them, going to the fields that were still untilled. Naim recognized them as they passed: Guru, Dina Nath, Karam Singh, Imam Din the wrestler. The men looked, with a peasant's silent suspicion, at the stranger in the unfamiliar garb, his face completely hidden by his hat and the upturned collars of his coat, walking by at this unusual hour. Naim wanted to stop and speak to them, but he didn't have the will. Only Imam Din stopped for a moment to look him up and down before walking on, mumbling to himself, 'Don't know, walks like Niaz Beg's boy,' then addressing his bullock, 'Year fourteen last brought this kind of cold to the world.' Naim saw his steaming white breath as he laughed quietly, striding towards the village. By the edge of the pond he picked up a flat stone and threw it over his arm. The stone skimmed the icy surface once and, with a single muffled bubbling sound, sank a yard further, throwing up tiny drops that gleamed in the light from the sky. Naim looked at the house on the corner and remembered Mahinder Singh and then all the others that had died who had never left him since, and for a moment he had a sense of having no home anywhere.

But that was before he saw the Mughals' house – his and his father's home. He didn't recognize it. As if in a trance, he walked up to the door and stared at it in disbelief. It was a big new door with scores of thick five-headed brass nails hammered into the solid black shisham wood all over it. Putting his hand out, he touched the glinting metal of the decorative nails. It was a rich man's door. Seized by sudden apprehension, Naim didn't have the nerve to knock at it. He stood there for minutes, until the sun came up behind him and from the neighbouring door emerged the figure of Ahmad Din, riding on the back of his bullock with hukka in hand and pipe between his lips. Naim pushed his wool cap up his forehead and said, 'Assalamoalaikam, chacha.'

Ahmad Din jumped down from the bullock's back like a young boy and ran up to peer at Naim.

'Ah – ha ha – ha ha ha,' he burst out, spreading his arms wide. 'Niaz Beg's boy? You, when did you come? What are you doing standing here?' The old man started furiously thumping at the door, shouting with the full force of his lungs, 'Hey, hey, you old lazy-limbs, look, your boy's come, your son, from whose medal's acres you got melons a maund in weight and by the income from that you have raised a palace and become a big chaudri. Why did you not send your new mare to fetch your son? The earth is hard with ice and you have made your son walk here, you rascal! Come on now, leave your women in peace and come out –' Suddenly the old man stopped thumping the door and turned to Naim, twisting one of his coat buttons. 'I asked after you many times. Your father said you were seeing friends in Dilli and Kalkatta. So many seasons with friends, I asked? He said you were a very important man and had friends high up. True, true. I asked after you regularly. Since my son died in the angrezi war everyone's son is my son.

Why don't you speak? Is it because of the cold? Tsk tsk! Once I had to travel all night in the month of Poh and I couldn't speak for three days because of a stiff tongue. It froze.'

The heavy door creaked and Naim saw his father's face. Ignoring the stream of condemnation pouring once again from Ahmad Din's lips, Niaz Beg kept staring at his son, and Naim saw that his father's mouth was hanging loose and his lower jaw was shivering – not from the cold but trembling on nerves that couldn't support it. He had grown very old. Presently, he stepped outside and started kissing his son on the face, the coat on his chest, his right hand and then the wood of his left, mumbling words that were only a sound with no shape or meaning. He pulled Naim inside the house and quickly shut the door on Ahmad Din. Ahmad Din stood there looking at the door, in his eyes the wilderness of his own loss, then shouting for the last time in a fast-fading voice, 'I asked after you many times, as your father can confirm . . .'

Inside, Naim looked at the house in amazement. The courtyard had been laid with bricks, a new pukka brick room had been built on the roof of the house – 'your room', Niaz Beg told Naim later, 'all yours' – and all the doors had been replaced with polished shisham wood. The older woman, Naim's mother, stood in the doorway of her room and was crying loudly, both hands half-raised to the sky. Niaz Beg found his tongue. He started shouting at her.

'Get the fire going, stupid woman. Don't you know that after the year fourteen this is the biggest cold that the sky has sent the earth? And stop hoo hooing – hoo hoo hoo hoo,' he mimicked his wife, dragging Naim into the room.

Shortly after, Naim was sitting in front of red hot coals with a jug of hot buffalo milk and a day-old roti that had been fried in butter. Talking constantly, Niaz Beg was saying, 'This is all from your income that came –'

'My income?' Naim asked, absentmindedly chewing the bread.

'Yes, yes, from your ten acres, and some of mine. But mostly from your land. After all it's the land that we won with our bravery, so why should it not give us good fruit? So much wheat that I sold to ten other lazy ones for seed and still the grain store is full. I laid the bricks out in the yard and built the room above for you and all the doors and everything with my own hands, these hands,' he spread his hands in front of him, and through their dry, cracked skin knobs of bones showed, cruelly swollen.

Ali, now no longer a toddler, walked silently in from the other room and stood by Naim. 'Have you brought something for me from the city?' he asked.

Naim looked at the child and for the first time he emerged from the state of mindless, limb-stretching comfort into which he had lowered himself. Taken a little aback, he touched Ali on the cheek. 'I didn't go to the city,' he said weakly.

Niaz Beg pushed the child away with his arm. 'Go. Don't bother him, he is tired. Let him rest.'

The old woman passed her hand over the nice spun-cotton sheet spread on the bed. 'There are eleven more like this one.'

'No need to shout about it,' Niaz Beg admonished, 'the whole village knows we have eleven more like this. In all a full dozen. No need to tell him. Let the boy rest.' Instead, seeing that Naim had finished his food, Niaz Beg pulled him up by the shoulder and dragged him outside. 'You see this mushki bullock? It is famous in all the villages here. Thieves came three times to steal it, but I was alert. They went away empty-handed. You've been walking all night. You need rest. Afterwards, I will show you the grain store.' Without a pause, Niaz Beg took him to the storeroom. Entering the room, he stumbled on the threshold. Naim saw that the old man's legs were thin as dry stalks and bent like bows.

'Baba, you've grown old,' he said, laughing.

Niaz Beg waved his arm all round the room, which was stacked with bags of wheat to the rafters. 'Look, all this with my own hands.' Then, remembering his son's remark, 'I am not old. I work. Men who work never become old. And I don't cry like women. Now you must sleep. When you get up, I will take you out.'

The sun had already covered three-quarters of the sky on its downward journey before Naim awoke. Niaz Beg was ready and waiting. They stepped out of the house together.

'This is where our acres start,' Niaz Beg said, standing far out in the fields beyond Roshan Agha's vast spread. 'You can't put a foot down without trampling on a root. I have looked after it bravely, seeing that we won it with bravery. Only two marlas of sugarcane were left, and I cut them while you slept. Finished. See those two girls peeling them now? Oh ho, they are three. Who is the third? Who are you?'

'I am Rehmu's daughter,' the third girl replied. 'Don't you recognize me, chacha? Have you stopped wearing surma in your eyes?' Sweating around the nose and breasts, which were visible through their loose shirts, wet from hours of labour cleaning sugarcane with small hand scythes in the sun, the girls laughed.

Niaz Beg shouted at them with embarrassment. 'Keep your heads and hands on your work. Young girls shouldn't let their tongues run free. Work, work, keep yourselves away from the devil!'

The girls looked at Naim and smiled shyly. Niaz Beg pulled his son away. 'We need a woman in the house. A young strong girl can manage the house on her own and help out in the fields too. I have made a room above the house for you. Do you like it?'

'Yes,' replied Naim.

At night, in the animals' yard just inside the main door of the house, the last of the gur was being made.

'This crusher,' Niaz Beg told Naim, 'I bought with my money. You remember we used to hire it from others and paid for it with the gur that we had made with our own labour? Now it is all ours. After all, it from the medal's land that –'

'Don't go on about it, Baba,' Naim interrupted.

'Why not? When I went with money in my pocket to buy the mushki bullock from the chaudris of Jat Nagar, people tried to stop me. They said nobody goes to the big chaudris to buy their cattle. But you know, when I went there they gave me a good seat to sit on, right next to themselves, and they mentioned your name with respect. After all, we won with bravery the medal from gora sarkar.'

'Baba,' Naim said severely, 'if you mention it one more time I will throw it in the fire. Be quiet.'

A great fire, fed by the crushed peel of the sugarcanes and their long dry leaves, burned under a huge wide-mouthed iron pot containing the furiously boiling juice that poured out of the crusher, pulled by the mushki ox. The cane crusher was always the gathering point for the men of the village wherever it was working, as much for the warmth of the fire on cold nights as for a cup of juice, a mouthful of hot gur, a round of hukka and gossip. Volunteers presented themselves to drive the oxen, feed the sugarcane into the mouth of the crusher and put the crushed peel into the fire. They talked for half the night about things that concerned them: the young about girls they fancied, the old about the weather, the crops, the strength of each other's tobacco, and later, when the sweet aroma of vapour arising from the ever-thickening juice in the pot had saturated the air and after it had been cleaned up with okra stalks and the dirt skimmed away from the surface and they had had a taste of the hot, yellowish pink gur and the night mellowed, they talked about their old loves, their faces showing the shy remembrance of their youth for ever gone.

The big door creaked and Hari Chand, the schoolmaster, entered. He quietly greeted the assembled people and went to sit by Naim who had earlier moved aside to sit on his own away from the crowd.

'Good to see you back,' Hari Chand said. 'You were away a long time.'

'Too long,' Naim said with a smile.

'I knew you were sent to other places, although not exactly where,' Hari Chand said with a questioning look.

'Oh, several places,' Naim said to him.

'I was told that our people lost track of you.'

'No they didn't, although I did go away on my own towards the end.'

Hari Chand was quiet for a while. Then he said, 'Were you happy?'

'It was work.'

'What are you going to do now?' Hari Chand asked.

'Nothing. I am going to stay here. Have you seen my father's condition?'

'Yes.'

'How is it with you?'

'Oh, much as before, much as before.'

Niaz Beg gave them a clay cup each full of hot gur with melted ghee swimming on top. 'Eat it,' he said. 'You give one of these to a horse and it will jump the wall. The cold – not since year fourteen . . .'

Naim ate it with relish. Hari Chand took only a couple of fingerfuls and put the cup aside.

'What do you think about the situation now?' Hari Chand asked.

'I don't think. I told you, I am doing nothing but staying here. I am tired.'

'I understand,' Hari Chand said. 'Everyone's work is cut out.'

Under a pale moon, they sat silently for a few minutes. Then Hari Chand got up, shook hands with Naim and left. Naim felt the other man's hand cold and heavy in his grip.

It was early when Naim awoke the next morning. His father was still asleep, gathered up under his quilt like a small bundle. This was one of those rare days when he didn't leave the house in the early hours to go out to the fields and stay there until sunrise. Naim went to the water pump in the courtyard and started pumping it. When all the cold water in the pipe had run out, he filled two buckets with the lukewarm water that fetched up from the bowels of the earth. With those he bathed, luxuriously pouring water over his head and feeling the grime of weeks wash away. Little Ali and Naim's cousin Rawal had walked out of their rooms and stood watching him. After Naim dried himself and put on his shirt and trousers, he grabbed Ali by the neck and tossed him in the air. The child landed smartly on his stepbrother's shoulders, gripping his head.

'I can ride the mare,' Ali said, pointing to the splendid white animal of whose purchase and value Naim had heard from his father at length the previous day.

'I can ride standing up,' Rawal boasted.

To keep up with them, Naim told a lie. 'I used to ride lying on my back when I was your age.'

'Really?' Rawal said, his eyes wide. 'Are there horses in Kulkutta?'

'Yes, they pull buggies.'

'Bullock buggies?'

'No, horse buggies.'

Niaz Beg had got out of bed. The old woman was getting on with preparing the food for her men. They sat on the floor around a very low table that Niaz Beg told his son he had made 'with his own hands', proudly spreading his hands yet again in front of him. He ate last night's warmed-up gur with butter first of all, followed by buffalo milk and a paratha and finally a melon. Naim had always been surprised at the contrast between his father's shrunken body and the amount of food he consumed. At times he had mentioned it and got the old man's answer, 'Horse and man, as long as they keep eating, they stay upright. They stop eating, they die.'

The old woman started weeping.

'Why are you crying, mother?' Naim asked her.

His mother kept quietly shedding tears.

'Tell me, what is it?'

'He,' she said, wiping her tears, 'slept here after two months. Two whole months, he ate my food and slept with that blood-sucker in the other room. Last night, only because of you . . . I pray you not to go away now.'

Naim blushed deeply. 'I am not going anywhere,' he said.

'Hold your tongue, you foolish woman,' Niaz Beg shouted. 'Give me some achar, go on, get up.'

Niaz Beg ate a whole pickled green mango and offered another to Naim. 'Eat it. When a buffalo's stomach gets heavy, a single achar mango does the job. Eat it. It will make your insides light, light as the wind.'

Naim laughed. 'I don't want the wind inside me.'

'Baba has much wind,' Rawal said, laughing.

Niaz Beg glowered at the boy. 'Hold your tongue. It is growing wings. One day I will cut them.'

They heard a noise outside the house. They listened. The low humming noise continued. There was the sound of hurrying feet. Niaz Beg and Naim got up together and went to the door. A group of villagers appeared running down the street, disappearing round the other corner. Following them came some women, all of them Hindu and Sikh, walking with irregular steps. Terror peeped out of their eyes, but no tears; they were mumbling words that sounded like low moans arising from a deep pain: 'They finished him. The Muslas finished him.' One by one they vanished into their houses, shutting the doors on the outside world. Picking up the scent, Niaz Beg and Naim went to Hari Chand's hut, where the schoolmaster lay, half in and half out of the door, his arms gathered upon his chest and legs spread wide. His throat had been cut. Out of his pulled-down shalwar his bloody genitals were visible: he had been crudely circumcised.

'They came in the night,' an old Sikh said to Niaz Beg, shaking his head.

'Did you see them?'

'No. They came from outside, not from here.'

Back in the house, Naim sat on the cot with his head in his hands. The silence in the village was so complete that the thought of a single living, breathing being seemed impossible. Everyone was waiting, waiting for something, or someone, other people, Roshan Agha, the police, God from heaven, anyone, to come and lift this pall of breathless quiet where not a sound arose from the hidden multitude. Naim sat still, with a voice saying over and over to him in his head, 'This has nothing to do with you, nothing at all.' His mother started crying. It was the first voice he heard. Then the horse neighed and the buffalo uttered a low, regretful moan. Some small children laughed in the distance. Slowly, the village began to come to life. But for hours no one came out of their houses and the streets remained empty, until the police party came. In the evening the police took the dead body away with them. The story told by the police was that 'the reality was different, it wasn't the Muslas, a cow was slaughtered and the militant Hindus flared up and killed Hari Chand when he went to try to calm them'. All this had happened in 'some other village', whence the body was brought back and dumped on his doorstep. Why was he circumcised? Because he was considered a 'sympathizer' of the Muslas.

The reality, however, as always in such cases, was never discovered. The dead man had no known relatives, no one to mourn him. The locked door of his hut, never lived in afterwards, for ever reminded Naim of death in the plural, as if it were not one man that had died there but all the dead he had known, depositing yet more on the heap of anonymous mourning within him.

Two months after Naim arrived back in the village, Niaz Beg met his end. Swift and sudden, it took barely twelve hours. The old man kept making plans for the next day right up to the last few moments, when he briefly wept. It was the second half of March; the mornings were still chilly. At dawn, Niaz Beg picked up his hukka and went out for the last watering of his wheat crop. He cut into the water coming from the main canal outlet and made little channels with his spade at several places for it to flow into his fields, constantly talking to it. 'First you took so long to come, and when you come, you devil, you are cold as ice, freezing the blood in my feet,' he said, standing ankle-deep in mud. 'But never mind, this is the last time before the harvest and I am going to suck up every drop of you. You go two steps and sink into the earth, eh? You lazy layabout, come with me and I will show you how many roots you have to wet, no man in the whole village has as much standing wheat as I have, I will tire you out or you can change my name to whatever you want, you wayward son of the river. When I was young I could stand in you up to the waist all night in the month of Poh, and now I am old you freeze my blood, eh? Shame on you. You just wait, wait, I am not going to give up until I am finished with you . . .' Talking thus, louder and louder to keep out the cold, he managed to water most of his field of rapidly paling crops before a neighbouring farmer came to claim his share of water.

The sun was up to a two-spear height when Niaz Beg returned home. He ate gur mixed with nuts and a cup of hot milk, smoked hukka for a few minutes and went out again to prepare the soil for the sowing of vegetables. Carrying the plough on his back and repeatedly taking the pipe of the hukka out of his mouth to poke the bullock in the behind with it to drive it ahead of him, he freed one hand by balancing the plough on one shoulder and rubbed his chest, swearing at the pain that had been roaming around under his ribs since the morning. 'If the boy had two hands,' he mumbled to himself, 'he could have helped me.' Sorrowfully, he swore at his son's disability and started tilling the land. By the time the sun was overhead he had turned the soil in the whole field. Back home, his pain kept bothering him. He made no mention of it. According to Niaz Beg, the one cure for a hundred ailments was work and more work. 'Every impurity of the body is washed away with sweat,' he always said. Rubbing his chest surreptitiously and grimacing, he still ate like a horse: two thick rotis of wheat flour kneaded in butter, with gram daal seared with fried onions, followed by a pot of lassi.

After another few pulls at the hukka, which had been refreshed on his orders by Rawal, he was up once again, shouting at Rawal to accompany him out to fetch fodder for the animals. Rawal picked up his tools – a length of rope and a hand scythe – and followed him out of the yard. 'You have eaten four times and they,' he said, pointing to the cattle and poking the boy in the neck with the sharp end of the scythe, 'have not eaten once. Have you no shame?'

'We are going, aren't we?' the boy said angrily.

Niaz Beg talked to Rawal on the way out, admonishing him for one thing or the other. But by the time he came back he had stopped talking. Lugging a large bundle of green fodder on his back, he was boiling with fever. At home, he threw down the heavy fodder and didn't have the energy to untie the bundle or serve it to the animals. He fell on his cot and lost consciousness. His two wives, panicking at the sight of him shivering like a twig in a storm, started massaging his chest with clove-seared ghee, until Naim told them to stop exposing him to the cold and cover him up with quilts. Niaz Beg did not regain consciousness until several hours later, when he briefly came to and called out for his son. He grabbed Naim's arm, felt that it was wood, a mistake he had never made in his full faculties, and shifted his grip to the good arm, holding it tightly to him. He spoke haltingly.

'I have turned up the earth for vegetables. Sow them inside four days or the soil will become hard. Take Rawal with you and get the seed from Ali's mother. Have you seen the mustard flowers blazing like fire? Phagan is already nearly over; soon it will be cutting time. I have watered the wheat for the last time, no more water there. It's going to be a heavy crop again this year, I can tell you. The gram crop will be ready in thirty days' time, but you don't have to worry about that, I will be up on my feet by that time. Nobody dies of working hard. I am going to go out to look for a woman for you as soon as I am up, don't you worry about that either. A woman is useful for a farmer . . .' He let go of Naim's arm for a second, then grasped it again, 'Ali is your brother, look after . . .' He wanted to go on but couldn't utter the words. He looked at his son with dumb eyes, and tears trickled down his temples. One of his hands shot out and grabbed at his younger wife's crotch under her waist-sheet, holding it tight. Lying thus on his back, Niaz Beg died quickly. The poor woman, her face red as beetroot, struggled to free herself from her husband's death-grip, finally succeeding after furiously pulling herself away, although she lost a small tuft of hair from her genital area that was wedged in the dead man's fist. She uttered a cry, as much of grief as of physical pain, and joined the other woman in wailing over their widowhood.

They kept the body at home during the night while the gravediggers got busy, not in the village graveyard but in a corner of the Mughal's land, for the burial the next day. In the morning the villagers came, those that were neighbours and friends and also those who disliked the deceased for his ill temper, his bragging and his new-found wealth. They sat on durrees spread on the ground in a circle in the courtyard, offering condolences. 'When my woman told me,' said Ghulam Hussain, a man well-known for being Niaz Beg's enemy, 'that chaudri had – had . . .' His face screwed up to indicate that he was overcome with grief, and just when Naim thought the man was going to break down and cry, he straightened up quickly, regaining his composure, and continued, '– had passed away, an arrow pierced my heart, here,' he thumped his chest, 'right here!' Despite the state of shock that Naim was in, he couldn't help imagining what his father would say at such deceit: 'Shut your tongue, you old thief, and be off with you!' Another man took up the wail, and then another, in the usual manner of peasants, whose cunning came not from malice but from the way they took life and death, grief and joy, the same as they did, in their proper time, the cycle of the seasons, the rising and setting of the sun each day, and thought little more of the passing of men than the unending change of colour of earth and crops.

A tonga stopped outside and Ayaz Beg stepped down from it. Slowly, he walked towards the house. The mourners sitting in the courtyard looked at this man whom they had last seen when he was a young man and calmly greeted him as they would someone returning from a night away from the village. Not Naim. He saw his uncle enter the house, supporting himself with a cane and, although he had spent the time since the death dry-eyed and numbed, now he leaned on the older man's shoulder and cried like a child.

CHAPTER 16

Naim took some while before he could settle down to a routine of living – for the first time – as an independent man in the village. Then came a shift in his circumstances so swift and sweeping that it altered the course of his life.

He had consolidated his father's, his own and almost ten acres of good fertile grace-and-favour land given by Roshan Agha to Ayaz Beg to mark his visit to the village after a long self-exile. Ayaz Beg, after burying his brother, never returned to the village again. Naim had twenty-six acres of land under him, two-thirds of which he gave to the muzaras on a half-share basis and the rest he kept for cultivation under his own supervision, providing the bullocks, the ploughs, the seed and anything else needed for the job, the tillers being his servants who took a share of the crop and whatever little money they needed according to custom. These sharecroppers and farm labourers in general had milch cattle, the produce of which they sold or bartered to supplement their income. Naim had built himself two brick rooms on his land outside the village and in these he now lived, looked after by a servant who fetched his meals, cooked by his mother three times a day. Sometimes he felt deeply his loneliness and the need for a friend, but he found that the ability to form friendships was lost to him, a wall-like curtain having dropped between him and the world. He still mixed with the villagers, often going to sit with them in the panchayat yard, a place for the common folk to come and go, using it for assemblies or just to exchange chat as they pleased. Being the owner of land and men in his own right and a hero on top, aside from having the advantage of an education, Naim was consulted by everyone about their problems, from small everyday matters to big affairs, and asked to give decisions that were accepted by all. He had attained a position in the village that was far higher than that of the munshi, the previous headman, who was only a servant and owned neither land nor men. Naim also went to his father's house regularly twice a week to sit with his mother and stepmother, to listen, mostly in silence, to their needs for food and clothing and to their woes, happy in the knowledge that the two women had now learned to live peaceably together.

Once a month, he went to visit his uncle Ayaz Beg, who had taken early retirement and lived in the old house in Delhi. It was on one of these occasions, as he sat at the table after the midday meal in his uncle's house, that Ayaz Beg handed him a thick, richly embossed card. The card, an invitation to the walima party of Pervez's marriage – the nikah ceremony of which was to have taken place two days previously at a family function – was addressed to 'Naim Ahmad Khan'.

'Will you come?' Ayaz Beg asked.

'Er – I don't know,' Naim answered.

'I got the impression that they would be glad to see you.'

'This is a busy time of the year in the village,' Naim said.

'I think it would be wise to go,' Ayaz Beg said to him.

'What do you mean?'

Ayaz Beg paused before answering. 'There is a chance,' he said, 'that we will regain possession of the land.'

'Which land?'

'The acres that we lost following the –' he stopped for a second, 'the case.'

'How is it possible after all these years?'

'Since your father's death there is a slight chance that we can have the decision reversed. After all, I was also one of the owners, and now you. And neither of us had anything to do with – with what happened.'

Naim thought for a moment. 'Do you really think it is feasible?'

'To be frank, it was Roshan Agha who first suggested it to me. I have already sent a petition to the governor. A separate one should go from you. In view of your services to the government, there is a real chance.'

A month later, Naim had his hair cut, put on a suit that he had had made soon after his return from the war but had not once worn, and went to Roshan Mahal with Ayaz Beg.

The house stood just as he remembered it, with only the addition of a garden-house, which, his uncle informed him proudly, was built to Ayaz Beg's own design. The paths and lawns of the house were a lot more crowded on this day than on the day Naim was last here to attend a party. Under the colourful bunting stretched across the garden, their strings tied to the rooftops, people stood, sat, sipped mango and orange juice, talked, made gentle gestures, moved leisurely about so that the entire assembly of men and women seemed, in a hum of voices, to be slowly floating and churning in space like currents and eddies in a great river. Among them, here and there, Naim could see the old familiar faces of people who had been young boys and girls when he had played with them on the very same ground.

'Hello, Uncle,' Pervez said, appearing from the side, 'adaab.'

'Assalam-o-alaikam, betay.' Ayaz Beg patted him on the head. 'Congratulations. How are you?'

'Thank you, Uncle. I am fine. Hello, Naim.'

They shook hands. Pervez held Naim's hand for several minutes, pressing it warmly, smiling, searching for the old acquaintance in Naim's eyes and finding it, no more than a spark but sufficient for a renewal. Suddenly, they found themselves surrounded by several of their group, followed by much shaking of hands and noise of greetings.

'Where did you go, Naim? For so long – so long,' asked Phoebe Gregson, the police superintendent's daughter, in her typical, too cheerful way.

'Are you deaf and blind, Phee, can't you see he's back from winning the war?' Arshad said, pointing with exaggerated formality to the entire length of Naim's erect posture.

'Oh good, good, good,' innocent-faced Talat, the only one who didn't seem to have aged a day since Naim last saw her, enthused, 'you are a war hero. Great! Are we allowed to worship you now?'

'We read it in the newspaper,' Shirin said.

'What?' Naim asked.

'Of your exploits.'

'It was nothing like that,' Naim said. 'It just happened by chance.'

'Hulloo –' someone from the back of the crowd cried. Sahibzada Waheeduddin proceeded vigorously to shake Naim's hand. 'Where have you been, old man? Oh, but of course you went off to the war. How wonderful! And you won fame, didn't you? Splendid. Welcome back. Welcome.'

For once Naim felt utter contempt for these young men in comparison to their counterparts in England and elsewhere in Europe who had fought and died in the trenches.

'Have you met Bilkees?' asked Shirin.

'Yes, yes,' the sahibzada injected, 'meet my wife . . .'

Bilkees Waheeduddin was a pale, slight young woman with fine, upper-class features.

'Bilkees, you know Naim?' Shirin said. 'No? Our old friend Naim Ahmad Khan. Now,' she paused, 'victor of wars.'

There was good-natured laughter. Naim joined in with a thin smile. He was mildly annoyed and embarrassed. He felt the general gaiety around him was forced and saw how hard everyone was trying to avoid looking at the unmoving arm thrust permanently in his jacket pocket. Someone called out from the side, and the group broke up, going in different directions in pairs, promising to meet up again in a short while.

Walking among the crowd, Naim was introduced some time later to civil service colleagues of Pervez and Sahibzada Waheed, who greeted him with customary politeness. Further on, he came across some minor zamindars, wearing their high starched turbans, standing in a group of four, one of whom stopped Naim.

'We heard you were in the war, young man,' the man said cheerfully, 'and you showed great bravery.'

'Who told you?' Naim asked him roughly.

'Oh, we all know,' the landowner said, looking pointedly at the sleeve-covered arm. 'We are proud of you.'

Naim thought the man was going to touch his arm. He abruptly turned and walked away. On the way to the veranda he was halted by Pervez's hand on his shoulder.

'Naim, meet my wife Naheed.'

Trying hard to lighten his mood, Naim said 'adaab' to a plumpish, fair-skinned girl, who, unlike any other young woman there, offered her hand to him to shake and spoke to him in English.

'How do you do?'

Slightly taken aback, Naim took her very soft hand for a second and mumbled a congratulation-cum-greeting. Pervez walked off, leaving the two of them standing there.

'I have heard so much about you,' she said to him.

'I am visiting here after many years,' Naim said.

'Oh, yes? But they talk of you as if you were never away.'

'Do they?'

A woman of about thirty, wearing a gold-threaded gharara, came up to speak in an urgent manner to Naheed, making her turn summarily to Naim to say, 'See you later,' and quickly go off with the woman. Naim felt immensely relieved. He ascended the four marble steps and stepped on to the veranda. Turning left, because that side was empty of both guests and servants, he started walking slowly along the long, curved black-and-white tiled veranda, pausing once or twice to look through the thick white columns out at the guests and hosts, mixing, talking, now a bit more animatedly, standing on the paths, on the grass, and sitting in the sofa chairs laid out on the lawn in the afternoon sun of late autumn. The years had imparted to his features a hint of roughness that sat attractively on his face. Women unknown to him looked from a distance at this good-looking young man walking all by himself behind the columns – his body held straight, arm in his pocket – with affection, and the English among them, these sitting mostly on the sofas, smiled boldly at him. Walking on, he met unexpectedly, one after the other, three people. First was Roshan Agha, emerging from an inner room and coming face to face with him.

'Adaab,' Naim said, touching his forehead with his hand.

'Good to see you, Naim,' Roshan Agha said, placing his hand on Naim's back, smiling but not looking him straight in the eye. He asked a string of questions in one breath. 'How are you? How are matters in the village? I am sorry about Niaz Beg's passing away. Are you faring well on your own?'

'Very well, sir, everything's all right.'

'Yes, yes. I wanted you to come. Come more often. Our relations go back generations. Anything I can do in the village, do not hesitate to let me know.' Roshan Agha hastened away, Naim saying 'Thank you' to his back.

Next was the aunt, coming down the stone staircase that descended from the upper storey near the end of the veranda. 'How are you, Naim mian?' she asked in her usual pinched manner, a forced civility that nevertheless expressed a half-formed disapproval of the world around her.

'I am quite well, khala,' Naim replied.

'It's been a long time,' she said.

'Yes,' said Naim, 'I have been busy.'

'So I have heard.' The older woman, who had all the time been looking past him at the people out in the open, moved sideways, seeming imperceptibly to shrink away from him and, without saying another word, stepped off the veranda, going on to join a group of women on the main lawn. Naim stood there trying to recover from his meeting with the woman. Just under the staircase was the last room in this wing of the house. Azra appeared in the doorway. She made no effort to step on to the veranda, nor did she utter a word to greet Naim. She stood there regarding him intently from head to foot with eyes at once warm and vacant, her gaze finally resting on the arm, of which only the jacket sleeve showed. Naim too was absolutely still, although his head, held high for so long, bowed ever so slightly as if bringing itself in line with Azra's. A whole minute passed. When she spoke, her lips quivered.

'I saw you once,' she said.

'Where?'

'In the village.'

'When?'

'The night khala and I were coming back with Papa from a visit there.'

'Where were you?'

'In the car. You were riding a horse.'

Naim remembered the evening. 'Did you see what happened there?'

'Yes. We were inside the haveli. It was awful.'

'Really? I thought you might have enjoyed it,' he said briskly.

'Why do you say that?' she asked.

'Isn't that how you treat the muzaras?'

'No,' she said. 'You are wrong.'

'The old man's son was killed in the war,' he said simply.

There was a brief silence. She kept looking him in the eye. 'I heard all about you,' she said.

'What did you hear?'

'That you went to the war. You were wounded.'

Naim's left shoulder stiffened, his face changed colour. 'Your war, not mine.'

What do you mean? I heard you insisted on going.'

'A mistake.'

'Why a mistake?'

'Everyone died out there.'

'People who go to war run that risk.'

'Yes. Those who avoid death get a pension, the dead get nothing.'

'I am sorry,' she paused. 'I also heard you were away again for a long time.'

Azra waited for him to say something. He quietly turned his face to look out at the brilliant sunshine falling on the very green grass and on the colourful dresses of the women that moved on it.

'You know, Naim,' Azra said, 'you are too proud of yourself.'

Naim shot back a glance and caught her withdrawing into the room, her white silk gharara flying in her wake, head bowed and hands half covering her face. Naim stopped where he was for just a second before he felt his old resentment evaporate. He went into the room after her. Azra was slumped in a sofa chair too vast for her, almost hidden behind many cushions that she held up as if to protect herself. Naim found it difficult to speak to her standing up. Azra was looking up at him but the set of her mouth also indicated a certain resolve behind her moist eyes. Naim slowly lowered himself to kneel beside the chair so that his face was level with Azra's. Looking in her eyes and seeing the determined conflict in them,

Naim knew, although until now he had been only dimly aware of it, that this face had always been within him wherever he had been.

He took Azra's hand and said quietly, 'I am sorry, Azra. I am – very sorry.'

Azra's eyes were on the verge of tears, but when she spoke her voice was without a quiver. 'Women are not without pride or shame. But they do have feelings.'

Naim heard, for the first time, a grown-up voice. He looked up in astonishment and saw not the young, carefree girl he had known but someone who had become an adult beyond his imagination. A servant, entering the room, stopped short at what he saw and tiptoed back into the adjoining chamber.

A month later, the following scene was enacted in Roshan Mahal. It took place in Azra's room where she sat on the edge of her bed, her back half-turned away from the only other person present in the room, who stood by the window. A sense of tension stretched across the room like a taut electric wire humming almost inaudibly as a high-voltage current passed through it.

'It is preposterous – most preposterous,' Azra's aunt said.

'Why, what is so terrible?'

'It's not done. Just not done.'

'Why not? Is he a servant?'

'That is not the point.'

'That is exactly the point.'

'Oh, Azra, don't you know, don't you just know? He is not from among us.'

'He is no muzara either.'

'Don't you understand, it has never been done before. How much more unhappiness will you cause Roshan Agha? You refused a perfect match with Waheed a year ago. Do you think that didn't cause your father pain? And now this – this p-p-peas–'

'Don't, khala, don't call him a peasant. I kept quiet the first time, please don't do it again. Isn't he educated? Does he not come from what you'd call a "pure-blood family"? Does he not own land?'

'Oh yes, a few acres, and those given to them by Roshan Agha. And some he got from the war, and at what cost? A cripp–'

It was as if a shock passed through Azra's whole body. She turned round to face her aunt and screamed, 'Don't! Don't utter that foul word, khala, don't ever call him that.'

The older woman's face drained of all blood. Her skin, already pale, turned ashen. She backed off towards the door. Trembling with a mixture of fright and anger, she said, as she went out of the room, 'You were always obstinate. And not normal.'

What occurred in the following few months was an upheaval that shook the house built by Roshan Ali Khan of Rohtak, titled Roshan Agha I, a pillar, no doubt not a major one but a pillar all the same, on which the governing classes of the Raj stood. Every means was employed to contain it; family and friends were all arrayed against the headstrong young woman. She was sent off to her father's house in the hill station of Simla, chaperoned by her ayah and a couple of servants. Bribing the ayah with tears and the servant with money, she sent messages to Naim. He came. Their trysts continued throughout her stay there and again, when she was brought back, in Delhi, more easily in the old city where they could use the annexe to the house of her dear friend Shirin. A year was spent thus, but in the end nothing availed Roshan Agha and the family. At the close of the following year, Azra and Naim were married off. No big feasts were held and no guests other than immediate family were invited to the nikah ceremony. A quiet affair as it was, news of it inevitably spread among the great houses of the country, becoming a minor scandal before it died down. It was, however, by no means an unprecedented occurrence. Cases such as these had been known among the high and the mighty, the rich and the well-known – including one in the famous Nehru family – but on most occasions the girl, for it was always a girl, was persuaded under unbearable pressure to step back from the line drawn by the family, or otherwise she was simply made to vanish, never to be seen or heard of again. Over the past hundred years, only two or three cases were known where the couple were allowed to unite and get on with their lives, mostly in relative obscurity. That, however, was not to be the case with Azra and Naim.

The modest wedding apart, Roshan Agha, who loved Azra more than any other person in the world, did whatever he could; he built the couple a large house, not in the city but in Roshan Pur at both Naim and Azra's insistence, Azra more for the sake of Naim than herself. Within months, they had settled down to village life, Azra planning and supervising the planting of a vast garden around the house – the first time she had done anything which could properly be called work – and Naim, now the supreme head of the village and all the lands that belonged to it, throwing himself enthusiastically into all the various duties that went with the job.

CHAPTER 17

It was the end of April and already it was too hot to expose human flesh to the sun. The comforting days of spring were over and now, quickly, in a matter of days, the sky would become a blazing sheet and begin to scorch the earth. It was the time of year when golden wheat swayed in gusts of dusty wind in fields as far as the eye could see, and those who had grown it spent their days impatiently sharpening the blades of their hand scythes, their eyes shadowed by fear of a storm or rain that would destroy their livelihood; it was the time when the first white buds of chambeli appeared like sugardrops on their green shoots, spreading the faintest whiffs of fragrance that told of approaching summer.

After a breakfast of sweet wheat porridge and tea, Naim and Azra made a round of the garden – Azra's big interest now in the place. Followed by Naim and two men who were actually share-cropping muzaras but had learned to tend a proper garden under Azra's guidance, she examined every shrub and plant and each tree as if they were pets with whom she was renewing acquaintance after her return from a two-week stay in Delhi. Stopping by the beds of winter flowers whose dying petals and leaves were falling one by one as the green summer plants began to bloom, picking a withered fruit from the young orange tree and looking up at the next to appreciate the little conical spheres, moustached and green, that would soon be ripe guava, she completed her round just as the sun became unbearable and sweat appeared on all their brows.

Ordering a jug of lemonade, Azra sat down under a tall bohr tree, whose fruit was the favourite of parrots who also nested in the deep crevices made by time and weather in its enormous trunk during its century-long growth. Resting his elbows on the waist-high boundary wall of the house that ran just outside the tree, Naim leaned over it, looking out. A woman was passing through the fields with a cane tray carrying her man's first meal of the day on her head. It would, Naim knew, be a couple of rotis with onion and green coriander chutney or a lump of mango achar. A crow flew overhead, casting a shadow over the woman's tracks. Wheeling down suddenly, it landed lightly on the tray and tried to beak out the bread from under the cloth that covered it. The woman lashed out and the crow flew away. The tray, which had not been touched by the woman's hand, stayed on her head in perfect balance with the practised swaying of her young body. Naim kept watching the progress of her torso through the standing crop until she disappeared.

The servant brought lemonade in a pot, two glass tumblers and the three-day-old English newspaper and placed them on the table. Showing the mildest of interest in the newspaper, Azra leaned over to look at the large photograph on the front page, reading the caption underneath it without picking up the paper. She poured some lemonade into the tumbler and leaned back to sip it. Although on her return from Delhi she had spent a joyful night in bed with her husband, there was a kind of tiredness, a sense of extreme indifference in her eyes, as if upon completing a tour of the garden her business with the world had come to an end. Things were not going the way either of them had envisaged. She had been going more and more often to Delhi and staying longer there.

'Come and have some lemonade,' she said to Naim.

Naim came back to sit in the other chair and filled a tumbler of the cool beverage for himself. They sat in silence for some time, listening to the parrots' raucous cries overhead, until the birds flew away, making a still shriller racket.

'Desai sisters,' Azra said, pointing to the photograph visible on the folded newspaper under the main headline.

Naim picked up the paper and read the caption under the picture.

'Picketing,' continued Azra, 'outside shops selling imported goods.'

'Yes,' Naim said.

'I met them in Delhi this time.'

'Did you?' Naim said, sipping his drink.

'You have heard of Jalianwala Bagh, haven't you?'

'Er – yes. To do with the Khilafat movement, wasn't it?'

'Rowlatt Act,' Azra said briefly.

'Er – yes. Many killed?'

'You don't even read the papers any more, Naim. What's happened to you?'

'You know I've been so busy.'

'You are just not interested any longer, that's all, isn't it?'

'I am. I know what's happening.'

'Do you? Then why are you not concerned? You worked for the Congress for a time after you came back from the war, didn't you?'

'It wasn't the Congress. Not exactly. Anyway, that was then.'

'Why? Has India become free?'

'No,' Naim said. 'But there are people working for it. Proper people.'

Azra looked at him quietly for a long moment. Suddenly she said, 'Let's go.'

'Where?'

'To Amritsar. Find out what happened.'

'I don't want to go anywhere. I mean I can't,' Naim said, looking away.

'Why not?'

'For one thing, the harvest is starting in a few days.'

'We can't go now anyway. There's Martial Law in the whole of Punjab. Have to wait, until a way can be found.'

There was a silence, full of unease and the sounds made by thirsty crickets hiding under the hot, cracked surface of the earth.

'What is the point?' Naim said.

'Point! You ask me what is the point? All right, I'll go if you don't want to.'

'What, on your own?' Flabbergasted, Naim said gently, 'Azra, aren't you happy – I mean, living here?'

Azra gave no reply but looked around without seeing anything. Naim suddenly became aware of a terrible fact: her life in the village had ceased to interest her. His heart panicked. He saw clearly that there was nothing there – not even the longing for a child – that involved her: she was utterly bored.

Roshan Agha, who could never say 'no' to his daughter anyway, was persuaded to go along with her proposal and proceeded to use his contacts among the people who mattered. As a result, Naim and Azra were included, although only as observers, in the inquiry committee that the Indian National Congress formed and delegated to produce a report about the events in Amritsar. As soon as martial law was lifted, the committee made its way to the Punjabi town.

CHAPTER 18

'This,' said the little hunchbacked old man, flourishing an expansive arm, 'is the place.'

The place, called Jalianwala Bagh, was no baghor garden in fact but a large yard, hedged in by a brick wall on three sides with a single exit on the fourth, which could well be taken for one of those places customarily used for tying up cattle or horses away from built-up areas in most cities. It was not, however, used as such but as a gathering place on any occasion for which people got together in numbers. The ground was corrugated baked earth with not a green shoot in sight – a place both close and desolate. Not so the ancient-looking man. He had skin like crumpled paper, and it was impossible to guess his real age or to decide whether the hump on his back was due to age or was merely the gift of his birth. With all that, he was quick as a rabbit, and very talkative. The inquiry committee had been talking to prominent social and political leaders, academics and lawyers in the city over the last few days and taking down their accounts. On their last day, when their work had finished, even their stock of pen and paper had run out and they were on the point of departure, they had come across this creature close to the spot. One of them had asked him an innocent question and that proved quite enough to get him going. He was a fisherman, now retired, he said, and he virtually dragged them back the short distance to the actual site, visited more than once by committee members who were now tired out and wanted nothing more than to leave the city. They were struck, however, by this man who had buttonholed them – by his appearance, for he resembled a four-legged primate with a withered face, his long arms starting from the curvature of his back and almost touching his ankles, and by his demeanour which matched his appearance, the sure-footed agility of an animal bestowed with several times more energy than size. With a single easy leap, he mounted the double-brick wall, sitting there now at eye-level to his audience.

'I saw what happened. Everything.'

'Tell us.'

'I am a fisherman,' the man began. 'So was my father before me. So you can say that I was born a fisherman, only three years old when I started going with my father in his boat to catch fish. My father caught fish and walked miles on his round selling it fresh from the bucket on his head, and those he couldn't sell he brought home, where my mother rubbed salt in them and hung them up to dry. Most times we lived well and in peace. But in the summer the river swelled up and the fish disappeared, swept away to God knows where in the muddy floods. Besides, the waters became too dangerous to row a boat in. Then my father grew bad-tempered for lack of a catch and he beat my mother and my mother beat me. Rain and the melting snow up in the mountains brought bad times for us. We became poor. That is when I got into the habit of eating raw fish.'

Horrified, Azra asked, 'Raw fish?'

'It is not bad. After getting a beating from my father my mother would be waiting for me at home to deliver me a return beating on any old excuse, like laziness, although I was not lazy. So I stayed out all day, hanging about the little ponds in the village catching small fish in shallow water with my hands, washing and chewing them to stave off hunger. I always kept a rock of salt in my pocket. I couldn't swallow the fish on its own in the beginning, but later I got a taste for it. When I returned home in the evening my mother would still beat me for loitering about. You could say that I had a bellyful of fish and beating. The summer brought trouble for us. War came to our home then. As the weather changed, life became good again. We had plenty of fish. My father would still beat my mother, but not for lack of fish.

'My mother was a wonderful woman. When she died I was eleven years old. Neither my father nor I knew how to cook anything, so we just boiled dry fish and ate it. That is when my father lost all interest in catching fish. He would catch only enough for us to eat and hang them up to dry for the next day. One day I saw what he was doing. He picked up a lovely fish from the net and gazed at it for a time. The fish had round black spots on its yellow skin. It was a leopard fish. After a minute, my father let it slip slowly out of his fingers into the water. I went up behind my father and heard him mumble, "You are beautiful, my hut is ugly, go back to your beautiful home." I stood there looking open-mouthed at him throwing fish after lovely fresh fish back into the river, saying to them, "You are so good-looking, we need only a few ugly old fish to eat. Go, go home."

'Then I knew he had gone away from the world. I waited patiently, and when we got to the shore I spoke to him. "That is it," I said. "You are not going to catch fish any more."

'"Who will bring in our food?" he asked.

'"I will," I said. "You are old and you are going mad."

'He raised his oar above his head to strike me, but I was faster on my feet and ran out of reach. "You are a little worm," he shouted, "worse than that, a dwarf."

'"I am a man," I shouted back. "I will show you. Look, can you eat a raw fish?" I grabbed a wriggling live fish, small mind you, and chewed it up in front of him.

'When he saw me swallow it he was tongue-tied with wonderment. He slapped his forehead and wailed, "My dear God, children of snakes and crocodiles are being born of humankind. What is the world coming to?"

'But after that he let me alone. I was twelve years old then and I started going out on the boat by myself and my father sat at the roadside selling fish from a bucket. Then he began telling everybody who passed not to beat their wife or she would die and they would be reduced to eating boiled fish and have dwarf crocodiles for children. People laughed at him. He wasn't paying attention to selling fish anyhow, so I took that job off his hands as well. Now I was doing both jobs at once. After some time he died of doing nothing and talking out of his head. For a time I looked around for a woman. But the women I approached were big and tall. I am small, you see. They made fun of me. Others were bad-tempered and told me to run off. After some time I gave up. I have seen everything.'

'I am sorry,' Azra said.

But the sun was going down and the others were getting restless, already regretting having been tricked into stopping by this babbling old idiot.

'Tell us what happened here,' one of them said to the man.

'Yes, yes, do not be impatient, my children. We can stop here until the end of the day. After that,' he gestured towards two white soldiers, rifles slung round their shoulders, standing by the yard's exit, 'there will be curfew. It is many days since I talked to someone alive like you people. Everybody in this city is going around like they were dead. I remember everything, even the time there was uprising by the Hindustani spahis, a proper ghadar, in the year '57, although that was during the last hundred years when I was a young boy. Also the red fever that spread when the old hundred years ended and the new hundred years began and many died. When I tell people about all those things they say to me, "You have lived a long life. What do you eat, old man?" I tell them, "Raw fish and boiled corn all my life." Then they say, "That is why you have a good brain."'

At this he bared the three teeth left in his mouth, and his listeners knew that he was happy, laughing soundlessly.

'Tell us what you saw here,' Naim asked him solemnly. 'We have to go soon.'

'Yes. I remember everything. Nobody talks to me here, these men and women you see on the streets, they have legs only for walking and hands only for buying food. They have lost their tongues. I can tell you everything.'

'Then tell,' someone said sternly.

'I am coming to that right now. Thank you for asking me, my children, my tongue was becoming a dry fish from keeping quiet in this dumb people's city. Well, did they not kill nine white men on the ninth day of the fourth month?'

'Did they? Who did?'

'Oh yes, sir, I saw every one of them. First the two, with whom I came to do direct business. No, they did not buy fish from me, although it is true that in my life I have definitely sold fish to three white people, two men and a woman. Or actually only two, counting the memsahib as half and the Anglo-Indian as also half to make one full. But never mind. These two, they only wanted to take my picture with a camera. After they had taken a picture of me sitting by my bucket of fish at the roadside, they laughed and threw a silver coin to me. I caught it in the air, and when I got a proper look at it I became dumb with happiness for some time, because it was a rupee, a whole rupee with the king's head on it, enough for me to buy things for many months. But I do not need things, so I saved it. Before I could say thank you to them they were on their way. They did not get far. Two men appeared from a street with naked swords in their hands. They thrust the shining weapons into the bodies of the two white men. One went straight through the first victim's belly, the other got stuck in the ribs of the second. The white men fell, bleeding and dying. Nobody came to tend to them. I was about to run, leaving even my bucket behind for fear that I would perhaps be also attacked for receiving a rupee from the white men, but the attackers disappeared back into the street from where they had come. Run away I did then, but not before picking up my bucket. Everyone around was running and vanishing away. Two streets further along I saw three white men badly wounded, all stabbed with sharp weapons through the chest or the side of the body, lying in the middle of the road. They had no cameras in their hands or anything. One of them was a beautiful young boy. He was either dead or he had lost consciousness, but there was no trouble on his face. I have seen much, in the time of the red fever I saw three dead bodies coming out of one house and have seen thousands of dead men and animals and fishes in the time of floods, but the picture of the young boy's body lying on the road with his hair mixing with blood and dust and no trouble on his face stayed with me for many days. Next I passed the Darbar Sahib and in front of it was another white man slumped on the ground. I kept my distance and had no wish to see how he died. One picture in my mind was enough. Running by the District Courts I came across yet another one spread on the pavement. I only glanced at it but could easily make out that it was a white man and dead.

'Nine men were killed that day, although I only saw seven with my own eyes. All the shops were shut quickly and not a single person was seen on the streets. Only ghosts lived in the town. But the ghosts were there all right, in the mohallas and dead-end streets, coming out of their houses and standing in little groups. It was like a net for fishes that is snipped with scissors at one end and gathers up in bunches in many places. There was no talk, only whispers, like the wind. But it was a bad wind. I was afraid. In my hut that night I could not sleep. The weather was not cold but I started shivering. I made a wood fire and lay down beside it. Still the sleep was absent from my body. I did not do much business that day either, and the fishes in the bucket gave off a stench because they were rotting in the heat of the fire. Thinking that this might be the reason for my lack of sleep, I decided to do something about it. As I cannot bear to see cats and dogs dragging around the fishes that I have caught with my own hands, I preferred to throw the older ones into the fire. Now, children, if you have spent your life with fishes as I have, you would know that the smell of fish roasting in the fire is the biggest cause of hunger in the world. Great hunger was born in my belly, but from what I had seen during the day my throat had closed up. So I sat there looking at my fish slowly burning, making a crackling noise with their eyes open and mouths still smiling. I could not watch those eyes and mouths go lifeless so I turned away and lay on the floor in my usual place away from the fire. After some time –'

'Please, please,' several voices, somewhat annoyed, arose from the listeners, 'enough about the fish. Tell us what happened after the killings. Please, it is getting dark.'

'I am coming to that right now. The next day, I saw the white woman and what happened to her. One,' the old man raised a finger, crooked with work and age, 'no white woman ever came out to the bazaar without a servant, usually a spahi with a rifle. Two, they are never on foot, always in a buggee, a tonga, a rickshaw or something. But this woman was not usual. She was walking and was all alone. In the middle of the bazaar she found people advancing towards her, groups of men with ugliness in their eyes, not only from in front but from behind her also. She looked this way and that, and sensing danger she stopped. The men on both sides halted a few yards from her and kept staring directly at her. The woman's colour was pale on pink like turmeric, and she was turning on her feet like a spinning top but only slowly, looking in all four directions. Then one man stepped forward and grabbed her dress by the neck. He jerked it down with force so that the dress tore right down to the hem. No, I forget, it didn't tear, there were buttons which broke, flying all over the place. At that moment all the men pounced on her. They knocked her down and fell on her, tearing all the other clothes off her body. There were fifteen or twenty men piled on top of her. They were beating her with their fists. It went on for only a very short time but seemed to me a very long time. At the end of it the men stopped all at once. One by one they stood up. They looked at the naked woman lying on the ground and ran away from view into the side streets. I wanted to run away too for I did not wish to be caught as a witness to this occasion. But then I saw a strange sight. The woman, whom I thought was maybe dead by now, sprang right up like a rubber doll and started running at full speed down the bazaar. She was barefoot and there was nothing on her body except two small pieces of cloth, one round her chest which she was holding with both hands and the other covering her hips. The sight of that woman running with her legs flying in all directions and the white flesh of her thighs and buttocks pumping and making little jumps in the sunshine is still in my eyes.

'This scene was such that although for the next two days the city was like a graveyard, yet I could not stay indoors. And because all the food shops were shut I was able to sell most of my fish, even those that were half rotten which I had placed on top of the pile in the bucket. I made some money which I saved on top of the rupee I got from the man before he was dead. Now I was left with only a few fishes which I was bent upon selling as well. What I did not know was that the third day was to be the day when life in this city ended. I had not even reached my spot in the bazaar when I saw large groups of people moving in silence from one place to the other. Later I realized they were not going to different places but procession after procession of them was heading towards this place where we are now. I joined one group and went along. I also attempted to hawk fish by calling out loudly with my usual words once or twice but was silenced by the ugly looks I got from fellows around me.

'When we got here the bagh was already nearly full of people, yet they kept coming. They were pouring in from every side. At one time it seemed that not another soul could squeeze into this place but men of all ages from young boys to old men kept coming. I was pushed along by the crowd towards the middle of the bagh, where I held my ground with the full strength of my legs. I also kept a hold on my bucket although it was becoming hard in the crush. I saw a man standing on a raised surface like an empty crate or something by the opposite wall. He had a long black beard and a green turban like a maulvi or a Sikh sardar, I could not make out which because I am small, you see, and could only see through holes in other people. He was shouting at the people while making wide gestures with his arms like a very angry holy man in the usual way. Nothing could be heard clearly from where I stood. Some time passed.

'When I had entered the bagh I did not see any goras, only our people from the city. But then a gora officer appeared. He pushed the shouting man down from the crate and mounted it himself so that he could be seen clearly. He started saying something that also could not be heard. But slowly the sight of a gora officer in uniform made the people fall silent. The gora spoke in Urdu. "Go away," he was saying, "get out, out, *out*," he shouted, "*now!*" There was complete silence for a moment. Then a shoe was thrown from the crowd. It fell well short of the gora. There then followed a hail of shoes coming from everywhere, not one reaching the gora officer but falling on the people in front. Sometimes when my boat strayed into the wild ducks' feeding ground they would take off in hundreds, forming a cloud that would make the sky dark. It was the same with the flying shoes above our heads. When the shoes finished and everyone was barefoot they started throwing their clothes. Shirts and vests and everything, making balls of them and pitching them forward, but being lighter than shoes they flew only a few yards and fell while men at the very front stood motionless, not daring to throw anything straight at the gora within sight of him. The silence was also broken. People were now shouting and chanting slogans, of a political kind at first and then, as always, the religious ones, with Hindu, Muslim and Sikh calling upon their own gods to do nothing special but only to rouse pious emotions which as I have seen always turn angry and more angry for God knows what reason. Looking at the men pushing and shoving with their naked bodies dripping with sweat, the white officer was getting more and more nervous until the moment of misfortune arrived.' The old man stopped speaking for a long minute.

'What, the firing?' his listeners asked impatiently.

'No, the fish.'

'The fish? What fish?'

'My fish. I was the unfortunate man. When there was nothing left to throw the man next to me started trying to snatch the bucket from me. I clung to it as long as I could but it was taken away and passed from hand to hand. Soon it disappeared from my sight. Then the fishes began to fly. They were good fresh fishes, too, which I had put right at the bottom to attract the last customers so they wouldn't think it was left-over stuff. The men picked out the poor dead creatures from my bucket and threw them. They too landed on the men in front. Except one fish. The man on whom it landed picked it up and threw it. I can understand his action from another point of view. You see, some men cannot stand the sight or the smell of fish. I have known such men, and they do not come anywhere near me. So this must have been one of these strange men, because he handled my fish as if it was poison and threw it fiercely forward as far away from him as he could. That was it. The fish struck the officer squarely in the face. The force was such that it made him stagger backwards while slapping away the slippery animal. He regained his posture and raised his arm. That was the moment.

'Nobody had so far looked around them along the walls. Suddenly the heads of soldiers appeared above the walls on all sides as if from nowhere. They started shooting. For a moment we did not know what was happening although we felt that something was definitely on because the noise of the people stopped. In the silence the rat-tat-tat of bullets was coming from all three sides. Within moments we became aware of people being hit and bleeding and falling, and then we were running. Except that there was nowhere to run. We were all packed against each other like fishes in the net as it is pulled up, and like fishes we were wriggling, but whichever way we turned we saw only other men. I imagine that is what fishes see as they wriggle in the hold of the net – other fishes. There was movement in the crowd, but it was going in circles like eddies in a river. It was a river of heads and bodies turning and doubling back on itself, and still the bullets kept coming.

'As luck would have it, men after men started falling, making room for others to run over them, and some who were weak although not even hit by a bullet fell in the crush and died under the feet of running men. I am small, but I am quick. My smallness worked to my advantage so I could slip through other men's holes without falling. Near the opening in the wall which is the only exit, as you see, there is a well. It is a dry well, but deep. I saw that people were so blinded by the bullets which chased them that they were running and falling into the well and others were falling on top of them. There were rumours afterwards that the well was half filled up by the men who could not get out of it. But who wanted to wait and confirm it at the time? I made good my escape. But no, sir, I tell you it was no escape.

'We were all running until we came to the bazaar and there was another scene going on there. This was the spot where the gori woman had been attacked two days before. On that stretch of twenty yards there were soldiers with rifles taking straight aim and everyone who came there had to drop face down and crawl. Not on their elbows and knees either. No, sir. On their bellies like lizards. There I saw another river of men squirming and slithering like a herd of pythons with their heads buried in the earth and faces bleeding in attempts to crawl, for which they were not trained. But they were in fear of their lives because whenever a head was raised a bullet came a hand's width above it. The crawlers had great difficulty. Not me, though. I was only three when my father threw me in the river and taught me how to lie on it face down without moving a limb or sinking. So I was familiar with the job and the fastest to get through the crawl. Only this little bit of difficulty on my back was higher than other backs, and bullets passed two fingers above it but did no harm to my progress. The crawling of men did not stop that day but went on for many days after until people stopped going that side and still the soldiers went to other bazaars and drove the people ahead of them with rifle butts to this place and forced then to crawl through it. Many days. Oh, children, what do you know about how this rebel city was punished.'

There was complete silence from the six members of the committee. They started to shuffle without moving away. Dusk was not far away.

'You should go now,' the old man said. 'Soon there will be curfew.'

'And you? Are you not going home?' Mr Deshpanday asked him.

'The soldiers know me and let me sit here until late. I will tell you how. They traced me to my hut from my bucket that they found in the bagh and arrested me. I expected the worst because it was my fish that started it all. They put me in a small room with many others and asked questions of each of us for seventeen days. Me too. They asked me who I knew in the city, who were the leaders, who the speechmakers, whether I was a Muslim or a Hindu or a Sikh or Christian. I said I don't know, I am only a fisherman. They asked what my father was, Hindu or Muslim. I said he did not know, nor did he tell me. He was a fisherman. And my mother? She was a great cooker of fish, I said, who could cook fish many different ways and beyond that did not know much. On the seventeenth day they let me go. I don't know about the others. They did not give me back my bucket, so from that day I stopped working altogether. That is how they know me and let me walk after the curfew. I am in no danger.'

In the failing light of the day they saw the last three teeth flashing in the old man's mouth and knew that he was laughing soundlessly with his mouth wide open.

CHAPTER 19

Although initially urged by Azra to give consent and later included, as a result of her efforts alone, in the inquiry committee, Naim had nevertheless returned from his trip to Amritsar a deeply affected man. Not so much by the hundreds that were killed, for life had always been cheap in India – claimed yearly by the elements as well as man-made starvation – as by the manner of their dying. A further jolt was provided by what followed. The government had set up a body, called the Hunter Committee, to conduct an inquiry into the incident. The unofficial report prepared by the Congress Party was submitted but never considered with any degree of seriousness. General Dwyer, known as the 'butcher of Jalianwala Bagh', was called up before the Hunter Committee. He had earlier boasted that he had 'put a loop through the nose' of the mutinous city and that in return his superiors in London were dragging him before a committee of 'nincompoops'. The Hunter Committee, however, completely exonerated him, although as a token of conciliation he was transferred from his post.

The effect of these events on Azra, although equally deep in the beginning, proved, by the very nature of the way she perceived such things, to be transitory. She had had her name and a photograph of herself displayed prominently in the newspapers as being the only woman member of the Congress inquiry committee, and the excitement and 'glamour' of that provided the momentum which took her some way along this path. Too soon, it wore off and she began to stay back. Naim, on the other hand, was riding this path, the fire within him reignited, washing away the bitter memories, the resentment and the wounded pride of the past, along with the inertia that had afflicted him since his return to the village. His feelings turned gradually into a passion that was to take him in the following years from one end of this vast land to the other.

Delegating the village work to the munshi and the management of his own acres to Rawal, now grown up, he let the Congress Party know that he was available for any work they wished him to do. He went and lived with the tillers of the land, eating and sleeping with them for days. It was a hard job to do – not to live day and night in their dark huts and eat their rough food but to break through their resistance, their sullenness nurtured through generations, and finally to spark their deceptive quietude into anger. Matters took a turn between him and Azra when Naim's groundwork progressed to an open defiance of what was known as the 'Landlords' Law'. It was triggered by an incident that occurred in a village not far from Roshan Pur. Naim had been staying with the peasants in the village for a few days. He was sitting with a handful of them one evening in a hut belonging to one of them, partaking of a round of hukka and chatting, when a noise arose outside. It kept coming nearer. Leaving him in the hut, Naim's companions went out to look. What happened next Naim saw from the doorway of the hut when the sounds outside, of men swearing and threatening, became louder. Three men, two of the landlord's relatives and a munshi, were demanding the owner's share of the crop, long overdue according to them, from the muzaras.

'There was no crop, not a seed, you know that,' the peasants said.

'Then put your thumb imprint here.' The munshi pushed forward a sheet of paper with an inkwell in the other hand.

'What for?'

'To show that you owe it from the next crop.'

'There were no rains. You were here, don't you know that? Then the floods took the earth away. How can we owe you anything?'

One of the munshi's two companions, both of them on horseback and carrying thick batons, poked the man who spoke in the neck, 'Come on, liar, your thumb.'

'Look at this,' the young peasant said, pushing his fingers into the deeply corrugated flank of his bullock. 'All four fingers go in the ribs, look. And this,' he lifted his shirt from the front, baring his sunken belly with the ribs showing starkly around his trunk.

One of the men on horseback jumped down and struck the young man on the knuckles of his hand with a baton. 'Your thumb,' he ordered.

The peasant hid both his hands behind his back like a little boy before a schoolmaster.

'Search the houses,' the horseman thundered.

The munshi went into an unlit house. A woman's voice arose from within. 'My man is not home, I am alone –'

'Lying slut.' The munshi dragged the screaming woman out to the door.

'Your thumb,' the second horseman was saying to an old peasant.

The old man was quiet for a second. Then he said, 'I would sooner cut off my thumb with an axe than put it on paper.'

The horseman laughed. 'Then you will not be able to cut the next crop, will you? You will starve.'

'We are starving now, can't you see?'

'Cut off your thumb then, go on.'

'I will,' the peasant said. The woman's screams shook the mud walls of the houses. 'I will cut it here, in front of you,' the old peasant repeated.

'Don't keep barking about it, do it,' the man taunted him.

The old man started trembling with the dumb rage of the powerless. All of a sudden, he turned around. He picked up a cleaver from inside the door of his house, placed his hand on the door frame and, before anyone could stop him, raised the cleaver above his head and with one precise stroke separated his thumb from the hand at the knuckle. He raised his thumbless hand, which was emitting a small fountain of blood, to the man on the horse and attempted to say something, but the words failed to come out of his twisted face, which opened and shut several times as if gasping for air. The peasant's old wife came flying out of the door, screaming, and fell on her husband. She gripped the little stump of the cut thumb and pulled it into her open mouth. Closing her mouth tightly around it, she began to suck it, vigorously swallowing the shooting blood. With a piercing cry from the depths of his chest, the old peasant finally spoke, addressing not the man on the horse but his three sons who stood supporting their father's body.

'Hear, my sons. Claim a thumb for a thumb, every one of you.'

The horseman who had jumped down remounted, dragging the munshi up behind him. Without another word, they galloped away.

The news that the peasants of a village had refused to pay the owner's share and that his men were afraid to go back and demand it quickly spread, reaching Roshan Mahal. That Roshan Agha's son-in-law, the virtual head of Roshan Pur, was backing the peasants made matters palpably worse. Roshan Agha, although he had close friends who were at the forefront of the independence movement, was of necessity loyal to the interests of his class. And to defy the Landlords' Law was to strike a blow at its very heart. It was also on this occasion that Azra, who had been spending more and more time in Delhi in Naim's absence from the village and was coming under increasing silent pressure from her disapproving family, had her first argument with Naim.

'Why don't you distribute your land before inciting others?'

'It's not mine,' he said.

'What do you mean?'

'The land that I was supposed to look after for a time is your father's. This house is yours.'

'You have your own land, haven't you?'

'Just enough for our family.'

Azra sulked for a few days. She still loved her husband, and whenever he returned to Roshan Pur she came back. Yet she kept continually arguing that the British government would crush any physical uprising as they had shown, but that they could be more effectively pressurized by events that got publicity in the world. To this Naim replied that for 'publicity' you need the participation of large numbers of people, and for that you need first of all to get them out. An occasion arose, however, that excited Azra's interest. It was the visit of the Prince of Wales to India.

All India Congress, seizing an opportunity of international significance, declared a boycott of the visit. Leaflets were distributed all over the country, asking people not only to stay away from public greetings being organized by the administration and from all the official functions in connection with the visit, but actively to demonstrate against it. The government, losing its nerve, banned the Congress Party and carried out widespread arrests.

Inside the big house in Roshan Pur, Naim and Azra lay alongside one another after a passionate hour of love, Azra lost in satiated thought and Naim having an occasional cigarette.

'Shall we go to Delhi?' she asked.

'It's the main venue. There will be a general strike, the city will be shut down, no point going there.'

'There will be demonstrations, though.'

'People will simply offer themselves for arrest.'

'Oh no, no arrests, please. How about Calcutta? We can go to your uncle's.'

'You know quite well he no longer lives there.'

'Sorry. I forgot.'

'Why do you want to go anyway?' Naim asked.

'I want to see the prince. He is such a beautiful man.'

'How do you know?'

'He looks so nice in photographs.'

'You can get yourself invited through your father to an official function and have your photo taken with him,' Naim said, with just a hint of sarcasm in his voice.

'No,' Azra said after a pause. 'It wouldn't be right. But you have contacts in Calcutta, I know.'

'Yes, some.'

'Let's go to Calcutta at least, please. Please, Naim, can we?'

Half asleep, Naim nodded.

'But promise me one thing,' she said.

'What?'

'That you will not get yourself arrested.'

'I will have no control over it if we go to a demonstration. Besides, it is party policy to fill the gaols.'

'Of course you will have control if you are not at the place where they are making arrests. Please, Naim, promise me that.'

Naim smiled quietly. 'All right. We'll see how it goes.'

Calcutta's Sadar Bazaar was gaily decorated with bunting and ceremonial arches as it was the main route through which the Prince of Wales's procession was to pass. The day had been declared a holiday in all educational institutions and government offices and, while most office workers and adult students had stayed away, young children from schools, boys and girls as well as their teachers, dressed in colourful clothes and carrying little paper Union Jacks, lined the route as far as the eye could see. Among them, strictly paced and armed with bayoneted .303 rifles, stood at attention Indian, Anglo-Indian and British soldiers. Police and army sergeants did their rounds up and down the road, keeping an eye on arrangements. On the footpaths behind these lines there were few onlookers. All the shops were shut and their signboards were turned over, showing blank metal and wooden sheets of all shapes and sizes. In this city of four million souls, all business had come to a stop.

Azra had written, in very large red letters 'SWARAJ – FREEDOM' on an equally large piece of paper and folded it. The plan was to stick it with the help of a metal tack on to a suitably sized signboard from a shop and hold it up for the prince's party to see and then quickly withdraw into one of the side streets. They chose a spot by a shop with an easy-to-handle wooden signboard that hung, turned over, by a piece of string. Also, unknown to Naim, Azra had gone to a photographer's shop the previous day and arranged, on paying the required fee in advance, for a man with a camera to meet them. Walking up the bazaar before they chose the spot to stop, she was constantly looking around, but the cameraman was nowhere to be seen. She and Naim stood behind rows of Bengali schoolchildren, interrupted at one place by white children massed together, all of whom were being instructed to practise waving their flags. Temporary gates, their bamboo stays completely wrapped in palm leaves and foliage, stood at regular intervals bearing big signs that read 'WELCOME OUR BELOVED PRINCE OF WALES' and 'LONG LIVE THE RAJ'. Occasionally, small groups of curious citizens emerged from one street and after a few minutes went into the next. The word was that the prince's procession was already on its way from Government House. As he stood there, Naim's mind went back to the time when as a child he used to pass here on his way to school. He remembered the bunch of coloured pencils he used to have in his satchel, each one a different colour of the rainbow, and an empty glass inkwell in his pocket which he had filled with butterfly wings of a hundred different colours. He used to take it out of the pocket of his short pants at night and slip it under his pillow. The inkwell stayed with him for a whole year, until one day, playing on the beach, he lost it. For a long time afterwards he didn't feel safe in his bed at night, as if he had lost a coat of armour. It surprised him to feel that after all these years the loss of the inkwell that sparkled in the sun with the colours of butterflies still grieved his heart like a lost love. He was brought back from his reverie by a voice near by. A man dressed in white, homespun-cotton kurta-pajama was loudly admonishing a few onlookers for breaking the boycott. His audience scurried back whence they came. The admonisher walked earnestly along the footpath, throwing a glance at Naim but stopping short of speaking to him upon seeing Azra with him. The movements of the police and military officers on the road quickened, indicating the imminent arrival of the prince's procession. There were ripples among the schoolchildren and their teachers, furious flag-waving and loud 'cautions' from officers to the soldiers.

'Where is the paper?' Naim asked.

'Inside my blouse,' replied Azra.

At the far end of the long straight stretch of the bazaar the advance party, mostly security people on horseback, became visible. Naim turned and tried to pull up the signboard hanging below the eye-line of the soldiers. The string holding it turned out to be wound round a nail in the wall. Instead of trying to unwind the string, he gave it a couple of panicky tugs and managed to break it. As he returned to his place, he saw an open police lorry, in the back of which was sitting the man who had been telling people to go home, accompanied by two others dressed exactly as bhe was, all smiling. An armed soldier stood guard over them. The lorry thundered by.

'Where is the paper?' Naim asked.

Azra gave no reply. She was looking intently towards the end of the road from where first signs of the approaching precession were beginning to appear. Soon after, the cavalcade came into view.

'Where is it?' Naim hissed.

'What?' asked Azra without taking her eyes from the road.

'The paper,' Naim said fiercely.

'Oh, here.' She fished out the folded paper from inside her blouse.

Naim snatched it from her hand, jerked it open with his right hand and tacked it on to the wooden board that he had gripped under his left arm. He handed the board to Azra, for it was she who was to hold it up as the prince's carriage passed, running a lesser risk, being a woman, of being arrested, as they had agreed. She took the board in one hand without looking and held it at knee level. Riders in ceremonial dress were now passing. There were about a hundred of them, riding four abreast, of all the religions and castes of India, wearing tasselled turbans and golden swords in their waistbands. Carrying shining spears in one hand while the other hand held the reins, they sat erect and solid on the backs of splendid beasts without a single inch of unbalanced movement this side or that as if they were mere extensions of their horses. The prince's carriage was now in clear view only a hundred yards up the road. The air crackled with the sound of horses' hoofs on tarmac and with the full-throated cries of sergeants, cautioning the soldiers standing on both sides of the road to be ready to present arms for a 'salaami'. The noise of the schoolchildren filled the air. The whole world seemed to boom with the military band leading the procession.

'Are you ready?' Naim asked Azra.

Azra did not answer, her eyes fixed on the prince's magnificent buggee drawn by six white horses. Her face glowing and eyes shining with extra sparkle, she appeared to be mesmerized. Just then a sign, written in electric light, was projected on to a tall gate a few yards ahead of the prince's carriage. It read, 'Tell Your Mother We Are Unhappy'. The prince looked up, seemingly amused. The sign disappeared. The Governor of Bengal, sitting beside the prince, looked less amused. Facing the two men and with their backs to the front, sat two British women wearing large hats. They did not see the sign. A few yards along the route, the sign flashed again on top of the gate with the same words. Everyone, except the prince, looked back. The source of that light was not discovered – either then or ever. Immediately after this, out of a side street emerged a group of men, their faces blackened with coal dust, carrying long narrow tablets hung by a thread round their necks with writing on them in bright letters: 'Tell Your Mother We Are Hungry'. The prince did not turn round to look, but there could be no doubt that he was aware of them. The men quickly drew back into the street. From the next street, as the carriage came level with it, a small herd of cows was driven out. Slung round the cows' necks were also placards saying, 'Tell Your Mother We Are Dry'. The royal carriage was now only a few yards from where Naim and Azra stood. 'Hold it up,' Naim whispered to Azra. 'Hold it up, hold it up. Azra, are you listening? Come on, hold it right up. Oh, for God's sake –'

The procession had passed. Azra did not move a limb. She stood frozen in her posture, her eyes locked upon the prince and his companions, the buggee, the two giant, resplendent guards standing on the footboards of the carriage on either side of him, still as statues. The procession now consisted of carriages, drawn by horses and even elephants belonging to the rajas and nawabs of southern India, high and low, trying to outdo each other in the flaunting of their splendour, their jewel-studded carriages and silk-dressed servants, but taking their place in the procession according to status, following in the wake of their future king. After having looked several times at Azra and the procession in turn, Naim felt paralysed too. The long line of people and animals passed. The soldiers kept standing at attention but the schoolchildren and their chaperons were starting to leave. The wooden board had slipped from Azra's hand and was lying on the footpath. She turned and looked up at Naim. Her eyes were dull and her shoulders, her back, the whole of her body had visibly sagged. She looked extremely tired and out of place. Naim put an arm round her and pulled her to himself. They started slowly walking back.

'It's all right,' Naim said after a while.

CHAPTER 20

Throughout the years of his activism, Naim had been trying to instil in people a sense of their power to achieve things by a new kind of force – a force of resistance without violence. He hadn't been entirely successful in this within the national movement. At times he grew disheartened and returned to Roshan Pur to spend long periods of inactivity. But he always went back. Finally, in the middle of the monsoon season in the year 1924, he had the following experience, which drew him into a different world.

He had been asked by his local command to assist in holding a public meeting in Jat Nagar, the largest village in the territory. He was to organize the gathering of people from twelve villages within reach of Jat Nagar. A couple of men were to come from Delhi to speak to the meeting. Naim sent his men out to inform everyone in all the surrounding villages about the day, the time and the place of the meeting, and waited for the day to arrive. As in the previous few lucky years, the monsoons did not fail to bring timely rain and it was not so heavy as to wash away the soil. The mood among the farmers as well as the muzaras and field labourers was good, for they were optimistic that the earth would give them grain that would see them and their animals through the year without hunger attacking their guts. They had time on their hands and the moment was judged suitable for meetings – jalsas – all over the country. Political meetings, although not covered by a blanket ban, were nevertheless actively discouraged by the government.

As the day came and Naim and his party of men arrived in the village, they did not see many police in the outskirts. Jat Nagar was a market town for grain and other agricultural produce, serving a hundred villages around. The market, a large compound made up of wholesalers' stores and shops with a clear area in the middle, was situated in the centre of the village. It was here that the meeting was to take place. Men in large numbers had gathered outside the village, and the speakers from Delhi had arrived the previous night. When this crowd reached the market square, they saw that the only entrance to the central area had been blocked by planks of wood, supported by stacks of bricks on both sides and tied to each other with ropes. The job had been done expertly and only in the past hour so that the news hadn't reached the people who had waited at some distance outside the village at the gathering point. There were police everywhere. Only their three-stripe chief constable was armed with a rifle; the others carried lathis in their hands. There was nothing the people who had come to the jalsa could do other than to first stand around and then to sit down on the ground where they stood, filling up the narrow bazaars and streets around the square. The shops had quickly been shut and the shopkeepers joined the crowd. It was a day when the sun, after several days of overcast skies, had come out and was stinging the earth with its direct rays.

The wet earth on which the men sat was giving off steam, creating in the absence of wind a mugginess that made it difficult for them to breathe. With the sweat pouring from them like water and the sun baking their brains, with no one to listen to, they were getting restless. They started raising the usual slogans. The police were strutting around, striking their lathis on the ground, abusing the men, telling them to go home and sit in their mothers' laps. The crowd was becoming angry. They had walked miles and didn't want to go home.

Suddenly, three men got up and charged, with all their body weight, at a plank that seemed a bit rickety. The plank fell, with the men on top of it. They had gained entry. More men followed the first three, pushing over the other planks. Naim, who was sitting near the front, ran in and went straight to the other side of the compound where some covered bales of cotton had been stacked. He mounted them and stood there, looking at the men pouring in through the opening. A lathi charge was going on outside, the police beating the men with their batons. Some men were bleeding from the head and the face. But the purpose of the charge, which was to disperse the crowd, was defeated as the men were driven instead into the enclosure, now fast filling up. As the square filled, the last men in re-erected the planks, closing the gap. The police were pushing from outside and the men from the inside. Naim was not scheduled to make a speech at this meeting, but as he was standing on a raised platform on his own and could not spot the two speakers from Delhi, who were lost in the mêlée, he started to speak. He wasn't aware of what he was saying, except that he knew he had to keep speaking, if only to say over and over again, 'Stay calm, stay calm, don't hit back . . .' The crowd, except for the few who were holding the planks up, began actually to listen to him, to sit down one by one and become quiet.

Naim was babbling on when suddenly something happened to his perception: the crowd that he had been seeing as an amorphous body composed of irregular heads and bodies began to appear as a solid mass, joined up by unseen strings, expanding and shrinking like a lake of rubber, and the strings, he felt, were in his hands – both hands, he thought happily – and he could pull and push and tug, draw and withdraw and direct this concentrated centre of power whichever way he wished. He even waved his left hand to the right and left, and people would obey the command, draw in or out, sit down and listen to whatever he was saying. He talked on . . .

Eventually the police forced their way and stormed in, raining blows of their lathis on the sitting men and arresting them. The head constable with the rifle came straight for Naim, mounted the cotton bales and put him under arrest. There was no time to escape. When the policeman pulled up Naim's second hand for handcuffs, he was amazed.

Azra had been spending long periods at her father's house. She met her friends, read newspapers, books, anything she could lay her hands on. Occasionally, when she got bored with her life there and knew that Naim was in Roshan Pur, she returned to their house in the village for a few days. They talked, exchanged news and very occasionally made love. The garden, having taken root, was growing more or less on its own, although like the life in the house it suffered from a general lack of attention, with the result that part of it, especially the less hardy part, was drying out year by year.

In another part of the village, one hot day, Ali and his friends were playing with conkers when a dispute arose among the children. There were accusations of unfairness and deceit. Some pushing and shoving took place, and a punch was thrown. Two of them were wrestled to the ground and kicked. The game broke up and everyone went home, leaving only Ali and Aisha there. Aisha was Ali's cousin, thrice removed, whose mother had come to visit Ali's mother for a few days. Ali picked up his conkers from the dust on the ground, loosened during the skirmish, and the two of them started walking away. Aisha would take a shisham leaf from the handful she kept in her shirt pocket, fold it between her thumb and fingers and, holding it tightly stretched at both ends, blow on one end, producing a sharp whistling sound. She called them peepees. After a couple of times the leaf would crack and begin to leak wind. She would then fish out another green leaf and start again.

'I could cut Suleiman down with my left hand for playing foul,' Ali boasted.

Aisha kept blowing the peepees until they reached the cool shade of a large shisham tree. They sat down underneath it. Ali started rubbing his conkers on the tree trunk to put an extra shine on them.

'Ali,' Aisha said, 'can you climb the tree?'

'I can climb any tree,' he answered.

'My leaves are finished. Go up and get me some more.'

'Why should I? You can go up yourself.'

'I can't climb it, it's too big.'

'Then get Rawal to do it for you.'

'Why?'

'You are always talking to him, aren't you? Why are you always talking to him?'

'I don't talk to him,' Aisha said.

'Don't lie. I saw you talking to him.'

'He talked to me first, then I talked to him.'

'See, you were lying. I saw him pinch you on the cheek. If you lie, I will pinch you too.'

'No, please.'

Ali pinched her hard on the cheek. Aisha started crying. Ali panicked. 'All right, all right, here, take my conkers, they are shiny, look, they have more shine than anyone else's. Take them all.'

Aisha's sobs slowed down but did not stop, still producing a low whining noise.

'I will go up and get you some leaves,' Ali said.

Aisha quickly became quiet. 'Go on then,' she said, wiping her tears with the back of her hand.

The tree trunk had few holes that could serve as footholds. After a struggle, Ali managed to climb up to the branches. 'Can Rawal climb this big tree?' Ali asked from above.

'Yes, he can.'

'No, he can't.'

'He is big,' Aisha said.

Ali did not answer. He started picking dry, yellowing leaves and throwing them down, ones that would crack when folded and be useless as peepees.

'These are no good,' Aisha said from below. 'Pick the green ones.'

'I can't see any green leaves here,' Ali said.

'I can. Lots of them.'

'Then get Rawal to get you them. I bet he can't climb this tree, there are no footholds. Can he?'

After a minute's silence, Aisha said weakly, 'No.'

'No what?'

'He can't climb the tree.'

'See, I told you.'

Ali then picked handfuls of young green leaves and dropped them on Aisha. Aisha ran around collecting and stuffing them in her pocket. Ali slithered down from the tree and the two sat there quietly, Aisha making peepees of the succulent, elastic leaves that gave out a good sound for several blowings. It was noon, and the sun was emitting rays of fire that drove the men from their work to seek shelter in the shade of dense trees, quenching their thirst from pots of lassi and waiting for the sun to slip a little from overhead.

'I am going home,' Ali said.

'Why?'

'I am hungry.'

The heat had sent everyone indoors in the village. As the two children approached their house, they saw Ali's old stepmother come out of the door and go into the next house. A tight white sheet of sun spread over the courtyard ground, making magic of the empty silence of a summer noon. Beside the old woman's room was a small hut-like cell of a room. There her milk was kept in an open earthenware pot on top of a bed of slow-burning dung cakes to prevent it from splitting in the heat. It warmed and gradually, over many hours, formed a thick layer of reddish brown fat on the top before the dung cakes beneath it quietly turned to ashes. Ali entered the little cell with a reed stalk in his hand that he had picked up before coming into the house, cleaning it on the way by blowing into it. He pierced the top layer of the milk on one side, taking care not to disturb it, and dipped one end of the reed pipe into the milk. From the other end he sucked the warm sweet milk from the pot. After swallowing several mouthfuls, he asked Aisha, 'Are you hungry?'

'Yes,' she said. 'I will drink from Auntie's milk,' pointing to a similar mud cupola by the door of Ali's mother's room.

'No,' Ali said, 'don't drink our milk. Here, take the reed, come, drink from here.'

Aisha sucked up the milk from the same pinprick of a hole, almost invisible, in the fat layer. As they came out the old woman entered the house and saw them. She ran after them.

'Stop, thieves, I am going to deal with you. Thieving robbers, stop –'

They ran as fast as they could around the woman and jumped through the open door, not stopping until they reached the old pipal tree, and on its huge roots they fell, breathless, their eyes streaming.

'Why are you crying?' Ali asked.

'My feet are burning,' Aisha whimpered.

'Hunh!' Ali said disdainfully. 'Excuses.'

'Why, you are crying too.'

'It's only the dung smoke in my eyes,' Ali said manfully. 'I never cry.'

'Rawal never cries,' Aisha said. 'He is a big man.'

'You are small,' said Ali to her. 'You should never speak to him. I am small, only one year bigger than you.'

They sat there talking until they knew that their mothers would be up from their afternoon sleep to protect them.

The next day, Aisha and her mother were leaving. Ali's mother had borrowed two mares from Naim's house to take her guests back to their village. As mother and daughter mounted the horses and said goodbye, two villagers passing on the other side of the pond called out.

'Chaudri Naim's auntie, may God be with you.'

They knew that the woman was really Ali's aunt, but Naim's name was used as a matter of pride.

'God be with you too,' Aisha's mother replied.

'Used to be some woman when she was young,' said one villager to the other afterwards.

Aisha's mother was riding a few yards ahead of her daughter. Ali was walking alongside Aisha's mount. 'I will go with you,' he said.

'Why?' Aisha asked.

'There are wolves on the way. They kill the horses and steal young girls.'

'Nobody can catch up with this mare.'

'Wolves run faster.'

'Do they eat girls?'

'No, they make them servants for their wives. I know, I once saved a young girl from the jaws of a wolf.'

'You did?'

'Yes.'

As the path levelled out, Aisha's mount quickened its step. Ali started running with it.

'I can run,' he said.

'Go back,' Aisha, a good rider, said to him. 'It will soon be at a gallop.'

'Never mind, I can run as fast as the horse.'

Soon, however, the mare, with Aisha digging her heels in, galloped ahead, disappearing in a cloud of dust. Ali went some way after it, then ran out of breath. He sat down on the low brick wall of a nullah bridge. It was then that he realized he had lost his shoes. He started walking back, his eyes to the ground. He found one on the way to the village but saw no sign of the other.

His mother saw his fallen face as he stepped into the house and ran to clasp him to her breast.

'What is it, my child? Tell me. Why don't you say something? Tell me, my love, what is it?'

'I lost my shoe,' Ali said after a while.

'Never mind, it was an old shoe anyway, torn in the front. I will ask your brother to buy you new shoes.'

'I don't want shoes from him.'

'Don't say that. Your brother is a good man. You should go and spend more time with him.'

By the time his mother and all the rest of the village were asleep that night, the boy had forgotten about the shoe. But he could not sleep. There was loss in his heart. For a time he cried quietly in his bed, then he went to sleep.

CHAPTER 21

There were no trials, no names or addresses, no court proceedings. Those arrested from all over were simply sent to different gaols, in some cases to other provinces of the country. After two days in his eight-by-six-foot cell, Naim had a distinct feeling that they had been locked up and forgotten. He didn't mind the hard floor he slept on or the brick walls pressing in on him from all four sides – he had done it in the past, although a long time ago. It was the food he couldn't swallow. The flour with which the thick, half-cooked roti was made had grit in it, and with it went a few grains of daal boiled in water containing no salt or chilli. He ate just a bit of it and, tired as he was after the events of the day, managed to fell asleep. When he awoke he knew the night had ended from the daylight coming in through the small barred window high up in the wall.

Strangely enough, he felt a connection with the place: they had taken away, as he entered the gaol, besides his shoes, belt and handkerchief, also his left hand. When he had protested, the gaoler said, 'It is a hard object, can be used as a weapon. It is safe with us, will be returned when you go.' Then the gaoler had laughed. 'If you go,' he had said. It came as a mild shock to Naim to hear it described as a 'hard object' and a 'weapon', so used had he become to feeling it as soft and alive, as much a part of himself as his other hand. He liked to believe that in this dreadful place his left hand was, as the man had said, tucked away in a safe place. In the absence of any light or hope inside his dark cell, this was one that gave him a vague sense of belonging; while the place held his hand, he was of it. Distressed by his deprivation, he was also somewhat comforted by the thought.

In the morning, two gaol officials opened the barred iron door of the cell and dumped a sack of wheat on the floor. 'Finish it by sundown,' ordered one, before they left, locking the door behind them.

The wheat was to be ground up as flour in the chakki – a heavy round stone slab atop a fixed stone base with a hole in it to pour the grain into and a wooden handle to turn it. Naim had no intention of doing it. But he found that anything, anything at all with which to busy himself, even the chakki, beckoned him to itself more and more as the time dragged on in the cell which offered nothing else whatsoever to do. The grinding required both hands, one to pour the grain into the hole and the other at the same time to turn the slab by the handle. With only one hand to do both jobs, Naim's work slowed down. In the evening he got into trouble over it with the ward overseer, a 'lifer' given the overseeing job for having served some years of his term with more or less good behaviour.

'What is this?' the ward overseer asked. 'You have not finished half of it.'

'I have only one hand to work with. Look.' Naim showed him the stump of his left arm.

It had no effect on the man. 'This is no concern of mine. You can go and push it up your mother's behind, you son of a bitch,' the man said flatly in a voice that showed no anger.

Naim's blood boiled. He got up and punched the ward overseer in the face. The man staggered, supporting his back against the bars of the door. His expression did not change, nor did he retaliate. He picked up the two sacks of flour and the left-over grain, and said as he left, 'You will get your punishment. You wait.'

Naim was surprised not so much by his own action as by the lack of reaction in the other man. The next morning two gaol officials came and questioned him.

'Did you strike the ward overseer?'

'Yes,' answered Naim. 'He abused me.'

'What did he say?'

Naim repeated the ward overseer's words. There was amazement on the faces of officials.

'You struck him just for *that*?'

'Yes.'

'You think this is your mother-in-law's house, you bastard? Come out, you will draw water for this.'

Naim's mood brightened as he felt the fresh air in his nostrils and sunlight on his face. Then he saw a round enclosure in the middle of the prison yard surrounded by tall iron bars. Inside it were six men tied to a long, horizontal wooden pole, pulling it like oxen to fetch up water from the well dug in the centre. Naim was led in. The gaolers gave instructions to the overseer – another man with a cloth badge on his chest saying 'CO 19' (convict overseer) – and left.

'I cannot do it,' Naim said as CO 19 advanced towards him with a rope. 'I have the use of only one hand.'

'Are you blind too, you cripple pig?' the man said. 'Do you see them pulling with their hands?'

Naim's ruse didn't work. He could see that the men pulled as oxen do, with their backs and legs, the rope looped over their shoulders and around the chest. His punishment lasted for three days, two hours each day. Naim finally understood that these men, gaolers as well as convicts, had no response left in them for their fellow men other than foul words, which came out without arousing any emotion in them. These harsh swearwords, the only tools these men lived by, had shed their meanings. When he realized this, Naim stopped taking what they said at face value as there was nothing behind the face.

At the end of three days Naim was horrified at the thought of going back to his cell, the chakki, the small barred window in the wall near the ceiling that showed only a still square of the sky during the day until a bird crossed it and the sky moved, and a rusty iron pot in the corner to use for answering calls of nature. During the ten-minute rest period he went and sat with CO 19. The overseer had a tiny piece of broken mirror in his hand, and with its help he was plucking white hairs out of his beard. As Naim sat alongside him the CO spread out his legs toward him, so that his new brown shoes, an extreme rarity in gaol, were right in front of Naim's face.

'Are you in for murder?' he asked, concentrating on the mirror to pluck out hairs with his thick fingers.

'No,' answered Naim.

'For thieving?'

'No.'

'For what then, sisterfucker? Did you rape her with your stump?'

'No,' Naim said. 'I made a speech for swaraj.'

'What is that?'

'Freedom.'

'Hah, freedom. I have sixteen more years to go,' the man said, showing his sleeve which had the year of discharge written on it in ink. 'I will be dead when my freedom comes.'

'Not your freedom, the country's freedom, the freedom of Hindustan.'

'What good is it? My mother and father will be dead before it comes. Me too.'

'Why then are you plucking white hairs from your beard?' said Naim, laughing.

The CO turned to Naim. 'Listen, you motherfucking stumpy, my beard is my own matter, nothing to do with you.'

'Look,' Naim said to him, 'I mean no harm. Actually, I want to ask you a favour.'

'You want some charas? I can get you as much as you like. You see my shoes?'

'They are very nice,' Naim said. 'Where did you get them?'

'The man was in for a short while for thieving. I supplied him with opium for six months. Before he was freed, he asked me what I wanted in return. I said my only wish was to have a pair of brown shoes, which I have never had in my life. He said, "Wait for three days, shoes will be outside the drain hole by the outer wall." A CO can go up to the wall. Same with this mirror, you see, nobody but us COs can have them. They can cut themselves and others with these, so no ordinary pig can have them, you see. Well, exactly three days it was. I had a job pulling them in through the drain hole with a stick and rope, had to go down on my belly to reach them and bruised my skull. But in the end I pulled them in.'

'They are very nice,' Naim said to him. 'I asked for a favour.'

'Say it, dumbfucker.'

'I want to carry on pulling water.'

'What? Don't want to go back to chakki?'

'No. I can do the water chukker. I am getting used to it. It is easy.'

The CO thought for a moment, fixing Naim with a stare for the first time. 'You will be back here anyway,' he said slowly.

'How?'

'That,' he pointed with his shiny shoe to Naim's empty sleeve. 'You can't do your share of chakki.'

Harnam, CO 19, was right. Every two days Naim was back from the chakki to the water chukker. These two hours left him breathless, weak and tired. But these were the two golden hours of his life when Naim could get out of the rank, dark, narrow cell and feel the wind and light seep into his pores.

The news of Naim's internment took a long while to reach Azra, who had been staying in Roshan Mahal. The whole village knew. But neither the munshi nor anyone lower than him had the courage to inform her. Naim had tried, without success, to get word to her through warders, discharged inmates, their visitors and any others he could find. Eventually she got suspicious. Naim had never remained out of contact with her for this long, always sending a letter or a message through a servant to let her know what was going on. She made a two-day visit to Roshan Pur, heard rumours, and finally got the truth by questioning Rawal, the munshi and others servants. Although she had led a life separate from her husband for years now, the spark of her love for him had never been extinguished in her heart. At the same time, still embarrassed before her family despite Naim's years of work, she did not want the news of Naim's incarceration to reach them, not just yet, if she could avoid it. Using her own contacts, it took her some time to find out where Naim was. Once she knew that he was in Lucknow gaol, she decided at once to go and see him.

But first there was one of Roshan Agha's regular parties to get through, where his friends gathered at the big house for lunch once each winter – the other annual event being a dinner in the summer – and it had become a necessary part of Azra's life to act as the official hostess in her father's house. A big demonstration was also planned a few days later by the Congress in Lucknow against the Simon Commission. It was an opportunity for Azra at least to watch the demonstration, if not take part in it, and go to see Naim in gaol in the same town.

It was a bright winter day in Delhi, the sun shining warmly on the green lawns of Roshan Mahal, wrapping itself around the white columns and creeping inch by inch up the veranda and the large windows and into the drawing rooms. The guests had a choice of seating – sofa chairs laid under large parasols, armchairs on the verandas and stuffed chairs and settees in the rooms – before they would all go in and sit round two long dining tables for a sumptuous lunch.

Most of the guests, attracted by the winter sun, were sitting out on the main lawn, drinking orange juice. There were few white faces on this day, although a European woman wearing dark glasses was on the lawn, taking the sun. Outside the house a long line of behlis and two motor cars stood along the road. Hiding her troubled face behind a practised smile, Azra was attending to the guests who had already arrived and receiving those who were just coming in, informing them of the seating arrangements and also that Roshan Agha was sitting with friends in the drawing room. The guests were handed over to the white-uniformed servants and offered drinks. They chose their places to sit, sipping drinks and fingering pistachio nuts and other dried fruit in the dishes laid on every side table.

A behli came to stop at the main gate and three men alighted. Two of them were in the traditional Marhatta dress – round white pumpkin turbans and long white coats – and the third, a thin-faced tall man with pale skin wearing gold-rimmed glasses, in dark Western clothes. After exchanging a few formal words with Azra, the three men went straight to the drawing room, nodding but not stopping to greet acquaintances sitting on the lawn and verandas. Roshan Agha got up from his high-backed chair, received them warmly and sat them near him. The vigorous conversation that had been going at the time and had stopped for formal greetings started up again. Roshan Agha's company in the room included large and medium landowners – Dr Ambedkar, who had estates in Oudh, Raja Sahib of Karam Abad, and others including an Englishman, while the two Marhattas were connected with the Servants of India Society. The talk so far had been carried along, with occasional promptings from the pipe-smoking Dr Ambedkar, chiefly by young Iqbal Singh, who, although owning an even less than moderate estate in Karnal district, had a respectable place in the present company owing to his intellectual status. Being a scholar, a published author and a serious political journalist, he was granted entry as honorary aristocracy. His latest topic had been literature and his hobby-horse Tagore, whom he thought second-rate.

'He is a romantic folklorist, nothing more,' he had been saying. 'If Yeats hadn't taken a fancy to his work he would not get published in English, let alone win the Nobel Prize.'

'Come on, Iqbal,' Dr Ambedkar said. 'Romantic folklorist? Really!'

'Look at his contemporaries in Europe. Far, far ahead of him. Take Rolland, the economic conscience that he possessed . . .'

At this moment the white woman in dark glasses, having had enough sun, had entered the room, making all the men stand up, greet and seat her in a comfortable chair. She immediately started talking in a low voice to the man sitting next to her.

'What I don't understand is why Indian children have their noses constantly running. I mean, the climate here being so dry, don't you think?'

'Yes, yes,' the man said, slightly embarrassed.

'But the French critics –' Dr Ambedkar began to say.

He was cut short by Iqbal Singh. 'Oh, the French critics, don't talk about them, they are only good at starting ever-bizarre movements in literature and what-not. It is their chauvinism at work.'

'Gothic architecture went from Asia to Africa . . .' someone was saying.

The woman in dark glasses overheard this and shivered as if in horror. 'Asia? Africa? Gothic? What nonsense!' she said in an even lower voice to her companion, continuing a largely one-sided conversation. 'Now their general behaviour, rude and rather primitive, could perhaps be labelled as Gothic.' She uttered a small bark of a laugh. 'But architecture? They *have* no architecture in Africa, you know.'

This bee-hum of talk was then interrupted by the arrival of the three guests from the last behli, the two Servants of India and the thin-faced pale man with spectacles. Iqbal Singh slowed down, seeing that they were now joined by one whom he considered his equal, the man with gold-rimmed glasses who was the editor of an English newspaper, and that the flow of talk would now inevitably tilt towards politics. During the brief pause that followed after everyone had retaken their seats, one of the Servants of India addressed the room without further ado.

'This demand for the British army to go is completely unreasonable. Their job is only to defend out country, and they did this in the war, besides raising an army from the undisciplined masses of India. I don't see why, when their presence does not conflict with the running of the country, the civilian transfer of power cannot take place.'

'True. Very true,' his companion added. 'We are manufacturing no armaments in India. On top of that these are the days of battles in the air, aeroplanes fighting with other aeroplanes and all that.'

'The greatest danger,' the newspaper editor said, patting with one hand an ashen cheek, 'is of dictatorship, for that is the direction in which the extremist parties are taking the country.'

A Kashmiri Brahmin, who had been sitting quietly in a corner, now spoke up with passion. 'Swaraj, Swaraj! What is it? This is the age of internationalism. The European and Socialist nations have fallen victim to isolation because of this madness of separatism and are now suffering from economic disaster. It will come, I tell you, it will come.'

'This "direct action" advocated by some,' the editor, sitting up straight and again patting his cheek, said in English, 'is not too far from terrorism – if not another name for it. There are constitutional means available.'

The woman nodded in agreement.

The Marhatta looked all round the room, preparing to speak. 'First of all, we have to be clear about our objective. The time has not yet come for us to take control of the entire centre. We don't want Defence and Foreign Relations. But Finance and the general administration must be in our hands. That means,' he tapped his walking stick on the carpet and raised a finger, 'only one thing: Dominion status.'

Iqbal Singh was about to open his mouth when the call for lunch came. Everybody left their words in the air and got up, making their way to the dining-room.

This was a class that was rich, fairly rich and very rich, educated, calling itself liberal, indulging in anything between idle talk and lip-service, with the chief objective of having a good time together, which gave it a sense of solidarity, besides the satisfaction of taking an 'active' part in the historical development of their country. This was a class of people that was to remain, despite 'reforms', largely intact and in command for many years – until the day of judgement was to arrive.

CHAPTER 22

In the middle of a procession of protesters against the Simon Commission in Lahore Lala Lajpat Rai, a well-known philanthropist and politician, was hit on the back during a lathi charge ordered by a British police officer. Consequent to the Lala's death some time later, which was believed to have been caused by the blow (the police officer was later murdered), the Commission acquired a notoriety that raced ahead of it throughout the country. A call had gone out for a demonstration against the Commission on the day of their scheduled arrival in Lucknow.

The nature of the independence movement was such at the time that nobody knew the exact aim of these demonstrations; they were carried through simply as a form of defiance. In the end, what the demonstration achieved in Lucknow was far more precise than anyone had hoped for.

Azra's aim too was rather vague. She had no intention of being a front-line participant, yet she wanted to have some part in it, if only to stand aside and watch it go by. Why she wanted even to be an onlooker was something of which she had not been fully aware. It was rather like an occasion that holds an unknown promise and thereby becomes attractive. Or perhaps it was more complex: mildly ashamed, within her milieu, of her life with Naim on the one hand, she desired on the other to gain respect in the eyes of her husband.

On the morning of the day, large groups of men, with a scattering of women among them, coming not from the city itself but from small towns and villages all around, began to gather at the Congress office in the city. From there they marched in their thousands to the railway station.

All along the front of the station there was a line of policemen, armed with rifles and lathis, facing the crowd. Behind them were the mounted police, reputed to be trained by the British cavalry, looking fearsome in their hard hats and dark uniforms. Between the mounted police and the station was a narrow strip of open ground, including a road, where a number of British army and police officers, a few Indian dignitaries and Indian and British administrative officials moved about. The demonstrators took in the scene and stopped a little distance from the line of policemen at the front. For some time they milled about, then quietly began to sit down. Unwittingly, Azra got caught up in the crowd and found herself near the middle of it. Half the people, mainly simple peasants from villages, sat on the ground, covering a large area, with the rest of the great mass standing at the back. Azra was at the edge of those who were standing, mostly city and town activists carrying black banners and placards. All she could see behind her was a sea of heads and banners declaring 'GO BACK SIMON', and in front of her another ocean, lower down, of black heads. She heard a party of peasants, sitting by her feet, speaking to each other and was amazed to hear them talking of their villages, of crops, of rain and of wives who were pregnant and could not put in enough work in the fields. One of them got out some tobacco from a fold of his tehmad while the other made a fire of a piece of wood in the clearing they created by drawing back a little on all sides. Thus they started a hukka that they had carried with them and each one took a pull at it to get it going and coughed and spoke of the quality of the tobacco that was stronger than the sharaab the Sikhs made from the bark of the kikar tree. They were little bothered about the demonstration, did not understand much of what was going on but were content to be there, among their own people.

Azra looked up and drew a sharp breath. Behind the line of mounted police she caught a glimpse of Pervez. He had been appointed an Extra Assistant Commissioner with the powers of a magistrate second class, but he was supposed to be at his post in Delhi. What is he doing here? she wondered. All at once she became extremely nervous. For the first time she became conscious not so much of where she was as who she was. Daughter of Nawab Ghulam Mohyyeddin of Roshan Pur, hostess in Roshan Mahal to people like the Chief Commissioner of Delhi, a visitor to the Governor's darbar on one occasion when she was a young girl, and sister of an administrative official of the realm! Had he seen her? She wanted to slip behind the standing crowd and leave. But she did not get the chance.

Suddenly, after a few impassioned slogans from the banner-carrying men, the line of policemen split apart and the mounted police behind them galloped towards the men sitting in the front, raising a small cloud of dust. The men were so surprised to see them that they barely moved from their places. As the horses reached the line of men looking up at them in astonishment, they were pulled up, their hooves shivering above the men's heads as they reared. The riders turned around, went about twenty yards, turned around once again and came back at a gallop. This time the men on the ground stood up and ran back, shouting, not finding the room to escape and falling over each other, dispersing, in their attempts to evade the marauding horses, to left and right. Behind the horses the foot police ran up and started a lathi charge. Everybody was now on their feet and running, bumping into others, knocking them down, their skulls being broken by lathi blows raining on them, splitting their faces, bloodying them. Screams pierced the air. Ducking through the scramble, Azra caught a glancing blow from a baton, giving her a bruise on her brow that oozed a drop of blood. She stopped, less from the effect of the blow than shocked surprise at what was happening to her. She saw a policeman, his face twisted with anger, raise his lathi to a man who, cringing before the impending blow, had his own face steeped in fear and hatred. She stood still for a moment, wondering how this place could bring two men, completely unknown to one another, face to face as deadly enemies. She turned and saw before her a young man taking photographs with a heavy camera, supporting its long concertina nose with a hand underneath it. Almost paralysed, she stood there, not even trying to hide the bruise on her face, until the camera clicked and simultaneously a lathi fell on the young man, knocking him down on top of his camera. Then she ran away.

With one look at Naim, Azra forgot all about the difficulties she had encountered trying to obtain, on her own, an appointment to see her husband in gaol. She couldn't believe her eyes. Naim looked about half his former size. She could not speak for minutes other than to nod and shake her head in answer to Naim's questions: 'Did you get my messages? I tried my best to send word. Are you all right?'

Finally she found her tongue. 'Naim, you are – so – thin. What has happened?'

'The food is not worth eating.' He laughed. 'As someone said to me here, it's not my mother-in-law's house.'

'I could have arranged to have it sent from the homes of friends here if I'd known,' she said.

'Don't worry, I won't die for a long time yet,' he said, laughing again. 'But you could try to get me out of here.'

'Yes. Yes of course.'

'Does Roshan Agha know?'

'Not yet – I think. Oh, Naim,' she wept. 'Why? Why did it have to happen?'

'Azra,' Naim said to her calmly, 'I did not set out to get myself arrested. It just happened. I am not the only one, there are hundreds more like me rotting in gaol. Look, I am healthy, except that I am thinner. It has done me no harm, it makes it easier for my feet to carry my weight. Look.' Cheerily he spread his arms to indicate his well-being. His empty left sleeve hung limply. He lowered his arms. Azra's eyes were fixed upon the sleeve. Naim began in embarrassment to twist the sleeve in his right hand. 'Oh, they took it away. They said it looked like a weapon with which I could shoot them.' He laughed yet again. 'But it is safe. I will get it back when I leave.'

'Dirty pigs,' Azra said angrily. 'Animals.'

'Listen to me, Azra, you shouldn't come here. It's not a fit place for you to visit. I'll be out sooner or later. Because there was no trial and no conviction, there is no fixed term to my imprisonment. I was even told recently that if I write a note regretting my actions and promising not to repeat them, I could be shown mercy and let out immediately. But I am not going to do that.'

'Why not?'

'It's not fair to the others. I'll be all right, you shouldn't worry too much. Tell me, how are things?'

Naim's mood had helped to lessen Azra's grief. 'We demonstrated against the Simon Commission,' she told him.

'Did you? Where?'

'Here in Lucknow. Didn't you know they were coming here?'

'We get no news from outside. What happened then?'

'Oh, you should've seen it, we were thousands and thousands. The Commission didn't even leave the train.'

'They didn't?'

'No. They heard the people shouting "Go back, Simon" and decided not to get off here.'

'You made them run? Wonderful.'

'Yes, isn't it? I wish you could have seen it.'

Naim laughed. 'Just now you were saying I should recant and beg for mercy.'

'That was just so you could get out,' Azra said, laughing lightly for the first time.

The guards cut short the meeting and led Naim away.

'I am having food sent to you from Shukla Auntie's house,' Azra shouted to him.

'No, don't, it will never reach me. I will be all right,' he said.

It was after she was gone and Naim was in his cell that he felt his need for Azra as he had never done before. The cell looked more like a grave than it usually did. As he passed his hand over his body he remembered the touch of Azra's hands and, strangely, remembered all the grave-like places he had been in, the trenches in the battlefields, the half-room in the south where he had spent some nights with a young girl called Sheelah. He had been lonely at times in those places, but never like this. This is the worst, he thought.

'Come on,' Harnam said to Naim the next morning during the rest period after the water chukker. 'The blind pickpocket is leaving.'

The pickpocket was an extraordinary man. He was a blind beggar, but begging was only a front. Being blind, he would bump into people in the bazaar. His skill was manifold. On first impact, he knew immediately, without touching them with a hand, whether the other was well-off or poor. Ignoring the poor, he would aim for the rich. Further, with the very same impact he figured out what type of clothing the person was wearing – a suit, a shalwar-kameez, a jacket or a shirwani – and where the money, the wallet, the valuables would be. Only then would his fingers go to work. Nine times out of ten he got away with it. The one time he was caught he would be sent back to gaol for a few months. All the long-term inmates knew him, but it was the first time Naim had seen the old beggar and heard the stories of his exploits and expertise. He had a home, a wife and nine children. He had taught his old mates in gaol some of his skills and volunteered to do the same for Naim, which Naim declined, laughing and thanking him for the offer. This time when he was gaoled his feet had bad sores on them. Every once in a while, the sores raised a tremendous itch. When the itch came he scratched at them with fury, cutting into the sores with his sharp nails, making them bleed. His own explanation for the sores was that 'business' had not been so good lately and feeding eleven mouths had become difficult. So when his old shoes fell apart, he begged for a time only for shoes and nothing else. But nobody gave him their old shoes. With his feet becoming worse, his day of discharge from the gaol arrived.

'Why are you laughing so much, you son of a blind bitch?' Harnam said to the beggar, landing a huge thump on his back. 'Because you are going out in the world? Don't worry, you will be back here before you know it.'

'What will you do first of all in the world, blind man?' asked another from the crowd that had gathered around him.

'Ah, first of all, I will go to my father's grave.'

'To say thank you to him for teaching you to pick pockets?'

'No, no, I have some money buried in the earth by the grave. Not much, mind you, only enough to buy some food.'

'That sure will make your wife happy.'

'Yes, yes,' the blind beggar said, laughing.

'So she'll drop a tenth puppy for you, eh? When will you pick the first pocket, eyeless pig?'

Suddenly, the blind man cried, 'Get away, get away from me,' as he started madly scratching his feet.

By the time his itching flesh was calmed, the sores were bleeding badly. There were tears in his blank eyes. The moment of his departure had come and everyone fell silent. Without a word, Harnam began taking off his shoes. He took his shiny brown shoes and thrust them in the blind man's hands.

'Here, take them.'

'What, your shoes?' the beggar said, feeling the shoes, turning them round in both hands, as if searching someone's pocket. 'They are mine?' he asked in disbelief.

'Yes.' Harnam gave him another thump. 'If you sell them, I will kill you. Bring them with you next time you come in, I want them back.'

The blind pickpocket began to laugh wordlessly. Naim was astonished to see this act of sudden generosity from Harnam, the same man who had told him two days earlier that he had committed six murders. These killings had been prompted by the behaviour of Harnam's eldest stepbrother, the son of the most senior of his father's six wives, who had usurped all their father's property and would share neither the lands nor their produce with the other brothers. The brothers, fearful of the strong man that the eldest was, went off to the town to do labouring jobs. Harnam waited for his chance, and one day killed his stepbrother, his wife and four sons, two of them as old as Harnam himself.

'What if the beggar doesn't return with your shoes?' he asked Harnam afterwards.

'I will kill him.'

'Really?'

'Sure.'

As soon as Azra stepped back into Roshan Mahal she felt the tension in the atmosphere. She spoke to the servants and learned that Roshan Agha had spent the last three days in his study on his own. She went to her room and lay down on a settee, trembling at the thought of going to see her father. But she had to go; there was no other way. She didn't want to see another member of the family before she saw him.

Roshan Agha looked at her with sad, tired eyes. He didn't extend welcoming arms to her as he always did whenever Azra returned home after even a day of absence. Nor did he speak to her. He lowered his eyes to the large notebook in which he was writing. At that moment Azra knew that Pervez had seen her in Lucknow.

'Baba –' wailed Azra. It had been a long time since she had spoken in a tone she had used as a child when asking for something she wanted.

Her father looked up. 'Don't you have something to say to me – something to explain?' he asked.

'Baba, Naim is in –'

'I know.'

'You know? You mean you knew?'

'Yes.'

'Since when?' Azra demanded, abandoning her pleading tone.

Her father looked at her silently for a moment, then said, 'All right, from the day he was taken away.'

'And you did nothing?'

'It isn't easy to do things quickly in cases like these, especially in the present circumstances.'

'You didn't even tell me?'

'I wanted to keep you separate from his actions. It's been long enough, he will not change. I think you are doing well to stay here –'

Azra's eyes filled with tears. 'He is my husband. His work and my staying here have nothing to do with it. I love him.'

Her father was taken aback a little by her vehemence. 'Come here.' He raised his arms. 'I am trying to get him out. I hope he learns his lesson from this. Come. Come to me, Ajjoo. I am sorry.'

Hearing her childhood name, one that was seldom used now, made her realize not just her father's love but also his grief.

Before going to bed that night, Azra shed all her clothes and took a long time rubbing sweet almond oil over her whole body and sat in a hot bath afterwards until it was nearly midnight, still slowly massaging her limbs.

The administrative authorities finally decided to respond to political pressure and hold trials. In a summary trial, Naim was sentenced with retrospective effect to imprisonment for addressing an 'illegal' meeting to a term exactly equal to the period he had already served in confinement and released at the end of the one-day proceeding. Trials like these were held in the cases of a score of other prominent men across the country. The rest of the hundreds who had been put in gaol were left there for long periods of time.

Additionally, in Naim's case, they confiscated the ten acres of land granted to him for war services, although they had no power to take away the medal for distinguished conduct with which he had been decorated. On the day of his release from prison he was received back in Roshan Pur by followers from other villages as well as his own, slogans were chanted in his honour and he was buried under garlands of marigold thrown round his neck, and he gave thought to nothing else in the euphoria of freedom. At night he lay in bed beside Azra and took her in his arms, clasping her with the whole of his body from head to foot as tightly as he could, inhaling her smell, listening to the beating of her heart and feeling the softness of her firm breasts. Azra too held him tight, wrapping her arms and legs around him, wishing desperately for this occasion to renew the passion that had slipped from her grasp. For a long time there was just the breathing of the two bodies, warm and willing but still and unmoving. Then Naim's grip relaxed. He rolled away from her and lay on his back, staring at the ceiling.

After a while, he said, 'The food. It's because of the food in there. It was like poison.'

'I know,' Azra said, raising herself on an elbow and putting a hand softly on his stomach, caressing his wasted body. 'It doesn't matter. I'll tell munshi to shoot some partridges. A few days of proper food . . .'

'I am sorry, Azra,' Naim said.

'No, don't be. You'll be all right before you know it.'

'I am sorry,' he repeated softly.

That night's failure brought back to him the extent of his loss, including the prime land of which he had been so proud, although he had at times been ashamed of it too. At times he had thought he had been far from brave in the war, that he had been afraid, the fear had filled his body and soul, he had not stood up and fought in the face of mortal danger, never fulfilled the norms of what people called 'courage' and the army 'gallantry'. Still, with the passing of time he had come to feel that the losses he had suffered were deserving of a reward. That night, looking, with a certain regret, at the unblemished flesh of his wife, to whom the passing years had done no harm, the seeds of real self-doubt began to stir in the depths of his mind. He regained his strength in time but not his vitality of spirit. He became morose and began to fear his wife and everything connected with her. He never resumed the duties he had previously discharged in the village or on Roshan Agha's lands. The promised return of their ancestral lands had not materialized. Naim now concentrated on cultivating his six acres, which were barely sufficient to feed the four mouths of his family and their cattle. He spoke less and less. Despite much effort, Azra remained unable to revive his soul. Eventually, she withdrew once again to Delhi, only occasionally visiting Naim in Roshan Pur. It took Naim a long time to come out of his shell, sparked once again by an incident in the uneasy relationship between himself and Azra.

It was the time when political awareness was beginning to awaken a sense of separate identity among the Muslims of India. A grand gathering had been arranged in Delhi to try and bring together all the Muslim parties in the country. For this purpose Sir Aga Khan, who lived in France, was invited, as an international symbol of Indian Muslimhood, to preside over the meeting. Naim and Azra wanted – Azra more than Naim – to go and take part in this significant national event.

They still slept together, in the same room but in separate beds laid alongside one another with a yard's space between them. Once in a while they made love – as they did on this, the night before they were to go to Delhi. Afterwards they lay in bed and talked in brief sentences, marked by long silences in between.

'Don't you think it was a good thing to invite the Aga Khan to preside over the meeting?' Azra asked.

'I don't know,' Naim said. 'We'll see.'

'He is famous.'

'Well, he is very rich.'

'But look at his life, so eventful. And so glamorous. I am excited. The day after is the New Year, we can go to Waheed's New Year's Eve party.'

'I don't want to go to any party. Only with you to the conference,' Naim said.

Azra was quiet for a few minutes. When she spoke it was with a deep sadness in her voice. 'Naim?'

'Yes?'

'I wish things could have turned out differently.'

Naim knew what she meant, yet still he asked, if only to say something, 'What do you mean?'

'Oh, so much. I wish you hadn't gone to prison, for one thing.'

It took Naim a few minutes to completely absorb what she meant. Very slowly, the entire climate of his feelings changed. He turned his head slightly to look at her. What he saw surprised him. He looked at her face, the swollen lips, the thrust of the chin, the pointedly raised breasts, round white thighs, and all he saw was a coarse sensuality, naked and without shame. He wondered how it was that he had been in love with this woman for so long. He got off the bed and went to stand by the fireplace. He was shaking. Resting his elbows on the mantelshelf, he took his head in his hands, trying to calm himself. After a while, he returned to his own bed. Azra lay with her back to him, her eyes wide open, trying to dream about the past and wondering how and where it had gone. It took most of the night to douse the flames of bitter sadness inside her and for her to sleep for a few hours full of dread. In the morning, the distance between them increased, she spoke calmly to Naim, telling him she was going to Roshan Mahal on her own. Naim was relieved. He felt the distance between them stretching to a new limit, although he knew that there still remained some grains of love – that insoluble residue of a union between him and Azra that would not come to an end in this one night. Before he had slept in the night, however, he had decided that, one way or another, he would have to get out of this hole into which his spirit had dived.

On open ground opposite the Jamia Mosque the stage was set for the All India Muslim Conference. All the Muslim political and religious parties in the country had come to participate. All manner of people, from Bombay to Peshawar, in their regional dress and headgear, were gathered there. A ceremonial gate of bamboo poles, tall trees cut for the purpose and wrapped in palm leaves, was erected at one end to serve as the entrance. A red carpet, lined on both sides with pots of winter flowers of all colours, led from the gate to the dais, a raised wooden structure covered with fine carpets and more flower pots all round. A high-backed chair, upholstered in golden silk, stood behind a large table, also covered with silken cloth of the same hue. At ground level in front of the dais were rows of chairs extending beyond the width of the platform. The first rows were of sofa chairs and behind them several more rows of simple, armless wooden seats. Behind the chairs there was an area for sitting and standing. This durree-covered ground was full of people, some sitting in the front, others standing at the back, the foot soldiers whose innocent perseverance and cheapness of life was the blood in the veins of every movement. They sat and stood unprotected from the sun under an open sky, their cheeks hollow but eyes bright with hope, looking up to their leaders who sat in the chairs and talked among themselves. The dais and the seating area was covered with orange tarpaulin strung up overhead with the help of bamboo poles and strong ropes. To the left and right of the dais in the front row sat the official delegates of each participating party. There was Sir Shafi, who headed the Punjab faction of the Muslim League. Among them was also the poet Dr Mohammad Iqbal. In the middle were the brothers Maulana Mohammad Ali and Shaukat Ali of the Khilafat Movement. On one side sat long-bearded Maulana Hussain Ahmad Madni and Shabir Ahmad Usmani of Jamiatul-Ulema-e-Hind. Each party had nominated twenty delegates who sat in prominent places in front of their followers. The rows behind them were occupied by the major and minor nawabs and jagirdars, dressed to the full in their jewels, medals and other finery, from the Muslim states and estates of India. Because of the Muslim custom of purdah, there were few women in the gathering.

After Azra's earlier change of heart and decision to go to Delhi by herself, Naim was not sure whether she would come to the conference. But as he entered the arena from the back, he had no difficulty in spotting her. She was sitting in one of the wooden seats in the last row, up against the first row of people sitting on the ground. Scanning the entire assembly, Naim could not see Roshan Agha, although he knew that the Agha had been planning to attend. Azra was sitting on her own, with the two chairs on either side, although they were in great demand, left vacant in deference to the woman present there, one who was not sitting in the very small separate enclosure reserved for women but with the men. Naim waded through the sitting crowd and took the chair next to her. She looked at him and there was no trace of the previous night on her face. Her eyes were bright and expectant. A few moments later the Aga Khan, surrounded by the reception committee, walked up the red carpet, a short, rotund figure in white morning suit, although it was well into the afternoon. He mounted the three wooden steps to the dais, took off his fan-shaped black hat to place it on the table, refused the rose garlands offered to him, stood his white cane against the arm of the chair and, acknowledging the slogans chanted by the sitting crowd with a wave of the hand, took his seat in the golden chair. Despite his prejudices, Naim thought the man had a striking presence. Without taking her gaze from the dais, Azra placed her hand on Naim's arm and whispered to him, 'Just listen to him when he speaks. I heard him once. Such beautiful English, with a slight accent.'

With a jolt, Naim's whole attention shifted to Azra, while his eyes remained fixed on the scene in front of him – men moving to and fro from one end of the dais to the other, talking, gesticulating, someone taking the microphone, men sitting behind him chanting 'Zinda Bad' and 'Allah-o-Akbar'. But he was neither seeing nor listening to it, like a deaf and blind man roaming in his thoughts: she is beautiful, she's coarse, she is loving, she is greedy, she is brave, she's vivacious, she is faithful, she is contradictory, she's a rich woman who gets what she wants, what in the world is she doing sitting here with me! The conflict in his heart took him away for a while from where he sat. When he returned to the present, Sir Shafi had finished a brief speech and was declaring at the end, 'I announce the merger of Punjab Muslim League into the All India Muslim League and from now on will follow its leadership –'

He was interrupted by the ear-splitting slogans of 'All India Muslim League Zinda Bad' and other such from the crowd. When the noise died down, Sir Shafi went on, 'Today the Muslim community of India –'

He was stopped short by a gentle rebuke from the Aga Khan, 'Muslim nation, not community.'

Sir Shafi picked it up, '– today the Muslim nation of India has been united as one on this platform.'

Naim's mind took a dip once again. Merge! Merge! We have merged and mingled, and yet remain apart, in large unknown spaces, echoing with suspicion. She is a better woman. No, just richer. I am a poor farmer. She is sitting by my side with her hand on my arm, lost in her own passions. Nothing to do with mine. Or with me. How have we walked for so long on the sides of this distant space, keeping within sight? Or am I totally in the wrong? Or is it love, as she says. If it is, it is a separate world . . .

He was brought back to the conference by the roar of the crowd. An important-looking man was at the microphone, saying, 'After counting the votes, I declare the resolution passed.'

Suddenly Maulana Mohammad Ali Jauhar jumped on to the dais, pushed the man aside and stuck his face into the microphone. 'We cannot accept this joint electorate in this way. Politics being the means of obtaining material benefits, we demand one-third representation at the centre and weighting in the provinces.'

The man who had been at the microphone covered it with his hand and started speaking to the maulana in fast, pleading tones. A man who had been speaking to the Aga Khan, bending down to his ear, saw the Aga nod and stepped over to take resolute possession of the microphone to announce an interval for tea, after which, he said, the meeting would be reconvened. The Aga Khan got up from the presidential chair. He put on his hat, picked up his cane and left the stage, saying to someone as he passed the microphone, heard by some in the audience, 'Keep a hold on Mohammad Ali, don't let him speak during the interval.'

Those occupying the chairs stood up and dispersed, while the sitting crowd stayed put, chanting slogans, having nowhere to go for tea.

It was to be years before the Muslim masses gathered under the banner of the Muslim League behind the leadership of Mohammad Ali Jinnah, albeit without the religious parties who advocated the precedence of Islam over politics. For the time being, the Muslim Conference remained merely a symbol of Muslim unity, the different factions of Muslims keeping their distance from each other, holding to their separate agendas. Naim and Azra exchanged a few words, Naim telling her that he didn't feel like staying for the next session of the conference and Azra trying gently to persuade him to stay not just for the day but also the next when the conference would formally end and the Aga Khan give an address. But in the end Naim went. He got out the same way he came in, through the back. Passing through hundreds of people sitting on their haunches, patiently waiting for something to happen, anything that would give them a reason to raise their voices in a slogan they had shouted a hundred times before as if it were the most precious thing they possessed, Naim knew what he had to do. He had no way of increasing his meagre landholding or earning a decent living, nor could he leave the big house and go to live in his two brick rooms or his father's house; he simply had no heart for it. There was also the stinging regret of coming away from Azra, an act over which, despite his willing heart, he had lost control. He imagined that he had decided, not at that particular moment but before that, perhaps during the night before, that he would put himself once again at the disposal of the party and this time go the whole hog. He couldn't suppress, however, a sneaking ambition mixed with the thought that some time in the future he might be considered good enough to join the leadership of the organization at some level.

He wanted to put the work on his land in Ali's hands with Rawal to help him with it. But it proved impossible. Ali, although only sixteen, had matured beyond his years and under the influence of his mother and the traditional enmity between step-siblings had never taken to Naim. During the time Naim was in gaol Ali had fallen in with a bad lot and was taken to the police station a couple of times under suspicion of cattle theft. Eventually Naim saw no alternative but to get him out of the village for a period before anything worse happened.

'Come with me,' Naim said to Ali one day when he went routinely to see his mothers.

'Where?'

'Out.'

They walked together along some fields, Ali leading the way without knowing where they were going, and Naim deliberately falling behind to keep his brother within sight and reach.

'Why don't you work on your land?' Naim asked him.

'What land, six acres? Not even enough for one man.'

'That is all we have,' Naim said.

'Thanks to you since you lost your own by going to gaol.'

'We can all eat if we work properly.'

'No. I am going to get more land.'

'How?'

'I am going to earn more money.'

'By stealing cattle?'

'Maybe.'

'You won't earn one paisa but end up in gaol instead.'

'It will not be the first time for this family,' Ali said sarcastically.

'Have you been pulling a plough?' Naim asked with a smile, unseen by Ali.

'No, why?'

'Your neck is like a bullock's.'

'Have you come out here to make fun of me?'

'You run with men who are bad characters. They are older than you and are criminals.'

'I can stand my ground with any of them.'

'That ground will soon be a prison yard.'

'What is it to you?'

'I will have to go and beg the police to let you off like the last time.'

'Nobody asked you.'

'It's my duty. You are my brother.'

'You are not my brother. You are son of your own mother.'

'Your mother and mine are both our mothers.'

'No,' Ali said belligerently.

'Haven't I looked after them?' Naim asked.

'You don't have to. I can look after my mother.'

'You have the brain of a pig in your head. You never come to see me in my house.'

'It's not your house.'

For a moment Naim didn't know what to say. 'And you fight with Rawal.'

'Rawal is a son of a bitch.'

'There is filth on your tongue,' Naim said decidedly. 'I am not listening to such talk. I am going to take you to town and leave you there.'

Without warning, Ali took off. Naim ran after him. The peasants working in the fields shaded their eyes against the sun and said, laughing, 'The young one's exercising the elder.'

The two ran on through fields mown and unmown, fertile and barren, startling wild pigeons and partridge and quail, which flew off in all directions, and rabbits scurrying away helter-skelter from under bushes looking for another shelter. Ali, younger and quicker, was putting ground between himself and Naim. A rabbit jumped out of a hole and struck Naim's legs. It rolled with the blow for a few feet before running off. Naim was out of breath. He stopped and sat down on a small mound of earth. Seeing him tiring, Ali stopped running as well.

'You catch a rabbit and cook it,' Ali said, laughing. 'It's good for running strength.'

'Shut your mouth, swine,' Naim replied.

'You can't catch me. You are old and heavy from eating too much.'

Naim knew his brother was right. He could never catch the younger man in a race. They were now a few yards from Naim's house. A thought struck Naim. He put two fingers in his mouth and let off a sharp whistle. Within seconds his two guard dogs jumped the boundary wall and fell on the boy. Naim leaped up and ordered the dogs away before they could do damage. He had his hand on Ali's neck, barely encircling the thick, coarse-fleshed stump joined at one end to hefty shoulders and at the other to a powerfully wriggling head. Having only one hand to use, Naim had to fall back on the trick he learned in the army of immobilizing a man by pressing on certain points in the neck. Ali was screaming to get out of the grip. Naim drag-walked him to his house. There he asked the servants to saddle a horse. That done, he mounted the horse and the servants lifted Ali up to sit behind him. Naim then had a rope tied round him and Ali and dug his heels in. The horse, carrying the two of them on its back, started running.

Halfway to the town, wriggling to get out of the bind, Ali asked, 'Where are you taking me?'

'To the cloth mill.'

'It's not even built.'

'It will be built. They are taking men on.'

'You want me to work there?'

'Yes.'

'I will run away.'

'I will take you back as many times as I have to,' Naim said.

'I don't know how to work in a mill.'

'They will teach you. You will learn a skill. You only know that our father went to prison before you were born. But you don't know that he had great skill in his hands.'

'You have no skill,' Ali said accusingly. 'You only have the skill of going to gaol.'

'Yes,' Naim said. 'I am sorry.'

Ali relented in his struggle to break free. 'What skill did father have?'

After a pause, Naim said, 'He made guns.'

'Real guns?' Ali was excited. 'Guns that fire bullets?'

'Yes,' Naim said. 'But he never made bullets and never fired them.'

Ali seemed disappointed. 'I want to make guns. And bullets.'

'You can't, it's against the law. But you can learn some other useful skill. You can get rich and buy more land by learning a skill.'

Ali had calmed down. 'All right,' he said after a while. 'Marry me then to Aisha.'

Naim half-turned his head to look at Ali. 'She is promised to Rawal,' he said.

'I will kill Rawal.'

'Shut up.'

'I am not lying. I will, I swear.'

'Don't talk nonsense,' Naim said to him. 'I will arrange it. Only if you promise to work away from the village for a while.'

'Let me out,' Ali said, squirming. 'The rope's cutting into my back. I won't run away.'

Naim loosened the rope. Ali jumped down from the horse and started running alongside it.

'You will arrange it?' he asked anxiously.

'I will try.'

'What does that mean? I make no promises if you don't arrange it.'

'All right, all right,' Naim said. 'Now be quiet. We are nearly there.'

At the cloth mill, still under construction, one of the first in the country, the man in the recruiting office asked, 'How old is the boy?'

'Sixteen years and eight months,' Naim replied.

'He is too young.'

'I can do all the work,' Ali said, pressing forward.

'According to the Factory Act –' the man began to say.

Naim leaned forward and shouted in the man's face, 'When I was sixteen they put a rifle in my hand and sent me to fight in the war. Look!' He struck his left hand on the table several times.

The man in the office was so shocked to hear the sound of wood tapping on wood that he entered the name in the ledger and hastily gave a chit to Ali to go and report to the electrician on site.

CHAPTER 23

Ali was out of his element in that foreign land of concrete and steel where no earth split open beneath his feet to reveal tiny green shoots that grew into big trees and plants to provide food for the living creatures as if they were faces of God. This machinery too was called a 'plant' by the engineers and mechanics and electricians; this was the first English word that Ali and others like him learned and began to use, though they did not understand it for it had neither food nor shade. It was still under construction and there were rumours that it would somehow in the end make cloth. Despite his discomfort, Ali stuck to it, eating and sleeping with four other labourers in a small room of brick and mortar, in the hope of marrying Aisha; he knew that as long as he kept away from the village and out of trouble his brother would not forsake either him or the promise he had made. On his days off Ali ran back to Roshan Pur and went to Naim's house, at times even spending the night in the house where his brother now mostly lived alone when he was not away for days on the instructions of the local organization. Naim had persuaded his own and Ali's mother to break their word to Aisha's mother regarding her verbal betrothal to Rawal in favour of Ali. The women – the older with much complaint, the younger more readily – eventually agreed, but not before extracting a promise from Naim that he would find another girl for Rawal to marry. Rawal was not consulted, nor did he openly say much. Ali was living on Naim's promise that he would have Ali and Aisha married as soon as the boy became eighteen years old – until one day an incident occurred which stopped Ali in his tracks.

Towards the end of the next year, Mahatma Gandhi, on his return from the Round Table Conference in London, launched his civil non-cooperation movement by publicly making salt on the sea shore at Dundy. Afterwards, he walked from village to village, gathering followers on the way. Naim had wanted to go and join the march, but he was hampered by two things: he was asked to go to Peshawar – not to take part but to report, as an eye-witness of the imminent events there, back to the organization; and, second, he wanted to get Ali's marriage over with before he left for anywhere. Ali and Aisha were married in a simple ceremony, presided over by Naim. Rawal had disappeared from the village for the day.

Two days later, a party of three men arrived from Delhi. Naim's house had been selected as the place in which to perform the token gesture of making salt. Naim knew that the news of it would reach Roshan Mahal and he wasn't sure how Azra would react to it. Further, there was the risk of being arrested by the police for breaking the law. In view of the latter, it was decided that they would disperse – the three men back to Delhi and Naim to Peshawar – the same evening.

In a sheltered spot in the garden of the house a huge, open-mouthed iron karah, used for making gur, was placed on top of a hole in the ground full of burning wood from a couple of dead trees, except that instead of cane juice in the container it was water from the well boiling over the fire. For fear of the police, only a few men from the village had had the courage to come round to attend the 'ceremony'. They all sat by the pot of boiling water, looking at it expectantly just as they used to sit waiting for gur to form from the evaporating juice. It being his brother's house, Ali sat on a three-legged wooden stool among them, assuming a place of importance, while Rawal wandered around, seemingly taking little interest in the proceedings. Naim sat with the three visitors on the back veranda of the house, out of view of the boiling water pot, writing a speech for one of the guests that the man was going to make at a meeting the following week.

The water in the pot boiled and boiled, and more was poured into the pot and more wood burned, and still it boiled down and there was no salt. Disappointment spread over the faces of those sitting and standing around. Naim and his companions were told the news. One of the three guests thought for a while and said that it had all been a mistake and why did they not think of it in the first place? Of course there would be no salt in the sweet drinking and irrigation water well. Then one of the villagers said that he knew of a well outside another village about ten miles away that had been abandoned because it created salinity in the land. Two men were sent to this well with two or three large milk pitchers loaded on to a donkey to fetch water from there. The rest of the assembly waited patiently in the garden. A hukka was started up anew and Bakhsh the bald had to be coaxed, known miser that he was, to produce tobacco in his turn. In the face of his resistance the men mocked him relentlessly for having a body like a hairless woman until Bakhsh the bald reluctantly got a little bit of tobacco from the roll of his turban, and then he wouldn't let go of the hukka pipe until, pulling furiously at it, he had burned half the fresh tobacco in it. They sat and smoked and gossiped and laughed thus until the two donkeys – two of the best in the village – arrived back, one carrying the two men, the other four pitchers full of water from the abandoned well. A fire was lit with more dry wood upon the embers, and the water was poured into the pot. Then everyone sat around looking to see what happened. The water boiled, and as it went down it left a layer of greyish matter all round the inside of the pot. Ali went running to the back veranda to tell Naim the news. All four men came to check. One of them scraped a little bit of the powder off the rim of the pot and put a grain of it on the tip of his tongue. Yes, it was salt, he nodded. A low shout went up from the men, shushed by Naim.

'It is salt,' the taster said, 'but not for cooking. It may even be no good for you.'

'But is it salt?'

'It is that all right,' the man answered. 'We have done it.'

The pot was quickly tipped over to pour the remaining water on the fire to douse it, and then the upturned pot was put on top of the ashes, concealing all signs of their illegal act. Then all the villagers, except for Ali and Rawal, went home, carrying no salt but only the pride of having defied the laws of the earthly gods that ruled their lives.

By now it was the evening. Ali was the only one left in the house other than the servants. He headed for home. After the day's hectic work, he wanted to have a night's sleep before going back to the mill. He was nearing the village when he heard quick footsteps. He turned round to see Rawal coming up fast behind him, sights firmly fixed on Ali. Ali had thought Rawal had gone home. He didn't have the time to steady himself before Rawal jumped on him, knocking him down. Ali sprang up after the first attack but was struck down again. Once again Ali wriggled out from under Rawal and was on his feet. He was still dazed by the assault but understood what it was about. For a moment he thought of running away from Rawal's clutches, knowing that he could outrun the other man. But he didn't want to give Rawal the advantage of victory in this fight. They wrestled for a minute, pushing and shoving. A passing villager saw them, stopped for a moment before continuing on his way home, mumbling, 'You never know when the police will arrive and the boys are playing games.' Rawal wasn't playing games; there was murder in his heart. Strong as Ali was, Rawal was a thirty-year-old man and tougher. Eventually, he got Ali in a bear hug and squeezed him down to the ground.

'I am going to kill you,' he said, sitting on top of Ali, his hands on the boy's neck.

Ali knew that this time it was impossible to get out of Rawal's grip. He was thinking fast. 'What for?' he asked.

'You think you can take her away and be happy? I will rub you out here and now.'

'It was my brother's wish – why don't you talk to him?' Ali said.

'I will finish you before Neem comes back.'

'And where . . . will you be . . . then?' Ali said, trying to breathe under the grip of Rawal's hands on his neck.

'Where?' Rawal said, increasing the pressure.

'I . . . can't . . . breathe.'

Rawal loosened the grip a little. 'Where do you think I'll be?'

'You will be in gaol. You will never get out. Your wheat crop will rot.'

'It will do your bitch mother good to starve.'

'So will your aunt.'

'Neem will look after her,' Rawal said.

'He is always away. If you kill me our house will fall to the ground.'

'I don't care. I don't care.'

Ali's words, however, got through to Rawal, somewhat slackening his determination to kill. But he wanted to inflict the maximum damage before letting go. He squeezed Ali's neck with all the strength of his hands. Ali's eyes popped out. Then Rawal started punching Ali's face, wrecking his lips and nose.

'You sneaked up on me in the dark,' Ali said, crying. 'Let me go and we will fight tomorrow. Face to face. In the daylight.'

'There will be no tomorrow for you,' Rawal said, mercilessly continuing to punch. 'I never want to see you in the village again, do you hear that? Take her and run away from here. If I see you with her in the village I swear I will kill you both.' Rawal pulled out a long shining knife from under his shirt.

'All right, all right,' Ali said, howling, 'I will not come back.'

'Go.' Rawal took his hands off Ali and stood up. 'Run.'

Ali ran on home, his face bleeding and a permanent terror settled in his heart. The very next day, he left the village.

Even before Naim left the train at Peshawar railway station, he remembered the promise he had made years before to Amir Khan, his fellow-wounded for some time in a foreign hospital. Both knew that they were no longer of any use for battle and would go home. Before they parted, Amir Khan had made Naim give his word that he would visit Amir Khan in his village near Peshawar if ever he passed that way. After all these years, Naim remembered the name of the village. The day was ending. Naim decided to look Amir Khan up and, in case he found his old companion-in-arms alive and well, spend the night with him. He took a tonga from the station. After over an hour and a dozen miles, the tonga stopped by a stony little hill.

'End of the road,' the tonga driver told him. 'Now you walk. Kaka Khel is on the other side of the hill.'

Naim climbed the narrow path to the top of the hill and got a view of the village. Under a moonlit sky, the village lay in the dark, with the dim points of lanterns visible in a few houses. But over on the far side a glow of light spread upwards, creating a halo in the air that enhanced the blackness of the rest of the village. Naim passed through unlit streets where men in great loose shalwars and huge turbans, rifles slung across their shoulders, passed him wordlessly like shadows. He stopped one of them and asked about Amir Khan. The man pointed towards the flood of light pouring from the house on the other side. As he neared the source of the light, he saw the walls of the house marked by torches of slow-burning oily wood, giving off the faint fragrance of burnt mountain pine. In the courtyard, a large crowd of men sat in a circle, with an old, long-bearded man in the middle, covering his ear with one hand, singing a Pushto song in drawn-out, high tones. Naim had walked into the middle of a celebration. Hesitantly, he entered the courtyard.

Amir Khan never got an artificial leg. Hopping on his crutches and peering at the newcomer, he approached Naim.

'Aha!' he smiled, showing his missing teeth. 'Naeem!' Balancing on one crutch and opening the other arm, he hugged Naim.

'Recognize me, you old devil?' Naim said. 'I thought you might have gone blind.'

'Why, I can pick you out among a thousand men any time. We are friends from bad times.'

He led Naim to the place of honour beside his own carpet seat on the ground. 'This is my friend,' he said loudly to the assembly, 'Subedar Naeem Khan, come specially to attend my son's marriage from Dilli. He is my friend from bad times.'

All the men got up one by one and came to shake hands with Naim. The old singer shuffled over. Sitting down in front of Naim, he began his song all over again. Amir Khan struck him over the head with his crutch.

'Shut up, you old fool,' he said. 'My friend has not come from far-away Dilli to listen to your babbling. Let me speak to him. Now, then,' he turned to Naim, 'tell me, how are you?' He bent down to look at Naim's left hand, then brought it up close to his eyes, examining it minutely. 'Good,' he said with satisfaction, 'very good,' before letting go of it. 'Wazir Khan,' he shouted. A young man answered. 'Come, come here.' Amir Khan turned to Naim again. 'This is my son. You have come at the exact right time. We are going to start off any minute to bring the girl home.' Then he said proudly, 'He is in the army.'

The boy, about eighteen, resembling but better-looking than his father, stood respectfully and looked at Naim with unsmiling eyes. Naim shook hands with him once again.

'I am going inside the house for one minute,' Amir Khan said to Naim. 'You talk to my son. Not long to wait now.' He hopped over to the house.

To go to the girl's house, they had to climb up and then down another hill, in the light of just two burning tree-torches and a few lanterns, along narrow and dangerous paths full of stones that rolled underfoot. Naim, being an honoured guest, walked under good light, but he saw that most of the others, especially the tail-enders, made their way over these precipices in total darkness with such ease as if they could clearly see the path.

The arena for the nikah ceremony – for arena it was, for a contest, as Naim later learned – was different from Amir Khan's courtyard in some respects. It wasn't in a house but was set in plain open ground some distance away from the girl's village, although the lighting was provided by the same kind of torches made from young trees, cut down and supported by surrounding their bases with heavy stones. Second, there was a small tent, erected on one side of the arena, with its curtains drawn shut. Third, there was food; behind the tent, whole lambs, skewered over iron stands, were being slowly turned and spit-roasted on wood fires, giving off saliva-inducing smells that carried on the air. The groom's party was received and seated.

After only a few minutes' exchange of pleasantries, which Naim thought were a bit tense and unsmiling, two men appeared, leading a live, well-fed lamb whom they stood in the middle and, leaving it there, withdrew. Presently, the sheet covering the opening of the tent lifted and a girl, the bride, covered from head to foot in red silk, silver ornaments sparkling on her forehead, neck and forearms, with only half of her face showing above the bridge of her nose up to the hairline, walked out, advancing towards the lamb that stood docilely where it had been left. The bride, a plumpish girl with fair skin and large black eyes, stopped by the lamb. She didn't look up or around her. Bending over, she tried to lift the lamb off its feet by putting her arms round the animal's legs and heaving it up. She could only move it a few inches off the ground. Then she tried lifting it with her arms slipped under its neck and stomach. She failed again; the lamb was too heavy. Finally, she knelt down, put her head under the lamb's belly, spread her arms to hold either end of it and raised it up on her back, stumbling a little but steadying herself, using the strength of her entire body. She stood with the lamb gently wriggling across her shoulders, her legs trembling under the weight. Now she looked up, but at no one in particular.

Wazir Khan, the groom, broke away from the crowd of his tribe, strode out to the middle and stopped some yards away from the girl bearing the lamb. Facing her, he swung his rifle from his side and lifted it to his shoulder. He took aim. Dumbfounded, Naim looked on. He knew nothing of what was going on nor what was going to happen. He had seen nothing like it in his life. There was complete silence among the nearly two hundred people sitting there as Wazir Khan stood with the sights of his rifle trained on the girl, who was now shaking under the load, swaying lightly to right and left. Almost imperceptibly, the barrel of Wazir Khan's rifle swayed with her, his finger on the trigger. Naim felt as if every one of the men in that large crowd had stopped breathing, and yet the boy with the gun stood waiting, still not pulling the trigger. It must have been a minute but it seemed a long time. Naim saw the flash a split second before he heard the report of the gun. The girl staggered but kept to her feet. The lamb, bleeding from the head, was twisting and trembling on the girl's back. She held fast until the lamb shivered a couple of times, hung its head to one side and became still. The girl let go of it. The lifeless body dropped with a thud to the ground behind her. Then she lifted her face and looked with a fearless gaze at her groom.

A great roar arose from the throats of the men, and with it a hundred rifles were fired into the sky. For several minutes the noise of shooting and men shrieking with laughter buzzed in Naim's ears. Leaving his crutches, Amir Khan had prostrated himself towards Makkah. After he had rubbed his forehead several times on the ground, he sat up and said to Naim, 'Alhamdulillah, Alhamdulillah.'

'Alhamdulillah,' Naim repeated with him. 'What happens now?'

'The nikah,' replied Amir Khan. 'If the lamb didn't get it in the head or the bullet hit the girl, my son would be killed. Alhamdulillah – honour is saved.'

They, the bride and the groom, had to win each other, Amir Khan explained later. The girl did not falter in front of the gun, and the boy killed the lamb with a single shot. If any of this failed to happen, said Amir Khan, there would be no wedding but war between the tribes. 'But do not worry,' he said, laughing happily, 'no one would shoot you. Everyone knows you are a guest.'

Soon after the bride withdrew to the tent, the nikah ceremony was performed and presents were exchanged, including the bride-price of thirty-five silver coins offered in a pouch by Amir Khan to the girl's father. All through this, except for a few minutes of the actual nikah when verses from the holy Quraan were recited by the maulvi, shots from rifles kept ringing out, echoing in distant hills until the food was brought out. Whole cooked lambs lay in round shallow trays, each one carried by two men. Amir Khan handed Naim a long knife for him to be the first to carve from the fattest lamb put before him. It was a mark of honour and Naim, with his good hand, put the knife to the lamb's shoulder.

'No, no,' Amir Khan said, pointing to the stomach, 'here, cut it here.'

Naim saw that the stomach had been opened and then sewn up with strong thread that somehow had been saved from burning. As he passed the knife over the cut, it ripped open and mounds of rice, cooked inside the stomach's lining of fat, poured out into the tray, fluffy and infused with cinnamon, cloves and cardamom. Nobody used knives to carve but sank their fingers into the tender meat and dug out handfuls of salted lamb to chew with the fragrant rice.

It was after midnight when the wedding party returned with the bride. Amir Khan had had Naim's bed laid out alongside his own in his room. Both tired out with the evening's proceedings, Amir Khan talked to Naim for a few minutes, passing his hand appreciatively over the smooth surface of Naim's left hand.

'You got a medal?' he asked.

Naim shook his head.

'I heard some talk about it later on.'

'No,' Naim said shortly.

Amir Khan was called out. Naim was at the point of dozing off when Amir Khan returned.

'Bad,' he said, shaking his head.

'What is it?' Naim asked him.

'Wazir Khan has five more days' leave to go, but the army wants him to report back.'

'Is he going straight back in the morning?'

'No, straight back now. The man is waiting for him outside.'

'Why so soon?'

'God only knows. Maybe there is need. Poor boy has not seen his wife's full face yet.'

When Naim arrived back in Peshawar the next day, it was early afternoon and the following scene was already being played out in a bazaar in the city. A brown-haired man, clad in homespun rough cotton shalwar-kameez, stood on an empty wooden box. He had a strip of the same cloth in his hand, in one end of which was tied a fist-sized solid piece of something. The man had the free end of the strip in his grip and, rotating it in a centrifugal motion above his head, he was shouting repeatedly, 'Salt, salt, salt . . .' This mantra-like call was being picked up by a large crowd standing around him. They were taking turns: the man, continuously rotating the rock over his head, would shout the word 'salt' three times and stop, whereupon hundreds of people would repeat the same word the same number of times in an enormous roar and then fall silent, waiting for the cue from the man on the box – and the whole sequence would start all over again. As if it was a game, this went on for some time. Naim stood at the edge of the crowd, looking around. He was surprised to see the people, Pathans who considered a gun an ornament, indeed as much a part of their person as a shirt or a shoe, present in the gathering that day with no firearms on them. There was a heavy contingent of police surrounding them, although they were not doing anything to stop this law-breaking crowd. The voices of the people, answering the man on the box, were gradually rising, in volume and tempo, until they reached a screaming pitch and, in the heat of the emotion, a few rifles, hitherto unseen, were raised above heads. On seeing this, another man, a thick-set Pathan of middle years, mounted the box and raised his hand to silence the crowd.

'No,' he shouted in anger, 'no firing. You were told not to bring your guns here today. If a single shot is fired, we will end this demonstration and leave. I appeal to the people who have guns to go and leave their weapons at home. Until you do that we will not go any further with the jalsa.'

A handful of men, who seemed to be volunteers managing the meeting, went into the crowd, heading for men who had been seen raising rifles. They took these men gently out of the throng. The thick-set man jumped off the box, yielding to the man who had been orchestrating the meeting. This man now began undoing the knot at the end of the strip of cloth. Inside was not a hard rock but a misshapen piece of white matter, which he proceeded to place in the middle of his palm. He raised his hand and, closing the fingers around the substance, squeezed it. It disintegrated into small bits. The man let them run slowly through his fingers and fall to the ground. Simultaneously from his audience rose an ecstatic howl, forming the words 'Salt . . . salt'. He lifted his arms, bidding them to be quiet.

'Tomorrow,' he said, 'we will hold protest demonstrations in front of the theatre. I want all of you to be there, every one of you.'

He dismounted the box. As he stood among his companions, a number of policemen, led by an officer, waded into the mass of people and arrested him and a dozen others with him. They pushed the men off in front of them, reaching a covered police vehicle that was standing by and quickly bundled them into it. The vehicle sped away. For a moment the crowd, surprised into immobility, stood still. Then they started running after the police lorry. The vehicle, which had to go through bazaars and populated areas, could not throw off its pursuers despite the best efforts of the driver. When it reached its destination, the main police station in Qissa Khwani bazaar, the hundreds chasing it were only a few minutes behind. The police, however, had time to get their prisoners into the station's remand gaol. The crowd of people outside came running up and stopped in front of the station. They were chanting slogans and shouting 'Let them go . . . let them go . . . let them go.'

All around them, in addition to the police, there was the presence of the army. Naim was still at the back of the gathering. As the slogans kept going, he thought there would be a lathi charge any time now. He had sensed wrong; there was no lathi charge. Instead, a British army officer, wearing an eye-patch, stepped forward and issued an order to the line of soldiers. The soldiers stirred. The officer shouted a second order.

'Garhwali Rifles, Company One, Platoon One. Fire!'

Not a single soldier in the front line lifted his rifle, took aim or fired. Astonished, the officer screamed his order a second time. Still there was no movement from the soldiers. A blue-eyed, fair-skinned Pathan soldier at the end of the line nearest to where Naim stood mumbled audibly, 'They are unarmed.'

The officer paused just for a second. Naim saw narrow red stripes, where the blood had gathered, appear across the paleness of his cheeks. Suppressing his anger, he spoke calmly.

'Those who have disobeyed, step forward.'

The front line of soldiers hesitated. As the order of their commander sank in under his angry glare, they took a step forward.

'Garhwali Rifles, Platoon Two,' the officer said, still in a calm voice. 'Take their weapons.'

Other soldiers from behind stepped forward and disarmed the front line. Then they took position.

'Platoon Two,' the officer – a Captain Wood, later infamously known as 'the one-eyed butcher of Qissa Khwani' – barked the order. 'Fire!'

The soldiers started shooting, firing their .303 rifles, the sound of smooth steel-on-steel sliding bolt for repeated reloading punctuating the terrifying crack of combined shot. The men in the crowd ran chaotically in whatever direction they faced, some straight into the bullets. Some of them got away, the rest either falling wounded or taking shelter in open drains and abandoned shops. The shooting went on for what felt like hours, concentrated into minutes.

There was a loud bang to one side and an armour-plated car, a parked army vehicle, burst into flames, the soldiers inside it jumping out one after the other in panic. The shooting stopped. The officer and his company looked towards the vehicle on fire. Their disarmed colleagues still stood under guard.

Slowly, a head began to emerge from under the burning vehicle. It was the head of a civilian, a Pathan. He was on his back, furiously crawling in that awkward position in an attempt to get away. Naim had sheltered himself behind a thick brick structure housing a water pump. His mind had completely emptied. Why, he wondered, looking at the man now moving his arms as if swimming in the air, does he not turn over and crawl out properly? Inch by inch, the man was sliding along the ground – head, shoulders, then chest. Below the chest, there was nothing, every shred of his body blown away. Unmindful of the soldiers, several men jumped out of the open drains and stood looking at the torso struggling like a healthy, strong person to escape the flames he may himself have helped ignite. Nobody went to his assistance. The ground in front of the police station was littered with bodies. When the shooting stopped, the police had pushed forward. Two constables came up and arrested Naim.

I was not supposed to get myself arrested, thought Naim as he sat behind the barred door of the remand gaol. 'I should have run,' he said to himself firmly. In a moment of thought as clear as that sunny day, he knew that in the flow of the great river that his life had been, this was the one thing he could definitely have avoided. He was making mistakes. He was not thirty-four years old and already he felt things slipping through his fingers. With a throbbing pain in his head, his whole body was feeling increasingly lighter as if it was about to lift itself and float like a feather in the air. The strong sun hit his eyes in a solid sheet, making them ache. Random thoughts passed through his mind. Between his half-closed eyelids he saw other men sitting with him and he thought: Who will cut their crops? He didn't even know if they had crops.

CHAPTER 24

Ali waited for Naim to return so he could go back to the village. A month passed and there was no news of his brother. He took his bride from her mother's house and went back to the one-room brick hut that he had acquired as electrician's mate in Shanti Nagar. There he waited and waited. Months grew into a year and then more, until slowly hope began to dry up in his heart. The mill was still being built, the machinery – looms and huge electric motors and a hundred other things – arriving from England and being erected, engineers, fitters, electricians and their helpers working twelve hours a day, later sixteen hours in two shifts.

Shanti Nagar, the housing colony so named after the daughter of the industrialist owner, had been built to accommodate workers and their families. There were three parts of it. Spread over a few acres were one- and two-room brick 'quarters' for semi-skilled and unskilled workers, mostly labourers. These were built in straight lines with open drains running through the streets that crossed each other at right angles. There was no vegetation, no shade except for the shadows of brick walls that moved with the sun, providing no relief through the eight-month-long summer that turned the barracks-like structures into airless ovens. There was open ground between this and the second part of the colony which consisted of 'houses', each with three rooms and stamp-sized front and back lawns. The 'officers' who lived in them – young diploma holders from technical schools and semi-literate older men who had risen through years of experience above the rank of foreman – made an effort to cultivate their patches, although they grew vegetables instead of grass in their little squares, thus taking the first step towards colonizing the colony. The third part of Shanti Nagar was set back and apart from the first two, on land specially chosen for the mature tahli, pipal and bohr trees that had grown there for years. It was a row of seven large bungalows, enclosed by boundary walls with wooden gates and long grassy lawns in front and back of the houses bordered by new-grown trees and flowers beds tended by gardeners. Here lived the British engineers and administrators, their company cars and jeeps parked beside their gates, forever being polished by servants. A metalled road led from in front of the bungalows straight to the factory premises, bypassing the other two parts of the colony which had to make do with dirt paths. There were concrete tennis and badminton courts laid to the side of the bungalows, and next to these was the Rest House, and in an extension of it a small clubhouse, reserved for the residents of the bungalows and no one else, save their servants, to use for social gatherings. Only the owner, Mr Dalmia, on his occasional visits, stayed in the Rest House and was invited into the club for a cup of tea. On site, however, the white sahibs were the owners of the colony.

The inhabitants of the three parts of the colony had no social contact one with the other, each group mixing only among themselves.

(In years to come, after the white residents of the bungalows had left, the middle order, those who lived in the 'houses' in the second part of the colony, took charge of different departments of the working mill and were upgraded to live in the bungalows. In addition to making use of all the facilities that went with the bungalows, to which they had long aspired, they took on the habits of their previous masters; socially they had little to do with the men working below them except when they came into contact with them inside the mill. The gulf between these two groups, one tiny and the other very large, remained in place until the end of time as if it were the natural order.)

At noon, during his fifteen-minute rest period, Ali entered the empty hut earmarked for any extra storage that might be needed later on but which was used for the moment by men seeking shelter from the hot sun to ease their weary limbs. A labourer, another peasant, was sitting on the floor, eating a roti with tomato and green coriander chutney. Breathing in the cool, restful air of still-damp bricks and mortar, Ali went to stand by the lone window of the hut. Idly, he opened half of it; a view of the land entered the room. There was nobody in sight; everyone, high and low, was taking the few minutes of rest sanctioned by the owners and had found some shade or other. Ali saw only the heavy pieces of machinery lying around, waiting to be fixed in their proper place, and mounds of earth and stone, but no green, no sign of life on that scorched earth pressed down by the vast white sheet of a fierce sun.

'Shut the window,' the man on the floor said.

Ali lingered by the window.

'Here,' the man said again, offering a piece of roti to Ali, 'I've had enough.'

'I am not hungry,' Ali replied.

The man threw the piece of roti to a pup that had walked in and was sitting by the man's feet, its eyes mild and moist and its tongue hanging out like the outstretched hand of a beggar. Ali shut the window. The burning view disappeared. He sat down by the wall, shutting his eyes and resting his head against the wall, his face a mask of bones showing on his cheeks and forehead and his eyes deep beneath them.

'Oh well,' the labourer said, 'a man has rights ahead of an animal. I come here every day and give a crumb to this rascal. When I go, what will it do? I don't know.'

'Where will you go?' Ali asked.

'Home, where else?'

Home, Ali thought, and shut his eyes again.

'You are not well,' the man said, looking closely at Ali. 'A man who works the land should not get ill.'

'I work on no land,' Ali said quietly. 'I am an electrician's mate.'

'Still, eat more. That is what you should do, eat more wheat.' He got up, picking up his spade.

'Where are you working?' Ali asked him.

'On the south side.'

'Doing what?'

'Digging ditches. For water pipes.'

The pup followed him out. A gust of hot wind had pushed the latchless window open. Ali got up to go. Through the window he could see the labourer, spade resting on his shoulder, walking away with a heavy, steady step, one, two, one, two, as if imitating some machine. The pup had stopped short and was looking at the man too, his ears up in ignorant expectation. The man's uniform gait produced an added sense of weariness in Ali. He turned his eyes away and went out into the blinding heat of the day.

A little before his shift ended, Ali put down his pair of pliers and the screwdriver.

'I am hungry,' he said to his electrician.

'The shift is not over yet,' his superior said.

'I want to go to the canteen.'

'How many knots have you done on the armature?'

'One hundred and sixty.'

'Not enough, boy.'

Ali did not pick up his tools. The electrician looked back to the foreman. The foreman was looking away. The electrician leaned forward. 'Are you well, Ali?'

'I want to go and have something to eat.'

The electrician stared at him for a minute. 'All right, go. Through that door, not this one, that door – don't let the foreman see you.'

Ali hadn't tasted tea until he started working in the mill. Now he had tea twice a day. In the canteen he sat on a bench and asked for a cup of tea, paying a paisa to the seller in advance. The middle-aged man poured tea into a clay mug from a large black kettle that he had simmering on hot coals with the same tea leaves in it that he had put in that morning.

'When will it be built?' he asked Ali by way of conversation.

'It is being built,' Ali answered.

'That I can see. But it's been years. When will it be finished?'

Ali drank his tea from the mug without answering.

'Do you have children?' the tea-seller pressed on.

'No.'

'Oho. How many years have you been married?'

Ali drank the last of the tea and glared at the man. 'Don't know,' he said and walked out.

'Don't know – don't know, ha ha,' the tea-seller laughed, turning to the other man sitting on the bench. 'These starving peasants come here looking for work, and as soon as they have one paisa in the pocket they don't have a nice word to say to anyone. Don't know, he says.'

Aisha lay sleeping in the cot, her mouth half-open and her fine muslin shirt, wet with sweat, clinging to her breasts. Ali stopped in the doorway looking distantly at her familiar form. The sound of his feet awoke Aisha. She left the cot and immediately started talking as if continuing a sentence that had been interrupted a second before.

'Where were you? I asked Rahim and he said he saw you leave the mill. I waited for you. It's so hot I fell asleep. The black tom stole the grey hen. I was cooking. The beast, why don't you kill it? Remember we killed this great big wild cat in the cornfield in Roshan Pur that year when –'

'Give me something to eat. I am hungry.'

'You would be hungry. It is so hot. Want to drink some water before you eat? No, it will kill your appetite. Better have a bath first, you will get hot-cold if you bathe after eating –'

'Give me food,' Ali repeated tonelessly.

Talking non-stop, Aisha went into the shadeless three-foot courtyard where she cooked under the open sky and warmed up the food. She brought in hot salan in a clay plate and warm rotis wrapped in a piece of cloth and sat down opposite Ali, waving one end of her dopatta over the food. 'Flies, so many flies, don't know where they come from, they're like locusts, swarms of them. You remember two years before we were married locusts came to the village? Like dark clouds over the sky. Us women caught them and roasted them over the fire to eat, they were delicious, and all the men went into the fields waving sheets of cloth to stop them landing on the crops. But they came down and did a lot of damage. Don't you remember, you told me not to eat them because they were no good for women, only good for men? I was Rawal's betrothed at the time. He saw us talking to one another and slapped me later. I think rain will come – the sky is shimmering with the heat and do you hear the kites screaming, asking for water? That's a sign. Eat up. Why, is it no good today? I know, Rahim's wife came and borrowed all my mint. You said yourself to give them whatever they want, didn't you? I couldn't say no. Some people came from the mosque asking for money. I shut the door on them. We never go to the mosque, why should we give them money? After a while they went away. I don't think they collected much money from round here. I did chase after the black tom, but he got away. And the grey hen laid eggs too. If I ever catch it I will strangle it. How fast I used to run in the village, do you remember? Nobody could catch me. I think you had something to eat in the mill. Don't blame me –'

'Shut up, Aishoo,' Ali said, pulling back his hand from the food.

'Something happen to you at the mill today? I know something has, you have not even finished your food, and you said you were hungry. Don't blame me –'

'Take these away,' Ali said, wiping his hands and lips with the cloth covering the rotis.

When Aisha returned Ali was lying on the cot. She talked on. The tall slim girl knew nothing other than to talk, bringing up over and over again their past in the village.

'Shut up,' Ali said to her again. 'Come here.'

She came and lay down by Ali's side, still talking. Ali put a hand over her mouth and rolled over. He lay on top of her for a long time before he found the stirrings in his loins. These two children of the earth of their homeland writhed under the dead weight of a foreign life cracking through their bones and making them weary.

HINDUSTAN II

As they are told not to spread dispute
among the people, so they reply that they are
but peacemakers.

– *Al Quraan*

CHAPTER 25

Azra sat on a stool in the window of her darkened room, leaning forward, her elbows on the sill and face in the cup of her hands, looking out on the rain that had been falling all day. When the day ended and the lights came on in Roshan Mahal, she had left her room unlit. She did not leave home all day, not knowing what to do with herself in the emptied state of her mind. Random thoughts, bereft of occasion or logic, came and went. A thick, greyish strand of hair, matching her eyes, had fallen on her forehead. She had wanted to push it up for some time but could not bring herself to do it. This typical winter drizzle, falling on the eucalyptus tree outside her window, through the lights in the garden and over the roads, the houses and beyond on the vast fields of villages far and wide, had ensnared her in its never-ending sounds of drip, drip, drip, covering the world in a damp quilt. In this busy world populated by a million drops, only her mind was empty – not just of objects of thought but of intention. Shall I push up this strand from my brow? she thought for the tenth time, but made no move to do so. The rain is still falling, she repeated to herself, still falling, over everything. Two servants passed across the veranda below her window. 'Bibi is sleeping,' one whispered to the other. 'Yes,' the other whispered back.

It took Azra an effort of the will to stir from her seat on the stool. She finally pushed up the strand of hair touching her eyebrow with the back of her hand. It clung precariously to the shock of unbrushed hair on one side of her head. She looked at her musical instruments lined up by the wall, unplayed for years. She walked up to them and lightly touched the cloth cover of one of them. A fine layer of dust covered the tip of her finger. They haven't dusted them, she frowned, then remembered that most days she wouldn't let the servants into her room. Stiffly, carefully, she removed the covers, dropping them on the floor: a sitar, a tanpura, a sarangi, a violin all stood straight up against the wall, their polished wood glistening darkly in the dimness of light refracted from the garden. She lifted a string of the sitar with a finger. Instead of letting go of it, she slowly lowered it in its place as though it were the hammer of a loaded gun that would make a bang if thrown. She came back to sit in the chair. In front of her were some blank sheets of paper. After a while she switched on the table lamp, picked up her pen and began to write.

'Dearest, dearest Shirin, you write to me after nearly two years and want to know everything. Why don't you come and see me? You are so, so far away and want to find out what is going on here. Is it fair? Well, it's been raining all day and I am sitting in my room writing to you, and it is late. That is how I am. Nothing drastic. In the day they have been celebrating somebody's birthday, couldn't go out because of the rain so ran about on the veranda and in the corridors making a racket. Sorry, it was Pervez's son Imran's birthday, you probably got an invitation so why am I telling you this? Oh yes, he is seventeen, that is why. I mean, such a lot of time has gone by so quickly, don't you think? How are your three? And Salim Bhai? You never write anything about them, or yourself. All you do is want to find out, find out after two years whether I am alive, and how. Just like you, good old Shirin, my dear, dear, I am. Alive, that is. Don't you think you'd know if it was otherwise? Only joking. Anyway, I joined the festivities downstairs but only for a few minutes. You know that Pervez has been putting more and more distance between himself and me over the years, did I mention it to you before? And Naheed, never been thick with me or my friends or anyone really. But don't need to tell you this, do I? Well, you wanted to know everything. I have a feeling that they have begun to look at me and everything about me as if I were no longer part of them. Khala too. Don't know why. Oh, I KNOW. They disapprove of me, that's it. At least with Pervez I can pinpoint the time when he began to cut me off. No, nothing to do with Naim. I think Pervez had accepted him. Not Khala, not Naheed, but Pervez, and Roshan Agha, they came to have a certain regard for him in the end. I don't know about now, though. So much has changed.

'What was I saying? Yes, it was the time when Pervez spotted me in the mob in Lucknow years ago. I am certain of that. But I am very fond of Imran, he is the sweetest boy in the world, the only one who comes and sits with me and talks about everything, as if to defy everybody. It was for him that I went downstairs for a few minutes. Roshan Agha is not keeping well, can't get rid of his cough. I am worried about him. Don't tell me off, please, but I feel responsible. Yes, guilty. Although he is the only one to whom I go without any qualms. When he clasps me in his arms and hugs me each time he sees me, something he has only begun or begun again to do after a gap of many years, all my bad sense about anything vanishes. I love him very much. Then a strange thing happens. As soon as I come away from him I start to feel guilty even more than before and the weight of it descends on me like a falling sky. And yet there is no wrongdoing, no fault, no error, no regret even. Just the way it happened. Can guilt exist without regret, or am I going mad? Naim's absence does not make it any easier. This time as you know there was a trial of sorts and they were sentenced for an unspecified time, but what is the unspecified time? Also it all happened in the Frontier and none of us knew anyone in that region. It is so, so far away. Well, not so far away as other places in the south, but strange, I mean nobody goes there. Why did he do it? I went to visit him once and he forbade me to come again. He is in fairly good condition, unlike last time. It's not that I miss him in myself – it's been too long and it's too late for that. Funny thing is that I can't picture his face in his absence. Every time I try to imagine his features I see blank. Don't you think that is very, very odd? I don't pine for his touch, only his presence. I am surrounded by holes – everywhere I turn there is a hole which is shaped like him. I breathe through holes in the air and my chest aches. Do you understand that, my dear, dearest Shirin? I think not.'

She didn't put her name at the bottom. She stared at the letter for just a moment and then slowly crumpled it in her hands into a ball, as if she had decided to destroy it even as she wrote the last word. After a few minutes, she yawned and got up from the chair. She was going to change into her night-dress and go to bed. Instead, she didn't even hang the clothes that she was wearing on the clothes-stand, dropping them on the floor one by one until she was standing naked in front of the tall mirror. She looked at her image, the circles around the eyes getting blacker, a fattened chin and thin shoulders above breasts limp and shrunk, never sucked by a baby's mouth, and the expanding hips, and she wanted to turn her face away from the woman in the mirror. But her gaze into herself had stilled her in a frozen posture with her eyes staring into the pain of battles she had fought, until a great fright gripped her and she began to shiver. She slipped under the quilt as she stood, and the rub of velvet on her bare, goose-pimpled skin made her aware that, despite the time gone by and the sorrow of it, the one thing she still wanted was Naim's presence, to fill the gap that had opened up in her life and calm the shivering of her heart.

Naim had years to serve yet, and Ali to live in his life without shade, before things would change. One rainy season cholera spread in several districts and took many lives, Ali's mother among the Roshan Pur dead. Aisha and Ali crept up to the village in the dark of the evening and were met by someone they dreaded: Rawal. He had stood in their path outside the village for hours, waiting for them. When he confronted them he had his foot-long knife in his hand which he waved before them.

'Put the woman in the ground and go back,' he snarled.

The couple caught the shine of the steel blade, too close to them, and knew they had no choice. They sneaked out of the village the next day as they had come, still waiting in vain for Naim.

Naim had been unwell in gaol off and on for some time. It was no commonplace complaint like a headache or indigestion or some such as could be diagnosed and treated, but every once in a while he felt dizzy. He had to lie down and would then be overtaken by a great weakness that seemed to penetrate to his guts so that he could move not one limb for hours, sometimes for days. His gaolers, not in the least concerned for the health of the inmates, considered him a malingerer, while Naim, wishing to dismiss it from his mind, put it down to the poor quality of life that he had been leading there over the years. One day, when he least expected it, he was told to go.

Naim took one look at the big house in Roshan Pur and came away. He went to stay in his mother's house. He found Rawal living in Ali's mother's room. Naim occupied his old room that his father had built for him on top of the house which had been lying vacant ever since he went first to live in his two rooms in the fields and then moved into the new house with Azra. Ali came to see him as soon he heard of his brother's arrival back in the village. This time he came without fear.

'I want to come back,' he said to Naim.

'Are you not happy there?' Naim asked him.

'Are you joking? I am fed up there.'

'Why, have you not learned any skills?'

'I have. I am a first-class electrician now.'

'Are you? I thought you were a mechanic.'

'I am an electrical mechanic. I can mend big motors.'

'Are you getting more money now?'

'Yes.'

'Then why do you want to leave?'

'Have you not looked at me? You were in prison so that is why you look like a ghost. But why do I look like this?'

Naim gave an embarrassed laugh. 'You have lost some weight, I see.'

'Some weight! I have lost half my life. Aisha has too. We work with machines there and their noise makes me go crazy. It is a prison. There are no trees there.'

'Have they not planted any new trees?' Naim said, wishing to divert Ali. 'Or flowers?'

'They tried. But the earth is not good. Only bushes and hardy creepers grow. There are some old trees, but they are in the bungalows where gora sahibs live.'

'You have not been coming to the village very often, I hear.'

'Don't you know why? Rawal threatened to kill me.'

Naim looked towards his mother, who looked away. 'He has old enmity in his heart,' she mumbled. 'What can I do?'

'But he has a wife and child now. Why is he Ali's enemy?' Naim said to her.

'What can I do?' his mother repeated. 'You were not here. I am only an old woman.' She started crying. 'You have lost everything. Just like your father.'

The room was full of smoke rising from smouldering dung-cakes on which the old woman had cooked a meal of a young chicken for the two men with separate portions of spinach. Naim got up to push the half-closed door wide open to let the air in.

'I will put the rascal right,' he said, and called out, 'Rawal!'

'He is not here,' Ali said to him. 'He went out when he saw me coming.'

'The rascal,' Naim said angrily, 'I will put him right.'

His one hand gripping the other behind his back and looking at the ground in front of his feet, Naim started pacing the room, as if in thought, while Ali finished the last of his butter-spattered roti, wiping clean the plate that had contained spinach cooked with fenugreek and green chillies.

'I had thought,' Naim said, still pacing the floor, 'that you could help me.'

'I will,' Ali said. 'I haven't forgotten how to work the land.'

'I don't mean that,' said Naim. 'I thought different.'

'What?'

'Among the workers. I did some thinking while I was inside. The next stage now is to wake up the labourers, all labourers, railway coolies, grain carriers, everyone who works as a casual worker on daily wages. But we can start with industrial labour. There are many of them in one place and they can be easily organized.'

'Organized for what?'

'More money, overtime payments, paid holidays, those things.'

'I can do that,' Ali said eagerly. 'I have many friends. I can go every day and talk to them.'

'That won't do,' Naim said. 'You have to be inside with them to be effective.'

'You mean,' Ali stood up, 'that I cannot come back?'

Taken aback by Ali's agitated state, Naim said to him calmly, 'Of course you can come back. I just thought that for the time being –'

'The time being? I have waited for you for years. Aisha – she has become barren. Waiting for you. We couldn't come back here for fear –'

'Don't worry about Rawal, he will do as I tell him. He is not bad, he has looked after the land and the house –'

'And your mother,' Ali interrupted him. 'You take his side because he is your mother's nephew.'

'Look, all right, if you do want to come back, listen –'

But Ali wouldn't stop. It was as if the whole vaporous mass of years of misery and fear had solidified into a weight that suddenly dropped on his heart in the face of ruined hope. 'He is your uncle's son. You have made him the owner of everything. I am nothing to you, not your mother's son.' He flung himself out through the door.

'No, no, Ali,' Naim ran after him. But Ali was already across the courtyard. At the main door, Ali stopped and turned.

'And he is living in my mother's room. My room!' he shouted.

'I will get him out of there,' Naim called out. 'Stop, Ali, I will get him out of the house. He is nothing –'

Ali had cleared the threshold and was gone before Naim could finish the sentence. Standing at the outside door, looking at the receding back of his brother running away, he said, almost to himself, 'He is nothing to me . . .'

Tears streaming down his face, Ali ran on until he had no breath left in his chest. He sat down on a large stone by the roadside. He put his hands on the craggy surface of the stone to support himself. A mile outside the village, this piece of rock had always been there. Nobody knew where it came from; there was no sign of its origin, a hill or a valley, for as far as the eye could see in this soft-soil flat land; nor any clue how and by what means the heavy stone, weighing tons, had been brought there. Nobody thought about it either, for the stone had grown to be part of the earth with age and had become invisible. Everything in Ali's mind too had become invisible. The sudden rage having subsided just as quickly as it came, his head was empty of thought. Once his breath levelled out, he got up and started walking. After he had walked for a while, passing other villages on the way, he found himself at the railway station. He sat by the railway line, full of a mass of figureless grief. A train came and he boarded a third-class compartment. He didn't know where it was going, nor did he think about it. There was no room on the wooden bench seats, so he sat on the floor of the compartment. He did not move for hours. At times he dozed off, only to be woken, in the middle of a dream he didn't remember, by the bustle of embarking and disembarking passengers, most of them peasants like him or small shopkeepers from villages and towns. It was a passenger train that stopped everywhere and took twenty-four hours to reach its destination. Ali had been lucky on two points: first, no ticket-checker came to look for 'free' travellers to demand money or throw them out, or if he came it was at a time when Ali had slipped under the nearest seat to sleep in peace for an hour or so, hidden behind and beneath a mass of bodies and left unspotted; second, he had a little money in his pocket to last him a day or two. By the time he left the train at the large and crowded station of the great city of Lahore, he had partially regained his sense of time and place and the shadow on his heart had shrunk to a dense spot, but one that was to stay heavy on his chest for the rest of his life.

He hadn't eaten for nearly a day and a night. He went to a tea stall and asked for a cup of tea. The stallholder, recognizing the accent of Ali's speech, asked him, 'Where do you come from?'

'Roshan Pur. It is near Rani Pur station.'

The stallholder, a man of thirty, immediately extended a hand to Ali. 'Shake hands then,' he said, smiling. 'I come from Ludhiana. I have relatives living near Rani Pur.'

Ali shook his hand.

'My name is Hasan,' the man said. 'What is yours?'

'Ali.'

'Have you come looking for work?'

'Yes,' Ali replied after a pause.

'I came last year. I was lucky. After nine months labouring I got permission from the railways to sell tea from this pitch. I know this town well. There are plenty of labouring jobs here. Have you anywhere to stay? No? Any money? Don't worry, I have a hut of my own by the river. There is only me and my wife. You can stay with me until you make your own hut. You can pay me whatever you figure is proper when you have money. If you are a hard worker you can earn enough by labouring in the markets. You see that road, if you follow it for a mile you get to the fruit and vegetable market. Lots of work there, loading, unloading for wholesalers, carrying for shopkeepers and customers. You are a young man, you will be all right here.

Have another cup, no charge, save your money until you start earning.'

'Thank you,' Ali said shyly.

'It is not every day that one finds someone from home,' Hasan said. 'So far away . . .'

This was the third stroke of luck for Ali. It was, though, not to be of much use to him as events turned out. After Hasan closed up the stall late at night, the two of them walked for miles on dark, abandoned roads and paths to reach the river Ravi. The hut was made of river reeds and cardboard, with irregular planks of wood, some driftwood, tied up cleverly in places to hold the structure together. Across the opening for the door hung a dirty piece of cloth serving as a curtain for privacy. Hasan and Ali ate a simple meal of roti and daal cooked by Hasan's wife. Ali found the husband and wife good-natured and cheerful. Afterwards, Hasan spread a thick sheet of cloth on the ground in one corner for Ali while the couple slept in the other corner by the hearth. So tired out was he that Ali felt as if he had only slept a wink before the sounds of the day awoke him. He accompanied Hasan to the railway station and from there, following his friend's directions, took to the road.

Still in a daze, Ali knew only where he was but not why, nor what he was going to do in that strange place and for how long. He was not going to go to the fruit and vegetable market and do a labouring job, for sure. He took some turnings, carefully making a note of them in his mind so he could remember his way back to the station. He also knew that he didn't have to spend his own money for a day or two, little that he had, for his food and lodging were already taken care of. His belly was full from what he had had, a big roti left over from the previous night, eaten with mango achar followed by a cup of tea at the hut, and another cup at the railway station before he started off. He liked the city. It was the first time he had been in a city as large, clean and well-built as this, and the look of it helped lift his spirits a little bit. The people, men as well as women, looked healthy and strong and they talked to each other loudly in a different Punjabi. Within an hour he found himself in a densely populated area, bazaars running into narrow streets and through to other bazaars. He wondered whether it was the centre of the city. There was an abundance of food shops where very fat men sat deep-frying pakoras of cauliflower, aubergine, onion, long green chillies and potato covered in gramflour batter, grilling fat morsels of lamb marinated in yogurt, mint and coriander and spiced beef mince kebabs on open coal fires; tandoor operators cooking hot naans one after the other with their quick-clapping hands; and sweetmeat makers with huge open-mouthed pans full of jalebis floating in bubbling syrup. The look and smell of all this made Ali wish he had more money in his pocket to buy some of it. He had to console himself with the thought that it was unnecessary because he was full up. He was beginning to enjoy just walking through this big city that he had only heard of, like Dilli, Bombai and Kulkutta. He thought with some bitterness about his brother who had been to all these places and many more. But also, for the first time since he arrived here, he felt a sense of pride that he too had travelled far from home to the centre of a city.

Walking from one street into a bazaar, he saw a change in his surroundings: the bazaar was quieter and, instead of going about their business, people were standing about, talking in low tones and looking towards the corner where the next bazaar began, running across the first. All the shopkeepers had paused in their business and were looking around with apprehension. Ali could not see anything unusual from where he stood. He walked on. As soon as he turned the corner, he was brought to a halt. About a hundred men, members of the Khaksar Movement, stood at attention, four-deep, shoulder to shoulder in straight lines, clad in their distinctive khaki uniforms and carrying clean, shining spades on their shoulders, a symbol of the movement's armed defiance. Facing them, a short distance away, were policemen, most of them Indian constables and sergeants, but heading them were white officers. On both sides of the street, parallel to the Khaksar lines, stood a motley gathering of men, chanting muffled slogans as if they dared not shout with full throat yet wished to express their anger. The Khaksar 'soldiers' stood motionless and mute with their bodies erect, perfectly disciplined in the manner for which they were renowned. Ali walked up the street and stood on one side among the crowd. The stand-off between the Khaksars and the police did not last for long. A white officer advanced from the police ranks. He was in a different uniform. He had no police insignia on his lapels and was wearing a solar hat, although he carried a revolver in a black holster. To Ali he did not look like a policeman either in his bearing or in the way he barked an order.

'Get back,' he said to the massed Khaksars, pushing the air with an open hand.

Nobody moved. The crowd on both sides of the street fell silent. The ranks of the Khaksars seemed to be made of stone with their feet embedded in the earth. The officer, a man of indeterminate years with a red face and a fine sandy moustache on his upper lip, turned redder. He unholstered the revolver and waved it in the air.

'Go back,' he shouted. 'Go. Disperse. Go away. All of you.'

There was a long moment in which the officer glowered at the men before him. He slowly raised his revolver. Suddenly a tall, hefty Khaksar at the head of a row of them broke ranks. He took two steps forward, raised his spade above his head and brought it down with its sharp end on the head of the officer, uttering a loud humph from deep inside his chest to back up the power of his enormous arms. The spade cut through the solar hat and the skull like a cleaver, sinking down to the eyes, and the head parted visibly on one side, an ear hanging lopsidedly under the mangled hat. The white man fell backwards, going slowly down on his feet, his hand automatically firing the revolver in the air. Soldiers appeared from behind with cocked rifles and started firing at point blank range.

It all happened so quickly that the men at the receiving end only moved after they saw bodies falling. Then they fled. They turned back, running, and were hit in the back, or they entered side streets or dived into shops, pursued by the soldiers. Some fell without being hit and crawled under the footboards of shops. Gripped by fear, Ali leaped up the three brick steps leading to the closed door of a house and started thumping on it with both hands. The bullets flying past him pinned him to the wall. Blind with panic, he pushed and kicked at the door, thinking fast at the same time about finding another escape route. Just when he was about to give up, the door was unbolted from inside and a woman's face appeared in the slim crack. Ali pushed the door open and threw himself inside. The woman quickly bolted the door. A woman of fading youth, she looked at the man's face for a moment and uttered a foul oath.

'Run upstairs,' she said, 'motherfucking pig.'

Dark narrow steps climbed straight from the door at a steep angle. Ali ran up, stumbling, falling and scrambling halfway up in his haste. The woman followed. They emerged in a room lit dimly by the sun coming in through dirty squares of glass fitted in two small shut and bolted windows.

'What do you think this is, your fucking mother's house?' the woman asked in anger. 'Who are you?'

Ali looked at her without answering.

'Are you dumb? I am asking you, who are you?'

'I don't know anybody here,' Ali blurted out.

'You are right, I don't know you either. Who are you and why have you barged in here?'

'They are firing guns,' Ali said.

'You think I don't know, you think I am deaf? You wanted to get me killed, you son of a dog?'

'I am a stranger,' Ali said. 'I only came to this city yesterday. I didn't know where to go.'

'So you chose my door. Are you a fool?'

'No,' Ali said, now almost blubbing. 'Forgive me.'

The woman calmed down. 'Sit down, now that you are here.'

She went to the window and peered through the glass. Down in the street the shooting had stopped. The woman had a masculine roughness not just in her voice but in the way she bore herself and walked.

'Why are you sitting on the floor?' she asked Ali. 'Get up, sit in the chair.'

Reluctantly, Ali sat straight up in the armchair.

'Why are you sitting like that?' the woman asked with a hint of a mocking smile. 'Lean back. Are you a peasant?'

'No,' Ali said, 'I am an electrician.'

She went to sit on the bed. 'You came to this city to look for work?'

'Yes.'

'This bitch city is falling down, haven't you noticed? Only dogs will live here. Go back where you came from. Have you any money?'

'N-no.'

'God help me,' the woman said. 'No beggar comes up to my room.'

'I thank you,' Ali said awkwardly.

'Oh, shut up. Have you eaten anything?'

'No. I am not hungry.'

'You don't look very fat. Are you very poor?'

'No – yes.'

'You poor beggar, don't even know what to say.'

There was a loud knock on the door below. The woman ran to the window to look. By the time she hurried back, they were kicking at the door. The woman pulled Ali up by the arm and, shoving him in front of her, went to a door in the back of the room, pushing it open. There were steps leading down. They were equally dark, with a ray of light filtering in through a hairline slit in the door at the bottom of the steps. Ali fell in the dark and rolled down a few steps, hurting his leg and an elbow. The woman caught up with him. A few steps up from the bottom, she slid a plank of wood in the wall to one side, pushed Ali in the dark hole revealed behind the plank and put it back in place. She rushed back up the stairs. The black hole was not a proper hiding place but an irregular space gouged out of the thick wall, perhaps left as such during construction. Hardly able to stand in it, Ali sat down, bunched up in a corner against sharp brick ends sticking out of the surface. The soldiers, having kicked the bottom door down, ran up the stairs and were all around her as she got back up.

'Where is he?'

'Who?'

'The man you let in.'

'I don't know what man you mean –'

The policeman cut her off with a slap on the face. The others were looking around the room, under the bed, inside the almirah, snatching clothes off the pegs and flinging them to the floor.

'Keep your hands off me,' the woman shouted.

The policeman slapped her again, twice, across the face. Then the others joined in. They punched her to the ground and kicked her. 'Get up, slut. Stand up, cheap prostitute . . .'

'Pigs,' she was shouting back, 'dogs.'

A young white officer ran up the steps into the room. The woman spoke to him.

'Are you finished killing men? Have you now started on women?'

Paying scant attention to her or to the men beating her, the officer quickly looked around and went to the door at the back. He opened the door and went down the steps. Three policemen followed him. They descended the steps and opened the door at the bottom, looking to left and right along the back street and came back up.

'I know nothing of any man,' the woman, slumped on the floor, was whimpering under the blows. 'I know nothing, you dirty sons of dogs.'

The officer raised a hand to stop the men. 'Nobody here,' he said, and motioned them to leave. They all followed him out of the room and down into the bazaar.

The woman lifted herself up from the floor, crying silently and pressing her hands to her sides. She went down to shut the door but found it had been kicked off its hinges. She clambered back up and after bolting the door of her room from inside she lay down on the bed, scrunched up on her side with her knees up to her chest, until her sobs stopped. Slowly, she got off the bed, her face screwed up with pain, and went down the back steps. She went all the way down to shut the bottom door and bolt it. On the way back up, she carefully removed the plank and gestured with her head for Ali to come out. Up into the room, she went back to the bed and lay on it, gathered up as before. Ali sat beside the bed on the floor.

'I heard the noise of men,' he said after a while.

The woman did not answer.

'Were they soldiers?'

The woman nodded weakly.

'Did they beat you?'

The woman let out a brief whisper of pain. Hesitantly, Ali put a hand on her arm and started pressing it gently. She shut her eyes and seemed to doze off. Ali rose up on his knees and began slowly massaging her shoulder and the whole length of her side with both hands. It was the first time since his marriage to Aisha that he had put his hands on another woman with such ease. The roughness around the edges of the woman's face when awake had disappeared as if her features had recovered their true contours in sleep. There had been an imperceptible shift in her appearance which made her look comely and innocent. He kept staring at her for a long time, taking the utmost care not to break the rhythm and pressure of his hands in case he woke her, listening to the tiny cries of pain and pleasure she gave out every few minutes or so. Eventually she opened her eyes and sat up. She felt her sides, her legs, and gripped her shoulders.

'I am going to bathe,' she said, softly pushing Ali away. 'Do you want to eat something?'

'No,' Ali said.

She went and looked down through the windowpane and saw an abandoned street with some dead bodies still scattered around and soldiers walking about.

'Dogs,' she said, 'dead dogs,' and went into the bathroom.

She was wearing a nice white shalwar-kameez when she returned, drying her hair with a towel. She went and sat in a chair. 'Get off the floor,' she said to Ali. 'What is the matter with you? Come and sit in the chair. What is your name?'

'Ali. What is yours?'

'Naseem.'

'It is a nice name. Are you feeling all right?'

'I am all right, nothing happens to me. I have taken many blows in my life.'

'Tell me about your life.'

'Why do you ask?' she said severely.

'I want to listen,' Ali said, putting his hand on her arm.

She shrank away from his hand. 'Don't touch me,' she said, but not with anger. 'You have nice eyes. But don't touch me. There is nothing to tell about my life. We lived in a village not far from here. My father worked in the zamindar's fields. The zamindar had his way first with my mother, then with me. My father came out to fight but was killed by the zamindar's men. After some time I ran away from there and came here. A nice woman here took me in as a servant. I was thirteen years old.'

'Have you not gone back to your village since that time?'

'What for?'
'Your mother?'
'Don't want to see her. I remember only my father. He was big and strong, and there was no fear in his eyes. Apart from him, I have not seen a beautiful man.' She got up from the chair. 'I am going to eat something. You want a morsel, or a cup of milk?'
'Yes.'
Ali went and stood by her side as she blew on damp wood to build a fire. Darkness had fallen outside.
'What was the trouble?' Ali asked.
'What trouble?'
'Outside.'
'It is all about mad dogs.'
'Who?'
'Musalmans and Sikhs.'
'What about them?'
'There is a place up the street called Shaheed Gunj. Musalmans want a mosque there and Sikhs want a gurdwara. Mad dogs fighting over mad places.'
The wood had just caught fire when there was a knock at the back door. Naseem swore and got up to go down the steps. She opened the door and stood there talking in whispers to someone. Ali went to stand at the top of the steps. There was a hole in the wall down there where he had spent what seemed a very long time. He felt the hard coins in his shirt pocket. He had found them tied up in a piece of cloth that had been pushed into a hollow between two protruding bricks cutting into his back as he sat there. He had pulled it out and undone the knot. In the pitch dark inside the hole he could not see, but feeling the contents in his hands he knew that they were several large coins. Moving his fingers over them several times, he identified them as silver rupees. This, he thought, was the woman's whole fortune secretly pushed into a hole inside the wall. This did not stop him from taking two rupees from the loose purse before tying it up at the neck and pushing it back in the hollow. Now as he stood listening to the woman below he made up his mind to give back the money. He could now make out the words from the woman's gradually rising voice.
'There is a curfew outside, damn it,' she was saying. 'Can't you wait until tomorrow?'
There was the pleading voice of a man in answer to her.
'At a time like this!' she said. 'Animal!'
After a few more moments, she half shut the door and climbed back up to the top.

'You have to go,' she said to Ali.

Ali looked at her in silence.

'Go,' she said. 'You can come back tomorrow during the day.'

'Let me stay tonight,' Ali begged. 'I will go tomorrow.'

'No,' she said sternly, 'I am busy.'

'There are soldiers –'

'No soldiers in the back street. Go now.'

Her expression had changed, the rough edges to her face and voice had returned. Frightened, Ali quietly went down the stairs and out the door. As he left he passed a bearded man in loose unwashed clothes who went in the door and bolted it from inside. The narrow back street was deserted. He did not know where he was or where he was going, except that he had to keep walking. For the first time since he boarded the train at Rani Pur Ali felt the unbearably aching pull of home.

CHAPTER 26

Before he could decide for himself what to do next, nature felled Naim. One morning he felt more than usually dizzy and lay down on the cot after breakfast. A while later, as he awoke from sleep, he found that he was unable to pick himself off the bed. He told his mother, who ran to the village hakeem. The hakeem, after examining Naim by poking fingers in his flesh and asking questions, declared that it was no different from a horse or a donkey whose body becomes hot-cold after a race and jams up. But the sick animal, he said, gets back on his feet – he flicked his fingers to indicate a speedy recovery – within two days with proper treatment. The treatment was the tried and tested potion, effective for both man and beast, of jackal-meat stock made with herbs supplied by the hakeem. The stock, said the hakeem, had 'hot properties' that would unlock the joints and perk up the flesh. Naim refused point blank to drink the stuff, although Rawal had set a snare and spent a whole night in a field of near-ripe wheat to catch the jackal. Eventually he did catch one, killed and skinned it and brought it home, and the old woman boiled it with herbs without Naim's knowledge. Naim wouldn't have it. Luckily, the stroke was not severe. His speech was not affected and a little voluntary movement began shortly to appear in his limbs. After the discarded jackal, the next best thing Naim's mother could do was to massage the paralysed left side of Naim's body with linseed oil seared with cloves, which she did three times a day, apart from feeding him hot chicken soup. Whether the massage worked or whether the body regained strength from its own natural resources was never definitely established one way or the other. But after two weeks Naim could sit up in bed with the support of pillows behind his back without feeling tired and could even move his leg and the half-arm on his left side a few inches every day by way of exercise. From the very first day, Naim had read all hours to while away the time, holding a book in his unaffected right hand. Books were stacked around him, some on the table and others on the floor beside his bed. That was what he was doing one evening by the light of a lamp when Azra appeared at the door.

It was not until a fortnight after Naim fell ill that Azra got the news from the munshi who had gone to Delhi, ostensibly to show the crop accounts to Roshan Agha's main munshi, called the manager, but also to let Azra know about Naim's condition. She had known of his release from prison and had been thinking – fearfully because Naim had not contacted her – of going to Roshan Pur. After the munshi's visit, she left for the village and went straight to the big house, which had been not just abandoned but neglected for years, for the servants, although they still received wages in money and kind for looking after the house, had taken to working in the fields to earn extra money. There was only the loyal old man who lived in one of the rooms in the outhouse. Confused and frightened, he ran out to collect the servants from the village and the fields. Azra, sitting on the thick roots, visible above the earth, of the great bohr tree, heard, as from afar, the sounds of doors and windows opening and shutting and of furniture being dusted and dragged about. She sat there, refusing the offer of tea or a meal, until the sun went down. The house was eventually cleaned and aired, made ready for her. But she did not go in. Leaving behind the small heap of fallen leaves she had made while she sat under the large tree and accompanied by the old servant, she came out of the main gate and headed for the village. The house was never to be lived in again.

It was evening when Azra stepped into Naim's house for the first time in her life. She lingered at the door of the courtyard. She could see the shadowy figure of Naim's mother, whom she had only met once before in all those years, moving about in the lamp-lit room. As Azra stood in the darkened doorway, the old woman came out and went into the next dimly lit room. On trembling legs, Azra crossed the courtyard and reached the door of the first room. Naim was sitting up in bed with his back to the door, reading a book. Hearing the footsteps, he said without turning his head, 'I don't want the massage just yet. Give me something to eat.' Hearing no answer nor a shuffle of feet, he turned his head to look. For a few long moments, inhaling successive short breaths, Naim stared at Azra's figure standing absolutely still in the doorway of his room as though it were a vision he had longed for from a former life, disbelieving it. The book fell from his hand on to his stomach as he tried to turn over to face the door, but his body would not cooperate. Azra walked into the room and sat down on the edge of the bed, her body touching his. She put both hands on his shoulders and gently pushed him back on to the pillows. Her hands resting on him and Naim gripping her arm with his one hand and making a supreme attempt to lift his left half-arm to touch her with it but failing, they kept looking at one another in silence until the old woman appeared carrying a cup of warm linseed. It took her a minute to recognize the woman sitting on her son's bed. She smiled a simple peasant's smile and sat down at the foot of the bed. She rubbed a little oil on her palms and started to massage her son's leg. Neither Naim nor Azra, locked in a gaze, paid any attention to her. Naim's eyes were once more seeing an image of the old Azra, but Azra saw that her husband's hair had receded almost halfway over his head and the several days' growth of beard on his face was more than half white. Wordlessly, Azra bent over and put her face close to Naim's. He kissed her on the brow, the cheeks and the lips but did not linger, raising her face with his hand to about a foot from his. Minute after minute, with their eyes alone, they renewed their acquaintance, until Naim's mother's hands became hot from rubbing and she left the room, taking the pot of oil with her.

'You have,' Azra spoke her first words, 'lost some hair.'

'No,' Naim laughed. 'A lot.'

'And your eyes,' she said, 'have become wrinkled.'

'Because they didn't see you for so long.'

'Are you cross with me that I didn't come?'

'You came once.'

'Only once,' she said with sadness.

'That was no place for you. Once was enough.'

'No, I should have come.'

'No, no.' Naim was quiet for a moment. 'You know, the hardest thing for me was the night. I kept busy during the day, but the night without you was like – like a mountain.'

'A mountain?'

'One that had to be climbed.'

'You spent many nights alone when you were here.'

'It is not the same. The place I am talking about has nights – nights – oh, I can't put it into words – like stone.'

'The words?'

'No, nights. Like they are made of stone and you have to scale them with nothing to hold on to and only on the other side is another day.'

'You know, Naim,' Azra said, 'a strange thing happens to me. Have I told you this before?'

'What?'

'This strange thing that always happens to me?'

Naim laughed. 'You have told me many strange things that happen to you.'

'No, this: I can't imagine your face.'

'What do you mean?'

'I know your face as well as my own – no, as well as my own hands. But as soon as you go away, I can't remember it, can't picture it in my mind. No matter how I try, I can't bring your features back to memory.'

'Well, I have been away a long time.'

'No, it has always happened.'

'From the very beginning?'

'Yes.'

'That means,' Naim said, smiling, 'that you didn't love me.'

'No,' Azra cried, pressing her hands down on Naim's chest, 'seriously, I have never understood this. I can picture everything of yours, your feet, legs, the way you walk, even your voice, the whole figure but not the face. Does it happen to you as well?'

'No, never,' Naim replied. 'Your face, your voice, they are always there, they alone carried me through all the stony nights.'

Naim's mother came into the room, carrying a tray on which she had two bowls of chicken shorba, mango pickle in a separate saucer and hot rotis wrapped in clean cloth. Carefully, she placed the tray on the table and walked out soundlessly, avoiding looking at her son and Azra, neither of whom looked at the food or at her.

'Uncle Ayaz died,' Naim said.

'I heard,' Azra answered.

'He was not happy with me. Never came to see me in gaol, not once. A few days after he died his old servant Aslam came to visit and gave me the news. Some time later, I dreamed about my uncle. He was standing at the door of the prison as I was walking out a free man. He handed me his favourite walking stick and walked away without saying a word. Now here is something that would astonish you, as it did me. When I came back to Roshan Pur, Aslam came to see me. He told me that my uncle had left his house in Delhi to me but all the household goods to him, his old servant, except just one thing – the silver-topped cane. He had brought it with him along with the papers for the house. Aslam had never mentioned it to me when he came to visit me in gaol. I asked him and he said that he didn't know about it until later when my uncle's lawyer read the will.'

'Is that true?'

'Absolutely true.'

'Amazing. He must have loved you very much.'

A shadow of pain appeared in Naim's eyes. 'Yes,' he said.

'Khala died last year,' Azra said.

'Did she? I am sorry.'

Suddenly, Azra took his face in her hands and said, 'Naim, promise me one thing.'

'What?'

'Say that you promise.'

'All right, I promise.'

'Come with me to Delhi.'

Taken by surprise, Naim looked at her without answering.

'Won't you?'

'What for?'

'You need proper treatment.'

'I am getting better,' Naim said, making a little movement in his left leg.

'You are deceiving yourself, Naim. You won't fully recover like this, and not here. You need a good doctor's treatment, in a hospital if necessary. Look, you promised.'

Naim was quiet for a few moments, avoiding Azra's gaze. There was an intensity in her face that he found himself powerless to resist. In the end, he closed his eyes and nodded. Azra lowered her head and began rubbing it on his chest.

Until now, Naim's life seemed to have led him by its circumstances not from the front but from behind, like a man being pushed along in a storm by gusts of strong wind, limiting his own movements to the resistance of his limbs. Now, in a life circumscribed by necessity, he had entered a different world – the unfamiliar territory of the mind. He could do no more than read and think. It was as if a skylight in the ceiling, cut through the roof – at which he stared most of the day and night – had opened up. Into this he was to step on hesitant, fearful feet, for the place beyond was in utter darkness, and he was like a child who presses himself on hands and knees against invisible barriers until his eyes begin to make out the shapes of things about him and then he stands up, extends his arms in front and walks, becoming familiar with the blackness. Occasionally, he indulged in dialogue, often with himself, at times with his doctor but rarely with Azra.

Dr Ansari, a cultivated man, renowned too for his political activities, and a friend of Roshan Agha, visited once a week to examine the sick man who lay in Azra's room in a separate bed, and he usually left Naim with a thought. At times it would be something as troubling as this:

'Are you a believer, Naim?'

'Believer in what?'

'God. Religion.'

'Why do you ask?'

'Because even in this day and age when science is making great advances and machines are taking over the work of men's hands and feet, belief in religion is still a force that a man can bring to bear on his life.'

'Which religion are you talking about?'

'Doesn't matter which, the main religions all have a common aim.'

'Paradise?'

'No, the provision of comfort and hope.'

'Even in illness?'

'Especially in illness. Let me explain. Illness, long-term illness, as for example yours, can drive a man to dark thoughts, sometimes to hopelessness. Religious belief can pull you out of that condition. It provides you with a focus for positive thought. The worst thing in a state of illness, as I have often said to you, is a negative attitude. External application of medicine alone cannot do the job. Putting it purely in medical terms, it can reduce the agitation of the mind and bring down the blood pressure.'

'So you advise me to use religion like some kind of pill?'

'That, my dear man, is exactly what I call negative attitude.'

'Don't you think I am a bit old to turn myself to this kind of thing at this stage?'

'You are never, never too old to become a believer.'

'Can I get back all that I have lost?'

'No one can. But you can start a new life. The past doesn't exist if you are a believer. There is only the future – a new future.'

When Dr Ansari left, Naim kept thinking about this – although he did smile at the doctor's passionate phrase, 'a new future'. The doctor's speeches sparked off trains of thought, but his vehemence had the opposite effect on Naim. The renewal not of life but a hollowed-out memory cast a shadow over his brow. 'What has belief in God or religion or whatever got to do with me, my everyday life, with me and Azra, she who picks up my arm and leg and exercises them but is lost for words, except the renewed concern she shows in her every movement? Who is she doing it for? For me or for herself? Why is it always like this between me and her, passion flaring with blinding light and then dying quickly, like a soft, hollow driftwood fire? Belief! What place does it have in lives that have gone wrong? All she ever says now is "when", "when I get better", "when I will walk into the world", into life again, when, when – the future, the coming into new life. What about the dead, what shall we say about them? Having made a compromise with death once and for all, why should we make any other? Belief! What has it got to do with love?'

Yet slowly, over months and years and without taking the good doctor's advice other than by exercising his muscles, Naim entered the physical world once again. Gradually the unfeeling flesh moved, dripping strength into the joints, and one day he stood up and walked. As he tread the floor, hobbling a step at a time on crutches, and later, leaning heavily on Azra, learning to pace the room and then the balcony outside it, later still shifting his weight from Azra's shoulder to a strong walking stick, he felt as if he had been born again. Born again or not, he had none the less acquired an altered vision of the world in which he had come to accept, with diminished resentment, his place in the house of a man he had disliked and dependence on a woman who, he thought, had once loved him.

It was a hot evening as, supported on the right-hand side by his stick and held lightly on the left by Azra, he came descending step by single step down the staircase and on to the long veranda, then on to the lawn for his prescribed daily walk. 'Can't we have a room downstairs?' he asked.

'I don't want to ask for it,' Azra replied. 'Besides, Dr Ansari said climbing the stairs is good for you.'

'Roshan Agha has offered you a whole suite of rooms on the ground floor.'

Azra looked up sharply. 'Who told you?'

'Pervez.'

'When?'

'He came up to see me a few days back.'

'Oh, so he is trying to be nice to you, is he?' Azra said, looking through the corner of her eyes to the far side of the lawn where Pervez, his wife, their friend Khalid and Khalid's wife sat around a table playing cards.

'He has visited me a few times,' Naim said.

'You never mentioned it to me before.'

'Didn't think about it. Why?'

'Oh . . .' Azra shivered as with revulsion, 'he's so two-faced. And that woman, his wife, cold fish.'

'Aren't you being a bit harsh on them?' Naim said to her.

'Naim,' she said, a look of shock on her face, 'how can you say that? You know he hasn't spoken to me for years. And you know quite well why. He has no right to see you behind my back.'

Sudden black clouds began crowding the sky and gusts of wind shook the trees in the garden. The cards flew off Pervez's table and the two men ran to pick them up from the grass. The women at their table laughed. Naim looked towards them and lifted his walking stick to answer their hands waving to him in greeting. Azra turned her back on them and started back to the house.

'Are we going back already?' Naim asked her as she led him on to the veranda.

'I think it is going to rain,' Azra replied, hurrying him away.

Darkness quickly fell. Laboriously climbing the steps, Naim was out of his breath by the time he reached his room and dropped himself on his bed.

'I need to do something,' he said after a while.

'What?'

'Something. Anything. I am fed up with having nothing to do.'

'You are not strong enough yet,' Azra said to him.

'I will never be strong enough if I don't do something.'

'You want to go back to Roshan Pur?' Azra asked. 'We can go, if you want. You don't need much medication now, just exercise.'

Head bowed, Naim sat on the bed for a few moments. Then he shook his head. 'No,' he said, in a faint but definite voice, 'I am all right here.'

Amazed, Azra went and sat by him at the edge of the bed. 'You want me to talk to Roshan Agha?'

Naim nodded silently.

Azra, now near bewilderment, made as if she was going to bury her face in his chest but stopped short, looking closely at his face. 'You never go to see Papa,' she said questioningly. 'He is not well.'

'I will,' said Naim, his face beginning to contort. 'I will go along with whatever he says.'

Azra, still unable to contain her astonishment, got up and started, with brief, nervous strokes of a feather-duster, to clean the little glass, copper, bronze and gold-plated ornaments, statuettes and replicas of birds and buildings that lined the mantelpiece. For the first time she had heard her husband speak in a way that signified a decline in his challenge to her world. Strangely, it upset her. She looked at the proud, handsome head of Naim bowed low and felt as if he had finally withdrawn from her the small, defiant pride that she had won from her union with him.

'Why don't you let the servants dust the room?' Naim asked her.

'I will not allow them in here. Don't you see how they look at you? They all pity you. And me. Do you think I get pleasure out of having nothing to do with Pervez or his wife? But I hate them for the way they treat you.'

'They treat me all right, I think.'

'Yes, politely, civilly, the way we were taught to behave with – with – never mind, you can't see it, but I can. You were not brought up like we were . . .' Even as the words left her mouth, she was startled by the sound of them. She froze, her hand holding the feather-duster, looking at Naim with unblinking eyes and expecting the old anger to rise in him. Instead Naim raised his head as if it were a heavy object.

'I am sorry,' he said, 'I have spoiled your relations with your own family.'

His words broke the spell. An unaccountable rage rose up in Azra. 'You couldn't spoil them if you tried,' she shouted at him. 'I have done that myself.'

Then just as quickly she fell silent. She dropped the feather-duster to the floor, went round and sat down on the other side of the bed, covered her face with her hands and began, as if mourning a lost treasure, silently to weep.

CHAPTER 27

Tired of waiting for promotion, Ali moved two hundred miles north to a newly built cement factory. On the basis of his years of experience and a successful test, he got a job as an electrician. His new job earned him more money plus other amenities such as a small kitchen and a latrine attached to his one-room living 'quarter'. These facilities gave little comfort to Aisha, however, for whom the distances proved too great to bridge. From the cloth mill she had been able go to her nearby village to visit her mother whenever she felt like it. The journey from the cement factory was possible only once a year, if that. The unfathomable disease which was the withering of her soul drove her to bed, where she spent most of the day and night, eventually losing all desire to eat. In the end she became virtually bedridden.

With her appetite Ali's also disappeared. For him work in the factory offered only the prize of 'promotion', and he did his job more or less competently by habit alone. His day began like this: he rose early to make tea, gave a cupful to Aisha and had one for himself, then went to the factory. In the beginning he used to take with him a piece of left-over roti which he ate with a cup of tea in the middle of the day. As he lost his hunger, he began getting through the day on just the one cup of tea from the canteen, until he went home and cooked a roti. He could never get the hang of swinging the dough ball between the palms of hands to make real chapattis, an art that belonged properly only to women who learned it in childhood. As a result he made a thick roti, which was just as well as the two of them needed no more than one. He boiled vegetables on alternate days and ate them with the roti, using a cup of milk instead on the other days. After he had finished three-quarters of the roti, he put the rest of it by Aisha's side. She took a morsel from it and complained of stomach ache and nausea. Ever since Ali stopped taking a roti to the factory for his midday meal, Aisha had insisted that he break up whatever was left into small pieces and throw them outside the house for the sparrows to eat in the morning. She believed that the birds, and the little sparrows especially, would bless her and God would make her well again. It didn't work, nor did the medicine that the 'doctor', actually only a compounder, who visited her once a week, this being another of the amenities that came with Ali's job, gave her to take twice a day. No matter how tired Ali was at the end of the day or how late he was getting to go to work in the morning or how much resistance Aisha put up to the taking of the medicine, he administered it to her first thing in the morning and again upon arrival home from work before he started anything else. Aisha wasted away in her cot until she became almost invisible under the sheets. Ali endured; he lost all the fat on his body but the grain and milk and greens that he forced himself to eat at the end of the day prevented his hunger from eating into his muscle.

He had one friend at work, a young labourer named Salim who lived with his mother in a cardboard hut they had erected some distance from the factory. The boy had attached himself to Ali in the hope of learning the trade from him if and when the chance arose in the factory for him to become electrician's mate. Salim brought a roti with him every day, tied up in a piece of cloth, which he ate at noon with wild berries and other such fruit as he could pick off bushes and trees on his way to work. Quite often he offered Ali a piece of bread or a few berries which Ali sometimes took and nibbled at. Salim never took his leftovers, whether roti or berries, back home with him but offered them to whoever was around, and if there were no takers he fed them to the factory dogs and cats, before shaking the crumbs off the dirt- and fat-soaked piece of cloth and tying it tightly round his head. Afterwards he would break into a simple song till the half-hour break was over and it was time to return to work. Salim's hopes for a step up in the world came and went during a brief labour strike that occurred in the factory.

Everybody knew that Ali was the one man in the whole works who could live on next to nothing and yet perform his duties. For this reason they gave him the title of 'Saeen', meaning in simple terms, Man of God, although Ali had never had any reason to be close to God, much less understand it. But there was one quality that had all the workers fix their sights on him as a possible leading player in what was going to come about. It was this: two years into Ali's work in the cement factory a labour union had been formed which, with the help of outside agents, had decided to strike in favour of their demands for better wages and facilities. The agents, some of them political workers of the Congress Party, had advised the labour force to go for a hunger strike as they did not think a simple walk-out would achieve much. They solicited Ali's agreement.

'Saeen, with you sitting on a hunger strike we can get what we want in two days, at the most three. What do you say?'

Ali stayed silent, saying neither yes nor no; he simply didn't feel involved in the affair.

'Saeen, Saeen, no harm will come to you, no harm at all, we know that . . .' they pleaded.

They did not get a nod from Ali. But they had already assumed that when the time came the 'silent Saeen' would join them.

The day arrived. The managers were well informed about the strike and were joined by a young man from Delhi, the son of one of the three brothers who owned the factory, for the occasion. In addition they had arranged for a police presence. About a dozen constables, carrying no firearms but simple lathis, led by a head constable from the local police station walked around the premises, going in and out of the main gate and generally keeping an eye on things. The workers of the four o'clock shift left their places without being relieved of their duties by the men on the next shift, who had in turn been stopped outside the gate by the leaders of the strike. They had all gathered outside the main gate, raising slogans against the Management. Ali went up to the gate and stopped. The workers outside called out to him.

'Saeen, come on out, your shift is finished. Run, Saeen, run, don't worry, there will be no hunger strike, we will win anyway.'

Ali did not run. Nor did he go with the foreman who had come up behind him to ask him, politely, to come back to the millhouse. Just before the police, gauging the situation, shut the gate and locked it from inside, young Salim broke away from the crowd of strikers and ran back into the factory. He stood by Ali's side, looking up at him. Half of the constables were outside the gate, keeping order but not otherwise interfering with the men. The rest of the police were within the boundary of the factory. Ali stood a few feet inside the locked gate, listening to an outside leader, a political activist lawyer from the nearby town, make a speech to the strikers.

'Brothers, labourers, the time has come for you to offer a sacrifice for the sake of just rewards in return for the labour you give. Until today, you have given your sweat. Today you are required to give blood. Hundreds of labourers and hundreds of donkeys have together spilled their sweat on this earth to raise these great factories, and the owners think there is no difference between you and the donkeys. But no. Can a donkey push dry stone into a crusher at one end and draw cement from the other? No, brothers, men do that, and you are men, not donkeys. And who buys the cement that you make? Not you. In your villages you and your old fathers and mothers live in huts made of mud and reeds while the cement goes to build great houses in big cities. Until today you have toiled for your masters' bellies. Today you are asking for the rights of your own bellies . . .'

At this point the crowd, getting restless, began chanting slogans. They started off simply with shouted phrases of 'We want bread' and 'Money to buy meat' which gradually became more complex as 'Long Live Inqalab', finally sloping off to the simplest yet emotion-packed religious ones as 'Allah-o-Akbar' and 'Hari Krishan Maharaj Ki Jai', which, although they had no connection with the business in hand, served to lift the workers' spirits to a higher level and inflame their passions. Some people turned round and tried to coax Ali to scale the gate and jump over to their side. He did not seem to hear their pleas. The foreman came up again and, taking hold of his arm, led him back into the millhouse.

'Toadies!' a few voices taunted him and Salim from behind. Entering the millhouse with a few other men that were rounded up, Salim and Ali got separated. Ali went and sat on the plinth of the grinding mill. A short while later, Salim came in, jumping up and down.

'Saeen, I have been looking for you.' In the roar of the grinding mill, Salim was shouting with excitement. 'I will be made electrician's mate, your mate. The manager told me himself, do you know, himself!' He sat down beside Ali.

The foremen, the engineers, the assistant managers, together with the general manager and the young son of one of the owners, were bustling in and out of different buildings – from the crusher through the grinding mills, the kiln, the boilerhouse, the workshops and the packing plant, making sure that the skeleton staff kept the plant running. 'Keep the chimney smoking' was their slogan, resounding in each building through which they passed. The electrical foreman, Ali's immediate superior, appeared at the door of the millhouse and shouted to him. The foreman's voice got lost in the ear-splitting noise of the huge revolving mills. He then put two fingers in his mouth and blew a whistle that reached Ali's ears. The foreman moved a hooked finger to call Ali out, leading him to the kiln platform. The three-hundred-foot-long kiln, where the pulverized mixture of limestone and clay was burnt at fourteen hundred degrees centigrade, was the heart of the factory. To make perfect clinker in the kiln was the job of the 'burners', men highly valued as skilled technicians. But the burners, not being supervisory staff, were out with the strikers and the kiln was being managed by the lone head burner, a man renowned for being able to look at the kiln from a hundred yards and tell the temperature inside it. Ali's foreman left him as help with the head burner and went away. The head burner told him to go and fetch a cup of tea for him from the canteen. Good food – meat, vegetables, rice and hot rotis – was being prepared in the canteen by the head cook, who was running around with great urgency to manage several pots on the boil at the same time. Tea was constantly on the hot stove and was provided, along with as much food as anyone could eat, free of cost to those who had stayed behind. Ali got two cups of tea, one for himself and the other for the head burner. They had barely finished their tea when the whole gang of officers climbed the few steps to the kiln platform: young 'Seth', the general manager, engineers, assistant engineers, general foreman, everyone. They were talking about the negotiations that their representatives had been conducting with the strike leaders. The most senior technical man among them took the welder's shade from the head burner and looked through the green glass into the blinding white heat where the slowly revolving kiln turned the pulverized powder into grape-sized round balls of incandescent clinker. Then the general manager made a brief speech.

'Well done, men. You have sided with the management and stayed beyond your duty time. For this you will be rewarded. We have one mission and one only, and that is to keep the kiln chimney smoking. With your help we shall show the traitors outside the gate how to run a factory with the help of a few faithful men. We will lock them out for ever. Just remember: *Keep the chimney smoking*. That alone will defeat the mischief of the slogan raisers.'

By the time he finished, a few labourers had brought some tables and chairs and laid them out on the kiln platform. Then they went back to fetch the food. There were three different kinds of food and they were all meat dishes, even the rice fried and cooked as pulao with lamb. The assistant engineers and foremen, who were not properly 'management', sat beside the higher-ups with looks of gratitude on their faces. But the lower-grade workers, even after much persuasion, refused to occupy the chairs alongside their superiors, although they accepted the food and sat on the ground to eat it. They couldn't believe what they were witnessing: these men, near-gods to them, whose place was way up there in the clouds, were sharing their food with the lowly, the ones who were as dirt and hardly deserved better; and sharing not only food but also talk, speaking to those sitting near their feet on the ground with pleasant, affectionate faces and cheery words. Like friends, the labourers thought; like friends. The meal over, the labourers took it back, the utensils, the spoons, the dishes, trays, tables and chairs. Ali joined them hauling the things back to the canteen.

He hadn't eaten much and was not feeling joyful like the others; during all the agitation, he thought of Aisha and remembered that he had missed giving her the second dose of her medicine. He hung around the canteen for an extra free cup of tea. As darkness fell, he wanted to go home. He found himself in the midst of pandemonium as he went back to where he had been directed: the kiln wasn't turning. Ali sprinted the last hundred yards to the point where everyone, from the general manager to the labourer, was crowding. The electrical motor that turned the main shaft of the kiln had gone dead. It was a hot end-of-May evening that made it impossible to go near the motor, for this was a spot that made men's faces burn even in the severest of winters. They all stood a few yards away from it, leaving the foreman and a 'senior' electrician, their heads and faces wrapped in their shirts and other dirty rags from the workshop, to work on it. The heat was so intense that the two men weren't even sweating, their bare bodies dry and roasted red.

'Where were you?' the foreman shouted at Ali. Silently, Ali tore off his shirt, wound it round his head and face and jumped on to the concrete plinth of the motor. Not until then did he see and recognize a third man, masked like the other two, struggling with a large nut on the side of the motor. It was Salim. Ali tried to get the spanner out of his hand, but Salim wouldn't yield. Nor would the nut. Under the eyes of not only the electrical foreman but all the owners of the whole factory as far as he knew, Salim was reluctant to give up the job for which he had volunteered. Straining his sinewy body, his chest lowered on the spanner handle and his fingers jammed on it, shoulder and arm muscles rippling like long thin fishes and his face contorted with effort, Salim was determined to move the nut that had seized as if this was a job for which he had been preparing himself for his entire life. Ali put his strength behind it as well by placing his hand on top of Salim's and pushing. The nut proved unmovable. The firing of the kiln was stopped and the smoke coming from the chimney at the other end got progressively thinner.

As the slogans of the strikers, still there outside the gate after five hours, got louder upon seeing the smoke disappear, so the faces of the officers grew more frantic. The chief engineer got so out of control that he started accusing the electrical engineer of being 'the most useless man in the world', disregarding the fact that the man might be good for some other things in his life. As the chief engineer's angry voice rose, so also did Salim's ceaseless efforts. Ignoring Ali's advice to let the machine cool down a little before going any further, he continued to wrestle with the obstinate nut, as if his promotion to electrician's mate would come there and then if only he could prise open the death-bite of the nut-and-bolt teeth with the last ounce of his strength. Suddenly, in the middle of a pull, Salim's hand slipped off the long spanner handle and he fell over on top of the motor. He didn't spring back up. For a few seconds they watched him silently as he lay with both arms spread wide on the hot casing of the motor. Then the realization came that Salim had simply keeled over.

Three men lifted the boy's collapsed body and laid it carefully, face up, on the ground. In Salim's bloodless face his eyes were half-open, fixed in a terrible gaze which seemed to look at nothing beyond the eyelids. Someone ran to fetch the 'doctor' from the works dispensary. The young rotund, bespectacled owner's son threw a glance up at the smoke stack whose emission of curling white cloud had turned to thin black strands, dispersing forlornly into the air. He turned his eyes away from it and had a word with the general manager, who in turn spoke to his assistant. The assistant manager, taking the chief accountant and an engineer with him, walked quietly away. The man from the dispensary arrived. He examined the unconscious Salim and shook his head in despair. The men put the body on a trolley and wheeled it towards the dispensary.

Within an hour, the assistant general manager and his team of negotiators had reached an agreement with the leaders of the striking workers. The gates were opened and the mob of workers poured in, chanting the usual slogans. Not many of their demands had been met, yet they were carrying two members of the management team on their shoulders in victory. The negotiators had proved cleverer than their labour opponents, giving away little but playing upon the gratitude of the lowly for merely being treated as equals across the bargaining table. Ali had earlier wandered off towards the main gate after they had removed Salim's body from near the kiln. He met the incoming crowd on the way. Few noticed him in their euphoria. He walked out of the gate into the night, thinking of Aisha without emotion.

CHAPTER 28

Anees Rahman was Personal Assistant to a member of the Indian Legislative Assembly – MLA (Centre) for short. He was both a relative of one of the only two Muslim members of the Viceroy's Executive Council, and a member of the ruling family of a small state in central India. Although he lived comfortably on a stipend from his ancestral state, he had no personal fortune by way of landholding or money. All he owned as property was two houses, one in Delhi and the other in a picturesque village situated on the banks of the river twenty miles from the capital. The only other thing of value he possessed was a fine education. Supported by his family, he had gone to England in the early thirties and qualified as Barrister at Law. He never practised the profession; he dabbled in politics but gave that up after a while. Helped by family contacts, he acquired his present non-governmental position and settled down in it. Although some years younger, he had been a friend of Roshan Agha and his family for many years. He had known Naim, but only slightly, barely a handshake or two and an Assalam-o-Alaikam. When Azra spoke to him, he agreed to take on Naim in a position in his office at the Assembly – rather less, it was understood, to get Naim to do any real work than to provide him with a place to go to each day and a routine to follow. Naim got an entry pass to the Assembly and a desk of his own in an office that he shared with three other staff. Once he got settled in, however, Naim found himself more and more involved in conversations initiated by Anees Rahman, and not always regarding work; Anees had found Naim an attractive listener to the outpourings of his active mind. Over a period of time the two men developed a personal friendship.

Azra had finally agreed to take a suite of rooms – a drawing room and two bedrooms – on the ground floor. Naim had amassed a great collection of books on various subjects. From books of general interest in the first year of his confinement, he had gone on to specialized reading, picking up books on a single topic at a time until he exhausted it according to his liking and ability, before going on to the next: religion, history, general science, ending with philosophy. This did not particularly clear his mind about anything; what he got out of it was a permanent habit of reading, no longer now for the sake of acquiring knowledge so much as to use it as a veil between himself and the world. Meticulously following doctor's orders, Azra would be seen by the early risers in the neighbourhood of Roshan Mahal taking Naim for a walk, her hand on his left shoulder while he carried his old walking stick in his right hand. Naim had almost fully recovered, his limp nearly gone, but like his reading the stick in his hand and Azra by his shoulder had become a comforting habit, one that served to hide his embarrassment from onlookers. On their return, they had breakfast together, the only occasion after the walk in the morning when they sat face to face, although they exchanged no more than a few words. Naim habitually skipped the midday meal in order to control the weight he had put on during his confinement, causing him high blood pressure. Azra always took her evening meal with Roshan Agha who, suffering from chronic diabetes and heart problems, was almost permanently confined to his room. Naim had dinner in his room and afterwards read late into the night. They had separate bedrooms.

The country was in turmoil. The Cripps Mission had failed and Stafford Cripps's offer of freedom 'after the war is over' had been rejected by the Congress Party. At the same time the 'Quit India' Movement was launched, which engaged in sabotage. Hearing reports of the blowing up of railway lines and suchlike, Naim was reminded of a part of his distant past but felt no movement in his blood. He had even given up reading the newspaper. Only Azra felt momentarily excited by it, reading the papers out aloud to Naim at breakfast. Getting a feeble response from Naim, she gave up after a few days. The war was at its height and a famine was raging in Bengal.

Anees Rahman, a short, stocky bull of a man, moved with the agility of an athlete, his energy never allowing him to stay in one position for long. In the middle of looking at some papers, he would jump up and go to the window to look outside, often talking quietly to himself while gesticulating busily with his hands. Back at his desk, he would no sooner settle down than leave his seat and go to the outer office to speak to one of his staff. He had also had Naim's desk moved to his own private office, placing Naim's seat opposite his own so that he could talk to him without having to get up.

One day he invited Naim to his house in the village for a stay over the weekly holiday. He picked Naim up at the end of office hours on Saturday afternoon and took him straight to the village. The journey took less than an hour. The village, although situated only a short distance from the river, was built on high ground, so that it remained safe from flooding when the river burst its banks during the monsoons. Anees's house was right at the top of the hill from where the eye could see mile after mile of the plains on both sides of the river. The whitewashed house was simple but solidly built, with large gardens and old trees, lush green lawns sloping away from the front veranda of the house. The two men sat in cane chairs under the shade of an amaltas tree. The air was very still. There was not a sound to be heard, not even the chirp of a bird in the garden, except for the hiss of water coming faintly over from the great river that somehow had the effect of increasing the silence. Naim thought it was the quietest place he had been to, and mentioned it to Anees.

'Yes,' Anees said. 'I have a rather agitated nature. I come here to calm myself.'

A servant laid out tea on the table. The sun was still up. After tea, Anees asked the servant to get his fishing tackle out. Within fifteen minutes they were sitting on two low wooden stools by the river bank with Anees's line in the water, the sinker bobbing on the surface and a small pot of squirming earthworms, dug up by the servant, by their side. Naim noticed the change in Anees: he had become quiet. Sitting absolutely still, gazing at the slow movement of the broad plank of water sparkling in the late afternoon sun, he seemed to Naim, for the first time since he had known him, to be in a reflective mood. There was a large family of refugees from Bengal living in the open on the bank of the river. They had not erected a shelter, nor did they appear to be doing anything towards the provision of food for themselves and their several children. There were only some rumpled dirty sheets on the ground by way of bedding.

Nodding his head in their direction, Naim asked, 'Aren't the village people doing something for them?'

'They get cooked food from the village,' Anees replied. 'But they don't want to stay. They are moving on to the city. At least that is what they keep saying. I think they have lost their sense of direction.'

Naim laughed drily. 'God help them.'

'What has God to do with it?' Anees said, unleashing another of his speeches on the unsuspecting Naim. 'It's a man-made disaster. And only man will suffer.'

A bit surprised, Naim slowly nodded, 'Yeees.'

'You have only seen the living,' Anees said, 'I have seen the dead in

Bengal. Piles and piles of them. If you can spare a day's supply of rice, you sell it. If you haven't, you beg. The difference between rich and poor is a handful of rice. No, not between rich and poor, actually between life and death. We live our lives according to simple rules. When we are young we read history and come to know of the disasters that befell our ancestors. From these lessons, we deduce some rules. Look before you leap, that sort of thing. My father gave me a book called *Golden Rules*. Did you read the book of golden rules when you were young?'

'I was never young,' Naim said, laughing.

'When we grow up we see that there is no such thing as a regular shape of history. Come floods, come epidemics, come famine. But they are never the same. Like each life, each disaster is different. There is a fixed pattern, it's called helter-skelter.' He laughed ironically. 'In order to form a reasonable pattern, we invent the idea of justice. When that doesn't work, we go further into helter-skelter and invent God. I will tell you one thing: there are no golden rules.'

This was yet another aspect of Anees that Naim witnessed: the man, no longer restless, sitting patiently like an old angler, giving quiet words to his desperation.

Later, as their friendship grew, it became, at Anees's insistence, a regular feature of Naim's life to accompany Anees to his village house once every two or three weeks. Gradually, there came a point when, one day, Anees told Naim the story of his life. He was thought of as a minor aristocrat, Anees said, an idea carefully cultivated by himself and others. He was nothing of the sort. He had been disinherited because his mother had been insufficiently respectable to qualify as a proper wife to his father, so she stayed in the position of a concubine all her life. The old nawab only married her on his deathbed, a marriage that became the subject of a dispute in the courts of law, initiated by the legitimate heirs, on the basis that the dying man was in no fit state to have reached a rational decision. In order, eventually, to avoid publicity, said Anees, he renounced all his claims in return for the grant of two houses and a reasonable sum of money as a yearly stipend. He had never, he said, been back to the state, although his wife and two children were being kept and well looked after there by the present ruler.

Naim, hesitant though he was in the beginning, now began to look forward to these trips to the house on the river bank in company with Anees, recognizing in him a companion soul in trouble. He also liked the place, as it reminded him of his own village. Being neither a believer – in anything! – nor the opposite but, as it were, shuffling somewhere in between, Naim took comfort from the silence of the vast plains and the memory of what had been left behind.

He did go back to his village once, when he received the news that his mother was unwell.

'Shall I come?' Azra asked him.

'No,' he replied softly.

'I would like to.'

'I am certain she is only sick with something minor. Maybe she only wants to see me.' He laughed. 'Really no need for you to go. She'll get well.'

But that was not to be. By the time he arrived at the village, she was dead. He was surprised at how little grief he felt at his mother's death compared to the time that his father passed away. What he felt immensely was the absence of Ali, someone to whom he hadn't given a thought for a long time. Naim's eyes searched for him.

'I have no enmity with him,' Rawal said. 'It was long time ago. I would like him to come back here. Only Aisha,' he said, with a hint of remorse in his voice, 'died.'

Naim sent Rawal to look for Ali at the cloth mill. From the information Rawal got at the mill, he travelled to the cement factory. On the third day, Rawal returned empty-handed. Ali had moved away from there, he said, and nobody knew where he had gone. Naim stayed in the village for seven days. During that time he went one day to Aisha's village to give his condolences to her family. The had no information about Ali's whereabouts either. Naim went back to Delhi, to his routine at Roshan Mahal and his association with Anees.

The war was over. A quarter of a million Indian troops had become casualties on the fields of Europe and elsewhere. Those who survived returned to a turbulent land. The struggle for independence had hotted up. Times had changed, and Naim saw Anees Rahman undergo a gradual transform-ation. Over the years he became mellower, then morose and finally bitter, although he never lost the attractive sides of his personality. He had started going back for short trips to his state to see his wife and two children, now grown up. He never stayed for long. 'I feel out of place there,' he would say as he rushed back to Delhi. 'Always will.' His physical energy had diminished. On one occasion he said to Naim, 'Life wastes us with such savagery,' and Naim felt that he was looking at a man who had died. He shivered at the thought of seeing his own image in the other man. But the two of them had by now become so firmly dependent on one another as friends, not least because they had none other, that they gravitated together, now more frequently, each Saturday to the riverside house which had become their place of sanctuary from the world. Once there, they would sit by the river bank or, if the weather did not allow it, on the veranda and talk, or not, descending into long silences. At times, when he became maudlin, Anees talked about death.

'It is easy, if you prepare yourself for it,' he would say.

'How do you prepare yourself for it?'

'If you have kept your moments whole, the moments of your lifetime, if you have kept them whole, death will hold no terror for you. Just as a moment in its completion passes to give rise to another, so will you pass through the moment of death to another birth. Only a divided moment causes pain, leading to a divided death.'

'So you think these, what you call moments of our time, can be made "whole" with the power of the mind?'

'No,' Anees shook his head, 'you design your time not with the amount of thought but with the volume of grief that you hold.'

Conversations such as these would at times go on at length before coming inevitably to their inconclusive end. They knew that their discourse, albeit largely one-sided in favour of Anees, was carried on not for the sake of imparting information, knowledge or wisdom but to provide a shade – of voice, or presence – as shelter for one another. During periods of silence, both felt like two separate mausoleums within which their spirits flew like imprisoned birds, striking their heads against the walls while outside the world rushed onwards on its inexorable path without catching their voices.

Despite their closeness, Anees never invited Naim to his house in the city where he mainly lived, although Naim knew where it was, having seen it from outside while driving past it as a passenger in Anees's car. Only on one occasion did Naim visit the house to call upon Anees un-announced, and that was towards the end of their time together as they knew it. It was a night when Naim couldn't sleep. He was feeling restless on account of something that had happened earlier in the evening. There had been a gathering of the family in Roshan Agha's bedroom. The purpose of the meeting was to discuss whether to move or to stay in the event that the partition of the country, which seemed increasingly likely, eventually became a reality. Roshan Agha was torn between two points of view. Having never worked on it, he had no attachment to the land itself; his loyalty lay with the ownership – of land and, by virtue of that, of people. On the other side was his late conversion to the cause of the Muslim League and their demand for a separate homeland for the Muslims to be called Pakistan. But these were the passions of an old and weak man, unable to force through his opinions. The meeting was domin-ated by Pervez. His arguments were rational: Roshan Agha will be able to claim, to the fullest extent, the lands in the new country abandoned by Hindus and Sikhs who will inevitably move back from there to India; and so far as his own career in the civil service was concerned, there would be unlimited chances for promotion right to the top as there would certainly be a severe shortage of Muslim administrators in Pakistan, given that there weren't many in the whole of India as it was.

'How do you know the Hindus will leave their lands and migrate to this side?' asked Azra.

'Don't you see what is going on? Already Hindus and Sikhs are beginning to riot, demanding that if Muslims want a separate country let them all go there. Besides, we have had reports.'

'Reports of what?'

'Of retaliations taking place in the north of the country, in areas proposed to become Pakistan.'

'I don't believe people will actually pull up their roots and go,' Azra said. 'Even if that happens it's bound to be a temporary phase. You can't deny nationality to people who have always lived here. It is unimaginable.'

'Well,' Pervez said, 'in that case, where's the problem? We can all come back.'

There was a brief silence, broken by Roshan Agha. 'What do you think, Naim?' he asked.

Everyone looked at Naim. Naim gazed absent-mindedly at Azra. 'I don't know,' he mumbled.

'A decision,' Pervez's wife spoke up, 'has to be taken on the basis of common sense.'

'Do you think you have a monopoly on common sense?' Azra said sharply.

Naheed shrugged in a couldn't-care-less way. 'Let's face it, Naim is –'

She was cut short by her husband. 'Naim has no great stake here anyway,' Pervez said, 'no family of his own, no property to speak of.' He was immediately embarrassed at having said that. 'I mean,' he stammered, 'I mean he is not tied down here, that is what I mean. He can go on living with us wherever we go.'

During the tense silence that followed, Naim left his chair and the room. Back in his own room, he couldn't read. He could hear the voices of the other four, who had resumed the discussion. Naim lay flat on his bed, with a book opened and turned face down on his chest, staring at the ceiling. He got up and paced the room, then came back to bed. In time, the meeting in Roshan Agha's room broke up. He heard Azra go to her room and settle in bed. Extra lights in the house were turned off as a routine by the servants, and in the bedrooms by the occupants. Night had fallen. There was complete quiet in the house. Still sleep was nowhere near Naim's head. He switched his bedside lamp off and switched it back on again several times. Finally, he thought a walk in the garden might do the trick. He slipped on his dressing gown, picked up the walking stick and went out, trying not to make a sound. He had regained full health but carrying the stick had become a firm habit. Walking on the grass wearing slippers, around which the dew drops touched his bare feet, he felt perked up. A cool night breeze blew after what had been a hot July day. There was more than usual lightness in his head – a thoughtless vacuum. Stepping easily on to the hard ground, he approached the main gate and walked out of the house without being fully conscious of it. He walked on.

It was midnight now and Naim was walking through a heavily built-up part of the city. He was looking closely, stopping and starting, at houses and shops. He was in an area he vaguely recognized. After a while he realized that his uncle's old house was in a mohalla just like this one. A momentary thought, that it was his house now and he had never looked after it, passed through his mind. He thought that if he tried he could probably find the house. After all he had stayed there many times. There was no street lighting and in the dark of the night he went on, peering at the shut doors of houses, until he found himself in an area that ceased to be familiar. He stopped for a moment and thought of retracing his steps. Suddenly a group of dark shadowy figures emerged from a street, running soundlessly on bare feet. They disappeared down another side street. A few minutes later two police constables, carrying lathis, appeared out of the first street. One of them shone his torch on Naim.

'Oi, who are you?' he asked severely.

'Me?'

'Do you see anyone else here, you sisterfucker?'

'No,' Naim answered.

'What are you doing here?'

'I am just walking.'

'Just walking? At this time? Are you a thief?'

'No, no. I am –'

The constable hit him on the left arm with his lathi, and then pulled back sharply.

'What is in your hand?'

'Nothing.'

The constable shone his torch again and Naim rolled up his sleeve to show him in the light. The constable struck his lathi lightly twice on the hand and looked up in suspicious wonder.

'What is your name?'

'Naim Ahmad Khan.'

The constable looked at his companion and said, 'A Musla.' Then he turned round and, pointing to the wall, ordered, 'Go and sit there, and wait.'

Naim went and sat on an upturned crate lying outside a shop. The two constables hurried down the other street and disappeared. Naim sat on the crate and waited. A half-hour passed. Nobody came, other than a dirty stray pup out of an open drain who looked up at the man sitting outside the shop. Naim raised his stick to it but the pup wouldn't move. It was now that he realized he had picked up his uncle's walking stick instead of his regular one without noticing. Tired of waiting, Naim got up and walked away.

Quite without knowing it, he was walking towards Anees's house. It took him the better part of an hour to get there. A weak electric bulb burned outside the door. After hesitating for a few minutes, he rang the doorbell. Nobody answered. He rang again, and again, until the spring-action bell exhausted its coil. He started knocking on the door with his stick. In the end, a sleepy servant opened the door. Naim had never seen him before, but he received Naim as if he knew him.

'Come, come welcome, nawab sahib ji,' the servant bowed low in greeting. 'Are you all right, sir, everything all right at this time? Every-thing all right here, only sarkar is sleeping. I will go wake him, he will be happy.'

Anees looked anything but happy as he appeared a few minutes later, trying to rub sleep out of his eyes and looking at his wristwatch. Wordlessly, he regarded Naim from head to foot for a whole minute, then put his arm round him and led him to the drawing room.

'Sit down,' he said and went to a wooden cabinet. He poured himself a whisky. 'You want some?' he asked, raising the bottle.

Naim waved his hand.

'I know you don't drink. You should, you know,' Anees said, coming to sit in a sofa beside Naim. 'Are you all right?'

'Yes,' Naim said with a small laugh. Strangely, he was feeling lightly cheerful.

'Good God, Naim,' said Anees, still not over his astonishment. He kept raising his wristwatch and glancing at it. 'What is the matter?'

'Nothing,' Naim said. 'I came out for a walk. It was hot indoors.'

'It was too. But at this time?'

'I walked around.'

'Long walk, wasn't it?'

'Yes,' Naim said, slowly nodding his head.

'The city is becoming dangerous, do you know that?'

'Yes,' Naim said, 'I think I saw them.'

'Who?'

'Dangerous people.'

'You did? Who were they?'

'Police constables,' Naim said, laughing briefly again.

His light mood failed to communicate itself to Anees. His face solemn, Anees was becoming increasingly worried. He leaned forward.

'Naim, are you feeling well?'

'Very well. Why do you ask?'

'Oh, nothing,' Anees said. 'You want tea, breakfast, coffee?'

'No, no, thank you.'

Anees sat quietly looking at Naim for a few minutes. Naim looked back and saw Anees as though from a long way away, almost disappearing in the distance.

Anees looked at his wristwatch again, finished the whisky in his glass and got up. 'Come on, I will drive you home.'

It was in the early hours of the morning when Naim entered his bedroom. No one except the chowkidar at the main gate knew he had been absent. He lay in bed, still trying unsuccessfully to sleep. He gave up as daylight came up in the window. He took a leisurely bath, got dressed and sat in his favourite armchair, an unread book in his lap, until it was time for breakfast and then off to the office.

Naim didn't find Anees at the office. He sat at his desk for a few minutes and came out of the office. Walking along long covered verandas, he emerged on the second-storey balcony that went all the way round the great building. Many a time he had stood there with Anees, looking out over the large square a couple of hundred yards from the Assembly. It had always been bustling with people going about their business in this the capital city of India. On this day, he looked out and saw a different scene. There was a crowd all right, but it wasn't of people moving in any kind of controlled motion. Pushing and shoving each other, they weren't going anywhere. Naim was reminded of Anees's phrase 'helter-skelter'. He smiled to himself. In the square, some arms were raised along with muffled slogans that reached Naim's ears. Presently, a contingent of police arrived. They formed a circle three-quarters of the way round the crowd, leaving the fourth side free for the people to move away from the Assembly building. For a few minutes the police attempted to scare-drive the men, and some women, away with raised lathis, then they stopped, rearranging themselves on the orders of someone Naim couldn't see. Moments later, the lathi charge began. The people started running, not just to the open side but whichever way they were facing, their arms flailing and cries rising from their throats in place of shouted slogans. Some who broke through the lines and rushed towards the Assembly were pursued by the police. A constable's lathi fell on the head of an emaciated man with coal-black skin who had come within fifty yards of the building. The man fell to the ground. Surprisingly, his cry of pain, heard by Naim on the balcony, was mixed with his last slogan: 'Jai Hind'.

Then a shiver ran through Naim. For a few moments he stood absolutely still, his body tense and his eyes fixed on a figure in the fleeing crowd. It is him, he said to himself. It's him! The figure of a man, the one who had turned this anonymous crowd into a familiar body, was appearing and disappearing between frantic bodies. Frantically too, Naim raised his cane in the air and waved it as if giving a signal, before he realized the futility of it; they were too far and going away. The crowd had drawn back and scattered. The man went behind a tree once and did not appear again, neither to one side nor the other. Naim walked several steps along the balcony to the right, then the left, craning his neck to spot him. The man had vanished with the crowd. Naim stood there looking at the tree, and in the branches of that tree he thought he saw something. It wasn't the man he had seen, it was a young girl in a mauve silk shalwar-kameez who was climbing up with her dress swept by a cross-wind against her round hips and thighs, their firm flesh trembling. In a second she was gone. Naim rubbed his eyes. The tree, although present in its bare ordin-ariness, seemed to be sliding back, as if the earth beneath it was slipping. Naim looked down at the floor under his feet; it wasn't an earthquake. He felt that he was himself slipping back. Suddenly he was seized by the feeling that not just the tree and the crowd and the man in it but everything – everything he had known – was receding, becoming too far and going away. Some words echoed in his head. Sitting by the shifting waters of the Jamna, Anees had once said to him, 'For every man there comes a time when he knows he has lost it,' and Naim had thought this another of Anees's little homilies at the time.

Naim came out of the Assembly building. The place was now almost deserted. Passing by the tree, he looked up into its dense branches and dusty leaves but as if he were little concerned. He kept walking away.

EPILOGUE

I am moved by fancies that are curled
Around these images and cling;
The notion of some infinitely gentle
Infinitely suffering thing.
Wipe your hand across your mouth, and laugh;
The worlds revolve like ancient women
Gathering fuel in vacant lots.

– 'Preludes', *T. S. Eliot*

CHAPTER 29

They were driving their mules and donkeys ahead of them and riding their bullock-carts, women and children and old men sitting beside their meagre household goods loaded on to the carts and younger men walking alongside with their hands on the side planks of the carts for support. They were a group of no more than fifty when they set off from somewhere outside Delhi. But within days this foot caravan increased in numbers to a thousand human souls plus their animals and in volume to a shapeless mass stretching back over a mile in length. Viewed from high up in the air, it would look like an enormous python, escaped from an ancient jungle, that had grown lumps and bumps down its stem and a thousand little toes, winding its way along the Grand Trunk Road. Despite the add-ition of innumerable others, the original fifty had stayed close together. They shared between them the intimacy of seniority and considered themselves in the position of informal leaders of the pack, although no one was leading and none were led. The assumptions of the first fifty were nevertheless strengthened to some extent by an important factor: a few police constables, who had been posted to act as minders by the author-ities at the outset, gave up minding when they saw the crowd swelling out of all proportions and instead stayed with the fifty, talking mostly to them on account of longer acquaintance, somewhere about the middle of the long line, thus forming a kind of nucleus to which the others – newcomers, hence considered outside the circle – looked for safety.

The column was formed in such a hasty and haphazard way that no concept such as 'safety in numbers' ever developed among them. Among the original fifty, however, had grown a feeling which was rather like the one between members of, say, a tourist party arriving in a city and finding themselves in the middle of a rebellion; they stuck together. The whole column was rife with rumour. Nobody talked about everyday matters, for there were none; there was only an 'each day', which was fed and gone through with 'news', passing from one end to the other yet quickly overtaken by another, thereby reducing the one passed earlier to nil. It was not as though there was a family of rumour-mongers that invented and propagated false news. The news was not false, and the rumours were not a figment of the imagination but of desire: they were always of good things awaiting them at the next stop. Based on intense hope, rumour was more real than the event, the latest being that at the Ambala railway station a whole train had been reserved to take them on board and that to this train was attached a contingent of armed police to guard them in addition to a full kitchen stocked with ample food.

Among the distinguished fifty was also Naim. After days of walking, his clothes had become ragged and dirty. He had not spoken to anyone in all this time. People had made attempts to talk to him in the first day or two but, getting no response, had given up, dismissing him as a half-wit, while some women, considering him a man of God, deferred to him. The women gave him a little bit to eat from their own share, which he took without a word of thanks in return, thus enhancing his image as a holy man in the minds of the women, who looked after him in small ways. There were a few carts on wheels in their group, drawn by bullocks, mules or donkeys. Naim, having lost his cane somewhere along the way, put his hand on the side plank of one or the other. The women owner-passengers of these craft vied with each other to have Naim's hand on their cart, believing that it would bless the cart and save them from evil.

A mile short of Ambala the monsoons overtook them. They ran under a pouring sky and reached the railway station drenched to the skin. The cart people picked up their belongings, men, women and children carrying on their heads the stuff, wrapped and tied up with string, to the station platform. There was no train reserved and waiting for them; there was no other train for hours either. The rumour went round that all trains were running late because of the rains and floods. They sat down on the platform and waited for their train. After three hours, a train came. Picking up their bundles, they all ran to the edge of the platform. It was not just the compartments that were full, with people pressed against each other back to front like too many cattle in a small pound, but as many people again were riding on top of the train, men, women and children clinging to each other to avoid falling off the wet, slippery roof, and on the wooden steps of each compartment more than a dozen of them hung on to the metal handles of the doors. Some of the bolder ones among those waiting on the platform attempted to put a foot on the steps and were ferociously kicked away by those already there. The engine whistled twice and pulled the train away. They all drew back. Some who were quicker occupied others' places under shelters by the walls of the station building. There were arguments and scuffles. In the skirmishes Naim's memory began to stir from slumber. He rushed through a small crowd in front of him and stopped facing his brother.

'Ali,' he said. This was the first word he had spoken in over a week.

Ali looked at Naim without speaking for several moments, then said, 'What's happened to you?'

'Nothing,' Naim said, smiling.

'This,' Ali said, moving his hand in the air along the length of Naim's body, 'is nothing? I didn't recognize you.'

'I recognized you. I saw you before.'

'Where?'

'In Delhi.'

'When?'

'Ten, fifteen days back.'

'That is impossible,' Ali said. 'I left Delhi two months ago.'

Naim looked blankly at Ali.

'You are wet,' Ali said. 'Wait here.' Ali went to the two bundles of his belongings stacked against the wall. An old man was sitting on top of them. Ali slipped his hands in the old man's armpits and lifted him to his feet. 'Don't sit on my things,' he said harshly to the man. Untying one of the bundles, he pulled out a thin khes and brought it back to a shivering Naim. 'Wrap it round you.' He took Naim by the hand and led him to the bundles of his stuff. The old man had replaced himself on top of them. 'Get off,' Ali shouted at him. The man calmly got up and sat down on the floor. Ali kept glowering at him while settling Naim on the bundles. 'Stay here, don't wander about. What's happened to you?'

'Nothing,' Naim said again pleasantly.

'Nothing!' Ali said, imitating him. 'You look a miserable wretch. Now don't get lost. I am going to get something to eat.'

Another train arrived on the second line away from their platform, going the other way. It looked exactly the same as the first train, compartments and footboards packed and more people on top of it than inside, except for one difference: these people were all Hindus and Sikhs, apparent from their clothes and headgear and from their demeanour. Naim's memory was beginning to pick up. Looking at the people clinging to the roof of the train, he remembered the trains of his childhood when he would see a man walking on top of the stationary train taking in water for the engine from a station pump and think that it was a tightrope walker from a circus in a railway uniform. The train stopped for a few minutes and pulled out, leaving in Naim's eyes the sight of a child screaming with its mouth wide open in a woman's lap in the rain on the roof of the train. Ali returned with a watermelon in his hands. He broke it in two with a punch and offered the red juicy flesh to Naim, scooping it out with his fingers.

'Eat it,' he said. 'I have a few more left.'

'Where?' asked Naim.

'In the cart.'

'You have a cart?'

'Yes.'

'With a bullock?'

'A mule.'

'Good,' Naim said, eating the melon. Both his tongue and his hunger had returned.

'What do you mean, "good"?' Ali said. 'They are already standing around the carts outside, hunh,' he uttered a dry laugh, 'praying just like us for our train to arrive.'

'Why?'

'So that they can steal our carts after we board the train, that's why. Sisterfucking bastards.'

Now they were waiting not for the train but for the rain to stop. After another hour, it stopped. They all put their belongings of tied-up large and small bundles on their heads and cleared out of the platform. Reloading the stuff, the women and the weaker old men on the carts, on the donkeys, the bullocks and mules without carts and on a few buffaloes, they took to the road, realizing that safety, not to be found in numbers or in trains, now lay only in time; the quicker they measured the earth with their feet the safer they would be at the end of it.

'Hop on to it, hop on, what's the matter with you?' Ali said, eventually grabbing Naim by the waist and heaving him up on to the cart. 'Sit, sit now, go to sleep, you're in a bad way.'

A few miles out of the city, the rain caught up with them again. There was no fixed destination now other than the road, so nobody bothered to run.

'Here,' Ali handed an empty gunny bag to Naim. 'Cover yourself, put it on your head.'

Naim placed it flatly on his head.

'Not like that, no, no,' Ali said to him, showing Naim his own conical hat he had made from a bag by pushing one corner of it into itself and sticking it to the other corner, 'like this. Have you forgotten?'

Naim started struggling with it. Ali interrupted him again impatiently, 'Give it to me. You will never get it right. Give, give me.' Then he checked himself. 'Oh, you only have one hand. I nearly forgot. You never told me what happened. I asked you many times to tell me the story of your hand, but you always said it was nothing. Do you lose a whole hand if nothing happens? And you don't say what's happened to you now. You don't look like a poor beggar if nothing happens either. Here, it's made.' He slipped the bag, now properly converted into a hat covering the head and shoulders, on to Naim's head.

'You tell me,' Naim said to him.

'Hunh?'

'Tell me what happened to you.'

'Why do you want to know? There's nothing to tell. You said I could not come back to the village and I left. And you gave my room to Rawal and his wife. I was born there. I had no father, no mother, no brother, how could I come back? I looked after Aisha. I loved her. But her heart had shrunk. There was no way out for her but away. And away she went. What do you know about having your first good meal of chicken and spinach in a long time and not given time to rest before being told straight away you cannot come back home? What do you know of not giving your head a good rest and losing your home and everything? You married the jagirdar's daughter and went to live in the big house and wanted for nothing. What do you know about these things? When Father went to gaol you went to Kulkutta and to Angrezi schools. Then you went into the army and got land in return, a full ten acres of good land. I asked you what you did to get it and you said, "Oh, nothing." You never told me anything, not about the hand, not about the land, not about anything, always nothing, nothing, except don't do this, do that, don't come back to the village. So why do you ask me now? I have nothing to tell, not to you anyway. Then you even lost the land because like a fool you went to gaol for nothing. That was nothing, if you ask me. But this time you told me all about it and wanted me to do as you did. I did not want to go to gaol so I stayed put in mills and factories. I learned a skill as you said but lost half my life, and the other half when Aisha went, you never knew that, did you? Skill! What is the profit in skill if I have no home and no electricity of my own? There were no trees.'

'What trees?' Naim asked.

'Trees. Trees. I told you once. You have forgotten everything. The cement factory was worse, only limestone hills and nothing else. The stone was exploded every day and there was the smell of dust and blasting powder, no smell of trees. I am talking of old trees, not new ones. Big old trees that you can climb and sit in the branches and play with the leaves. Aisha made peepees with tahli leaves.' Ali stopped to swallow tears in his throat. 'You never grew trees, only took them on in the house they built for you when you married the rich woman and became the owner of the village. Where are they now, I ask you, your rich relatives? All gone. I knew it was no good, if you asked me, it was no good from the start. You have lost everything. What kind of skill is that? Fool's skill.' He put his hand out to point to the moving column. 'Everything!' He turned to glower at Naim's hat covering his head and face. 'I know everything. You became ill. I stayed away, but I got all the news about you. I had a hope that you would change your mind. But first you got yourself into gaol all over again, then you became ill and went to live in their house in Dilli and were treated by a big doctor. Who was there to treat Aisha and me? Homelessness, huh? You say nothing to everything, but I say nothing as well, I have nothing to tell you. This motherfucking rain, when crops are dying it doesn't come, now we have no crops so it comes and comes. If these fuckers stopped for a bit we could get under the cart and save ourselves from it. But they keep running, the fools don't know that you can't run away from rain but only get more wet. But can you tell them this? No, sir, they go on running as if they have to catch their mother's wedding in time. There's two rotis in the bundle next to you. You can have one. Eat it with melon when you feel the hunger. Or better let me know, I keep forgetting you can't untie the knot on your own. You were lucky, with only one hand you had servants to do everything for you. Where are they now? Are you feeling hungry?'

Naim's head of hat shook. 'No. Tell me more.'

'Tell you what?'

'What happened to you.'

'Nothing to tell. Why don't you sleep, it will do you good, put some strength into you. Go to sleep.'

Naim's hat shook silently again.

The column kept moving until the day ended and darkness fell. They could see the lights of a city in the distance. Fearful of going into or near it, they stopped in a large uncultivated field surrounded by trees. The rain had stopped. They opened up bundles of their belongings, collected fallen twigs or broke them off the trees to start small fires, kneaded the dough with water they carried with them in pitchers, cooked rotis and ate them with whatever they had, some achar or chutney or two-day-old cooked daal or with just salt and water. Those who didn't have anything to cook bought a little from those who did, with money or else by bartering clothes, shoes, even weapons such as long knives that they had kept to defend themselves in the event of an attack. The animals ate from the plentiful grass and foliage that sprouted everywhere in the days of the monsoons. After feeding their bodies they sustained their minds in the dark of the night by passing rumours from mouth to mouth. There were special camps, it was said, set up by the government in big cities where they would be housed and fed and guarded by the army and provided with proper transport for their journey onwards, all this being based on their concern for safety, food and conveyance in that order. The night, however, they spent, as they had done several before, under an open sky and occasional showers, shivering in the wet wind. Ali bought some milk from the few buffalo-owners who milked them nightly and sold the milk. They ate a roti each with milk and went to sleep, covering themselves with sheets and gunny bags under Ali's cart, only disturbed once during the night by the mule splashing its urine on them.

At dawn word passed through the column from one end to the other. For once it wasn't a rumour but the news of an actual event: the first death in the column. It was of a young man travelling on his own carrying no bundles of belongings but only the clothes on his back and no money or valuables on him, found dead where he lay in the night from exposure and possibly starvation, but most probably because his spirit had given up and let the body go. Nobody knew who the young man was. But because it was a death from natural causes, sent down by the will of God, it was holy and required to be treated as such. The maulvis took over the proceedings; all the rituals of the funeral had to be observed. An atmosphere of piety rippled through the whole column. It served to brighten up the mood of the men, women and especially children by restoring at least part of the old order of daily life. They rummaged through their bundles to pull out whatever fresh clothes they could find and changed into them. They lent a little bit of water from their pitchers to those who did not have it for wetting, if not thoroughly washing, their hands, feet and faces by way of ablution before they stood, thousands of them, in straight row after row, the children happily organizing themselves alongside their elders who admonished them to stay still in the presence of God and his angels. Massed thus, they stood solemnly in the field facing the body of the unknown man, laid on the ground wrapped in a white shroud that had been donated by the richest family in the column who owned a good cart, two horses and several metal trunks full of belongings. Before the namaz janaza, they listened to a speech delivered by the head maulvi:

'Brothers, we have proved before our God that we value and respect our dead. Today, an unclaimed person, whose name even we did not know and called him simply "Man" for the purpose of the namaz, is being blessed with a janaza bigger than many famous men get when they pass away. Look around you, more than a thousand souls, just imagine – more than even two thousand –'

After he finished the speech, the maulvi led the namaz, in which everyone except the women and the animals participated. A hole had already been dug in the ground. The corpse was lowered into the grave and each of the 'mourners' threw a handful of earth on it, including the women, in orderly fashion, until the hole not only filled up but a great mound of earth eventually formed on top of it. After the service was over, they hastily picked up their things and the column started moving. It was the largest grave anyone had ever seen, this mound that they had made for the unknown man, and they were justly proud of it, looking back at it for a long time until they came to a bend in the road and it disappeared from view. Never afterwards in the brief life of the column would death be accorded such honour. For they were soon to enter a province in the fields of which death stalked its prey in the shape of marauding Sikhs and Hindus on one side of the border and Muslims on the other – the province of the Punjab, across a map of which the good judge Cyril Radcliffe, after much concern and absent-minded deliberation, drew a line in red ink dividing it in two, each half going to a different country.

Despite hopeful rumours of a 'safe' camp with free food established for them at each 'next' stop, the column had begun to distrust railway stations and even cities, bypassing them although staying close to the road. They stopped for provisions, chiefly water, near small villages and only towns where they saw the dome of a mosque or a green rag of a flag flying above some holy 'mazar' signifying Muslim habitation. In most such places they found none of their kind, and no longer were even the signs of Muslim living allowed to remain in the abodes of those who had fled. The sense of fear grew with every mile they covered, until it became a solid mass that travelled by day and night alongside them. After shedding the notions that there was safety in railway stations, camps and the passage of time, their number one priority now was speed and, although speed was but a dimension of time, for them it existed in its own right, measured in terms of the 'quickness' with which they could take the decision to switch to another route, change direction or leave a stop-over spot in order to evade attackers, real and imagined. They started getting rid of their old clothes by throwing them by the wayside to lighten the load on the carts and the gradually weakening animals so they could pull along more easily, and indeed at times they became more a stampeding herd than a moving column.

Nobody wanted the discarded clothes, but many old shoes, already worn and holed, were picked up and put on regardless of size by those who had totally ruined their own during the march. Those who owned milch cattle quadrupled the price of the milk they sold; those who had pitchers stopped giving water to others, and instead put a cash price on it. Starvation became a reality and at every stop-over they left behind many sick people, the disabled with swollen feet and not a few who had died quietly in the night, along with others who simply refused to get up and go any further, waiting among the familiar dead under a blistering sun for someone or something to arrive and help them reach their end one way or another. No one looked back for them.

Luckily, the column suffered no real attack until they reached the outskirts of Amritsar; there were only intimations of the danger from the dead bodies strewn along the roadside, among the fields and around villages and cities. Successfully skirting these, they felt shielded from evil by a similar column of refugees going ahead of them that had borne the brunt of the attacks, thus easing the situation for them who followed. This view was confirmed by a quite extraordinary sight at one place. There was a horde of Sikhs and Hindus, sitting by the wayside, their spears, swords and long-handled cleavers, and also their clothes, covered in blood, as if they were waiting to kill the new arrivals. The refugees failed to see them until they turned a corner and found themselves on top of them. The people on foot started running while the cart-owners began furiously to beat their beasts. Hardly one of the attackers moved; they remained still, looking at the fleeing herd with nothing more than tired unconcern on their faces. After the column had cleared the danger spot, it dawned on them, from the scores of dead bodies over which they had stumbled, that the attackers had killed so many so recently, possibly only minutes before, that they could not be bothered to do any more of the same. The people in the column felt doubly beholden to the ones who had passed before them and fallen; they silently recited holy verses from the Quraan to bless their souls and to thank God for providing them with the shelter of the freshly dead so that they themselves would live.

There were rare stretches of ground that were comparatively tranquil. They would take refuge under a growth of dense old trees around a field or in a small forest and make forays into villages disguised as Hindus, or those who had beards would wrap sheets round their heads to look like Sikhs and pick up drinking water and other sustenance. They would come back and sell the food that was surplus to their own needs at a profit to those who had not had the heart to venture into dens of danger. All the wells had been contaminated by the rainwater overflowing into them from the ground, so clean water was only to be had from pumps dug in people's houses, thus fetching the highest price, especially from those who were dying of thirst. As their destination came nearer, hopes of survival grew, and acquiring money finally took priority over everything else. Those, however, were the marginally happier days . . .

Back in Delhi, Roshan Agha's family were at the airport, waiting for their flight. They were sitting in the superior lounge of the air terminal with their hand luggage on the floor beside the sofa chairs; Naheed was gripping a large handbag containing her jewellery in her lap with both hands and a half-satisfied expression on her face, while Azra, sitting away from her, looked blank, her empty hands resting lightly on the arms of the chair. Roshan Agha was in a wheelchair between the two women. There was bewilderment on his sallow face. Pervez and Imran were away at the check-in counter in the departure hall, haggling about getting on board the aircraft nearly fifty locked containers as accompanied baggage. 'I am Assistant Commissioner, Delhi,' he was saying, 'I have opted for Pakistan. We are all going. I want all this as accompanied baggage, none unaccompanied. I was given assurances by Mr Mehta, your General Manager. This is his card, you can speak to him . . .' Their flight was delayed for two hours, then for several hours more for unknown reasons. They all waited in the comfortable lounge, sipping ice-cold water. Outside, in the arrival and departure halls, there was pandemonium approaching a riot. It was hot and humid. Sweat pouring from their bodies, drenching them and their clothes, a thousand people were pushing, shoving, swearing and screaming to get to their uncertain future.

Naim was lucky in two respects: one, few were more worldly-wise than Ali, who was always the first to go into nearby villages at stop-overs posing as a Hindu traveller from the next village, speaking the local dialect and getting provisions; and, second, he had money in his pocket. He came back with water and food for the two of them and dry cut grass for the mule, all bought with cash. Every time he returned with his purchase, Naim asked him, 'Has your money not run out yet?'

'Why do you keep worrying about money?' Ali would reply. 'I have enough for us. I have worked all my life and earned it and kept it. I am not telling you how much I have.'

'Where did you work?' Naim once asked him when the column was on the move.

'Everywhere. Kulkutta.'

'You went to Calcutta?'

'Yes. I wanted to join the army. Do not imagine I wanted to get rid of my hand or win a medal. I only wanted to go to Burma.'

'Did you go then?'

'They said we would go. But we did parades and nothing but parades. One day I said to the sergeant, "The day you were born your mother's milk split in her teats and you became a coward." They put me under guard for three weeks and then kicked me out.'

'You were lucky,' Naim said.

'Why, because I did not lose my hand?'

'You would have been taken prisoner by the Japanese and died there.'

'I wouldn't. If I were to die I would have died in the factories.'

'But that was later when the war started,' Naim said. 'Where did you go before that?'

'I came here to Punjab. I was in Lahore once before but only for two days, it was no good then. But I liked the city. After Aisha passed away I came back here and got jobs in electric shops for three years.'

'And then?'

'Then what?'

'Where did you go after that?'

'Dilli.'

'You were in Delhi?'

'Yes. I could get work anywhere.'

'How long were you there?'

'Many years.'

'But I was there too. I went back to the village once and sent Rawal looking for you. He couldn't find you.'

'Just as well. I would have killed him. I hope he is already dead.'

'Don't say that. Not at a time like this.'

'And his wife and child, I hope they are dead too. Hey,' Ali turned to an old man walking alongside the cart, 'take your hand off the wood, puts a drag on the animal.'

'What did you do in Delhi?' Naim asked him.

'Have you become a fool? Worked in electric shops, what else? I saw you there once.'

'Where?'

'I was sent to do some work in your big house.'

Naim sat up. 'Where, when, what work?'

'Mended a short-circuit in the kitchen.'

'And you saw me?'

'You came out of the house and got into a black car and went. I asked the maid and she said you were bibi's husband and you went every day to work in the Viceroy's office.'

'And you didn't stop me?'

'How could I?' Ali said.

Naim was quiet for a long time.

'This,' said the old man, as if talking to himself, his hand still on the side plank of Ali's cart for support, pointing with his other hand to the dead bodies that lay in the fields they were passing, 'is history.'

'Oi, you old beggar, stuff your history in your mother's hind legs. Don't you listen? I told you to take your hand off my cart, the poor animal is already dead finished. You want a blow of this before you will listen,' Ali said, raising the cane in his hand that he used for beating the mule.

'Let him,' Naim said. 'Leave him be.'

'He's putting a drag on it,' Ali said sullenly.

The man wasn't very old, he only looked like it with his scraggly beard, dirty face and torn clothes. Naim liked his face; it had a rounded softness to it, although the cheeks had sunk.

'What's your name?' Naim asked him after a while.

'Jamaluddin.'

'Where do you come from?'

'Aligarh.'

'Nice town,' Naim said.

'Very nice. I was born in the city and stayed there all my life.'

'What did you do?'

'Taught history at the University.'

'You were a professor?'

'I was. Now I profess nothing. I taught old history, rajas and maharajas and the Mughals and English kings. Waste of time. This,' he pointed again to the corpses in the field, 'is history now. I shall be teaching this next to the boys and girls so they don't forget. Only what you don't forget is history.'

'You'll never get to your next history if you keep yapping like that,' Ali taunted him again.

'Hop on to the cart,' Naim said to the man.

The professor took an awkward leap. Ali looked angrily over his shoulder and started beating the mule, which broke into a gallop under the whip. The man hung half off the back of the cart. Naim pulled him in.

That night, after safely bypassing the city of Amritsar, they heaved a sigh of relief. Jalandhar and Amritsar were the main danger points, teeming with Sikhs inflamed by the sight of Hindu and Sikh refugees fleeing in similar columns and trains from the opposite direction and arriving with nothing to show but tears. Past Amritsar, they knew they were now within striking distance of the border. They relaxed and set down for the night in a field sheltered by trees and with no village in sight.

'We'll be all right,' Ali said, crawling under the cart for a few hours' rest. 'We will go to Lahore. I know every part of the city. I can get work there any time.'

'No,' Naim said to him, 'we will go to the village.'

'What village?'

'Any village. We will get land there and work on it.'

Ali gave Naim a look of suspicion in the dark. 'How can we get land?'

'We will put in a claim in return for the land we left behind.'

'Have you got papers for the land in Roshan Pur?'

'No.'

'Then how?'

'We will do something,' Naim said. 'If nothing else, you have money, we will buy land.'

'It's not enough to buy land, only for a month's food for us. I am not throwing my money away on some land when I can get paying work the very first day.'

'No,' Naim insisted. 'It is good to work on the land. We will grow our own food, don't have to rely on anyone else. Good open air as well, healthy life.'

'You know how many other things we need to grow a crop?'

'Yes, yes, we will do something,' Naim said again.

Ali kept looking at Naim as if he thought his brother had lost his mind. 'My money is not for you and your foolish ideas,' he said. 'It is my own money.' He turned away, putting an arm under his head on the ground.

Just before dawn they were attacked, for the first and last time during their flight. A horde of Sikhs, armed with spears, swords, daggers and lathis, took them by surprise. A few of them were on horses, the rest on foot. The horsemen were looking only for women. They simply went round the column and grabbed young girls, flinging them sideways over the front of their horses and galloping away. The half-darkness of dawn came alive with the screams of girls as young as ten and eleven being snatched and taken away. Older men on foot lifted older women, at places two men subduing and carrying away a powerfully flailing woman. Most of the group, merely enraged with the passion for revenge, simply killed, sinking sharp weapons into the bellies of men, women and children. The smell of fresh-spilled blood filled the air. Many people in the column, even some who owned carts, got up and fled on foot, leaving everything behind, including the carts, which were seized by the attackers. Ali kept his head. He pushed Naim up on to the cart and drove the mule, beating it fiercely with his cane as well as the reins amid the yells and cries of the attackers and the attacked, not minding whether he ran over his own people as they fled on foot. He had only gone a short distance before a few of the invaders jumped at the mule, catching hold of its mouthpiece. The cart came to a halt. Other Sikhs pulled Naim off the back of the cart.

Ali let go of the reins and turned round. 'Don't take him,' he begged, 'he is sick.'

They beat Naim on the head with lathis.

'No, no, in the name of Parmatma,' Ali put his palms together in front of their faces, then bent down to touch their feet, 'in the name of Guru Gurnanak, don't beat him, he is not well, look, look here.' With trembling hands he rolled up Naim's sleeve and quickly unhinged the wooden limb, holding it up to them. 'Here, see, he has only one –'

A lathi fell on Ali's hand, knocking the wooden arm to the ground, and another on his head.

'Here,' he wept, 'wait, wait.' He took out the money from the secret inner pocket of his shalwar. 'Take this, take the lot, I have no more,' he pulled the secret pocket inside out to show them, 'nothing, take everything – just – leave him –' They grabbed the money. Two lathis fell simultaneously on Ali and Naim. Naim fell in a motionless heap on the ground. A spear's blade shone near Ali's eyes. He glanced back for a way out and saw several men on top of his cart, holding the reins. He turned and ran. The Sikhs pursued him a little way, then, diverted by other prey nearer to them, gave up the chase.

A half-mile down the road, Ali ran out of breath. The voices behind him had died down. He sat down in the dust on the ground, looking fixedly at an ant-heap while he tried to regain his breath. After a few minutes, he turned to take a look at the desolate landscape behind him, scanning the width of it with his eyes. Then he raised his face and both his arms to the sky and let out howl after dry, animal howl, the pain in his eyes not letting the tears come.

CHAPTER 30

'Rai Manzil' was a sprawling, solidly constructed double-storey house built in the 1870s by Rai Bahadur Kaidar Nath, a big local landlord, in the outskirts of Lahore. After his death, his two sons and their families lived in the house until July 1947. The Rais, Rajput Hindus traditionally close to the Muslim culture, were nevertheless swept up in the frenzy of Partition, worked up daily by columns and trainloads of refugees arriving from India with tales of atrocities visited upon them by the Hindus. Receiving information on the quiet from their friends, the two families left secretly for India under the protection of the army authorities. When a Muslim mob attacked the house a few days later, they found neither the residents nor any valuables in the place. In their anger, they put the building to the torch. The fire succeeded only in burning down the eastern half of the house before it was brought under control – mostly by the efforts of Muslim neighbours who feared the conflagration would spread to their own equally large houses.

What was left of the Rai house, however, was more than sufficiently large to accommodate a family. Pervez's friends in the Civil Service who had already taken up jobs in Pakistan soon showed him round a few grand houses, and from these he chose Rai Manzil, which was a roomy house with extensive wood panelling and masonry cornice-work on the ceilings and parapets along the roof and a large mature garden left untouched by the arsonists. With the four other members of his household, Pervez slipped into the house just as easily as he did into his job as Secretary, Education, in the new provincial government. His son, Imran, who had done his MA in economics in Delhi, took a teaching job at the Punjab University while preparing himself for the Civil Service competitive examination. Naheed and Azra took a few months to settle down, Naheed organizing the house and the servants and Azra looking after her sick father and the garden. The wing of the house that was still standing was in reasonable order, the only damage a slight blackening of the walls where the smoke from the other wing had touched them. Naheed had all the rooms whitewashed under her supervision while Azra hired a gardener and went round having the lanes and the lawns cleared of fallen leaves, dead birds andweeds and seeing that the fruit trees of citrus, guava, jaman and shahtoot were properly pruned.

After the essentials had been dealt with, Pervez began gently to prompt Naheed and Azra to take up jobs in the Education Department where, he said, he could easily have decent posts created for them – 'Just for the sake of helping the new generation in this country in which we have invested by choosing to live here.' But, realist as he was, he could see that if things didn't quite work out all the able-bodied members of the family would have to pull their weight merely in order to keep a large house and its staff going. Although they had quickly lodged a claim to 'evacuee property' in lieu of the estate they had left behind in India, it was being processed for proper allotment at a snail's pace by the Rehabilitation Department while local people, non-refugees, were walking into evacuated houses and vast land-holdings and taking possession by force of men and arms. Having no such resources at his command, Pervez, despite his senior position in the government, had to wait patiently amid the administrative confusion created by tens of thousands of claims, small and large, true, untrue and false, and not enough staff to deal with them. In the new country, since refugees held no papers of domicile and no proof of property ownership, their 'claims' were without substance and had to be recreated.

The fortune of Pervez's family (now no longer Roshan Agha's) had meanwhile been considerably depleted on account of a wrong decision in Delhi: having been unable to get all their luggage on to the aircraft as accompanied baggage, and since they were not prepared to part with even a single piece of it for any length of time, they had decided, after prolonged and ill-tempered discussions, to take the train. The train was attacked at both Jalandhar and Amritsar stations by Hindus and Sikhs, who overpowered the police contingent accompanying the train and killed and robbed the passengers. The five members of the family were fortunate to have escaped death or injury, but they were deprived of most of their baggage, looted or lost. They were, however, able to hang on to their handbags which contained all their jewellery. They also escaped with some cash that had been sewn into the lining of their clothes. The cash quickly went within the first two months of their arrival, most of it on making the house habitable. Selling off the jewellery – the family heirlooms – was anathema to them. As a result, they began to live within much reduced means, which meant only Pervez's salary. Azra never complained, but Naheed constantly did. She would not, she said, set foot in a tonga or any such thing; she had to have a car and chauffeur. So a proposal that she should out to work in a girls' college came to nothing. The household subsided into a dreary routine, waiting for their claim to be settled. At one stage they were made the offer of an equally large tract of land in adjustment of their claim, but it was hundreds of miles away in the uncultivated wilderness of the province of Sind, and Pervez rejected it. The house, though, had been allotted to them in the name of Roshan Agha. Their days and evenings were spent making plans to rebuild the burnt-out part of the house as and when they got their hands on their claimed land or, preferably, compensation for it in cash.

Roshan Agha meanwhile had risen above everything that went on around him: he was dying. Soon after they arrived in Pakistan his diabetes ceased responding to treatment, and the disease began to attack his vital organs. From the very first day, his main concern had been less with getting his estate back than with changing the name of the house. 'RAI MANZIL' was etched in big black letters into a white marble slab right up on the façade of the house. He couldn't bear to look at it. It got so that eventually he stopped going out altogether to sit on the lawn on pleasant autumn evenings. The first thing he asked of his son on Pervez's return from office each day was whether the 'ordinance' had been issued. Every day, he waited. The government had forbidden by law the altering of names and signs of businesses and buildings, including private homes, until it completed its inventory of 'evacuee property', after which a new ordinance was to be issued allowing changes of use and name. That it would take some time was known and accepted by all in the family, and anyway nobody was much bothered whether or not it was allowed. But for Roshan Agha it became a matter of life and death. In the end, it proved to be literally so.

He had asked Azra to find a stonemason. Azra got one through the gardener. Roshan Agha interviewed him and, having satisfied himself about the workman's skill, engaged him. He was asked to bring back two things the following day: a large marble slab and a wooden board of equal size. The man returned the next day with a donkey cart on which were loaded the two required items. Roshan Agha ordered the marble to be stood against the wall in a corner of his room, and the wooden plank to be brought to him where he lay in bed. After receiving detailed instructions from the sick man, the stonemason sat on the floor and wrote the words 'ROSHAN MAHAL' on the wood. It didn't come out at all right, so he was asked to change the script. He changed it. Roshan Agha was not satisfied. The workman altered the script yet again. Roshan Agha shook his head and told him to go away and return the next morning. This went on for almost two weeks. The stonemason would continuously change the shape of the words and his master would reject it on one account or another. Despite the fact that the man, hardly educated enough in the first place to write more than a few words, ran out of scripts that he knew and then some more, he persevered because Roshan Agha had about forty old silver rupees in the pocket of his gown of which one, a fortune to the poor man, he tossed to the mason every third day. Several times, after examining the writing on the wooden board, Azra had said, 'That's it, Papa, exactly as it was on Roshan Mahal.' Each time Roshan Agha would shake his head. The curvature of one letter, the line of another, the look of the whole word or the balance of the two wasn't quite right; it wouldn't do. The daily toil of the stonemason would go on. After a fortnight of this activity, still reluctantly, tilting his head this way and that to view the script from many angles, the old man brought himself to approve the final lettering and gave the mason the go-ahead to etch it into the marble in indelible colours. Another week, and the marble slab was ready. It stood against the wall in Roshan Agha's room, the stonemason on orders to be ready to report at short notice, while the Agha waited for the ordinance to be issued. All five members of the family were thus in a state of continuous alert, so to speak: Pervez for his promotion to the Federal Secretariat, Naheed for the claim on the estate to come through, Imran for the date of the competitive examination to be announced, and Azra for an imaginary face to appear out of the air and restore her memory in all its detail.

Roshan Agha ran out of time; his kidneys began to give out. Fighting for his life, he still asked Pervez every single day about the ordinance.

'There is a way,' Azra said to Pervez one day.

'What is it?'

'Tell Papa that the ordinance has been issued.'

'What, just like that? What if he insists on putting up the bloody sign straight away?'

'Put it up so that he can see it once. He hardly ever goes out.'

'Don't bet on it, he might sit there every day looking at it.'

'Look, Pervez, it will ease his days. We ask the mason to stick it up temporarily. By the time someone from the government comes round, we can take it down. Who cares about these things anyway?'

'It is a question of my job, Azra,' Pervez said doubtfully.

In the event, things were made easy all round. A few hours after Roshan Agha heard the news from a reluctant Pervez and gave the order for the slab to be put up first thing in the morning, he sank into a coma. He was moved to a hospital, where he died three days later without regaining consciousness. His other wish was to be buried within the perimeter of the house; this was granted to him. Instead of the common graveyard, he was interred in the grounds of 'Rai Manzil'. There were no postal or telephone contacts with India, so Pervez telephoned a few families he knew of who had migrated to Pakistan. Their letters of condolence, along with their regrets at not being able to participate in the funeral, arrived a few days later. The mourners included the remaining four members of the family plus three of Pervez's colleagues. Three house servants made up the rear of the namaz janaza.

Having no one to look after any more and nothing to take with him, not even the mule and the cart, Ali ran on through fields and forests, making it to the Wagah border. From there he headed for the Lahore railway station. Both times that he had been in the city, once for two days and the second time for nearly three years, he had found his friend Hasan at the tea stall. This time Hasan was nowhere to be seen. Lost in a crowd of thousands of refugees fighting to get into or on top of the trains leaving for India and others arriving in trains from the other side, Ali's legs gave way beneath him. He slumped against the green-painted iron railings of the station platform and closed his eyes. He had no desire in his heart – not even for a morsel of food if he could get it down to his appetite-dead stomach – stronger than the desire to sleep. Here, finally, there was no one after him to take his life or his possessions; his life, good enough only to take revenge on across the border, was worth even less on this side either to him or to other Muslims, and he had on him no more than a shirt, torn in many places, and an equally ragged shalwar. He had lost his shoes. In these unusual times, what had been a fatal threat to him on the other side proved to be his greatest asset on this: his name, and his genitals. Some time after he collapsed into sleep, he was woken by a kick on his shins. He opened his eyes to see a group of men and boys, some as young as ten, armed with swords and long knives.

'Who are you?' one asked him.

'Refugee.'

'From where?'

'Hindustan.'

'What is your name?'

'Ali.'

One of them cut the string of his shalwar with a knife. Lowering the garment, they saw that he was circumcised.

'Musalman,' they said, a hint of disappointment in their voices.

They turned their attention to a newly arrived train from the north full of refugees going to India. A mob attacked the train. Ali saw a boy, hardly sixteen, shoot a crude home-made pistol into the face of a child who was looking out of the carriage window. The split-second-disfigured face of the child disappeared back into the compartment without a sound. A very fat woman came running awkwardly up the platform and suddenly came to a halt, face to face with the group of men that had questioned Ali. They raised their swords. The woman lifted the front of her muslin kurta, baring two enormous breasts that hung down to her navel. She put her hands underneath them and lifted them up, pushing the swollen, fleshy teats into the men's faces.

'Look, look at them,' she wept. 'I am your mother, don't kill me –'

Feeling his empty guts rising to his throat, Ali turned his face to the railing with a groan, soon sinking into a deep sleep once again. When he next awoke somebody had his shoulders in their hands and was shaking them. It was a woman.

'You have been lying here for two days,' she was saying to him. 'You want to be dead?'

Ali had barely enough energy to open his eyes. He couldn't move.

'Come on,' the woman said, 'can you stand up? You can't even speak, you wretched man, you are half dead already. Who told you to sleep here? Come, put your arms round my shoulders, come, oh, you dead body, make an effort. Yeees – like this, stand, stand up, up –'

The woman walked him out of the station. Ali slumped again. The woman took nearly half an hour to drag-walk him to her hut at the edge of a sprawling refugee camp two hundred yards from the station. Inside the hut, she dropped him to the floor, herself out of breath. She warmed up some milk in a dented pan, black with soot on the outside, and put the milk to Ali's mouth in a cup.

'Open your mouth,' she said to him, 'it's only milk, not poison, it'll put some life into you. Sit up. Ohhh –' She put the cup of milk on the floor and dragged Ali up by the armpits to sit him against the wall. 'Now, open your mouth, here, that's it, drink it up, swallow it . . .'

Ali tried to swallow the mouthful of milk and immediately threw up. The woman cleaned up the front of his shirt with a corner of her dopatta and put the cup to his lips again.

'Don't worry, just get it down – swallow.' She put her hand under Ali's shirt and passed it gently over his stomach. 'Your belly is sticking to your back, I can feel your spine from the front, no wonder you can't swallow anything. Drink, don't worry about throwing up, drink.'

'I can't,' Ali said his first words.

'I am not surprised,' the woman said, laughing lightly. 'At least you can speak. I saw you at Ambala station. You had an old man with you and two bundles of things. I was in the train. You tried but couldn't get on the train. Nobody could, we were already dying inside with everybody on top of us. When I saw you here at first I thought you were dead. There are so many dead lying around. The second time I was there today you had turned over in your sleep and I recognized you. I bent down and saw that you were breathing. I go to the station every day to look for my son. We were together but got separated when the train was attacked at Amritsar. I know he is alive. He is only six, but he is clever. I will find him one day. See, you can swallow if you really try, you have half a cup of milk inside you. You will be all right. Now you can go back to sleep. Here, lie yourself down on this quilt, it's soft, give your bones a rest.'

The woman tended to Ali in her hut, gradually getting solid food down his throat over several days. The second time Ali opened his mouth it was to answer the woman's question about his name.

'Ali,' he said.

'My name is Bano,' she said.

By the fourth day Ali could sit up on his own, and on the seventh he walked.

'What do you do?' was the next thing he asked.

'Clean houses. What did you do in your home over there?'

'Worked with electricity.'

'Worked with electricity? What's that?'

'I mend electricity.'

The woman laughed out loud.

'Why do you laugh?' Ali asked her.

'I have never seen electricity,' she said.

'You clean houses, have they no electricity?'

'They have. But I can't touch it.'

'Why not?'

'Not allowed to.'

'I can get work,' Ali said suddenly.

'What work?'

'Electricity work.'

'For money?'

'I will get money for it. I did it here before.'

'Here? When?'

'Some years ago.'

'You know this city?'

'Yes. All of it.'

'And me a stranger here bringing you home from the station!' Bano said, her eyes mockingly wide. 'I don't believe it!'

For the first time in weeks, Ali laughed.

'You are not strong enough,' Bano said to him. 'Wait some more. You can give me money when you earn it from – electricity?' She laughed again.

By the time a fortnight had gone by, Ali walked out of the hut. He returned after a few minutes and lay down on top of his quilt on the floor. Still weak in his legs, he also lacked the confidence to venture far on his own, although he knew all the streets and alleys of the city.

'If you get me some clothes,' he said to Bano, 'I can go out to the city.'

'I will get you clothes,' she said, a slight alarm in her voice, 'but stay here, get some food into you first.'

'And shoes,' Ali said.

'Yes, shoes. I will try.'

Dressed in a clean shalwar-kameez and shoes a size too big that Bano got him from the owners of houses she cleaned, day by day Ali went further and further into town, finally, by the end of the month, reaching the shop where he last worked. The Hindu owner-electrician had fled and in his place was a white-haired man, fiddling with a switchboard.

'Are you a refugee?' he asked Ali.

'Yes.'

'From where?'

'Everywhere,' Ali said, laughing a little. 'My village was near Rani Pur.'

'I am from Jalandhar. Sit down. Here.' The man handed Ali the wooden board with screwed-on switches and sockets and wires hanging out of it. 'Let's see what you can do.'

Twenty minutes later, Ali handed the board back to the man.

'All the men who knew anything here were Hindus. Can't find good men any more.' The white-haired electrician tossed Ali an eight-anna piece and told him to start coming to work at his shop the following day.

Back in the hut, Ali gave the silver piece to a wonder-struck Bano. 'Eight annas? For only three hours? What did you do?'

'Only half an hour. This is just something so that I go to work every day. I will get ten rupees a month.'

'God help me.' Bano put her hand to her mouth. 'I get a rupee a month from each house and it takes me a whole day to do three houses.'

'You get clothes and shoes too,' Ali said, laughing.

'Only sometimes, for myself, an old shalwar-kameez or something. This was the first time I asked for a man's clothes and the begum asked me if I'd got myself a man. I told her no, they are for a poor refugee boy. There is a sick old man in the house, mad too, I think he will die soon. They gave me his clothes and shoes.'

'They are nice clothes.' Ali said. 'You never wear clean clothes.'

'My work is with dust and muck. What do I want to wear clean clothes for?'

'You can wear them when you come home.'

'Why bother for such a short time? It's dark here anyway. None of your electricity here, now or ever.'

'When I get my money I will give you more than you earn from cleaning. Then you can stop work.'

'No. I would die of not working. I would die of remembering my son all the time.'

For the first time in Ali's presence, Bano began to cry. Ali took her dopatta in his hand and wiped away her tears.

'He will come,' he said to her. 'I am sure he will come. As you say, he is clever. Where is his father?'

'I don't know,' Bano said. 'He went away after a while.'

'Where was your home?'

'Nowhere, although we lived in a village in Bihar when I was small.'

There was silence in the hut for a few minutes. 'Tell me more,' then Ali said to her.

'What is there to tell?'

'Tell me how you lived.'

'My mother and father died when I was young. My brother and I lived in other people's houses. After some time Madan, he was my brother, ran away. I was ten, old enough to start working in houses, all cleaning work, we were cleaning people, not allowed to touch any other thing. My brother returned one day and took me away with him. He had fallen in with some wild people. They were outlaws, mixed up with dangerous things. We wandered from place to place. Many new people came to stay with us and then went. One time my brother went out and did not return. It was like that with those people. They were looking for death. I ran away from there. I did not like cleaning homes so I got work in shops and factories, still cleaning work, but at least they were shops and factories and not homes full of women and children. There I met Kamal. He was half owner of a shop. I liked him. He said he would marry me if I became a Muslim. I didn't know about these things. He only asked me to repeat some holy verses after him and changed my name to Bano.

After my son was born my husband took up with another woman and went away. I wasn't angry with him. But I knew I had made a great mistake. Not by marrying him but changing my religion. If I hadn't done that I wouldn't be a refugee today. But I am not angry with him or me. I made a mistake for love.'

'You don't like cleaning homes?'

'No. I am doing it because there is no other work here. But I keep looking. One day I will get work in a shop or a factory, in a big shop or a big factory. I can do hard work.'

'When I start getting money from my job,' Ali said, 'I will give you all of it.'

'You don't have to. I will get my own work in a big place.'

It was late at night. The last of the monsoon clouds were hovering above the earth, thundering in the distance. With clean clothes on him and a half rupee that he had earned and given to Bano, Ali's heart was big.

'Your clothes are dirty,' he said to her. 'Go and change them.'

'What, now?'

'Yes. Go on.'

Bano got up and went a few feet to the other wall of the hut where her bundle of clothes lay. She pulled out a shalwar-kameez from the bundle. Turning her back to Ali, she quickly took off her kurta and shalwar and put on the thin white silken suit. But Ali had had a glimpse of the straight body of a woman who was perhaps ten years older than him but who had a sinewy, arched back and slim hips with not an ounce of fat on them, moulded by a lifetime's toil as though cut from black stone. She came back to sit by him.

'Is it all right now?'

'Yes,' Ali said, looking at her with unblinking eyes. She looked back.

'You should eat more if you want to go to work every day,' she said to him.

'I will,' he said.

The flame on the wick of the lantern began to flicker, indicating the last of the oil. Bano reached out to blow it out. She did not go to her side of the hut but lay down beside Ali on the soft quilt on the ground.

'You can keep your money,' she said to him in the dark, 'but don't go away after a while.'

'I won't,' he said.